AN
UNFINISHED
STORY

ALSO BY BOO WALKER

Red Mountain
Red Mountain Rising
Red Mountain Burning
A Marriage Well Done

Writing as Benjamin Blackmore

Lowcountry Punch
Once a Soldier
Off You Go: A Mystery Novella

AN
UNFINISHED
STORY

BOO WALKER

Published by Lake Union Publishing, Seattle

www.apub.com

Amazon, the Amazon logo, and Lake Union Publishing are trademarks of Amazon.com, Inc., or its affiliates.

ISBN-13: 9781542019446
ISBN-10: 1542019443

Cover design by Caroline Teagle Johnson

Printed in the United States of America

For Riggs

Chapter 1

Boxing Up the Past

St. Petersburg, Florida

"This is our forever home," David had promised as he carried her across the threshold of their new waterfront dream house shortly after their honeymoon in Bonaire. The word *forever* was a term Claire had exhaustively pondered, ever since the police chaplain had knocked on the door and shattered her happy world.

That was three years ago today.

Driving the white VW convertible David had given her for her thirty-fifth birthday, Claire pumped the brakes as their house came into view toward the end of the cul-de-sac. Was it "theirs"? Or just "hers" now? Considering she was selling, her question didn't really matter anymore.

She had the top of the convertible down, and the February morning air was lower-seventies crisp. A flock of white ibises with their long orange beaks flew in a V shape over the house and across the neon-blue sky, which was as translucent as the water and only a shade lighter.

Where were the black clouds, the rain, the thunder and lightning? Today had no right to be so Florida, so epically stunning. You would think three years might muddle the past, making it less sharp to the touch, less invasive to explore. When asked last week by a widow in her support group how badly it still hurt on a scale of one to ten, Claire had admitted that she lived mostly nines and tens, with the occasional waves of happiness that felt more like delirium.

Their two-story house stood on the southeastern tip of St. Pete on the island of Coquina Key. A 1960s design with a white brick exterior, it wasn't the fanciest house on the block, but the panoramic views of Tampa Bay more than made up for it. Claire had transformed the inside with an artistic, midcentury vibe—the kind of place you never wanted to leave.

Claire rolled into the driveway and paused to revisit their last moment together, between the two pygmy date palms flanking the front stoop as David had rushed off to work.

"You're really not going to tell me who's coming to dinner tonight?" she'd asked, crossing her arms.

"Oh, c'mon." He'd tucked in his crisp yellow button-down, walking backward down the steps. "I thought you loved surprises." She could still hear his Michigander voice so clearly.

"I like surprise flowers or jewelry. Convertibles even. I'm not sure I like surprise guests. What if he or she is allergic to something?"

"This *person* will love your shrimp fajitas; trust me." He'd finished tucking in his shirt and buckled his belt, so skinny after training for yet another marathon. When she'd rolled her eyes, David had leaped back up the stairs and kissed her. "I love you, baby. See you around five."

"How much do you love me?" she'd asked.

He'd put his clean-shaven cheek to hers, and his warm breath had tickled her ear. "Infinity times infinity." He'd been on top of the world lately, so infectious with his thirst for life.

Those had been his last words to her. And she never did find out who was coming to dinner. No one had been in the car when it crashed, so Claire assumed David might have planned to pick up the person. Nothing else made sense. Claire remembered smiling as he'd pulled away in his 4 Series BMW—the one that would be totaled by a bastard drunk driver that afternoon.

Some of the widows at the meetings talked about how they wished they could have redone their last moments with their spouse, maybe said something different, hugged them a little harder. Looking back, remembering how connected she and David were, it was as if they had both been saying a last goodbye that morning and hadn't known it.

Claire grabbed a brown paper bag from the shotgun seat and climbed out of her car. She walked across the crunchy fresh-cut grass to her neighbor's house, a one-story rambler with the most well-kept yard on the street. Hal must have heard her and called out from behind the vinyl fence on the side of the house. Walking through the gate, she found him on his knees in the garden with a handful of old tomato plants he'd pulled from the soil. Beyond him, the turquoise of Tampa Bay shimmered in the sun.

"Good morning, young lady." He tossed the plants into the pile behind him. The nearby trees were noisy with birds. "It's nice to see you so often lately."

To show respect and to meet his eyes, she momentarily lifted her glasses. "Getting ready for the new season?"

He was eighty years young, a longtime widower, and the best neighbor Claire and David could have asked for, always quick to lend a hand.

He wiped his brow with his arm. "Still trying to figure out Florida gardening. I swear, as much as I love living down here, I miss that rich Ohio soil. But I wouldn't trade this weather for the world."

"That makes two of us." She held up the brown bag. "I brought you your favorite biscuit. Bacon, egg, cheese, and avocado."

"You're a doll, Claire. I swear your place makes the best in town." He pushed himself up slowly and dusted the dirt off his knees. "How's the moving coming?"

"It's pretty much done. Just a few odds and ends left." She wouldn't dare mention the one room left untouched. There were many reasons why she hadn't entered David's office since the day he died, but those excuses expired today. She could see in her mind's eye the doorknob that often haunted her dreams.

Hal reached for the bag with one of his shaky hands and smiled with all the kindness in the world. "Will you let me pay you this time?"

She returned her warmest smile, thinking he was one of the good ones, a reminder of the light at the end of the tunnel. "Don't be silly." She watched a green anole lizard climb up the A/C unit on the side of the house. "So how's your heart?"

"Still ticking."

"C'mon, Hal, don't sugarcoat things. What did the doctor say?"

Hal sighed. "I'm approaching the end stage, Claire."

"Oh, Hal." Claire choked up. She didn't know what was worse: dying slowly, or the flick of a switch, like David's death.

"It's nothing to be sad about. Truly." His hand holding the brown bag was shaking. He looked up to the sky. "Soon, I'll be with Ruby, dancing up high."

Claire took a step forward, holding back tears. "What can I do for you? I'm serious. If you need a ride to the doctor or an errand run, please call me."

"I will, Claire. Please don't worry about me. How are you doing with all this, by the way? I can only imagine saying goodbye to your house isn't easy."

Claire took a moment to change gears. "Selling the house has brought it all back, honestly. I wish I could be stronger sometimes." She paused, swallowing her sadness. "I just need to close my eyes and channel my inner Hal whenever times get tough."

He sprayed off his hands with the garden hose. "Let me tell you something, if you'll allow an old man to pass along the small bit of wisdom I've collected."

"If you tell me time heals all, I might just throw myself into the water, Hal."

A quick headshake as he dried his hands with his shirt. "No, I'm not going to tell you time heals all. The one thing I know for sure, Claire, is that life demands that we get back up and keep fighting, no matter how badly we've been knocked down. I'm going down swinging." He opened up the brown bag. "And now I'm going to eat a biscuit."

She smiled. "I'm so lucky you're in my life."

Hal peeled back the foil on the overstuffed biscuit and prepared to take a bite. "I'm the lucky one. And you know what makes me happier than anything?"

"What's that?"

"Seeing the fight in your eyes, the way you're coming back. David would be proud of you, kid." He took a bite and wiped his mouth. "Oh boy, this alone is worth sticking around for."

Claire sat with Hal on the back porch while he ate his biscuit and then left him to work on his tomato plants. Walking along the seawall, she crossed into the Bermuda grass of her own backyard, glancing at the pool where she'd once imagined future children splashing about. She looked left to the dock that stretched out into the bay, where those same children were supposed to catch their first fish. She had always sworn that she'd be a great mom, that she'd make up for her own mother's failures. Never had she considered she might not get the chance.

Deciding she wanted one last look from the end of the dock, Claire worked her way down the planks, breathing in the memories. When she and David had realized they weren't able to have children, they'd bought a boat, something to do with their time. They'd kept it tied to this dock, a twenty-three-foot center console Sea Ray, and in some ways it had saved their marriage. The sunset cruises, the day trips to Bunces Pass. It had been their window into finding fun again.

Claire stood at the end of the dock with Tampa looking back at her from across the bay. Her long, sandy-brown hair whipped in the cool sea breeze. The high-rise linen shorts and sleeveless top she'd chosen to wear weren't cutting it now. She hugged herself to fight the chill.

Hearing the whine of a diesel engine, Claire looked right to find a family of four speeding across the water in a ski boat. They were watching the white wake bubbling up from behind.

As they passed directly ahead, two bottlenose dolphins suddenly emerged, their dorsal fins knifing through the water. When the mammals leaped into the air in tandem, the two children—swallowed by oversize life jackets—thrust their skinny arms up high, and their joyful yelps echoed in the empty chambers of Claire's broken heart. But only when the woman driving the boat turned to kiss the man beside her did Claire let her first tear of the morning fall.

Unable to bear watching the happy family for another moment, she exchanged a wave with the mother and then turned away. It was supposed to be Claire out on a boat. Her husband, *her* children! With tears splashing the dock, she walked the planks back toward the house.

There would be no boys or girls hauling in a catch from the dock. There would be no children jumping on a trampoline. No wedding receptions in the backyard. And the worst part: no grandchildren. The family tree of Claire and David Kite had stopped before it had even begun.

Winding around to the front, Claire walked through the memory of their last conversation and entered the front door of their not-so-forever home. Her photochromic lenses quickly adjusted. Save a few boxes in the corner, the house was vacant. A ray of sunshine sprayed the bare cherry floors. Claire felt as empty as the house looked. She could see straight across the open living room and through the giant windows to the bay, where the happy family was making large circles in the boat.

Feeling for an uncomfortable moment like she wasn't alone, Claire whispered, "Hello. Is anyone here?"

Though there was no response, she sensed David's presence and was both uplifted by and afraid of the idea of his ghost. She had a sixth sense about things, and that was a big part of what fueled her trepidation to clean out his office. Oh God, what might she find . . .

Each step toward his office was like wading through emotional quicksand. She climbed the stairs with heavy feet, her footfalls like a ticking clock. She glanced into the empty master bedroom on the left and could still see their modern Scandinavian bed. Her imagination offered a quick glimpse of David and her cuddling in the sheets, watching one of their favorite shows on the television hanging on the wall.

A bitter taste hit her tongue. Damn him for leaving her.

Swallowing the rage that loved to surprise her at times, Claire passed the guest bedroom and reached the door to his office. Eyeing the aged bronze doorknob that had swollen to ominous proportions in her imagination, she stopped and listened. So many times toward the end she'd come to knock on the door, and all she'd heard was David muttering as he wrote his next book. Sometimes, in the quiet, she could still hear him reading his words out loud in a sort of whisper.

Claire briefly fell back in time and almost knocked on the door. "David, dinner's ready."

"Okay, honey. Let me wrap up this chapter."

"Please don't let it get cold."

"Just a few more words."

Those were great days. Somehow they'd dug themselves out of the darkness of being childless and had rediscovered themselves and each other. The same year Claire opened her café, David had committed to run his first marathon, and a chase to get in the best shape of his life ensued. Then he was biking, too, and training for triathlons. The mouthwatering sight of David peeling off his shirt was still etched into her mind.

Then one day, having found motivation in a novel that he'd recently read, he'd started writing again. Rediscovering the passion of his college years, he'd become as obsessed with words as he had with road bikes. His writing was one reason why Claire hadn't cleaned out his office yet, why she hadn't sold the house. She hadn't found the courage to read what he'd been working on the last year of his life, and she knew it was in there waiting for her. His final words. The only words he had left to say.

The identity of the guest to the dinner that had never happened was one of a few questions that had plagued her in the silent moments she hadn't filled with distractions. Maybe that answer was waiting.

Claire finally turned the knob and pushed open the door to the office. Nothing had changed in three years. Claire had demanded that no one touch David's stuff. She would do it when she was ready. Her parents and friends had advised her many times to move on, but she'd stood strong against them. Selling the house now was forcing her to do something she still wasn't completely ready to do.

A framed and signed photograph of David's favorite Tampa Bay Rays player, Fred McGriff, hung on the wall straight ahead. Fred was lifting his batting helmet toward the crowd, a thanks for their applause after a home run. His uniform read "Devil Rays." It wasn't until 2007 that the Rays dropped "Devil" from their name. Thinking about the Rays, she couldn't help but ponder the other big question still lingering after three years. As much of a Rays fan as David was, why had the police found a New York Yankees hat with the tag still on it in his car when he'd died?

Though Claire's eyes often glazed over when his talk turned too "inside baseball," she was well aware how much he disliked the team he called the Evil Empire. "How can you support a squad that buys their way to the World Series?" he'd said on more than one occasion.

Several feet away from the floor-to-ceiling window, his Victorian pedestal desk faced the water. Claire choked up but then broke into a smile when she saw the sepia-colored globe next to the computer monitor. They'd once committed, in writing, to let it decide their next vacation destination. Claire was to spin the globe, and with his eyes closed, David was to place a finger on the spot. His pointer had landed on Ohio. True to their word, they'd booked a trip to Cincinnati to watch the Rays beat the Reds. She barely knew what a curveball was, but they'd ended up having one of the best trips of their marriage.

Claire lowered her eyes to the drawers with thick iron pulls. The novel David had been writing—the one she'd promised not to read until he'd finished—was probably in one of them. Not that this novel was such a big deal. He'd penned a couple of amateur whodunits after graduating from the University of Florida as an English major. Finding himself frustrated in attempting to get published, he'd gone back to school to learn architecture, a more lucrative profession. His writing had fallen by the wayside. Still, these were his last words, and no matter how insignificant they might be from a literary perspective, they meant something to her.

Letting apprehension get the best of her, she couldn't quite muster the bravery to go to the desk. Not yet. She retrieved several boxes from the hallway and taped them together. Returning, she began stacking the books from the bookshelves into the boxes.

Claire stopped when she reached a first-edition, signed copy of *Napalm Trees and Turquoise Waters* by Whitaker Grant. The cover featured a man staring at a palm tree that had been snapped in half in a hurricane. She opened the book to the inscription.

To David. I hope you pick up your pen again. The finest words always come after breaking through the barriers. ~Whitaker

Though he hadn't written anything in years, Whitaker was a local celebrity. After they'd turned his award-winning book into a movie, it would have been difficult to find anyone in Florida who didn't have his or her own strong opinions of whether or not the movie had done justice to his miraculous piece of fiction.

Eschewing anything too popular, David had been one of the holdouts and showed no interest in reading it until Fate played her part. A couple of years after the release of *Napalm Trees and Turquoise Waters*, Whitaker had begun showing up at her café to write his second novel. Claire hadn't wanted to bother him but had loved his book and couldn't help but approach him to say thanks. As they'd talked, she'd admitted her frustration with her husband, who had not yet read the book. She'd joked that David must be the only one along the Gulf who hadn't. The next time he came in, Whitaker had given Claire an inscribed copy to pass along.

The hardhead he was, David hadn't picked up the book for a few more years but finally gave it a chance. He'd finished it one night while they were lying in bed together, and he'd rolled over and said, "I can't believe you didn't make me read this book! Life changing, really."

"I know!"

"Makes me want to write again, Claire."

"You should."

A month later, she'd heard him muttering in his office, a sound that drove her crazy at the time, but now it was all she wanted to hear. If only she'd recorded him so that she could replay it while lying in bed on the sleepless nights.

Claire smiled sadly at the memory and set the book aside. The little bungalow she'd just bought on Pass-a-Grille didn't have room for all of David's books, but she'd certainly find a spot for this keepsake.

After filling and taping up a few more boxes, she turned back to the desk. It was time to face the music. Claire approached David's ergonomic chair and sat down. His muttering grew louder in her heart. She touched the dark wood of the desk and again felt his presence.

A sound nearly knocked her out of the chair. A cuckoo bird poked its head out of the clock on the wall to signify with a loud chirp that noon had arrived. Another memory fired, and she could see David's giant grin as he'd unwrapped his Valentine's Day gift one year to find this absurd clock. The chirp reminded her that she needed to get back to her café to close. She was a manager short.

With gnawing trepidation, Claire rifled through his drawers. When she pulled open the bottom one, she found the composition books resting next to a collection of pencils held together with a rubber band. Her heart kicked at her chest. She'd asked many times if he'd let her read what he was writing, but he'd stood firmly against it. "Only once I'm finished," he'd said. "Promise me."

Though she did make the promise, she'd constantly teased him, sneaking into his office and peeking over his shoulder while he was distracted by his craft. It became a game of sorts and always ended with David twisting his head, dropping his chin, and lowering his reading glasses to the tip of his nose, then looking at her with eyes the color of graham crackers, gently reminding her of the promise.

Surely, that promise didn't hold up in death.

Or did it? What would he have wanted? For her to toss the pages away unread? He'd want her to enjoy his last words, no matter what they might be.

Unsure of how to proceed, Claire hesitantly reached down and shuffled through the stack. There were three composition books, parts one through three of the third draft. She chose *Saving Orlando #1—3rd Draft*, which was written on the line in the white space in the middle of the cover. With her heart racing, she opened to the first page. She wondered what the title meant, what David knew about Orlando, why he would write about it.

Being an architect and a lover of design, David had handwriting that would be better termed as calligraphy and would rival John Hancock's finest letters. In his tight black script, it read:

Claire, you're busted! I knew you'd try to read it. Seriously, you made a promise to me. It's not ready.

A brief relief from the sadness graced her, thinking of all the times she'd teased him with her clumsily covert attempts to read a line, and the way he snapped his composition book shut and explained that he didn't have much more to go.

She fingered the letters, felt the indentations in the page. David's hands had been here. His heart had been here. She bit her bottom lip and held back a cry. "What am I supposed to do now, baby?" she asked silently. "There's no way I'm not reading it."

Firm on her decision, she turned the page and read the first line:

The boy first came to me in a dream, a bolt striking from the sky.

Not the typical entry into a whodunit. Claire kept reading. Though there were still corrections and erased passages, the sentences were easy to follow. As her eyes bounced from word to word, beautiful images appeared in her mind. She flew through the first chapter and, at once, felt sad that David wasn't here but also glad that he had left this treasure. David had written something far from a mystery, taking a piece of his soul and putting it onto the page.

He wasn't writing about the city of Orlando. Set in modern-day Sarasota, the story began with a single man in his late thirties named Kevin catching an eleven-year-old boy breaking into his car. The boy's name was Orlando.

How had David never mentioned this story? She was desperate to keep reading, desperate to find out what happened. But she had to get back to the café, the only stable piece of her life. If she let that slip, she was sure she'd lose her last, white-knuckled grip on life.

Chapter 2

Unhappy Customers

As she crossed from Tampa Bay to the Gulf along the southern end of St. Pete, "96 Degrees in the Shade" by Third World easing through the speakers of her open-topped convertible, Claire stewed over the contents of David's book. What was she about to read?

At a stoplight, she dug into her purse and found the pack of American Spirit cigarettes hidden in the secret pocket. Setting them in the cup holder, she wrapped a scarf around her hair, the first step in hiding the cigarette smell from everyone in her life, especially her employees. She slipped on the windbreaker she kept for such occasions, zipped it up, and then pulled a latex glove over her hand.

Once Claire was moving again, her hair blowing in the salty breeze, she lit up. Smoke filled her lungs, a sweet taste amid the bitter. Today was one of those days when she could easily justify this nasty new habit of hers.

As she puffed away, she caught herself thinking of the overall unfairness of being human. Sometimes, all you wanted was a good cry, but life rarely gave you the space. Claire should have been able to go home and lie in bed all day reading David's book, curled up with an arm around a pillow as if he were still there—as if he were that pillow. There were still tears that needed purging.

That was not how life worked, though. Not only did she need to finish cleaning out his office (and read his novel), but she needed to keep her café running. Wasn't it funny and painful at the same time that in addition to the struggles of life—death, sickness, even simple house chores, the never-ending lack of time—you still had to keep up a day job to survive? Not that her café was just a day job. It was her dream, but sometimes she wished she could push the "Pause" button on it for a few days. As the owner, she couldn't be gone for long or the whole place would fall apart. That was life. We had to put on our best happy face, close the door on all the troubles that do their best to pull us down, and somehow pretend that everything was all right. One big Bob Marley song.

Claire loved her occupation and probably would have been bored otherwise. In fact, on the right day, she'd admit to herself that she had a nearly unhealthy obsession with the café she'd opened almost a decade before. What saddened Claire today, and all these days, was that she knew she wasn't some strange exception. Her life wasn't any more painful than the next. No, not everyone had lost a husband or a spouse, but the planet was a jumble of struggling people fighting to keep the roof from falling down on their heads.

Maybe there was some comfort in knowing and remembering that everyone suffered. At least, she thought, amid all the pain, everyone was in it together. Whether you lived in Boulder, Santa Barbara, Santa Fe, heck, even Bangkok, or, in this case, St. Pete, life dealt you blows that sometimes made it hard to get out of bed.

Taking a last puff and dropping her cigarette butt into a nearly empty bottle of water, she drove the Pinellas Bayway over the bridge leading to Pass-a-Grille, a beach town that, for most of the last ten thousand years, had been a Native American fishing village. Compared to its northerly neighbors closer to Clearwater, Pass-a-Grille was sleepy and tranquil, just the way Claire liked it. And just the way she remembered it from when she first came to visit her grandmother here as a teenager.

She removed the scarf and glove and crammed them into the glove compartment. After taking off the windbreaker, she stuffed it under the seat. Then, with a deep breath of salt air, she soaked in the view. Surely she could find some energy and healing in the divinity of the Gulf.

Ahead, the grand Don CeSar hotel, the big pink palace that defined the landscape and had served as a beach stay for such legends as F. Scott Fitzgerald and Franklin Roosevelt, stood proud and tall against the backdrop of the various shades of blue water. Like a warm breeze, the beach atmosphere brought Claire a tiny serving of peace.

Swinging a hard left, Claire drove along the beach, passing between the giant palm trees that lined the main thoroughfare. Pass-a-Grille was a peninsula, a tiny piece of land with the Gulf waters on one side and the channel on the other. A decent golfer could knock a ball from the sand over into the channel on the other side from even the widest stretch.

Claire stopped along the channel a block short of her café to perform her typical regimen after sneaking a cigarette. A pelican was sunbathing with open wings on an old wooden post jutting out of the glittery water. No one other than a couple of widows at her meetings knew Claire smoked, and she was intent on keeping it that way. After rubbing her hands together with the organic hand sanitizer made of lavender essential oils, she sprayed two pumps of natural mint freshener into her mouth and then popped in a piece of Spry peppermint gum.

She flipped down the visor and looked at herself in the mirror. Retiring her contact lenses, the oversize designer glasses were part of her new identity, the one she'd adopted upon leaving Chicago in her twenties. A new look for a new Claire. She touched up her shiny lip gloss and dusted her cheeks to give some more color to her sun-kissed skin.

Named in honor of her father's old diner in Chicago, which she'd helped run until he'd died in her midtwenties, Leo's South was tucked into a small lot on the channel side of the peninsula. After parking in the owner's spot, she looked out over the water, out to the stunning houses on Tierra Verde with their long wooden docks boasting gazebos and beautiful yachts at the end. That kind of beauty made her believe she might see David again, even if that meant they both came back as seabirds in the next life.

Ever since opening nearly a decade ago, Leo's South had been an institution. In the wake of their inability to have children, this café had become Claire's baby, and she wished her father could have seen it come to life. She wasn't solving the world's problems, but she was adding a little light to this already colorful blip on the map. Novelists had penned fine books here. Artists had sold their first works. Eckerd College students had collected their first paychecks. Business deals had been hashed out over avocado toast and huevos rancheros. Countless families had connected for their first meal after arriving for their weeklong beach retreat. No, she wasn't curing cancer, but she'd created a place that was as much a part of Pass-a-Grille as the dolphins, the seahorses, the stingrays, and even the sand upon which it was built.

David had helped design the building. Though his expertise had been in designing modern condominiums and office buildings for the budding downtown of St. Pete, she wanted beach-town simplicity. Where he was worried about hurricanes and would have designed some sort of Category Five hurricane-proof structure ready to handle anything from weather events to nuclear disaster, she wanted something light and airy with barely any structure at all, a posh tiki hut with sand on the floor.

Her lenses lightened as Claire started into the café. The ping of silverware hitting plates and the laughter of the happy guests met her ears in a glorious symphony. Her father would be so proud of her. Leo had taught her everything, most of all the importance of simplicity. The same one-page menu, along with a fresh catch of the day, was served from seven to two, every day but Mondays, and they were all out the door by three. Keep it simple. Keep it amazing.

She was happy to hear Jimmy Cliff singing through the speakers. Some of the servers had been changing the music when Claire left, and she didn't particularly share their taste. Leo's South had a laid-back air, and the music needed to fit the ambience. She played mostly reggae, though she allowed some old-school soul from time to time.

Her café was an extension of her own style: colorful boho chic. The floor was white, powdery sand, and on one wall hung a No Shoes Allowed sign, which Claire had assured the inspector from the health department was a joke. Potted tropical plants filled every available space. One of her favorite ideas to date, an Oriental rug stretched out over the sand, enhanced by an overhead crystal chandelier. The driftwood tables on the rug offered the best seats in the house.

"How we doing?" Claire asked the teenage hostess, who was three days into the first job of her life.

"It hasn't slowed down once," she said, wide eyed and short of breath.

Claire flashed a smile. "'Tis the season." February was the height of snowbird season and was typically one of their best two months.

She walked behind the bar, waved at Chef Jackson frying eggs on the stove and Paulie pulling a tray of biscuits out of the oven. She said hello to Jevaun from Jamaica, who was mixing up a line of screwdrivers, the aroma of fresh Florida citrus rising brightly into the air. His long dreads were tied up and wrapped in a net.

In a heavy accent, he said, "That Jimmy Cliff sounds good, yeah?"

Claire had thought she was a reggae aficionado until she'd hired Jevaun. "It's definitely brightening up my day. What's new with you?"

"Oh, just the birds and bees, my dear. *Mi life irie.*" She knew he was working two jobs to pay alimony for a wife who'd run out on him and child support for twin boys he never got to see. But Jevaun still found a way to smile.

"That makes me happy." She stole an orange wedge. "I'm gonna go make the rounds."

He looked at the next drink ticket in line, fully devoted to doing his part well. *"Do yu ting."*

Claire glanced back at the kitchen and then bounced her eyes around the room at the servers running around trying to keep the guests happy. She would never have made it through losing David without everyone at the restaurant. This was her family.

Coming out from behind the bar, Claire dodged one of her servers, Alicia, who was ushering a tray of food. Claire glanced at the omelet on one of the plates, a mixture of duck and chicken eggs from a tiny farm in Palmetto, topped with fresh mint and dill from the large herb garden surrounding the perimeter of the patio out back. The plating was just as she wanted it.

Claire visited with each table, staying a little longer with the guests she knew. When she stepped outside to the crowded patio, a friend waved at her from a two-top in the corner next to one of the long, raised garden beds spilling over with herbs.

Didi, an older woman from her widows' support group, was seated across from a much younger man.

"You're very sweet to come today," Claire said, straightening her glasses.

Didi looked stylish in her St. John dress, and her dark hair was pulled back, exposing stunning emerald earrings. Admiring her friend's clear skin and elegant smile, Claire could only hope she'd age so well. Didi set down her fork.

"Darling, I don't need an excuse to come eat at my favorite restaurant." Didi's dialect stemmed from sixty-plus years living within close proximity to Central Park—a lady who'd enjoyed countless performances in her box seat in Carnegie Hall and who'd sent her children to the same private school she'd attended so many years before.

Claire had met Didi at one of the group meetings, and Didi had become her mentor. Along with Claire's desire to age as gracefully as Didi, she hoped she might one day recover as triumphantly. Not that

Claire wanted to start dating again—she wasn't there yet—but she at least wanted to get her life back.

Didi gestured toward her table guest. "Claire, meet Andrés. He's just moved here from Barcelona and is doing some sort of tech-start-up venture."

Claire turned toward Andrés and took his hand. "Hi."

"It's a pleasure to make your acquaintance, *señora*," he said in a heavy Catalonian dialect and then confidently drew her hand up to his lips for a kiss. Admiring his arresting eyes and thick waves of brown hair tucked behind his ears, Claire almost broke into a laugh. The man looked like he belonged in a magazine ad for an expensive watch. Didi had outdone herself yet again. Her dark-skinned lover wore a crisp white shirt with three buttons undone, exposing a bare, perhaps waxed chest.

Claire was about to look at Didi with a dropped jaw when Andrés said, "Didi says very nice things about you." *Things* sounded more like *sings*, but Claire could follow him.

"That's very kind of her. She's a master of embellishment. How was your meal?"

Andrés held up a pinched index finger and thumb. "The black beans were exquisite."

"Thank you," Claire said proudly. "They *are* delightful." As a nod to the Cuban roots of the area, they did a rice and beans with an over-easy egg placed on top, decorated with perfectly ripe Florida avocados. That dish had been part of what had helped them establish a foothold early on in their career. Andrés might have been the thousandth customer to pay such a compliment.

Claire had met several of Didi's younger lovers in the past two years, but she still found herself taken aback almost every time. First of all, how had Didi gotten in the mind-set to chase men after losing her husband? Claire wasn't sure she'd ever remove her wedding ring. But more than that, Claire was surprised and, quite honestly, impressed with the men Didi had dated. She was indeed charming and stunning, but these younger studs fought over her, and she quite often broke their hearts in the end.

"How's the packing going?" Didi asked.

"I'm almost done," Claire said in an enthusiastic tone.

"Oh, that's great. And you were so worried about it. Look at you."

"I know!" Claire set her eyes on the rainbow table mat. "Everything's fine." Claire didn't want to tell Didi the whole truth. Because as a matter of fact, nothing was fine.

"Please excuse my French, but you do know what F.I.N.E. stands for, right?" Didi answered her own question: "Fucked up, insecure, neurotic, and emotional."

Claire's laugh was stopped short when she heard a customer behind her raise her voice. She spun around. Three tables over, a woman in a wide-brimmed black hat was verbally attacking Alicia.

Claire excused herself and crossed the restaurant. Standing next to Alicia, she looked at the four casually dressed women sitting around the table. Claire noticed large sparkly rings on all their fingers.

The one hot in the middle of a rant turned her angry red eyes to Claire. "These are the kinds of servers you hire now? I remember when this place used to be so good."

Claire caught herself feeling intensely defensive. She wanted to snatch the floppy hat off the woman's head and smack her with it, but Claire bit her tongue and kept her hands to herself. As a restaurateur in the modern world, between social media and the legions of review sites, one bad experience could be detrimental to your business. In no time in the history of the world had the notion of "the customer is always right" ever been more important.

Before Claire could get in a word, Alicia wagged a finger in the air. "She seriously doesn't need this right now!" Everyone on the staff knew today was the third anniversary of the day David had died, so Alicia was being extra protective.

Claire turned to Alicia and put a hand on her arm. "It's okay; let me take it from here."

Alicia gritted her teeth and eyed the woman.

"I got it," Claire said, lightly pinching her arm. Alicia finally took the hint.

As Alicia walked away, Claire looked back at the red-eyed woman, whose entire body was tensing. The other three ladies at the table were dead silent. "I'm so sorry you're dissatisfied. What happened?"

"She's just awful. Ever since the moment we sat down, she's been screwing up. Twenty minutes to get waters. Another twenty before we can even get our order in. At this rate, we'll need dinner menus."

Claire let her speak, though she knew the woman's embellishments were over the top. Knowing that no matter how perfect a place you created, there would always be someone who'd find something to complain about, Claire took her words with a grain of salt and focused on how to best snuff out the problem.

The woman kept on, the wrinkles in her forehead becoming more pronounced with each syllable. "We've got a gluten allergy that was made clear early on, but this girl brings toast out with the omelet. When we said something about it, she couldn't have been more rude. Said we didn't tell her. I don't know if you're the manager or whatever, but we've been visiting Pass-a-Grille and coming here for years. It used to be something special."

Talk about cutting to the bone. Claire could have unleashed hell. Venomous words loaded onto her tongue, but she suppressed them—at least she did at first.

"I'm so sorry. Sometimes we don't get it right, and it sounds like this is the case today. Alicia is a really good person and good server. Maybe she's having a rough day. Could I give you a gift certificate and convince you to give us another shot while you're in town? I know we can do better."

With an unforgiving attitude, the woman said, "I would expect that at the very least." She turned to her friends and shook her head. Then back to Claire, "How sad the owner let it fall to pieces like this. I know it's not your fault. Ugh. Probably some family business and the parents are letting the kids take over."

Scrambling to suppress the volcano of anger erupting inside her, Claire stared the woman down. "Actually, I own this place. Leo's South. Leo was my father, and he owned Leo's Diner in Chicago for forty-five years. My husband died three years ago today. Today!" Claire paused for effect. "But I didn't stop working. I didn't want this place to slip. I didn't want my husband's death to be some excuse for letting Leo's South fall apart. Instead, I did everything I could to not only keep up our standards but to make my restaurant better. Not just to make it better for you! To make it better for my husband! He built this place!" She started pointing. "He put in that stove. Built the bar. He ran the wiring. David gave me this place, my dream. Leo's South is his, too, and it's just about all I have left of him!" And she added less aggressively, "So I'm sorry it's not *special* to you anymore."

To say you could have heard a pin drop would not have done the moment justice. You could have heard a gecko sneeze from across the bay in Tampa.

Claire covered her mouth and took a giant breath, realizing what she'd said. She couldn't imagine the story her eyes must have told as emotions rushed over her. David was suddenly speaking to her, telling her to calm down. She could hear his voice in her mind. "Simmer down, honey." Closing her eyes, she nodded to him.

Finally, Claire looked at the ladies, ending with her eyes on the unhappiest of them. "I am so sorry. That was too much."

The woman looked like someone had stuffed a hard-boiled egg into her mouth. The patrons at the other tables were attempting not to stare.

Claire let out a sigh. "Your meal is on me. I'm so sorry, really. As you can tell, it's been a hard day." Without much more to say, she ended with, "I'm going to excuse myself."

Not a peep came from the table.

Claire attempted a smile and sneaked away with the past pecking away at her like turkey vultures on roadkill. The last person she saw before disappearing through the green door into her office was Didi, waiting in line for the restroom, showing a concerned facial expression.

Sitting down at her desk, she glanced at a picture she'd taken of her father. More than once over the years, he had gently cautioned her, "Don't air your dirty laundry in public." He'd also told her, "Never let them see you sweat." Both rules had officially been broken today.

A knock on the green door. Didi entered and closed the door behind her, shutting out the craziness of the busy café. She sat across from Claire in the wicker chair.

Claire straightened her glasses. "I know you're not going to ask me if everything's okay."

Didi took her time responding. "I'm not sure what I want to say." Shaking her head, she continued, "As you know, I don't have all the answers."

Several moments passed, and Claire liked having Didi in the room, but she didn't know how to break the silence. Finally, Claire told the truth. "I honestly don't feel like I'll ever get to where you are. There's no way I'm going to wake up one day feeling all giddy and excited about life. Look at you. I'm never going to be so carefree, running around with some Spanish model."

Didi sighed. "Claire, I still have my moments."

"What could possibly pull me out of this awful feeling that is constantly dragging me down? And don't tell me it's another man. That might be your secret, but it's not mine."

"I don't know what your answers are, Claire. There's no magic formula to get over losing the love of your life. Though I think you'll find another man to love one day, you'll probably have to learn to love yourself again first." She shrugged. "But what do I know?"

Another wave of emotions rushed through Claire, and she had to close her eyes and breathe through them. She put her hands behind her head—fighting the nausea—and looked at Didi. "I miss him more than anything, and the hole in my heart aches. The hurt is indescribable, like someone has ripped my rib cage open and left me to die." Hot tears filled her eyes. "I can't bear it anymore."

Didi rounded the desk and wrapped her arms around Claire. "Stay strong. That's all I can tell you. Try to tap into your stronger self."

Claire cried into her friend's shoulder. "How can I stay strong? I'm not strong. Nothing about me is strong." All she wanted to do was curl up and finish David's book, to read his words, to be close to him again.

Her friend released her and wiped one of the tears from Claire's cheek.

Claire removed her glasses and wiped her eyes.

"You don't ever have to say goodbye to him. He's in your heart, Claire. He'll always be in your heart." Didi stood straighter and touched her own chest. "Find him here. Feel him. And talk to him. Ask for his help. That's my magic formula. Not these men who chase me around. My secret is that my husband is here in my heart, and he wants me to be a fighter and to carve out a new happy life for myself. He wants me to be happy. What does David want from you?"

"I . . . I wish I knew."

After a long hug, Claire said to Didi as she was leaving, "By the way, you're one wild woman. He's a catch and a half."

Her friend perked up with a sinister lift of an eyebrow. "He's delicious, isn't he? Great on the eyes and even better under the sheets."

Claire couldn't hold back a smile. "I have no idea where you find these men."

She raised her hands, palms up. "They're falling from the sky! What can I say?"

After a shake of the head and one more smile, Claire said, "Thanks for being in my life."

"See you tomorrow afternoon at the meeting?"

"Yeah, for sure." Didi blew Claire a kiss and disappeared back into the madness of the café.

Claire sat and stared at the wall for a while. Sometimes that numbness of being all cried out was the only peace she could ever find. She loved her friend for her honesty and encouraging words, and though much of Claire didn't believe she had the strength to overcome, a very small part of her believed that she would. That she had to. Her dead husband would demand it.

Claire touched her heart and whispered, "Are you out there somewhere, David?"

Chapter 3

SAVING ORLANDO

After locking up, Claire climbed into her convertible and drove north, back toward the Don CeSar hotel. David's novel rode shotgun.

Claire couldn't help but see the parallels between her adult life and that of the hotel. Opening in the late twenties, the Pink Palace was welcomed with a flurry of excitement, drawing the rich and famous from all over the world. Those booming times were like the first years of Claire's marriage to David. After fighting off the early impact of the Great Depression, the untimely death of the hotel's owner had led it on a downward path of disrepair, only to be bought for a song by the US Army, who converted it into a military hospital during World War II. Shortly after, the army even abandoned the building. The southern sunshine and salt air had eaten away at this glorious feat of architecture over the subsequent thirty years.

That was just about how Claire felt right now: exhausted and worn down. But there was a bright side. New owners in the seventies and renovations over the next few decades had restored the Don CeSar to its former glory, and the hotel was back in business. Claire hoped the Don's story was just a few years ahead of her own.

Claire's new house was on the beach side of the main drag, still a half mile from the Don but only two blocks from the sand. After David died, knowing she could never spend another night in their house, she'd rented a spacious two-bedroom condo downtown. But a few months ago, as part of her intended comeback, which felt like the eleventh round of a boxing match, Claire had committed to rediscovering her love of the beach and started to house hunt.

Hidden amid giant supermansions with fast cars in the driveway, her little two-bedroom was a dreamy place to live for a single woman in need of healing. She'd been fortunate enough to see the real estate agent hammering the FOR SALE sign into the grass and was signing papers that same afternoon. How about that for spontaneity? Her new home was simple and beachy with a brick chimney and a tin roof that sang in the rain. A quick bike ride away from the café; a two-minute walk to the sand; a perfect place to relaunch.

She parked her car on the street and, with the box of David's possessions resting under one arm, circled to the front porch. Though not as chic as her café on the outside, her bungalow was certainly bohemian. Seashells, dream catchers, and driftwood. Claire had only been here two months but had read at least four books in the hammock and rocking chairs while breathing in the salt air.

She kicked aside an Amazon delivery and entered the living room. "Guess who's home . . ."

Her one-eyed tabby cat named Willy jumped down from the back of the couch, stopping on the cushion before landing on the rug.

Claire put her things down on the coffee table and reached down to swoop him up. "I hope you're having a better day than I am." She held him to her chest and bathed in his purrs as she ran her hand along his back.

Following the last hurricane, Claire had raced back to Pass-a-Grille after the evacuation to make sure the café had survived. She'd found Willy hiding on the patio with a hurt eye, probably a result of flying debris. The vet who'd stitched him up guessed he was about two years old. Claire considered Willy to be one of the great blessings of her life.

"You wouldn't believe what I found," Claire said, setting Willy down. He followed her through the house as she related the events of the morning in brief.

Throwing on a kimono, Claire made a cup of chamomile in the seventies retro kitchen made most apparent by the vivid orange counters. The one picture she had of David and her from the summer they met caught her eye; it hung on the wall above the counter. Being fourteen, she had the bird legs of a skinny teenager and wore blue rolled-up shorts and a T-shirt with a palm tree on it. The photo had been taken when Claire had flown down from Chicago to St. Pete to spend a month with her grandmother Betty.

Betty seemed to always have one foot in the sand and had introduced Claire to the magical properties of the Gulf. Every morning, they'd scour the beach in search of sharks' teeth and starfish and then settle into chairs under an umbrella to read until lunch. Claire could still taste the salty tears she'd shed on the return plane home at the end of the summer.

Not only had she fallen in love with the beach, but she'd fallen in love with a boy on the beach. The young man in the photograph was five shades tanner than her, with hairy legs, and as handsome as could be. He'd grown up in a huge family in Tampa, and they'd rented a beach house every summer on Pass-a-Grille. He'd seen her walking the beach by herself and said hello. Her first love.

They saw each other again the next summer, but then the flightiness of youth and the miles between Florida and Illinois proved to be too great to carry their relationship forward. They lost touch, and Claire didn't see him again for ten years. At the age of twenty-five, after Claire's father had died and she'd sold the diner, she moved south, taking a job assisting a wedding photographer. During one of her first shoots, David was one of the groomsmen. He took one knee later that year, and she'd said yes.

The whistling pot brought her back to the present. After dunking the tea bag up and down and then discarding it, Claire carried the cup back into the living room, where she fished out the composition books. It was time to read.

Moving to the porch, Claire settled into a rocking chair with Willy curled up on her lap. She petted him while sipping her tea, smoking another cigarette and watching the cars with out-of-state license plates pass.

When she was ready, she thumbed through the pages she'd already read, found the second chapter, and fell back into David's story, back into his arms. He hadn't let her read his old mysteries, insisting that they were trash, but now she wondered. Maybe she could dig those up too. David had been such a good writer. She knew that from his emails and letters he'd written over the years, but to read a story he'd created caught her off guard. He'd had true talent.

Claire burned through the first composition book in two hours. Willy had settled onto his favorite perch: a bamboo table by the door. Climbing into the hammock, Claire tore into the next book.

A notion settled in. David had written this book as some sort of cathartic exercise—a way to heal from his pain. He'd put all the hurt she didn't know he had into these pages, the sadness of being infertile, of never becoming a father. It wasn't a sad story by any means. Anything but! Claire felt great inspiration pulling for the main characters. But disguised in those words were the layers of David she hadn't known existed.

David had still wanted to be a father, even after he and Claire had agreed to stop trying. She'd forced him to stop bringing it up, to let go of the idea of parenthood. And she thought he'd been on the same page, that he'd moved on.

Claire's bottom lip quivered as it became all too clear that her husband had never gotten over their misfortune—his low sperm count. After their attempts to get pregnant and the grueling effects of negative results—and then what they believed was a sure-thing adoption that fell apart at the last moment—Claire had drawn a line in the sand. As difficult as it had been to say goodbye to her hopes of one day becoming a mother, she felt she knew what was best for them. "I don't want to talk about babies anymore, David. We have to let this go. I'm too hurt. I'm tired of being pricked and pried apart. And I can't take one more up and down."

Being the wonderful, loving, and supportive husband that David was, he'd given her a tight hug, encasing her with his love. "All I need is you, baby."

The man who'd grown up the oldest of five.

The man who was an uncle to seven and counting.

Her husband who had confessed to wanting four children (two boys, two girls) on their first date.

All I need is you.

Clearly, he'd needed more. David was the man in the story, and this was his way to experience fatherhood. Claire knew exactly why he hadn't let her read what he was working on. If she had, she would have known how much he'd been suffering, and without question, she would have blamed herself.

But the guilty feelings weren't enough to keep her from reading.

As the sun fell and she reached the third composition book, a budding idea took a firm hold. One of the most painful parts of grief and loss was how the memory dimmed. The legacy faded. Shortly after David had died, their house had filled with people. Casseroles spilled out of both refrigerators and freezers. Each day, lines of people had come to pay their respects, reaching a giant crescendo at the funeral, where hundreds of people turned out. A few weeks later, Claire hadn't had as many visitors. She hadn't received as many phone calls. Most of the casseroles she'd either eaten or given away. Soon, it was the occasional drop-by from her dearest friends. Six months later, David's memory was fading, and by the year anniversary of his death, his name was barely uttered. Here she was three years later, and even she was supposed to have moved on.

The buildings he'd designed, which Claire would always stop and admire, were all that would survive. Well . . . and his desk and chair.

And this book.

Claire had the idea that if she could get it published for him, she'd find a way to keep him alive. Or at least it would be a way to preserve his legacy, more words than any gravestone could hold. And perhaps it would help quell the guilt that was bubbling down in her depths. Maybe she could make right her wrong.

Claire returned to the final pages. She could feel the end of his story coming and hadn't felt so invested in the characters of a book in her entire life. Had David intended this to be the last draft? She'd never know, but the story might be publishable as it was. Why hadn't he shared it with her yet?

And then.

There were no more words.

Halfway through the third book, the story stopped midsentence.

Claire flipped through the blank pages, hoping to find more words. Nothing.

Leaving Willy back inside, Claire ran to her car and, under the glow of the moon, sped across St. Pete. She so hoped this wasn't a sad story. Was that why he wouldn't let her read it? When she reached their home, she ran up the stairs and raced into his office. She spent the next two hours searching for more words. Where were the other drafts? Had he tossed them? Had he hidden them somewhere?

She moved around his office like a madwoman, desperately pulling books off the shelf, opening drawers. She even knocked on the walls and floors, looking for hollow spots. It was soon evident that he had not finished his story. He died with words left to give, a story still to tell.

No one would ever know how it ended.

Lying on the floor amid the boxes of his books, Claire cried herself to sleep.

She woke puffy eyed in the middle of the night, not quite aware of her location. Whitaker Grant's book—the one inscribed to David—lay next to her head, lit up in the moonlight. She stared at it for a long while as her eyes and mind adjusted.

The realization of what she needed to do wrapped around her like David's arms when he'd last come to find her at the end of the dock. For perhaps the first time since he'd died, she felt hope, an almost impossible hope, like discovering a lost diamond ring in the waves. It was as if she'd suddenly found the answers she'd been looking for, and Claire was shocked, even saddened, that she'd waited three years to go through his office.

This book had been lying in a drawer collecting dust for three long years. His unfinished dream. As though wearing blinders, she felt a desperate need to get this book finished.

And Whitaker Grant was the one to do it. She knew that with all her heart, as if David had appeared to tell her so.

Chapter 4

DISTURBING THE PEACE

Whitaker Grant was on a Sunday-morning stakeout. Not the typical stakeout. And the absurdity had not been lost on him. He couldn't hold on to a marriage or drop a lick of weight. He certainly couldn't write another novel, but by God he would catch the man—or woman—responsible for not picking up dog poop in his neighborhood.

Wasting precious writing time, Whitaker hid behind tinted glass in the wayback of his aging Land Rover with his eyes glued to a pair of binoculars, watching for possible offenders in the park across the street. Since his divorce, he'd been living in a bachelorized house along Clymer Park in the tiny city of Gulfport, which bordered St. Petersburg. Lined with tall palms and oaks dripping Spanish moss, the park stretched for three blocks and featured lush gardens and local artists' exhibits as part of an art walk.

Whitaker was still in his bathrobe, and an empty box of Cheerios lay by his side. Seeing an unfamiliar man walking a springer spaniel through the grass, Whitaker leaned in with intense scrutiny.

When the dog finally took a squat, Whitaker readied himself. What exactly he'd do once he found the culprit, he was unsure. But this had to stop. Such a grand crime cut Whitaker to his core. Three times. Not once! Not twice. Thrice, he'd gone for a stroll around the park in his efforts to shed the ten extra pounds that had sneaked up on him, only to step in the excrement of a dog with a negligent owner. That third time, as he'd hosed off the poop, he'd committed to find this person.

The action in the park slowed for a while. He noticed a cute woman Rollerblading and wondered what her story was. He hadn't slept with a woman since his ex-wife, not that anyone would be surprised by that fact. Between his 1970s mustache and general disregard for style, he wasn't exactly the catch he used to be. Some men weathered a divorce and then ran like wild horses toward the closest women. Whitaker's divorce had only led him further into a lonely depression. A depression he was well aware of and disgusted by.

Whitaker glanced back at his little house, which was about all he had left after the settlement. Lisa had stayed in their mansion near the water, which was paid off courtesy of his novel. He'd asked for enough cash to buy a little house and to buy some time. Oh, and his wine. Considering he was the one who'd curated their robust collection, she hadn't argued. She was always content with a glass of sauvignon blanc anyway. He'd moved the collection to a wine-storage facility on Fourth Street and visited every once in a while. Though sadly, since he'd lost his wife and his muse, there weren't that many days worthy of popping corks on good bottles.

Still hungry, he pulled the bag of Cheerios out of the box and shook the crumbs into his mouth. He washed it down with the last of the lukewarm coffee in his travel mug. He always bought his beans from the same roaster in St. Pete, an establishment where the owners happened to be big fans of his writing. With the hazelnut hitting his taste buds, he tried not to think of what the owners would say about his recent habit of taking his coffee with an overly generous amount of creamer. Since the writer inside him had died, Whitaker's love of subtlety in coffee and wine had perished as well.

A suspicious-looking man walking a mini-poodle—or at least a mini-something—strutted by Whitaker's house. Was this the guy? The poop Whitaker had stepped in was more medium size, but Whitaker would be the first to admit he hadn't mastered the proportions of dog size to poop size yet. Hopefully, his limited PI skills (PI standing for *poop investigation*) would be enough to bring the perpetrator—or poopetrator—to justice.

Just when Whitaker thought he'd succeeded, the man extracted a bag from his back pocket, snapped it open with a shake, and reached down obediently to collect his dog's droppings.

Whitaker cursed in disappointment.

A few minutes later, his phone rang. Without looking at the display, he knew exactly who it was and the purpose of the call. And he always picked up for his mom. She was one of his favorite people on earth.

"Hi, sweetie," Sadie Grant said to her son. "I hope I'm not waking you."

"Oh, c'mon. I've been writing all morning."

In her typically jolly voice, she said, "Good for you. Well, I don't want to disturb you—just making sure you're coming over later."

"I wouldn't miss it for the world," he said, knowing there was no way out of this one.

"Honey, I know your sarcasm better than anyone. Don't toy with me."

Adjusting his position, he asked, "Why do you insist on everyone getting together when we don't get along?"

"Oh, honey, who cares about a few hiccups along the way? We're family. The Grants must stick together."

Whitaker could see her pumping her fist in the air. *The Grants must stick together!* He imagined his entire family, every Grant in Florida, marching down Beach Boulevard chanting, "The Grants must stick together! The Grants must stick together!" As if they owned St. Pete before the Native Americans did.

"I think you're confusing hiccups and hurricanes," he said. "Besides, I really need to write, Mom."

Whitaker scanned the park for more dogs.

"Don't do that, Whitaker. It's never the same without you."

Whitaker sighed. "What time does it start again?"

Still happy as can be, his mother almost sang, "The bouncy castle should be operational by three. But come over anytime. Did you get a present for your nephew?"

"Of course I did," Whitaker lied, wondering what he might find in the house worth wrapping. And where to find wrapping paper, tape, and ribbon.

"By the way, I just told your brother. We're hiding the liquor. There's plenty of beer and wine, but I don't like having everyone hammered on liquor. It shows our bad side."

"Bad side? We have a bad side?"

Her "Whitaker Grant" sounded like a reprimand. "I'll see you at the party."

"When is it again? Next week?"

"Whitaker, stop your shenanigans. See you in a few hours."

After ending the call, she flooded his phone with happy animal emojis, and Whitaker decided that the day baby boomers discovered emojis had to be the beginning of the end. How could someone be so happy all the time? Though she was brilliant and sharp, Whitaker had to wonder if part of her was insane. Why all these determined attempts to keep getting the family together? The Grant family took all the "fun" out of dysfunctional.

After another thirty minutes of the stakeout, Whitaker felt bored and decided to hang it up for now. Sundown might be a better time to expose this creep. That was when these people were more likely to break the pick-up-your-poop rule—in the dark when they could get away with it.

"Not anymore," promised Whitaker, climbing out of the Land Rover and returning to the house. "Not anymore."

Whitaker hung his binoculars on the coatrack next to the umbrella. In the kitchen, he poured himself another cup of coffee and destroyed it with creamer. While stirring the concoction, his mind wandered into book land. Although the words weren't flowing like they used to, he'd been typing some. That was the difference between now and the good old days. Where the man who had won copious literary awards, sold his book to Hollywood, and even for a moment made his father proud, was a respected writer, the man erratically running around in his bathrobe on this Sunday morning was a typist.

As the typist made his way to what could barely be called a third bedroom, Whitaker interviewed himself out loud. More and more lately, he was talking to himself, the banter of the lonely.

"Mr. Grant," he started, with Walter Cronkite–esque authority, "what do you do for a living now? Are you writing again?"

In his best washed-up Whitaker Grant accent—one he'd mastered considering he was one and the same—he answered, "No, I'm just typing. I don't have any more stories to tell. Nothing of consequence, at least."

"How are you paying the bills with this typing?"

"Oh, I'm not really. Still living off a few royalty checks, but I'm also dabbling in investments, advising folks on where to put their money."

"What do you know about banking?"

"One of the benefits of being Jack Grant's son. I was studying stock charts before I could read. Because I have somewhat of a name in the area, my clients tend to find me."

"Don't you miss writing? I can't imagine typing has the same creative return."

"Oh, no. Typing is much more fun." Whitaker threw his hands in the air. "Of course I miss writing, you bumbling fool! I'm lost in a world of words, and I can't get my fingers around any of them. They're everywhere. All I see . . . letters and words. But I can't wrap my hands or head around a damned one."

"I see," Walter responded with a twinge of pity. "You're screwed, aren't you?"

"Royally, Walter. Royally."

Nevertheless, Whitaker needed to sit down and get started on this typing venture. He felt sure that if he kept pecking away, the typing would turn to writing again, though the doubt and fear swollen inside him didn't leave much room for a creative outburst.

Like the rest of his house, the third bedroom–turned-office was a mess. Whitaker would do one of his monthly cleaning sessions soon, which was well overdue. In the meantime, he just didn't care.

A fold-up card table for a desk, covered with mail. Food particles on the rug, dirty laundry on the floor. Two of the three light bulbs on the ceiling fan dead. Sometimes you needed to worry about surviving. Then once you figured that part out, you could worry about the details of surviving with style: cleaning, shaving, that sort of thing.

Today, Whitaker was alive and sitting down to write. That was about as great of an accomplishment as the typist was capable of at the moment. Whitaker brushed aside a stack of books from his chair, let them fall to the floor, and dropped into his seat. Prepared for battle, he glanced up to find inspiration from the movie poster based on his bestselling novel, *Napalm Trees and Turquoise Waters*, hanging on the wall. He couldn't help looking at the framed photograph to the right of the poster, a shot of him and his ex-wife, Lisa—dressed to the nines—standing on the red carpet moments before the premiere in West Hollywood. Her lava-red hair long and wavy, the freckles he used to touch one at a time—connecting the dots, her soft skin, the two young lovers' hands clasped together as if nothing could ever sever their connection. What happened to the man in the photo? Whitaker looked back at Lisa. When she left, he left. Mystery solved.

Whitaker had always been attracted to redheads, and when Lisa had crossed his path one day at a book signing, he'd asked for her number. Those were the days when his game was strong. His confidence was unparalleled during those beautiful years after the release of *Napalm Trees*. The young redhead had been flattered, and why not? He was a big deal back then. The critics had called him a national treasure, a burgeoning genius. *Napalm Trees* was "a tour de force, a literary behemoth!"

Napalm Trees was indeed considered literary fiction, but not the kind that would turn into required reading in college. His novel was page-turning fiction meant for book clubs. It just so happened to be quite literary. What? Whitaker couldn't help that his silver pen painted scenes so vividly that a reader might tumble into the page through his wormhole of words. He rolled his eyes at his own sarcasm.

The typist unfolded his laptop. He'd written his last book on a laptop that he'd dubbed Excalibur. The screen used to come to life with the excitement of taking on the world. When he'd set his fingers over the keys, that computer had begged for words like a stranded man in the desert desperate for water. If only a laptop could keep up with the times. Newer technology had led to Excalibur's inevitable doom. Something about writing a hit book and making a lot of money had made Whitaker want to upgrade. If only he'd known that he was tossing his finest ally into the trash, he would have put up with its constant freezing and need to be restarted for the rest of his writing career.

As part of his regimen of procrastination, Whitaker always needed to restart his computer before words were written, something about starting fresh. As the computer rebooted, he sat there cracking his knuckles and watching the update bar. When the computer—still unworthy of a name—finally came alive with a welcome sound, he surfed his favorite sites. Anything to delay dredging up new words.

Of course, there would be no writing until he'd checked emails. He never knew what might be waiting for him, good or bad. Was he procrastinating? Yes, indeed. Still, he had several hours to write before his afternoon get-together with family.

Whitaker hadn't gotten far in reading emails when he came across the latest communique from his agent in New York. It was the same old message: When will you have something for me to read? I can find us another publisher. Might even be able to get another advance. Don't give up.

"Oh, good," Whitaker said through gritted teeth. "Another advance that I will have to pay back when no story surfaces."

If only people knew how impossible it was to put words on a page when your life depended on it. This sort of pressure from his peers was exactly what made writing now so much more difficult.

"I'm typing, dammit. I'll have your book soon enough. Get off my back. There's no blood left to suck."

Breaking away from the writing business, Whitaker took time to enjoy an inappropriate email from his brother. After a final bout of laughter, he checked his social media sites. Though *Napalm Trees* had hit stores before the social media uprising, Whitaker had built a strong and active following over the years. Much of that certainly had to do with his often careless and unfiltered rants, but, nevertheless, at least he still had a voice. Someone had posted in his group about a possible sequel to the movie. Whitaker read the comments, amazed how many conclusions these people could make on complete hearsay. Claiming the final word, he typed I have not been made aware of a movie.

Finally, it was time to get to it. The typist closed his internet browser and opened up his latest novel in Microsoft Word. It wasn't that he'd gone completely dry. It was just that the last ten years he'd written a series of unfinished novels. Somewhere between one page and halfway through, he'd decide that his premise sucked or that the writing was pedestrian at best, and that there was no way he'd show the world that this was his follow-up, that this was his best attempt to outdo his last one.

This new novel could be good, though. To change it up and catch his readers off guard, he'd decided to write a period piece. He wanted to explore life in the twenties in St. Pete, those days when Joe DiMaggio and Marilyn Monroe were allegedly sneaking around in their affair, and Frank Sinatra was crooning and chasing women at the marina in Tierra Verde.

Best of all, he knew this story was the right one because he was giving back to the city that had blessed him with his first novel. In return, he'd write another love letter to St. Pete, a novel oozing over with the magic of his beloved city. The premise was that a bootlegger was trying to escape his ties to the Mafia and become an honest man. His agent had said the book might be a bit off brand but that he could sell it. His agent really meant, "I'll take whatever I can get at this point."

After putting on one of his favorite Paco de Lucía albums, he lifted his fingers and straightened his back. *It's time,* he thought. With the effort of attempting to lift a car by oneself, Whitaker tapped the first key. Because the story would be in first person, "I" was a logical choice.

I.

I am.

No. Terrible verb.

I walked.

Even worse.

I ran.

Whitaker nodded his head.

I ran through the wild.

"What is this, Whitaker? You ran through the wild? No, no. You're a bootlegger and a family man. Everything you do is for your family. And you just want out."

Paco wailed on his flamenco guitar as Whitaker typed: I want out.

Ah, there it is. I want out. Who is he talking to? A crime boss. An Italian. Matteo.

Whitaker said triumphantly, "I want out, Matteo."

There, he did it. He'd written the first line. "Thank you for the soundtrack, Paco."

Feeling like he'd broken the tape at the finish line of a race, he pushed back from his chair and raised his hands in the air. "Victory," he said. "It's a start, Whitaker. It's a start."

Taking a break, he ambled to the kitchen and opened the refrigerator. In place of the capers, cornichons, freshly caught fish, farmers market vegetables, and fine cheeses of yesteryear, the fridge was now a wasteland of items fit to make quick-and-easy meals. Heinz might have agreed to sponsor him if he'd asked. After processing the realization that he needed to toss out half of it, he fumbled around until he found a carton of Chinese food that was a few days old. How many days, exactly, he wasn't sure. After a positive assessment, he grabbed a fork and dug in. No need heating it up. He was just looking for a little fix, something to stop his stomach from growling.

Halfway through, as soy sauce filled his taste buds, he said with a mouth full of food, "Coffee and cold moo goo gai pan. Couldn't pull this off when I was married. There's that."

Noticing the time on the range clock, he felt frustrated that the hours were getting away from him. He wanted to get more writing done *and* treat himself to an hour or so of video games before this family thing. Every part of him wanted to call his brother with an excuse, but Riley would never let him live it down.

He cast an eye toward the door leading to his office and then to the hallway leading to the living room. Write more or kill zombies? Internally justifying his choice to kill zombies, he prided himself on finally getting that first sentence. Sometimes the first sentence was the most difficult.

Whitaker moved a wrinkled shirt out of the way and plopped down onto the black-and-white houndstooth sofa his parents had handed down to him. They replaced their furniture far more often than they needed to. He set the Chinese food down and grabbed a controller. Pushing a button, the game started, and in no time he was dropped into a foreign future world where his avatar was wielding a giant gun. With this level of technology now available, who said gaming was for kids only? He circumnavigated a boulder and climbed a hill. The zombies started after him, screaming wildly as they jumped and flew around him. Whitaker pulled the trigger and let his automatic weapon wreak havoc on these decaying meat bags.

As the dopamine began to satisfy Whitaker's brain, a knock came at the door.

"Ay dios mío," he said in Spanish, the language he often slipped into when he was angry. Also fluent, his ex-wife had started the habit and had truly mastered it by the end of their marriage.

Whitaker paused the game as a zombie was making a run at him. Shaking his head, he said, *"Qué tipo de persona molesta a un hombre el domingo por la mañana?"* What kind of person bothers a man on Sunday morning?

He eyed the front door. Wasn't everyone supposed to be at church? Slinking lower on the sofa so that he couldn't be seen through the window next to the front door, he lowered the volume and returned to battle.

Chapter 5

No, Thank You, Goodbye

The knocking didn't stop. Someone out there was determined. Cinching his robe tight, Whitaker crept across the house to a window in the dining room. He peeked and saw the back of a woman with light-brown hair and long, tan legs waiting on the stoop. Who in the world? Perhaps someone interested in pushing her religious beliefs. Or someone selling something. With those legs, probably the latter. Either way, he'd better answer it and run her off, or she'd just come back at an even more inopportune time.

Whitaker walked to the front foyer and cracked open the door about two inches. "How can I help you?"

She was about his age. The rims of her glasses reached from her eyebrows down to the bottom of her nose. That was the style these days, Whitaker thought. She wore a romper with thick stripes of white and faded blue that fit tightly around her skinny waist. He attempted to stop his gaze from descending again but took a quick glance all the way down to her bright pink flip-flops and painted white nails. Whitaker pulled open the door even farther.

Though she looked like she hadn't slept all night, Whitaker found her arresting. Nerves he hadn't felt in a long time dizzied him. It occurred to him that he'd seen this woman before, but he couldn't place her. The big glasses, the seductive eyes and lips—as if a red rose had a face.

"Hi there," she said. "I'm . . ." She stopped and took a breath.

Why is she nervous? Whitaker wondered.

Stabilized, the woman touched her chest. "I'm Claire Kite." When the name didn't register, she said, "You probably don't remember me, but we met at my restaurant. I own Leo's South on Pass-a-Grille."

That's right, he thought. He flashed back to the days when he was single and used to type in her restaurant, a couple of years after *Napalm Trees.* He couldn't remember the specifics, but he remembered her. "Oh, yeah, sure."

Whitaker realized he shouldn't have opened the door. He couldn't imagine what he looked like, the robe, his wild and shaggy hair probably all over the place. "I used to love Leo's, but it's been a while. How can I help you?"

"I don't even know where to begin, really." She looked down briefly. "Can I come in?"

"Umm, I'm not exactly prepared to accept guests. Sorry. The place is a mess." He looked down for a wedding ring and noticed a stack of composition books in her left hand. The books covered her ring finger. "You're not some kind of journalist on the side, are you? I'm not doing interviews." *Other than the ones in my head,* he conceded silently.

Stay out of it, Walter.

"No, I'm not a journalist. I just need a few minutes of your time to explain. It's very important. To me, at least."

Whitaker thought for a moment. No way was he going to let this beguiling woman come in and see the disaster he'd become. Cold Chinese, zombies frozen on the television. Still, he was intrigued. What did she want from him? The pleading and sadness in her voice suggested that he needed to hear her out.

He pinched his mustache. "Would you please give me a moment? Let me put some clothes on, and we can sit out front. Can I offer you an ice water?"

Claire smiled. "Yes, absolutely. Thank you."

Whitaker ran up the stairs and pulled on a pair of blue shorts, which had become more difficult to button. Until recently, he'd always weighed around the same as he had during his college days at Emory, so the idea of wearing anything larger than a thirty-two-inch waist terrified him. He pulled on a white T-shirt and rushed into the bathroom. As he gargled mouthwash (no time for brushing), he couldn't help shaking his head at the man in the mirror. He was still tall, thank goodness. No one could take that from him. But what was this mustache he'd grown? Between that and the unkempt wild hair, he looked like he belonged on a sailboat much farther south, running drugs. Of course that would be looking at him in a more positive light. His father would tell him he looked like a redneck who lived with his hound dog in a single-wide trailer in the middle of Florida.

There wasn't much more he could do for his appearance while she waited, but he wondered why he even cared. It had been a long time since he'd cared what anyone thought about his appearance, but he felt this strange need to attempt to impress her. He shrugged and pointed at himself in the mirror. "Be nice."

After a quick stop by the kitchen for her glass of water, he found Claire waiting in one of the two chairs on the front porch. A pot with a dying fern hung above her head. She stood when Whitaker came out, but he waved her back down. Sadly, a daunting engagement ring and wedding band clung to her finger as if to say, "Don't bother."

Almost relieved that he wouldn't have to attempt a quick dusting off of his cobwebbed charm, he handed her the drink and took the seat opposite her. The sudden intimacy of the little porch made him uncomfortable. He wasn't the confident man around women that he used to be, especially around this one.

A towering kapok tree was in full bloom in the middle of the yard. He'd spent many hours in awe of this tree, the giant tropical red flowers coming to life on the tree's stubby, leafless branches. He couldn't help but think of a Tim Burton film whenever he took the time to appreciate the wicked beauty of the kapok.

While Claire explained that she wasn't a stalker and that a friend living nearby had told her where he lived, Whitaker scanned the park for any scandalous dog walkers. No dogs, only a man tossing a baseball with his two sons on the other side near a statue.

"Anyway," she said nervously, "I'm sorry to bother you on a Sunday morning."

"It seems important." They met eyes, and then Whitaker quickly looked back to the park. One of the boys attempted to catch a poorly thrown ball.

God, she is beautiful, he thought, as their first encounter a decade before started to come back to him. He remembered being as attracted to her then as he was now.

"My husband died three years ago yesterday."

Oh. A kaleidoscope of butterflies migrated back to his stomach. He spun his head back to her, both death and possibility knocking on his door. When he met her eyes, though, it was the stone-cold sobriety of widowhood that pulled at his heartstrings like the puppeteer of the lonely.

He gave her his full attention.

Claire sat up straight, placing her hands on her lap. "You probably wouldn't remember, but years ago, you were writing in my café, and I walked up to your table and introduced myself."

"Yeah, I remember," he said. To be clear, he remembered typing there, not writing. His well had already dried up by the time he'd started visiting Leo's South.

"I told you I loved your book, but that my husband, David, hadn't read it yet. You came back a week later with a copy for him. David didn't touch it for a couple more years, but when he finally did, it hit him hard." Claire shuffled her feet in her pink flip-flops and took a breath. "In fact, he started writing again. He was an English major in school and wrote a couple novels—mystery kind of stuff—but couldn't get them published. Went on to be an architect and let go of the writing thing. Until he read your book. Then it was reading and writing all the time. Up until the day he died."

Whitaker wasn't sure what to say. Apparently, she felt a need to share this story so badly that she'd shown up at his door on a Sunday morning to do so.

"He died without finishing it."

Whitaker nodded again. She wasn't about to ask him to finish it, was she?

"I read it yesterday for the first time," Claire continued. Before she could get out another word, her face melted with sadness, and she dropped her chin.

Whitaker wasn't very good at taking care of anyone else. He had been at one time, but those days felt distant. His inability to get outside himself was most certainly the culprit; he knew that. Either way, he had an urge to rise and comfort her. To whip out a white handkerchief and pat her tears. Alas, he had no white handkerchief. In his current state, the only comfort he might have offered her was a turn at killing zombies inside—the best (healthier than drinking) release for pain he'd found to date. He decided to let her take her time until she could get it all out.

"What he's written is special, and it needs . . ." She wiped her eyes.

"Can I get you some tissues?"

She shook her head and wiped her eyes again. "He wrote something great, and it needs to get out there. I want you to finish it. I'll pay you, of course. I'll do whatever it takes."

"Why me? Because my book from ten years ago inspired him? That's a far stretch."

"I think it's a pretty good reason. And I see a part of you in his writing. Not the setting, though I think you both come from the same school of description. And your prose is obviously more elevated. But it's in the tapping deep that I see similarities." Her gaze flitted all around, occasionally meeting his. "When I read *Napalm Trees*, I felt like you'd put it all out there, like you didn't care what people thought about you. You just wanted to be true, all else be damned. That's what his book reads like, like his story needed outing, all else be damned."

She finally settled and looked at him with pleading, almost irresistible eyes. "You inspired him to write again in a new way, and I believe that you are meant to finish this book. Not just because you inspired my husband to write. It's because you're one of the best writers in Florida, and he and this story deserve you."

Whitaker watched a lizard run up the wall. "Thank you for the compliment, but I haven't released anything in ten years. Life's kind of gotten in the way."

She processed his words with a few slow breaths. Then, with great determination, she asked, "What if this story is meant for you?"

Whitaker's eyes bulged, and his head floated backward at the notion. He could see that the idea of it being meant for him was her magic bullet, the words she'd been saving for the right moment. "Claire, I'm into the cosmos and meant-to-bes and aligning stars and all that. But I'm not abiding by the laws of the universe right now. You've caught me in a pretty low moment." He saw no need to lie to her or pretend he was anything more than a has-been caught in a constipated rut.

Claire shook her head again. "You can't say no."

Something about her words struck a dissonant chord, and he suddenly felt as if a squire were racing to clad him with armor for protection. A cautious voice warned, *Stay true to the course.*

"I have to say no," he said. He didn't want to, that was for sure. To say no to a widow in need felt below even him at his worst.

"Whitaker Grant, I'm asking you from the bottom of my heart. Will you please finish my husband's novel?"

He scratched his head and mumbled, "I want out, Matteo."

"What did you say?"

"Nothing, sorry. Just talking to myself." This moment was nothing to make light of, and he knew that. Smiling and awkward jokes in the midst of sadness were Grant family traits. "Look, I'm so sorry for your loss. I really can't imagine what you've been through. You're a brave woman to get out of bed every day." He clasped his hands together. "But I can't finish your husband's novel. Frankly, I can't even finish my own. I'm not your guy."

Her shoulders sank. "You are. I know you are."

"You can't know that."

Whitaker watched a flock of white ibises land in the front lawn and peck into the dirt. Though getting paid to write was tempting, this wasn't exactly what he'd been gunning for. The last thing he ever wanted was to follow up his hit novel with something he'd ghostwritten. He hated himself for his selfishness, but he had to put himself first. He might only have one shot left.

"Seriously, I'm a year away from hanging up this frivolous profession. You don't want me touching your husband's novel."

A tear rolled down her cheek, and the air left Whitaker's lungs. He'd only known her a little while, but her pain hit him like a dear friend was suffering. *No, don't go down that road, Whitaker. Don't let pity or your attraction to her win out. You must hold strong.* In his mind, he held out his arms so that the squire could finish assembling his armor.

"Will you at least read it?"

I want out, Matteo.

"Look, Claire, if I read every book that people asked me to read after I found some success, I wouldn't have a moment to do anything else. Even after ten years, people stop me at least weekly." In his grandpa accent, he said, "Have I got a story for you! Back when I was a . . ."

Claire didn't find him funny. "I'm not a random fan begging you to write my story." More tears came, and she struggled to get her words out. "I'm asking you to preserve my husband's legacy. And to get paid doing it."

He sat back and crossed his arms. "You're asking me to write another man's story, to climb into someone else's head. I'm sorry, Claire. If I'm able to finally tap into some creative energy, I'm going to put it into my own work. Not to finish what your husband started."

Claire leaned toward him, sitting at the edge of her seat. Her ice water sat untouched on the brick wall next to her. "Will you please just read it? I'll pay you."

Though he was tempted—for the money and to get a bit closer to her—he knew agreeing to read it wouldn't be right. He'd be leading this poor woman on. "If I agreed to read it, I'd still tell you no. And it would hurt you much worse. So no, I will not read it." He sliced his hand through the air. "Not even for money. Writing is a very personal thing . . . at least for me. I can't pick up where some random guy left off—no offense to your husband."

Claire wiped her eyes and looked up with new resolve. "What if you haven't been able to write because this story has been working its way to you? What if you telling me no right now is the same as spitting on your destiny?"

How could he possibly answer those questions? He wasn't a ghost-writer, dammit. Who had enough creative juice to share it in the name of charity? Besides, what if he let her down? If this project were truly meant to be, he'd feel it more. It would be calling him. Right now, he just wanted Claire to take those composition books and leave.

With finality, he said, "I'm sorry, Claire. I think it's a noble idea, and I hope you find someone. But it's not me." He stood. "Can I walk you to your car?"

Claire's face had changed from hope and determination to anger. He could see that she wanted to say more, to perhaps even cut him down with harsh words. Something about being selfish. After she stood, she didn't make eye contact with him again.

As the widow descended the steps of the porch, she said with her back to him, "Thanks for listening."

He started to say something else and opened his mouth. The words—all lame and pointless—died on his tongue.

Chapter 6

FATHER AND SON

Though Claire hadn't left his mind, and he felt terribly conflicted and even ripped apart by letting the young widow down, Whitaker's impending meeting with his family dominated his inner dialogue. No more words were written that Sunday. All the typist had done was slay zombies and pass out on the sofa. An alarm woke him, and a headache set in as he realized it was time to get ready. He showered and shaved but kept the mustache. There was something rather artistic and rebellious about it that appealed to him, and he fit in wonderfully with the vibrant array of outcasts living in Gulfport.

Whitaker's body was tensed to the point of pain as he drove his geriatric Land Rover toward his parents' expensive waterfront property north of downtown. What could go wrong this time? The possibilities were endless. As a loose belt slapped the engine, he couldn't help but marvel at the absurdity of life.

If it wasn't he and his father bickering, one of his siblings would bring some drama to the table. Somehow the Grants had missed the memo that, during family get-togethers, it was best to avoid topics of a sensitive persuasion, such as politics, religion, or dietary preferences. Whitaker had witnessed a disaster several months ago when his sister, with her heavy-left-leaning beliefs, had preached to Jack until the arteries in his neck had nearly burst.

There was always one dedicated member of a family—one brave soul—who tried to hold everyone together. In the Grant family, that dubious charge was taken up by Whitaker's mother, Sadie, the loyal and fearless Floridian matriarch, mother of three and wife to a pain in the ass. It was she who had intervened only seconds before Jack dropped to the floor from a heart attack.

Unlike a family tree sprouting branches, Whitaker's take on the Grant genealogy was that the Grants worked their way through the generations like cracked glass spidering outward . . . until it one day would shatter.

Using the logic that the worst part about getting a shot from the doctor was the agonizing anticipation leading up to it, Whitaker cranked up a Miles Davis album and let the loud music take him away from the impending birthday party.

His thoughts forced him to miss his right turn, so he took Central Avenue instead. Always promising a spectacle, Central would be a more distracting drive anyway. As he'd described in *Napalm Trees*, the upper crust of St. Pete had been infiltrated by young blood that pushed hard against the conservative values that had built this city years ago, and the result was a beautiful mix—or mess, depending on who was talking—of Republican and Democrat, native and snowbird, young and old, straight, gay, brown, black, white, or whatever, all working together to make this city one with which to be reckoned. It was a city as receptive to impressive graffiti as it was to the next high-rise.

Due to the disproportionate number of retirees that had once filled the Sunshine City, people had called St. Pete "God's Waiting Room." With the surge of youth the city was experiencing, God would have to wait a lot longer than usual to collect his souls.

Whitaker drove by an army of construction workers assembling yet another expensive, LEED-certified building under one of the many cranes that hovered over the city. A giant white sign read: GRANT CONSTRUCTION. BUILDING ST. PETE FOR GENERATIONS. His father was indeed the third generation of Grant Construction, and unless his sister—a feminist attorney—decided to don a hard hat, their father would be the last. His brother had already gone down his own path.

With the family's latest project in the rearview, Whitaker passed a glass-blowing studio where he'd once taken a date, a New Age center where he'd had his palms read, and a CBD store that he surely would have visited in his teens if it had been there. He then drove by a tattoo parlor where a seventeen-year-old, Emory-bound Whitaker had gotten his first and only tattoo—a quill pen in all black ink up high on his right arm—for no other reason than his father had forbidden him from doing so.

Below the tall, skinny palm trees that reached higher than many of the taller buildings—though not as high as the cranes—the happy citizens of St. Pete (some of them certainly as high as the cranes) moved along the sidewalks with great pride. Proud they lived down here and not in the Midwest or Northeast, both of which were currently suffering from winter blizzards. And proud because something special was happening here in St. Pete: the artists, the refugees of all kinds, the aura readers, the coffee shops, the breweries, the museums, the festivals, the cultural diversity. Whitaker knew exactly how they felt, because he shared the same feelings.

He wound his way through the intricate streets that led to the fingers of land sticking out into Tampa Bay, eventually reaching his parents' house. The mansion was the *exact* monstrosity one might picture when wondering what type of home an extremely successful construction company owner might own. A six-thousand-square-foot beast on deep water with more bedrooms and bathrooms than some small colonies could put to use. Whitaker wasn't opposed to money by any means, but sometimes seeing this house made him wince.

Since there wasn't room at his brother's house for a bouncy castle, Sadie had offered to host the birthday party here. Sure enough, a giant bouncy castle bubbling over with happy kids, like a popcorn machine popping corn, stood in the middle of the immaculate front lawn. Apparently, his mother had neglected to mention that the party was dinosaur themed. A banner hanging from the house read: LET'S HAVE A DINO-MITE PARTY! Several of the kids and even a few parents wore dinosaur tails. Someone had carved a watermelon into an impressive T. rex opening its mouth. Clusters of adults stood nearby, munching on catered finger foods and pounding rosé and cold beer and probably talking about the best private schools, or the stock market, or the next coach for the Bucs. Whitaker was already wondering where they'd hidden the liquor.

He parked close by and grabbed his nephew's present, which—for purposes of environmental concern and a lack of supplies—was wrapped in a Trader Joe's paper bag turned inside out. Present under arm, Whitaker forced a smile and moved toward his family.

"Uncle Whitaker!" his five-year-old nephew screamed from the top of the bouncy castle.

Whitaker gave a big wave. "Happy birthday, old man!"

"What's the present?"

"I'll stick it on the pile. You'll see soon enough."

The typist worked his way through the crowd, saying hello to people he'd known most of his life. Four generations of Grants. No one had more cousins and uncles and aunts, nephews and nieces. To his dismay, nearly all of them mentioned something about his writing career. After hugging and kissing and making small talk with half of them, he finally made it to his mother.

Sadie was not born a Grant, but to marry one was to cut your roots low and be replanted into dangerous Grant soil. He saw his mother as a brave yet aloof southern equestrienne riding the white flag of surrender into a bloodbath of familial dysfunction, the female Don Quixote of Florida.

Sadie was a doll. Born a doll and had always been a doll. A southern belle without the accent—at least without much of one. As southern belle as you can be growing up in Florida. For every native of Florida who had shucked an oyster, cracked open a boiled peanut, or polished off a bowl of grits, there was a snowbird's child next to them saying, "What in the world are gator bites?" No, you couldn't really be a southerner, not with all the northern and midwestern influence. But Sadie was a doll, as innocent as a flower, and everyone in St. Pete loved her. How could you not love someone who couldn't stop smiling?

"I'm so glad you came," she said loud enough to be heard over the kids screaming in the castle twenty feet away.

"Me too." Whitaker kissed her cheek and detected the familiar hints of gardenia from the perfume she'd worn for as long as he could remember. He was careful not to mess up her hair, which she'd kept the same way for forty years, a sort of bulbous helmet hardened by hair spray. The only change over the years was from brown to gray. Whitaker appreciated that his mom had let her hair gray without hiding behind dye. This devil-may-care attitude carried over to much of her life. She wasn't afraid to show her gray hair, and she damn sure wasn't afraid to show the scars and weaknesses of her family. In her aloof, high-pitched tone, she would ask, "Why be ashamed of being human, Whitaker?"

If only that insouciance had rubbed off on him. If he looked back, maybe it had, but years of fighting an artist's battles had made him start to overthink things and worry too much.

Doña Quixote looked down at the present in his hand. "Do I need to inspect it? No more fireworks, right? And you know Miles can't have dairy."

Whitaker sipped the beer someone had handed him. "No dairy. No gunpowder." She didn't say a word about anything sharp.

Sadie moved in and whispered into his ear. "Be nice to your father. He wants to talk to you about something."

"What did I do now?"

"Nothing, honey. Just hear him out."

What in the world could that mean? Whitaker wondered.

When he finally ran into his dad, Whitaker's clenched teeth compromised his fake smile. He could feel the rest of his family watching this encounter, as if Whitaker were part of a bomb squad approaching a man in a suicide vest. Or was Whitaker the one in the vest?

Both men were known to fly off the handle. The last time they'd been together, Whitaker had unleashed a rant that had cut to the core of his father. Though he thought the man deserved his fair share of harsh words, even Whitaker knew he'd stepped over the line, and he'd even gone as far as apologizing the next day. Somewhere down there, deep into the sludge, his father was a good man. It was a lot of sludge, though. Epic quantities of thick, PTSD-riddled sludge.

Jack stood two inches shorter than Whitaker, but he always looked down on him. Even if Jack were four feet tall, he'd still look down on his son. Though he'd been as strapping as Whitaker in his early years, according to Sadie, Jack had aged rapidly after the war. He had lost most of his hair and walked with a slight limp from a helicopter crash in the Mekong Delta. The hardhead that he was, he refused to use a cane. When the army had shipped him home from Saigon with his broken leg, he'd also brought back an unknown stomach worm that ran his immune system into the ground and nearly killed him.

Though the man had some rough edges, he'd been a good father. Perhaps overly stern, but certainly better than many others out there.

Staff Sergeant Jack Grant reached up and tugged at Whitaker's longish hair. His mane was by no means of ponytail length, but he'd let it go wild since the divorce. "I'd forgotten I had another daughter. Should I call you Whitney? You haven't seen your brother, have you?"

"Off to a good start, aren't you?" Whitaker said. "I'd forgotten where my humor came from."

Jack adjusted his Vietnam Vet hat. "Just pulling your chain, son." He offered a hand, and the men shook.

"Mom says you want to talk about something?"

Jack looked around and nodded. "Why don't we talk on the boat?"

Before he could say no, Whitaker found himself following his limping father around the side of the house. The landscaping could have won awards. They entered the backyard through a white vinyl gate, passed the saltwater pool, and walked down the short dock to Jack's pride and joy, a forty-one-foot Regulator sport fisher with four 425 engines hanging off the transom. Climbing aboard, Whitaker took a seat on the bow, and his father dug two cold beers out of the cooler.

He tossed one to Whitaker. "Finally got our first sailfish of the year yesterday."

Catching the can, Whitaker said, "Nice."

"She was a big one. Almost worth mounting. Pulled in a couple hog snappers too. It's that time of year."

Whitaker hated talking about fishing with his dad. Though he'd inherited his father's sense of humor, he'd not acquired his father's love of fishing. In fact, much to Jack's disappointment, Whitaker was prone to seasickness and had only once dared to go deep-sea fishing with Jack. With his father's Poseidon eyes on him, Whitaker had spent the majority of the day heaving over the rail.

Jack took a seat on the bow cushion across from Whitaker and cracked open his own beer. "I've been thinking." He paused, waving at a stand-up paddleboarder cutting through the channel.

"That's good to hear, Dad. I was worried you were going senile."

"No, the hamster's still spinning the wheel up there. At least for now." Jack smiled, confirmation that somewhere deep within his father's grim reaper shell was the slightest bit of light. What was funny and sad at the same time was that little light was what Whitaker wanted most in the world. To see that light, to feel a bit of love and approval from his father, was up there or even beyond the importance of writing another book.

They both watched a sailboat maneuver the narrow inlet and then Jack asked, "What would you think about coming to work for me?"

There it was. Forty years in the making. Between the grind of managing construction workers and the potential agony of working for Jack Grant, Whitaker and his other siblings had never taken to the idea.

Jack looked proud, like he'd just offered Whitaker a kidney. "I want one of you to take over this business, and I think you have what it takes. You'd have to learn a lot, and I'd make you work from the ground up. But I'd pay you well . . . and you'd take over the company one day. There's a lot of money to be had."

Whitaker considered the best way to say no. But he wasn't very good at walking on eggshells. "I'd rather you sell the company and leave me some money."

Jack shook his head. "Sorry, Whit. I don't feel right giving you a bunch of money to sit around and keep pretending you're writing."

Ah, the sting of Jack Grant.

"I am writing, Dad. And I have a job too."

"You and I both know that's temporary. You were never cut out for the corporate world. And wait until the bear market comes. You might second-guess this new career."

Whitaker couldn't argue with him.

"Come work with me," Jack said.

"Dad, I couldn't build a birdhouse."

"That's fine. You'll learn. You could finally put all those languages you learned to work. Well, Spanish, at least. Besides, when's the last time you think I picked up a hammer? You're good with people, and that's what matters." Jack adjusted his hat. "We'd need to clean you up some. Nothing a decent barber can't fix."

Whitaker appreciated the job offer, and it was kind of his father to come to his aid. But there was no way in hell he would join the family business. "The truth is that I'm writing again. I know I hit a dry spell, but I'm coming out of it. If I took a job with you, I'd be saying goodbye to writing forever."

"Can I be honest back with you?"

"That's one thing you always are."

Jack nodded. "You're a good writer, and I'm proud of you for what you've done. Even if you don't write another book, you've done more than most writers alive. There's something to be said for that. But there comes a point where you have to take life a bit more seriously. Time to start thinking about a new family again. Time to let go of these childhood dreams and . . . become an adult."

"Don't go there, Dad. Who says we all have to raise a family? I'm forty. I'm not sure that's even in the cards anymore. Lisa was the one pushing me. Without her, I'm not sure I'm father material."

"I think you'd be a great father, but fair enough. You don't need to force it if you're not interested. But behind every good man is a good woman."

Whitaker's headache was raging. He hated these conversations.

Unsurprisingly, Jack wasn't done. "We are the sum of our choices, Whit. All the little choices we make as humans create who we are. It's like the construction business. When I build a project, it's one good decision at a time. We start with a strong foundation, and then we take every following detail seriously. That's why my buildings stand the test of time. When I look at you, I see a big pile of bad decisions. I see a building falling apart from the inside out."

Whitaker crushed the empty beer can in his hand. "Thanks for the vote of confidence."

"I'm sorry, son. I don't want to be the dad who crushes your dreams, but it's been ten years. Some people only have one book in them. Nothing wrong with that."

A nauseated feeling rose from his stomach as Whitaker stood and started to leave. "There is no future without another book. That's about the only thing I know these days." He jumped up onto the dock. "Thanks for the beer."

"Whitaker, look at you. What is this mustache and the long hair? You're a good-looking guy. Quit trying to hide it."

Whitaker ignored his question. "I appreciate the job offer."

As he walked back around to the front of the house, dodging the others at the party, he wondered why he hadn't allowed himself to escape this madness, why he hadn't packed up his Rover and hit the highway.

But he knew. Because St. Pete had given him his first novel, and he knew she was going to give him another one.

Avoiding the dinosaur crowd around the bouncy castle, Whitaker walked the property line toward the street. Thinking he'd successfully sneaked away, he heard his brother's voice.

"Whit!" Riley yelled. "A buck knife? Who gives a five-year-old a buck knife?"

As he was wrapping it, the gift had made perfect sense, but upon hearing his brother's condemnation, it became painfully apparent how out of touch Whitaker was with parenthood. He waved his brother away and found a pace somewhere between a walk and run as he cut loose the anchor of his family and put his eyes on the Rover.

For some unknown reason, Claire popped into his mind. And Whitaker wished she could have seen this entire episode. Then she'd know the mess he'd become. If she could swim around in his mind for a little while, she'd see how wrong she'd been to track him down. He was in no condition to help someone else.

Chapter 7

CHASING SMILES

"Let go," the teacher was saying as she slalomed between the beach towels of the six yogis taking Shavasana during their early-afternoon session. "Let all the tension drift off with the breeze."

Claire had joined the new studio since moving to the beach, and they offered daily sessions on the sand. She was no stranger to yoga, but since David's death, she'd abandoned her practice for more intensive and mind-numbing workouts, such as running and spin class. Returning to her practice was a part of her commitment to healing.

But the end of the class, the Shavasana—the part most found the easiest—proved the most uncomfortable for Claire. So much quiet. The screaming of silence, where the seeds of her fury quickly sprouted. Sometimes it wasn't about David at all.

Her mother was always an easy target, the woman who'd left Claire and her father to marry another man and have more children. Half brothers and sisters . . . ugh. After David had died, her mom suggested she come back to Chicago to live with them for a while. Thanks but no thanks.

But sometimes it sure as hell was about David. Anger at him *and* the man who'd killed him. Anger at BMW for not making a safer car. Even anger at herself for being angry in the first place!

Today, though, no matter how hard she tried to deflect him, Whitaker kept inching his way into her mind. What kind of selfish bastard could ignore such a request, to finish the book of a man who'd died before his time?

When the teacher summoned them back to their bodies, Claire began to wiggle her toes and regretted wasting her last few minutes of her practice trapped in a whirlwind of thought. At least she'd shown up to class. *One day at a time, Claire.* Oh, how badly she needed to attend the support group this afternoon, and something was telling her she needed to finally tell her story.

With one more focused exhalation, Claire opened her eyes to the sky and the birds zigzagging above. She was the first to collect her beach towel and thanked the instructor as she made her way back down the beach. For a brief moment, seeing her feet cut across the sand transported her back to the summer she had met David. What had tripped her up and at the same time quickly endeared him to her was how polite he'd been when Claire had introduced him to her grandmother. "Hello, it's very nice to meet you . . . Yes, ma'am, my family rents a house here every year . . . Yes, ma'am, I'll bring her back by seven sharp . . ." He was only just on the edge of becoming a man, and Claire remembered thinking what a man he'd be.

Closer to her house, she walked into the brisk water, brushing the sand off her knees and elbows. Flashes of silver darted about, the beautiful madness of minnows circling her. *Saving Orlando*, saving the project, drifted through her mind as she waded deeper, the chill widening her eyes and stealing her breath. She'd been considering other writers all morning. Why did it have to be Whitaker? Sure, the signs had pointed in his direction, but he wasn't exactly the man she thought he'd be, and that frustrated her.

If she took a moment to think about it, she might have imagined Whitaker more like the handsome intellectual she'd seen when he used to come into the café, only a few years older. When she had approached him at his table that first time, he'd had this glow about him, an exceptional confidence, like he'd found his purpose. He'd flirted with her mildly, tamely—until she'd flashed her ring. Had she not been with David, she might have flirted back.

The man she had met today had been worn down. Though part of her was furious with him, another part pitied him. He wore his troubles like a billboard plastered to his forehead. Claire would have loved to think that he had the answer to all her woes, but life wasn't always such a nicely wrapped present. No doubt there were plenty of starving writers who would happily accept money to write, but Claire wanted to choose the absolute perfect one. That was what David would have done for her.

—

A couple of hours later, Claire sat in a circle with twelve other widows in a meeting room of a nondenominational church in the middle of St. Pete—this particular group had been created specifically for women. An unused portable podium occupied the corner. A fold-up table by the window offered coffee, lemonade, and a variety of pastries.

Claire was so nervous that she'd polished off her drink and still felt dehydrated, like she'd eaten a ball of cotton. She'd told Lashonda, the woman who ran the group, that she was finally ready to speak, but even as the words came out of her mouth, she was questioning her decision.

Though she'd been attending for more than two years and there were women newer to the group, Claire still didn't feel like an insider. As she looked around the room, she saw many veteran widows who had already climbed out of their own loneliness, and Claire had listened to their stories each week with hope that perhaps she wasn't too far behind in her own metamorphosis.

It was here that Claire met Didi, who was currently sitting three people down. Didi looked impeccable in gold hoop earrings; a short, white linen dress; and blue high heels. On the other side of Didi sat

Lashonda, who had been attending even longer than Didi. She'd gotten her PhD at Purdue and had a psychology practice in St. Pete, so she'd naturally fallen into the role of running most meetings.

Lashonda turned to Claire after running through a list of announcements. She had short silky hair and a bright smile. "There's one of us who has had some major breakthroughs recently. Claire, are you still interested in speaking this afternoon?"

Claire forced herself to nod, set the cup down on the floor under her chair, and sat up straight. She had never been afraid of public speaking; it wasn't that. It was just that there was so much to tell, and she was suddenly wondering if she was ready to be analyzed under the microscope.

Claire controlled her breathing and looked at the other widows, who came in all colors, shapes, sizes, and ages. More than half of them had already shared, and Claire knew all their stories. It was time that she got it over with. Maybe it would feel good.

There was no going back now. "I hit the three-year mark yesterday." It was so quiet in the room, but she pushed on. "A lot of you speak about two to three years as being the time when life gets a little easier. I guess I'm not as far as I'd like to be. I'm still sad and sometimes so angry I can't see straight."

A few nods, "me toos," and "yeps."

Claire fingered one of her necklaces. "I'm selling our house. Finally. It was empty for three years. Mostly empty. I'd cleaned out every room except his office. I couldn't bring myself to go in there and box up his things. It was all I had left of him. How could I throw it all into storage or give it away?"

Claire glanced at Didi. "It was only as I realized that I couldn't keep paying the mortgage forever that I put the house on the market. Yesterday, I finally marshaled up the courage to go into his office. And I found a pretty big surprise." Claire elaborated on the discovery of *Saving Orlando*, finishing, "His story stopped midsentence, which broke my heart. He'd died without finishing it."

Looking up, she found the women listening intently.

She thought for a quick second how beautiful it was she'd found this wonderful book of David's, and a smile erupted from inside her. This bright smile was so out of place for this room and for Claire. But it was as real as the warmth of the sun. "Something deep within is telling me that if I can get someone to finish it, then I can maybe turn the page of my own book."

Claire's smile faded as she moved on. "I thought I'd found the perfect author—the guy who wrote *Napalm Trees and Turquoise Waters*—but I went to see him today, and he told me he wasn't interested. That was really hard to hear. I thought he was the right guy for the job." She lifted her shoulders. "But I know I can find someone. Healing is different for everyone, but I feel like I'm doing the right thing by trying to give my husband this gift. It's like one last hug to say goodbye."

Claire clasped her hands together. She looked down at the floor and wondered what to say next. Was that enough? Maybe for now.

Lashonda thanked her, and then another woman took the floor. Once those who wanted to speak had gotten their chance, Lashonda wrapped up the meeting by inviting everyone to dinner and a salsa class in Gulfport.

Going out dancing was the worst idea Claire'd ever heard, but afterward, as the women began to leave the room, Didi homed in on her. "It's Lashonda's birthday. There is no way you're not going."

Claire sighed and looked off to her left.

"I'll tell you something that I believe with full conviction," Didi said. "David wants you to have dinner with the ladies, then put on your dancing shoes and go salsa." She offered a quick shimmy of the hips.

Claire shook her head with a half smile. How could she argue? It was Lashonda's birthday. Almost all the other women were going. Besides, she was tired of being the downer anyway.

Eight of them occupied two tables on the sidewalk outside of Rita's, one of the quintessential beach bars of St. Pete. A Grateful Dead jam set the laid-back mood. Claire checked out the locals, many without shoes or shirts, all of them shaggy and tanned sun worshippers holding Sunday boat drinks in their hands. A green-and-red parrot was resting on the shoulder of a patron a few tables down. Across the street, preventing a panoramic view of the water, stood the Gulfport Casino, which had been around for more than one hundred years. It was where the Sunday evening salsa classes were held.

A server with a nose ring promptly delivered their piña coladas and margaritas. The widows all toasted to Lashonda and then broke into smaller groups to talk.

Sitting next to Claire, Didi said, "I'm glad you're here."

Claire looked at the other widows and then at the other patrons celebrating life. "I feel like I don't belong."

"Why's that?"

"Because I'm the only one not smiling." Claire pushed aside the festive cocktail parasol and took her first sip.

After Didi had done the same, she said, "Well, I'd say the best way to relearn how to smile is to surround yourself with happy people. I always love coming to Gulfport. It's the Key West of St. Pete. Where else can you find this kind of vibe?" Then Didi pointed toward the tall buildings of downtown. "Over there, people are worried about 401(k)s and promotions. Here in Gulfport, they're worried about dying without living. It's a neat thing."

"I do need this. Sometimes I feel like my brain goes straight to work the moment I wake up. Then it's pedal to the metal all the way to bedtime."

"That's why Leo's South is doing so well. But I bet your café wouldn't go under if you took a few days off."

Another sip. Pineapple and coconut. "Days off? What are days off?"

"They are these very fine chunks of time, typically several consecutive days, where you focus on yourself and not work. You don't check email. You don't even answer the phone."

Claire rolled her eyes and changed the subject. "Where's Andrés today?"

Didi waved her hand. "I'm playing hard to get. He called a few times, but I ignored him."

"You're too much."

"I'm telling you, Claire. If you ever do go back on the dating market, just talk to me. The things I've learned as an older woman. I just wish the twenty-year-old Didi had known what the sixty-something-year-old Didi knows. I would have saved myself three marriages and maybe had an orgasm before my forties!"

A smile played at the corner of Claire's lips. "You didn't have an orgasm until your forties?"

"I was well into my forties, believe it or not. How about you?"

Claire looked around nervously, like she was suddenly naked in church. "I was blessed early with a good lover." Claire recalled her first orgasm, the night she'd reunited with David after more than a decade of lost years. The assistant wedding photographer. The groomsman. The ultimate cliché. An explosive evening. Needless to say, he'd learned a lot since their clumsy and sandy attempts on the beach as teenagers.

"Look at you, Claire Kite. You see? You've got this in you!"

"Anyway . . . ," Claire said, taking more long sips. As her mind often did, she fast-forwarded through the years of David all the way to the end, to dark places. The crash three years ago. The guest he was supposed to bring. The empty seats. The meal gone cold. The knock on the door. The visitors. The casseroles. The mysterious Yankees hat. The funeral.

"What are you doing?" Didi asked. "You just checked out on me."

Claire snapped out of it, releasing an exhausted breath. "Sorry."

"Where did you go?"

"Where do you think?" Claire pulled the cocktail parasol from her drink and spun it back and forth with her fingers. Needing to share the details, Claire elaborated on her visit with Whitaker, how she thought he might be the one.

Didi looked across the street and out over the water, obviously debating her next words.

Claire side-eyed her friend. "What is it?"

"I'm not sure you want me to tell you what I think."

"When has anything stopped you from speaking your mind?"

Didi shrugged her shoulders. "I like the idea . . . no, I love the idea of getting David's book finished. But I feel like you're putting lofty expectations on what completing it will accomplish. I think you have to ask yourself why. That's not going to be an easy answer if you really dig deep. Do you want to make him famous? Do you want to make him as famous as Whitaker? Is it just that you want to preserve his legacy? Or do you think this is somehow going to bring him back?"

"Of course it's not going to bring him back." Claire tapped her foot. Getting his book finished was the least she could do for David after smothering his dream of fatherhood. "I know it's not going to bring him back," she repeated. "It's a way for me to honor him."

A loud cackle rose from the other table.

"I just fear that this could be a false direction, a false calling. You might think you hear David talking to you, but it could actually be your sorrow begging for some light."

"Well, yes, if it is my sorrow begging for some light. What's wrong with that?"

Jerry Garcia sang the first line of "Scarlet Begonias."

"I guess what I'm really trying to tell you is that convincing Whitaker Grant or some other writer to finish your husband's story isn't necessarily the solution you're looking for."

"No, I know. But it could be one of the steps. He had something to say, and I think if I can get the book finished, I'll know exactly what."

"Ah, there it is. What's getting it finished by someone else going to tell you?"

Claire stirred her drink and took a big sip to quench her growing frustration. "It's hard to explain. I feel like I'm supposed to do this for him. Like he's out there, watching and waiting. There's a story that needs closure. He wants Whitaker to write it."

"You are the one who needs closure. David didn't know he would die prematurely. I mean, I get it. I'm the one who told you I talk to my dead husband. But this is different. I think it's a beautiful idea, but I don't want you to be let down with the results. Even if this book is as good as you say it is, and you convince someone to write it, *and* it gets published. Even if all that, you need to know David will still be gone no matter what."

"If you were anyone else, I'd leave the table." Claire resisted the urge to hammer her fist down. "Please don't treat me like I'm crazy."

"I just don't want you to tie your emotional health to the outcome of this book. It sounds like Whitaker is not even the right guy."

Claire fell back in her chair and crossed her arms. She bit her lip, her anger giving way to sadness. Attempting to escape further, she looked away and nearly lost her breath when she saw him.

Whitaker Grant.

"Are you okay?" Didi asked. "I'm sorry, Claire. I should have kept my big mouth shut."

Claire twisted her head back to Didi. "You know why I feel like this is not a false calling?" Without waiting on a response, Claire motioned with her head. "Look over there. See the tall guy with the mustache? That's him."

Chapter 8

The Woman in the Black Dress

Whitaker needed a stiff drink. He pushed through the crowd on his way to the bar at Rita's. Where else did people dance away their Sunday afternoons to the Grateful Dead? He did a double take when he saw a man with a parrot on his shoulder. More and more, Whitaker resembled the regulars there. And he was certainly becoming one.

The blonde bartender greeted him by name, and he ordered a double rum and Coke. The writer would scoff at such a pedestrian concoction. "Coke? What are you . . . sixteen?" But the typist loved it.

While waiting on his drink, Whitaker revisited his meeting on the boat with Jack. Though a job offer from his father wasn't the biggest shock in the world, it was still a punch to the gut. Not an insult, more like reality knocking on his door. Would he sling mutual funds the rest of his life? Even the thought made Whitaker want to sneak one of the plastic cocktail picks in the shape of a sword from the bartender and jab himself in the eye. No way could he sit in his Bank of South Florida office and pretend a stock surge was what kept him up at night—or got him out of bed in the morning. Not that there was anything wrong with banking, but it simply wasn't his personal dream.

He'd proved that he did have the creative juices to make a living writing. And even if he took money out of the equation, all the people who wrote him and stopped him on the street had validated his ability and, dare he say, talent. He'd affected people's lives; what was better than that? Of course, writing for a living was different than typing or procrastinating for a living. No one paid for procrastination. Which was a damned shame, actually. He'd be a billionaire. He could teach college courses on the art of not getting things done.

Back in the old days, standing in the afterglow of his book's release, one of the most common questions people had asked was, "How do you avoid writer's block?" Whitaker could still see his confident younger self unable to even imagine writer's block. "It's a mind-set," he had told them. "You have to put your butt in the chair and make something happen." Whitaker would always finish with his most important thought on the matter. "One word after another. If you do that enough, the muse will write the story for you."

When the rum drink came, he took down half the dark liquid in a large gulp. "Ahhhh."

"Easy there, killer," the bartender said. "We might run out."

Setting the glass down, he said, "Run out of rum, I'll switch to tequila."

They shared a smile.

Whitaker put an elbow on the bar and fell back into his thoughts. Apparently, the muse was gone. *One word after another.* As if! Typing a word these days was like removing a tooth. Writing a sentence would be removing an entire rack of pearly whites. Sadly, it all came down to pressure.

The limelight had become an anchor. It wasn't simply "one word after another" anymore. Each word had to be great. The people demanded it. So did his agent, his publisher. It was quite obvious, even to Whitaker, that he was putting unfair expectations on himself. But it was in this world of fear that the writer ("a vermouth spritz if you have a decent vermouth, an Americano if not") had died, and the typist ("double rum and Coke, no preference on the rum") had been born.

With nothing left but two large cubes, he shook the glass. The ice clinked like dice. The syrupy Coke had melted down the sides like the legs of a viscous Sauternes. *Writing used to be fun, didn't it? Wondering what might happen next. Getting to know a character that only exists in your mind. Toying with word choice and sentence construction until everything was just right. It wasn't a bad way to spend your mornings.*

The bartender slid the next drink across the bar, and Whitaker snatched it like a five-year-old reclaiming his toy from another child.

"Bottoms up," he mumbled, thinking this one would surely kill the pain.

Whitaker felt eyes on him and suddenly became terribly self-conscious about his overindulgence. He was used to eyes on him. He liked Gulfport because they'd let him be anonymous, but there were always a few people from outside of Gulfport catching sight of him for the first time. "Isn't that the guy who wrote . . . ?" Weren't writers supposed to be able to get away with their fame? Everyone in the country knew his book, but not many knew his face. Except in the Tampa area. He'd enjoyed too much press, especially with the movie.

He looked about. Each table was full of modern-day hippies bobbing their heads to the music, telling stories, and laughing. The Grateful Dead played louder and louder, drawing everything they could out of each tune. Whitaker was appreciating the view to the water when he saw her.

Claire Kite.

Quickly averting his eyes, he turned back to the bar. Staring at his drink, he wondered if she'd seen him. Was she there for him? That would be quite a stalker move and not something he'd put past her.

Unable to resist, he turned his head again. Claire was sitting with several other women at a plastic table on the sidewalk. Her arms were crossed, and he could tell she wasn't in the best of moods. It reminded him how much pity he felt for her. To lose your partner to premature death was not something any human should be forced to endure.

Whitaker had an urge to go say hi, but it would only muddle his message to her. She'd been so sure he was the right person to finish her husband's novel. If they ran into each other, she'd use that as justification that she was right. It was meant to be.

He turned back to the bartender and ordered the grouper and chips. The second double began to take its toll, and he fought off further considerations of accepting his dad's offer. He fell into a worthless conversation with the man next to him at the bar. When the food came, Whitaker scarfed it down. As he was wiping his mouth with a paper napkin, he turned back toward Claire's table. He craned his neck to see past a circle of people raising shots.

Claire and her group were leaving. This was his chance to say something. To be a kind citizen.

He didn't take it.

Whitaker watched them cross the street to the Gulfport Casino. He didn't know what was going on over there, but his curiosity was piqued.

Settling his bill, he moved rather recklessly in their direction. The rum had given him the courage to follow them, though he had no idea what he might say if he ran into Claire. He circled to the right of the old building, working his way to the water, which the sun had painted the colors of flames. The temperature was slowly creeping back down toward the seventies. He could still smell the fried seafood and hear the commotion from the bars across the street.

As he eyed the group of maybe thirty people forming in the center of the large windowed ballroom, he considered how deceptive the word *casino* was in the name. Perhaps it had been a casino back in the old days, but from what he'd heard (though he'd never been inside), the Gulfport Casino now served as a gathering place for dances, weddings, and bingo.

Whitaker hid by the corner of the window and watched her. He'd never seen such a sad woman in such a captivating shell. The writer back in the old days might have come up with some poignant analogy in nature, but the typist standing there gave up after attempting to translate what he thought about her into words.

Though she didn't look miserable, Claire looked awkward and out of place. He imagined how beautiful she might be *if* and when she smiled.

"Whitaker Grant," a voice said. Whitaker spun around, feeling like he'd been caught spying, which, in fact, he was.

One of the women from Claire's group was approaching him on the sidewalk.

"Oh shit." Whitaker ducked his head and attempted to camouflage himself behind a palm tree. He placed one hand on the trunk to steady himself. He resisted an urge to run.

"Are you hiding from me?"

Knowing he was busted, he stepped out from behind the tree. "Actually," he said, stroking his mustache, "I was seeing what was going on in there." They were alone on this side of the building, the only sounds coming from the bars on the other side of the street.

With her heels, she was as tall as he was. "Is that right? I was starting to think you were following us."

Whitaker bit his lip. "I guess you saw me across the street. And who might you be?"

"I'm Didi, Claire's friend."

Whitaker fixed his collar with fidgety hands. "Well, this is awkward."

Didi took another step forward, crossing her arms. "Claire told me about the book. She said she asked you to finish writing it."

Whitaker nodded, glad to be bypassing the discussion of why he was spying.

Didi pulled a strand of black hair away from her eyes. "Why don't you accept her offer?"

Whitaker smiled falsely. "Did she send you out here?"

"No, Claire doesn't know you were staring at her through the window. I snuck out."

"It would be nice if you didn't tell her."

"Will you hear her out?"

Whitaker sighed and could feel himself swaying. How embarrassing this entire episode felt. He turned away from her, toward the orange water. Pivoting back, he said, "Here's the thing, Didi. I can feel her pain. It's almost like she and I are going through some similar things. If I were in Claire's shoes and someone agreed to read the novel, I'd get my hopes up. I don't want to get her hopes up."

"Why wouldn't you want to write it? She says you haven't written anything in ten years and that she's offered you money. Is there something else pressing in your life?"

"Aren't you bold?"

Didi brushed a hand through the air. "I'm too old to filter."

"I kind of like you," Whitaker said.

"So . . . what is it? Are you too busy and rich to deal with the project?"

Whitaker put a finger on his chin. "As you can most likely detect, I'm not that together right now. The last thing I want to do is take on the responsibility of attempting to finish a piece of work that Claire holds so dear to her heart."

Didi took a step toward him. "Then I just have one more question. What are you doing spying on her?"

Whitaker scratched his head and pulled at his long, curly hair. Before he could stop himself, he admitted, "I don't know."

"Maybe you should hear her out."

Whitaker half smiled. "Please don't mention to Claire that you saw me out here. I need to be anonymous right now."

"You need to be anonymous? What a sad thing to say." Didi turned and began to walk away. "I can tell you really care, so I'll let you two work it out."

Chapter 9

SALSA NIGHT

Claire had never been more uncomfortable in her whole life. Not even when Benji Solomon tried to make it to first base in ninth grade. Though she used to dance for fun in high school and college, attempting salsa petrified her. Why in the world had she let Didi talk her into this absurd idea?

It was not that the ballroom crowd there was intimidating. Not at all. In fact, they looked like the nicest group in the world. She didn't know where Didi had run off to—perhaps the bathroom—but the other widows had melted into the crowd of dancers.

Claire was standing by herself in the corner of the large room, feeling like she was back in high school hoping a boy might come ask her to dance. She turned and looked out a window, chasing safety in the still water. A woman was working a small Sunfish, the sail taut with an easterly wind. Claire craved the protection of solitude and wanted to trade places with the sailor.

Soon the instructor, an older man in fancy shoes and a crisp guayabera, clapped his hands and asked everyone to gather around. Claire hesitantly joined the group in the center of the large wooden floor and noticed Didi returning just in time. Claire pushed away the thought of escaping and told herself that she needed to have some fun for once. All the other widows had giant smiles. Why was she so hesitant?

After thanking everyone for coming, the instructor sent them all to find partners. The ladies Claire had come with turned to the men or women next to them.

Claire turned to Didi, the safe choice, but her friend had already linked up and was giggling with another man. Claire suddenly felt light-headed, and she crossed her arms and looked down at the light-wood floor. Oh, how she wanted to leave, to be a sailor on a tiny boat surrounded by water.

Then a man with a genuine smile appeared. "Can I be your partner?"

Claire met his eyes and smiled back. He was twenty years older and wore a Hawaiian shirt tucked into blue shorts pulled up well above his belly button. A woven belt held him together.

"I'm Billy," he said with an easy South Texas accent, sticking out his hand.

"Claire," she said in a tremulous voice, wondering how she could so easily manage a large staff at a restaurant but feel vulnerable now.

"I have to warn you," he said. "I'm terrible at this. Please forgive me, dear."

Claire raised her hands in surrender. "I've never danced salsa in my life, so you're already doing better than I am."

The instructor clapped his hands again. "Now everyone spread out; make some room." Claire and Billy moved away from the crowd and found their own space on the floor. "Face your partner."

Billy smiled at her, as if assuring her that he wouldn't bite.

"Ladies, we'll go over your steps first. Men, you'll do the opposite." The instructor performed as he spoke. "Back with the right, two, three, up with the left, two, three. Now try it."

Claire almost tripped over herself. "Oh God, I'm really bad at this. These don't even feel like my feet."

"It's okay," Billy said patiently, his laid-back Texan intonation easing her.

Determined now, Claire said, "Okay, here we go." She counted again and focused on one foot at a time, switching her weight with each step. She felt like she was trying to pat her head and rub her stomach simultaneously. "I'm never going to get this."

"So long as we're done by my tee time Saturday morning, I've got plenty of time."

They were soon attempting their moves to the music. "Oh, wow," Claire said, "this adds to the challenge. Can you tell there's no Cuban leaf on my family tree?"

"The only Cuban leaf I'm connected to is the cigar I enjoyed last week. It took me a year to learn what you just figured out in ten minutes."

During another attempt, the instructor approached and put his hand on her hips. "You're getting it, but loosen those hips. Have a little fun with it."

Fun, she mused. She didn't even know what *fun* was anymore.

But she and Billy eventually fell into their rhythm, and like an impostor, a smile planted itself on Claire's face. But she couldn't deny, impostor or not, it was a smile that had deep roots, one that she couldn't have hidden had her life depended on it.

Claire covered her mouth. Though this *was* fun, she felt guilty. A dark voice inside her was stomping her foot, demanding, "Fun isn't allowed." And yet something felt right about what she was doing. She wanted to snap at the ugly voice and tell the little monster that she had every right.

Round and round they went, switching partners, adding new spins and various footwork. Toward the end of the hour, Lashonda and Claire paired.

As they attempted their moves, Lashonda asked, "Have you seen Claire, by chance? She was here earlier. The one with the sad heart on her sleeve."

Claire caught her drift quickly. "I can't believe you all talked me into this. But I'm so glad you did."

The most genuine smile in the world. "Good for you for stepping out. I couldn't ask for a better birthday present."

Though she wasn't necessarily accomplishing anything, Claire had a strong feeling that she was doing something so much more important than getting the monotonous checked off, like something to do with selling the house or running the café. The warrior inside her was breaking through, and she was getting down to the marrow of her life again. It wasn't about trying to get by. That was all she'd done for so long.

It was about honoring David's memory by living life to the fullest.

Why had this been such a difficult vision to see? Why such a difficult concept to wrap her head around? Hadn't everyone been telling her this for years? Was it really this simple? A few little smiles as she stumbled around attempting to dance salsa?

Perhaps.

Claire spent the next two days packing and working with the movers to empty the house. She visited her old home one last time after the cleaners had wiped away the last of her and David's life together. It was Tuesday morning, a few hours before the closing.

She climbed the steps and entered his empty office. She looked where his desk had been and, for one last time, imagined him sitting there.

"My friend Didi says she talks to her husband, so here goes. David, give me the strength I need. I know you don't want me to be sad. It's taken me three years to figure that out. But how do I find happiness? I enjoyed a glimpse of it on the dance floor two days ago, but how do I add to it?" She took in a giant breath and tried to feel his presence. She listened, as if there might be a whisper coming from above.

"I know you can't talk to me," she finally said. "Even if you're listening, I know you can't respond. Just know that I want to make you proud. Please do what you can to give me a boost every once in a while. I'm going to need it." She shrugged. "So here I go. I'm off to the closing. I guess the one thing that makes me happy is that saying goodbye to this house isn't saying goodbye to you." She choked up and touched her heart. "You're inside me forever. You're not allowed to leave, okay?"

Locking up, she descended the steps and climbed into her car. Almost out of habit, she reached into the glove box for her latex glove. But as she began to snap it on, she shook her head. David would forgive a lot of things, but not smoking.

With a guilty little smile, Claire took a detour from her usual reggae and found a salsa playlist. As the rich Latin beats filled her convertible, the welcome taste of hope hit the tip of her tongue.

Chapter 10

I Hear Thunder

After a brutal Wednesday dealing with needy clients, Whitaker came home with every intention of writing. Something about his father offering him a job made him desperate to find his words again. It was no secret that it was his father who'd given him a story in the first place. It didn't take much effort shaking the napalm tree for the Vietnam vet to fall out. In other words, post the release of *Napalm Trees and Turquoise Waters*, everyone knew the Grants a little better. Of course, Whitaker's characters only mildly resembled those in real life.

"I stole a few things from friends and family," Whitaker would say in interviews, "but it's just my imagination hard at work."

"How about the father in the story?" they'd asked. "I know your father was a vet too."

"The father in the story is a completely unfair, diminished view of my dad. It's who he *could* have become after the war, but thankfully he returned intact." *For the most part,* Whitaker would always add internally.

That father was a PTSD-riddled tiger of a man who was relentless in life and work. He was still fighting the Vietnam War every single day. Jack Grant, however, had dealt with his demons in a much more impressive way. Whitaker would always end his interviews with, "Jack Grant is my hero. The man in the book is an antihero. It's just that . . .

knowing a vet so intimately as you would when you're raised by one, it's easy to let your imagination run with how much worse it could be. That's where the palm trees are poisoned with napalm and the turquoise waters are dyed red with blood."

Jack Grant was Whitaker's hero in a lot of ways, but when it came down to it, no man in the history of business could remove a suit and tie like Whitaker Grant. The moment he closed his front door, his tie was flying in the air and his suit jacket was falling to the floor. He kicked his polished loafers toward the wall and shucked his ironed black pants into the corner. Letting the suit wrinkle and leaving the businessman in the foyer, Whitaker dressed in basketball shorts and a T-shirt and headed toward his office.

Entering his writing space always felt like he was jumping out of a helicopter into a Vietnamese jungle. Never did going to war get easier, and that was exactly what sitting down to fill a blank page was: war.

I Hear Thunder (the working title of his newest work, the one that began with "I want out, Matteo") had led to many more words and sentences. Like *Napalm Trees*, he'd begun to feel the character, starting to see through the eyes of this man.

The problem was Whitaker kept getting in the way of himself. *Napalm Trees and Turquoise Waters* had been a thrill to write. He could remember countless times when he was pounding the keys with his foot tapping and heart racing, and he could barely wait until he could share the story with the world. Where was the joy in this one?

The warrior typist sat in his chair, rebooted his computer, and stared at the movie poster until the final beep sounded. He couldn't help but take a quick peek at Lisa and him at the premiere again. She was still his cheerleader, even after leaving him. That was, in fact, the last thing she said to him. "I'm pulling for you, Whitaker. I can't love you anymore, but I'm your biggest fan." No one could imagine how hard hitting her last words were.

Stalling, he checked his social media accounts. A fan had posted on his Facebook wall, telling Whitaker that he'd rewatched the movie again and absolutely loved it. The fan suggested writing a sequel.

Not for the first time, Whitaker bounced that notion around in his head. The producers had made the same request. Being the prideful artist that he was, Whitaker had answered the publisher the way his heart wanted him to. "It's not a story that has a second piece to it. It's done." His agent disagreed, but Whitaker had assured him, "I've got more stories. Let's not chase sequels. It's a path that doesn't always go so well."

"Mario Puzo didn't do that bad of a job."

"I'm no Puzo. These characters have had their arc; they've already faced their worst nightmares. To revisit their stories would be a travesty, even if it filled our pockets with gold."

His agent had said, "Let's worry about more money now and travesties later."

Whitaker responded to the man on Facebook's post with: Imagine if Pat Conroy had written The Prince of Tides, Part II: Tom Wingo Goes to Disney World. No, not going to happen. Before he officially posted his reply, Whitaker realized he had no business comparing himself to Pat Conroy. Instead, he retyped his response: Have you ever seen One Flew Over the Cuckoo's Nest Two? Me neither.

Not quite ready to tackle his next masterpiece—and not for the first time—Whitaker tossed around title ideas for a sequel. *Napalm Trees and Turquoise Waters II: Hunt for a Cool September.* Whitaker smirked, enjoying a moment of flexing his creative muscle, which seemed to thrive more in the absurd. Or better yet: *Agent Oranges Dangling on Citrus Trees.* Even Jack Grant would laugh at that. The title was almost good enough to write a book around.

Whitaker came up with one more that satisfied him: *Napalm Trees II: Attack of the Viet Cong Snowbirds.* Considering snowbirds and the Viet Cong both came from the north, Whitaker decided that he did indeed still have some wit left in him.

With that out of the way, Whitaker opened up *I Hear Thunder*. He scrolled down to see how far he'd made it: 543 words. Three days of work. An amateur effort.

"Saul Bellow could type five hundred and forty-three words while he was brushing his teeth," Whitaker mumbled.

He looked at the cursor flashing on the new line. The engulfing white space below. "Just start, you damned typist. One word after the other." The cursor taunted him with each flash, like a big middle finger telling him he had nothing important to say. "C'mon, Whitaker," the cursor said. "Are you scared, you little weenie? Do I put the fear of God in you?"

As if he were stabbing a flag into the top of Mount Everest, Whitaker brought his index finger down onto the "R" key with a triumphant, thunderous jab. The cursor revealed an *r* and then moved to the right, flashing once again.

With the little bastard taking the upper hand, Whitaker sat back in his chair and laughed at the idea of writing for a living. Even if. *Even if* you could get past all the doubt in your head and put together enough letters and words to make up the necessary word count for a novel, you still had to create compelling characters who either grew or were broken by their choices. And the plot needed to grip the reader like it was grabbing their testicles or their female bits. Above all, the story needed to move quickly. Pacing, pacing, pacing! People didn't have the attention span they used to.

Even if you'd done all that once, and succeeded, you had to do it again, but better. The readers expected every sentence to sing. No such thing as trying to make the new one as good as the last. You had to do better. You had to one-up yourself.

Feeling a rush of anger at the cursor, Whitaker hit the "R" button again.

He jabbed it several times in a row.

rrrrrr

"How about that, you twinkly little shit? I'll *r* you to death. You'll be singing pirate songs all the way to the landfill. Rrrrrrrr, you ugly blinking bastard!" He mashed the *R* key again, this time holding it down.

rrrrrrrrrrrrrrrrrrrrrrrrrr

"Damn, that feels good!" So satisfying that his other fingers wanted to get involved. He set them free.

D;hfiwejf;kjewkfjkewjfkwjdskfj
dfkjsdlkfjkladsjf;kj
Dlfadskjfkljasd9uweiroujq
Dfhoi23ejiqjeoir

"There's your fucking word count! Let's keep going." He let his fingers dance again, another burst of word graffiti.

A staccato piercing sound came from the other room—two chirps. Probably one of the smoke alarms. Ignoring it, Whitaker took a deep breath and reread his work. There was no gold to be mined from his burst of inspiration. His agent would shake his head. His publisher would shut the door. His dad might spit on him.

One last irritating chirp sealed the writing session's fate, and he pushed away from his desk. No way would he get anywhere with this nonsense screaming at him. Barreling out of his room in a fit, he opened the utility closet in the hallway and was surprised at his organization. Amid a stack of cardboard boxes crammed into the closet, he found one labeled "Batteries and shit . . ."

In the living room, Whitaker eyed the fire alarm above the sofa. A bag of Doritos had been left open on the coffee table. The zombie game he'd been enjoying lately was frozen on the television. He hopped up onto the sofa and changed the battery on the alarm. With a green light and chirp of acceptance, the fire alarm seemed to be satisfied.

It was too tempting to collapse onto the sofa for a quick few minutes of game play. He unpaused the game and dropped back into an alternate reality where he was a meathead Special Forces soldier well equipped with several futuristic guns, trying to save the planet from the zombie apocalypse. He moved to the edge of his seat as he rained down terror.

The guilt of not reaching his writing goal hung over his head, and he eventually paused the game. Returning to his office, Whitaker faced the mostly blank page again.

"I don't get out of this chair for five hundred words. Period."

Another chirp from the living room.

His teeth ground against each other, and he resisted the urge to slam his fist into the keyboard. "Now I truly know that there is a God. And he's a sadist who likes picking on writers."

Whitaker looked up through the ceiling. "Are you enjoying yourself?" Thinking of Russell Crowe in *Gladiator*, Whitaker raised his hands, palms up, and asked the popcorn ceiling with all the fury he could muster, "Are you not entertained?"

This time, Whitaker stomped back to the fire alarm, screaming obscenities. How could anyone accomplish anything with the interminable curses of being human? He ripped the battery out and returned to the closet, where he found a tester. Sure enough, it was dead. Why would he put a dead battery back into the box? What an idiot. Testing several more, he finally found one 9V battery with a bit of fight left.

Whitaker plugged the battery into the fire alarm and—voilà!—a green light, a satisfactory chirp.

Weary from his battle and feeling creatively listless, Whitaker retreated to the kitchen to plan dinner. As he opened the fridge, he heard movement in the living room.

"Anyone there?" he asked, looking for a weapon to protect himself.

With a quickening pulse, Whitaker extracted a knife from the butcher block. It was a paring knife, the smallest in the block. He quietly set it down and drew one much larger. Butcher knife in hand, he crept across the kitchen and entered the living room, prepared to fight the intruder.

It was indeed an intruder, but the knife wouldn't be necessary.

"Good afternoon," his mother said, while folding his business slacks.

"Mom!" he said, trying not to yell. "You can't just come in here."

Sadie Grant, dressed as if for a ladies' luncheon, looked at him like he'd said something absurd. "Whitaker, you should be ashamed of yourself." She looked around the living room. "I didn't raise you to live like this."

"I'm serious, Mom. You can't just walk into my house. I'm forty years old." He raised the knife. "I was about to stab you."

She looked at the knife and then back at him. "Don't be ridiculous."

"Ridiculous? It's the twenty-first century. There is crime in this neighborhood." Whitaker set the knife down on the coffee table. "I'm tempted to call the police."

Sadie ignored him and continued to fold. "Please pour me a glass of chardonnay. I'm parched."

Chapter 11

ALWAYS LISTEN TO YOUR MOTHER

Returning from the kitchen with her wine, Whitaker joined his mother in the living room. Ashamed of the digital slaughter paused on the flat screen, he found the remote and turned off the television.

The Doña Quixote of Florida was humming to herself and folding clothes from the pile of laundry on the chair. Her bulbous gray hair was styled the exact same way as he'd last seen her. And the time before that. "The door was open. I knocked."

"I was writing. What if I were in here with a woman?"

"Oh, are you dating again?" She turned to him with such enthusiasm that it was almost as if he'd told her of an impending grandchild.

"No. I mean, I'm open to whatever comes my way. But I haven't met anyone lately worth pursuing." He questioned those words as they exited his mouth.

Sadie shook out a wrinkled polo shirt. "You should get out more."

Whitaker drew in a breath. He reminded himself that she meant no harm and there was no point fighting back. He had to let her be a mother and grandmother.

Sadie was humming as she continued folding the clothes. "How's the writing coming along?" Only his mother had the guts to ask, and only she could get away with it.

Taking a pair of boxer shorts, Whitaker joined his mother in helping fold the clothes. "Every time I think I'm getting close, the words stop flowing. It's a game of persistence, and I'm struggling right now." Whitaker shook his head. "The strife of an artist."

Then good ol' Sadie cut to the chase, the reason she'd graced Whitaker with a surprise visit. "Did you give your father's offer another thought?"

Whitaker laid down the shirt he'd folded. "I had a feeling you had an agenda today."

"A mother can't come by and see her son?"

He took another pair of boxers. Something about his mother folding his underwear didn't feel right, so he tried to stay ahead of her. "I know when you're up to something."

She folded in silence, waiting for his reply.

"Though I'm going through a difficult phase, I'm not sure I'm ready to hang up the writing gig. And you know as well as I do that taking that job will consume me. The money would be nice—"

"Not to mention the *security*," Sadie interrupted while straightening the collar of one of his short-sleeved button-downs. "You'd have a guaranteed job for the rest of your life. Can you say that about working for the bank?"

"If I took the job, I might as well rip out my soul and bury it in the backyard while I'm at it. Look at Dad. He works too much and is miserable half the time. With the bank, I can at least leave my work at the office."

"Your father is not miserable. He might still be dealing with stuff from the war, but his job gives him a reason to get out into the world." She united a pair of socks. "St. Pete wouldn't be what it is without your father and Grant Construction. You did a great thing for this city with your book. You've both given to your community. Imagine if you joined him and continued to write. The Grant Powerhouse."

Whitaker shook his head. Why was it that the Grants felt this need to take over the world?

Sadie whistled a short melody. "It doesn't take ten years to write a book. I know you're trying, but . . . trying to make a living with your art can sometimes cause problems."

Whitaker gave up folding and walked to the window. A green lizard missing half its tail was doing push-ups on the sill. The reptile dashed away when it noticed the typist approaching. "If there's one thing I know, it's the dangers of mixing business and pleasure. But I don't want to be defeated. I have another book in me. I know I do."

Sadie ignored him. "Let's face it; you need a woman, and you need to consider starting a family. It's not all about you anymore. Selfishness is the business of men in their thirties." Clearly she and Jack were in agreement.

Indecisive on which bait to take, he finally chose her most consistent argument. "We all know you want more grandkids."

While taking a break from folding to sip her wine, Sadie replied, "Of course I do. I also happen to think you would be an amazing father. Look at the way your nephew looks at you."

She was slashing open the wounds of his failed marriage. Lisa had told Whitaker the same thing about being a great father. "Just let me get one more book done, and then we'll focus on babies," he'd promised her.

"My body is ready now," she'd replied, and then dramatically stuck a finger in the air to emulate a second hand on a clock. "Tick, tick, tick."

As much as Whitaker had loved Lisa, that little movement of hers might have been the most exasperating gesture on earth—not to mention an added impediment to his writer's block. The selfishness of his thirties, indeed. No question that he and Lisa would still be together if he'd been on the same page about parenthood. *Tick, tick.*

Sadie was still going. "You have a way with kids, and you owe it to the world."

Whitaker heard his brother scolding him about the birthday present. *A buck knife?*

"I really appreciate your life advice," he said, "but, seriously, I'm going through a rough patch, and I need to deal with it on my own. I know you want me to have a serious job and a family, but I'm not there. Did you ever stop to think about the poor woman who would have to put up with me?"

"Who hasn't had a total collapse?" Sadie asked. "You post-baby-boomer generations think you're the only ones who have struggled internally. The only way to learn to live is by crashing hard a few times."

He collapsed onto the sofa. "Then I'm learning well, believe me."

Sadie sat in the comfy chair next to the sofa and set her wine down on a coaster. "I only have a few more minutes before I need to get to the club to meet Joe and Nancy. Let me just say this. Don't turn down your father yet. Keep mulling it over. Think about living a more normal existence."

"Not everyone wants a country club life."

She nodded slowly. "That's true, but you should be a bit more open to testing it out."

Whitaker smiled sarcastically. He never did like country clubs. Every time he joined his family for a meal there, he felt like an outsider.

They spoke a few more minutes, and Sadie kissed him on the cheek on the way out. He told her he loved her and closed the door. The tension in his shoulders was palpable.

His mother was right. Making a living with your art was not always a good idea. Had he not enjoyed a taste of making good cash with his book, he might already happily be running Grant Construction. He might be a great husband and father. He might be mowing his green lawn at his house on the water, honing his golf game at the country club. Dropping his kids off at private school. Listening to his wife tell him about her Acroyoga session. He might be hosting Tuesday poker nights for the fellas.

But all that seemed so much less interesting than writing for a living. There was nothing like those moments when he'd sit down with his story and quickly lose himself in his own imagination. That feeling of tapping in, drawing creative fuel from some outside force, was better than any drug on the planet. The high was so lovely that he could still feel what it was like, even though he hadn't enjoyed more than a taste of it in years. The high was so addictive that he could easily spend the rest of his life chasing it.

Whitaker glanced out the window by the front door to make sure she'd left. A man he'd seen before, wearing Converse All Stars, was walking a chestnut-colored pit bull across the park. Whitaker had a strong suspicion that this might be his guy—or at least one of them.

He slipped out the front door and sneaked to the edge of his driveway. Once he was sure he'd gone unseen, he dashed across the street into the park, finding refuge behind a giant oak tree. The park was lush green and well manicured all year round, courtesy of Florida's tropical climate and the fine City of Gulfport landscapers willing to brave the conditions.

The dog walker was talking to the pit bull, perhaps coaxing him to poop. Where were the poop bags? Had he gotten lazy today? Whitaker hoped so. The man and his dog reached the opposite end of the park, falling out of Whitaker's view. Blending in, the typist walked briskly as if he were getting some exercise. As if!

During the excitement, the muse finally came for a visit. He suddenly had a great idea for a poop sign. Seeing a bench, he recalled the scene in *Forrest Gump* when the girl on the bus said, "Can't sit here." Whitaker considered putting a picture of the girl on the sign with the caption *Can't shit here.* He grinned and said self-mockingly, in his mother's voice this time, "Witty Whitaker strikes again." Couldn't write a book, but maybe he could start a stupid-sign business.

Seeing the dog spread his legs, Whitaker sped up, preparing to run. When the man turned back, Whitaker spun the other way and feigned analyzing a nearby bird-of-paradise.

Only one thing could feel as great as writing another book or drawing a smile from his father, and that was catching this man red-handed. How long had Whitaker been spying on dog walkers? Weeks. He'd put true effort into it, as if the mayor had tapped him on the shoulder with this important task. An agent for MI6, a mission to save the world. *This message will self-destruct in five seconds.*

To finally have come to a conclusion, to have solved the mystery, was so gratifying that Whitaker considered taking himself out to dinner. A bone-in rib eye and a bottle of Washington State Syrah. Didn't James Bond always dine after catching the bad guy?

Ready to finally nab the perp and celebrate his victory, Whitaker turned away from the bird-of-paradise just in time to see the man pulling a bag from his dog's collar. How could Whitaker have missed the poop-bag dispenser attached to the dog collar? Oldest trick in the book!

Returning to his house in failure, Whitaker decided he certainly didn't deserve a steak. He finished off a bag of boiled peanuts and fell into a deep sleep on the sofa.

A midnight chirp stole him from his dreams. Whitaker sat up so fast that he hit his knee on the coffee table. He looked left and right, wondering where he was. As his vision settled, he realized he was in his living room, and it was still dark outside.

Another chirp sent his heart to pounding in anger. Had the battery already run completely out of juice? Enraged, he jumped onto the sofa. Seeing a reflection in the window, he realized the absurdity of the scene: a middle-aged male in his underwear standing on the sofa in the middle of the night waging war with a fire alarm. He removed the battery, hoping that might stop the chirp.

Nope, it didn't.

Whitaker cursed and went to find another battery, but he came up empty. The fire alarm screamed while he desperately searched the other boxes. He marched back down the hallway screaming in Spanish, *"Cállate!"*

As if the fire alarm had a mind of its own, it chirped over and over, one shrill shriek every five seconds, taunting him like the cursor on the blank screen.

Whitaker jumped back onto the sofa and ripped it from the ceiling. Or at least he tried. The hardwired line was still attached. Red, green, and black wires. He was no handyman, so the colors were irrelevant. He was half-asleep anyway, and the piercing scream made rational thought impossible. As he tugged at the wires, the dangling alarm began to break free. Only one intact wire remained. Out of pure stupidity and in the haze of the madness, he reached for the wire.

A trembling shock ran through him as he fell backward and hit the coffee table, his shoulders slamming into the wood. He rolled onto the floor, still shivering from the electricity.

Looking up toward the free wires, Whitaker began to laugh. What an absurd, miserable existence he was living, and this moment of being attacked by a fire alarm pretty much summed up his whole life.

Chapter 12

CRAB CLAWS AND SHARK JAWS

On Thursday, Claire woke to yet another day of feeling good. Ever since saying yes to dancing salsa, she'd felt like the universe had started to open up to her. She stopped by the café to help open, but once the tables were full, she left her shoes in the office and strolled the two blocks to the beach. Smiling at the beauty of the morning, she took her first steps onto the sand and felt as light as a feather as the sun's rays bathed her in warmth. Was there softer sand in the world? *One small step for woman, one giant leap for womankind.*

For a while, Claire watched a cruise ship she guessed had left the port of Tampa as it floated along the horizon, destined for Mexico. Then she walked north, at a snail's pace, looking down at the shells, returning to the girl strolling this same tide line with her grandmother. What had changed since then? Betty had now passed. Claire had loved and lost. The Don CeSar still stood tall and illustrious. The houses of Pass-a-Grille were fancier, more modern. But this little stretch of beach was still undiscovered, a slice of the 1950s. Hopefully, no writer would ever put her little treasure on the map.

A thought had hit her when she'd woken to this beautiful day. What if she had accepted Whitaker's rejection too easily? She wasn't the type who gave up. Especially when it came to her love for David.

No way on earth she was going to let Whitaker Grant say no. Life often served up surprises. And challenges. Just because people said no didn't mean you couldn't change their minds. David wouldn't have let Whitaker say no. Look at the way he went after getting in shape, the way he dived into writing. Once he'd committed to something, nothing could stop him.

Claire noticed a crab leg sticking out of the sand. She picked it up and opened and closed the pincers. "I'm coming to get you, Whitaker Grant," she whispered in a creepy, Wicked Witch of the West voice. "You can't say no to me forever."

Dropping the claw to the ground, she jogged back to the café barefooted, ran in to grab her sandals and keys, and left with nothing more than a wave to Alicia. Returning to Gulfport, Claire was disappointed to find Whitaker's driveway empty. She pulled in and put the convertible in park. It was nine thirty. Maybe he had a day job. He'd surely made a good amount of money with his novel, but she didn't know if it was enough to retire. Of course, his family was wealthy from their construction business, so maybe they were supporting him.

A voice from the neighbor's yard startled her. She whipped her head around.

An old man with a long face and hollow cheeks was smiling at her. He carried a rake in his hand, and Claire thought he looked like the man holding a pitchfork in Grant Wood's famous painting *American Gothic*. "Ya lookin' for Whitaker?" he asked in a deeply southern tongue.

"I sure am," Claire answered, glancing at the rake again, making sure it wasn't a pitchfork. "Do you know where he is?"

"Prolly at work."

"Oh, I guess the morning is over, isn't it? Where is he working now? We're old friends."

"Still over there at the Bank of South Florida, far as I know. That's what he told me, least. He used to write, you know. Wrote that big movie."

"I do know." *And he will write again,* Claire thought. She thanked him and backed out of the driveway. She pulled over along the park and searched for the closest bank branch. With a glance at the composition books in the passenger seat, she reaffirmed her decision not to take no for an answer.

Parking at the far end of the lot, she entered the white, four-story building under a sun-bleached yellow awning and found herself standing in the bank lobby under bright fluorescent lights. Her photochromic lenses lightened quickly. Two lines of people waited for the next available teller. Sitting behind a desk, a woman with gorgeous curly black hair welcomed her.

"Aren't you lucky?" Claire asked, her eyes on a fresh bouquet of sunflowers resting on the filing cabinet. A small card dangled from a straw bow.

The woman lit up. "Aren't I? They're from my son. He's stationed in Germany, about to go to Afghanistan. But he's thinking of me on my birthday."

Claire smiled in sympathy. "Aww, what a sweetheart. Happy birthday."

"Thank you. Now, how may I help you?"

Back to the mission. "Does Whitaker Grant work here, by chance?"

"He sure does. Let me check and see if he's available." After a quick call, she said, "He'll be here in a moment. You can take a seat right over there."

Claire sat in one of the chairs in the waiting area, watching people tend to their banking needs. But on her mind was the woman's son stationed in Germany. Claire touched her stomach, wondering what it would have been like to be a mother. Would she have been a good one? Definitely better than her own mother, who had all but abandoned her and her dad.

A few minutes later, as Claire reached for one of the magazines on the table in front of her, Whitaker appeared. He looked surprisingly put together in a suit, reminding her more of the man she'd met years ago.

Claire felt her nerves fire as he drew closer. "Can we talk?"

Whitaker clasped his hands at his waist. "You don't want to give up, do you? I can see it all over your face." He looked down at the composition books in her hand. "Are those what I think they are?"

Claire stood. "Give me five minutes. If you still have no interest, I won't bug you again."

After a long pause, he conceded. "Come on back."

She followed him down a hallway with beach photographs hanging on the walls and turned left into an office. He gestured for her to sit, and she sat across from him. Other than his nameplate, there was nothing marking this as his office. No pictures. Nothing to reveal his personality. Only a laptop, a phone, and a few stacks of paper.

"How long have you been doing this?"

"Almost a year now." He loosened his tie and leaned in, resting his elbows on the desk. "Did you close on your house? You mentioned that was coming."

Claire fidgeted with her hands. "Yeah, on Tuesday."

"I imagine it was pretty tough."

Claire nodded and whispered a yes.

"Hey, do you guys still serve that oyster omelet?"

Claire welcomed some small talk. "We do."

"I used to love it. And I haven't seen it on a menu anywhere else in the States. Right after college, I backpacked from Bangkok to Singapore, and the oyster omelet became my street food of choice."

"When were you in Thailand? I did the whole backpacking thing too. Didn't cross into Malaysia, though. My girlfriend and I got waylaid in Phuket."

"Sounds like a song, doesn't it?" Whitaker said. "Waylaid in Phuket." Catching Claire totally off guard, Whitaker broke into a quiet country song reminiscent of George Jones. "We were waylaid in Phuket. Nothing to eat but an omelet."

Claire couldn't help but smile.

"The beers they poured were tall. And the woman I loved was . . ." He ran out of words and searched for them on the white wall. "The woman I loved had . . ." He shrugged, as if giving up on finding a workable rhyme. And then as an afterthought, he added, "claws."

He was actually funny. But how did he know about the claw?

"Are you done?" she asked, stifling a grin.

Whitaker shrugged his shoulders. "Couldn't help it. Anyway, this would have been almost twenty years ago."

"Ah, long before me."

"Yeah, I'm a dinosaur." When he smiled again, she could tell she was breaking through to him. He was a nice guy, and nice guys do nice things.

She sat back. "Well, that's where our oyster omelet came from."

"I'll have to revisit it soon." Whitaker beat a nervous rhythm on his desk.

It was as if all the joy had been sucked out of the room.

He sat back in his leather chair. "See this office. This suit. That lobby out there. It's my life for now, and I'm kind of good at it. My writing isn't up to par. I mean . . . I have a story coming along, but I'm not up to a new task. What I'm trying to say is . . . you don't want me to write your husband's novel. I'm currently deleting everything I type. It's almost like I was gifted one book, and that's it. Time to move on."

This was her moment. She had to be strong. Sitting up straight and finding her courage, Claire said, "You're the *only* one I want to write his novel." She took a slow breath. "I sold the house, and I have money. You can have everything I have left after I pay off my debts. I don't care."

Trying to cover all angles, she decided to push harder into the cosmic with her appeal. Pounding her fists with each syllable, she repeated what she'd told him at his house. "You're. Meant. To. Write. This. Book." Even as she said it, she wasn't sure she believed her own words.

Whitaker smiled sadly and threw up his hands as if she'd just charged him with treason. "I hate to disappoint you. Truly. But I think you're mistaken."

Claire sat back in her chair with frustration. She set the books on his desk and fired a finger at the first composition book. "I'm not some girl thinking her dead husband's novel is the best thing in the world when it's not. But you sound like you're out of stories." She opened her hands. "I'm giving you one." She realized she was raising her voice. Lowering it, she added, "And I'm willing to pay you to write it."

Feeling like she was making progress, Claire made a show of looking around the room, the cheap furniture, the barren walls. His ego needed to be fed. "This isn't you. Why aren't you writing? The world deserves to read more of your words."

Whitaker looked at his watch, a silver Rolex.

She was losing. "I'll pay you one hundred thousand dollars to write the rest of it. He's already done all the hard work."

Whitaker's eyebrows floated up, and she saw some temptation.

She didn't care about the money. She could live off the café. All she cared about was getting this book done by a reputable author, preferably this guy. "You can even put your name on the book if you want. I don't care. It's not about making David famous. It's about getting his story out there."

Whitaker tapped his fingers on the desk. "It's a tempting offer, but what you don't understand is that a writer, a *true* writer, can't step into someone else's style. It won't be authentic."

"You could figure out his style; don't play dumb with me. I'll pay you five thousand just to read it. If the story doesn't strike you, then give it back." She dusted off her hands. "I pay you, and you're done."

Whitaker flashed a smile, and again Claire saw the charm of the man who used to come into her café. Why couldn't he just say yes?

Lowering his voice, he said, "If I agreed to read even the first of those books, you would never let me off the hook."

Claire could hear and see that he cared. Maybe there was some substance behind his ego. She put her hands together in prayer. It was now or never. "I swear to God I would."

"Honestly, I'm tempted to take your money. But the project isn't my cup of tea. When and *if* I finally tap back into the source, it's going to be with a book that I start. Do you know how many people approach me with a story?"

Claire resisted the urge to roll her eyes.

"I'm the one who has to sit with these characters for hundreds of hours." He jabbed his thumb to his chest. "They have to be my creations."

"You can change as much of his book as you want. How could you possibly not accept one hundred thousand dollars?"

"Because, Claire, I can't take someone else's story and run with it. That's cheating." He paused to think, starting to speak a couple of times before retreating again. Finally, he touched his chest and lowered his voice. "The part of me that wants to agree is not the part of me that you want as your writer. I would let you down; trust me."

Biting her tongue, Claire pointed to the composition books again. "You'd be lucky to put your name on this project."

"I don't doubt it. And I'm really not trying to be a jerk. I want to help you, and if you were asking something else, I'd happily oblige." She sensed the defeat in his voice. "It's just that you're asking the one thing I can't do. I feel like I'm carrying the bones of my writing back from war. I need to go put those bones back together and then figure out how to make the dead come alive again. I really have to get back to work. I'm so sorry."

"You *are* sorry," Claire admonished. "And I'm not talking apologetic. You're a sorry person. Your ego is getting in the way of doing something amazing." She shot a finger at him. "You think you're an artist. An artist would see the beauty in this project. He'd see the beauty in doing something for someone else."

Whitaker stood. "I wish you the best, and if you'd like my help finding someone else, let me know." He handed her one of his Bank of South Florida cards.

Swallowing her own defeat, she looked at the card and tossed it back onto Whitaker's desk. She collected the books and turned and left him. She wasn't sad. She was angry. Not just angry at Whitaker.

Angry at the world. Why this pull to Whitaker? There were so many authors in the world, so many who could bring out the best in David's novel. So why all these signs? Was it because Whitaker was meant to write this novel? Or was it something deeper? The frustration she felt toward him dizzied her.

Whitaker watched her go. For someone he barely knew, she had a very fine ability of making him feel like the biggest jerk on earth. He scratched his head, wondering why he was so against saying yes to her. Was he that much of a hardheaded eccentric that he couldn't ghostwrite? What was wrong with ghostwriting, anyway, especially with money on the line? One hundred thousand dollars. He wasn't making much more than that with this gig.

The guilt rode Whitaker hard, and he couldn't take it anymore. Hoping he could catch her, he charged out of his office. A coworker stopped him to tell a story, but Whitaker replied he was in a rush. Leaving the building, he scanned the parking lot. A kid was attempting ollies with his skateboard on Central. A homeless man was dragging a bag of empty cans. Whitaker finally found her convertible on the far end of the lot.

"Hold on," he said, running to her.

As he approached the car, he was caught off guard. Claire was wearing a head scarf and a latex glove and smoking a cigarette like her life depended on it.

"What in the world are you doing?" he asked.

Claire quickly stubbed out the cigarette as her face flushed. She reached under her glasses and wiped a tear from her eye. "It's a habit I picked up recently. A bad one."

"You're way too beautiful to be smoking." Though he meant what he said, he regretted crossing that line immediately. How dare he hit on a grieving widow. Shame on you, Typist.

Claire flushed red.

Whitaker reached for a lifeline. "I've picked up a few bad habits myself lately." He waved his hand. "No judging here. Listen, I don't want to get your hopes up, but I'll read the story. I clearly have nothing better going on."

Black to white in a blink. He'd never seen such a transformation in a person. Her sad face lit up in a wonderful way, like a volcano erupting, a caterpillar metamorphosing into a butterfly, a distraught child finding the golden Easter egg.

Realizing what he'd done, Whitaker held up a finger. "But I'm not promising anything. This is what I was afraid of. If the story doesn't jibe with me, I can't write it. And I refuse to write it unless it speaks to me. I need you to understand that should I decline, you need to respect my decision."

Claire was nodding like a Tampa Bay Rays bobblehead. Did she even hear him? She reached over to the passenger side. "Can I write you a check?"

"I'm not going to take your money. Yes, if for some reason, I decide to write the book, I will. But I'm not going to let you pay me to read it."

She handed him the three composition books. "Please take care of them. They're the only copies."

That notion scared Whitaker as he took them with both hands. He wasn't the most responsible man of late. "I will. I'll take them straight home after work."

"When do you think you'll take a look?"

"The next few days."

In a move that nearly took his breath away, Claire placed a hand on his. "Thank you. Seriously."

As he smiled at her, he wondered what she was thinking behind those dark lenses and panda bear eyes. "You're very welcome."

He was the one who broke eye contact, and a dangerous thought passed through him. Was he agreeing to help her because he liked her? Did he think he was some knight swooping down to help a damsel in distress? Regardless of the reason, Whitaker needed to at least read the story. Then he could tell her no officially—a conversation he dreaded like no other.

⌐

Claire felt alive. So damned alive. The world was finally making sense. Though she'd promised him she wouldn't get her hopes up, she knew he would agree to write it now. It was meant to be.

Riding back toward the beach on Central, with Buju Banton singing "Wanna Be Loved," she lifted her arms high in the air and screamed at the top of her lungs. Some random person sitting at a table outside of a taco joint yelled back. Claire waved. She didn't care who could see or hear her. Today was a victory in so many ways. Most importantly, she was doing right by David. He deserved this more than anyone.

After her fit of exaltation, she turned down the reggae and called Didi. "He's going to read the book!"

"What?"

"Yeah. Whitaker Grant. I went by to see him at his work, and he's agreed to read it. I didn't even have to pay him."

"That's amazing," Didi said. "I'm so happy for you."

"The last two days have been . . . it's like I've finally turned the final corner. That's how it happens, isn't it? The pain doesn't really go away, but you move it around a little bit, almost like giving it less light and water. I still have a hole in my heart, but it's not as all-consuming. I was sleeping through life and didn't even realize it."

"Good for you," Didi said.

And there it was. It had taken three years, but Claire had broken through to the light.

Chapter 13

WHERE ARE THE ZOMBIES?

As the hues of dusk colored Clymer Park, Whitaker settled down on the front patio with the three composition books in his hand. Watching the park for a while, he noticed a proud osprey perched on a high branch on the dead limb of an oak.

Back down on the ground, a lone woman speed-walking a goldendoodle piqued his interest. She was working her arms back and forth like a cross-country skier. Never one to shy away from distraction, he spent a few moments thinking of more sign ideas. Coming up with clever poop memes could be so enjoyable.

We have video. We know where you live. If you don't pick up after your dog, we'll send our grandson to poop on your lawn.

So angry. He didn't need to be the fascist of the neighborhood. What about a kinder approach?

If you forget a poop bag, raise your hand and wait for assistance.

Oh, he's adorable! And yet . . . his poop in my yard is not.

How about hashtags?

#PoopHappens . . . ToNeedToBePickedUp

Weary of all the feculence, Whitaker glanced at the first composition book: *Saving Orlando #1.*

What in the world did the title mean? It occurred to him on the drive home that he'd neglected to ask Claire the premise of the story.

Was the city of Orlando in trouble? Was this some kind of sci-fi attack? Was Mickey Mouse in trouble? Was an asteroid coming?

Whitaker crossed his legs and opened to the first page. He read David's warning to Claire, asking her not to read it. His heart sank. Though he had felt badly for her, something about reading David's note to her made it so much more real. With the flip of a page, Whitaker had now stepped into Claire and David's intimacy.

On the next page, he read the first line.

"That's not bad," Whitaker said. "But where are the zombies?" He read the sentence again. "A first-person point of view is a brave choice, David. Let's see if you can pull it off."

Whitaker kept reading. After several pages, he nodded to himself, acknowledging that this guy, David, wasn't that bad a writer. Not to mention the finest handwriting he'd ever seen.

Whitaker had almost reached the end of the first chapter when his phone buzzed in his pocket. Reaching for it, he saw a text from a friend. Just saw Lisa on a date with some schmuck at the Birchwood.

The idea of his ex-wife going on a date wasn't a complete shock, but it didn't sit well with Whitaker. Did he still love her? Nah, it wasn't that. He was lonely, but he didn't crave her anymore. But if he had his preference, she'd remain single the rest of her life. He set the composition book on the ground and surrendered to the memory of her.

Lisa was an obstetrician fresh out of her residency. She was by all accounts smarter and funnier than Whitaker, but he loved trying to keep up with her. Not only Whitaker's parents but the entire Grant horde had loved her and welcomed her into the family, and, in a lot of ways, the two were married long before he'd even proposed.

Where he was flighty and always thinking about characters and stories, she was put together and businesslike. The only way they'd done couple things was if she'd organized them. Whitaker flew by the seat of his pants; Lisa kept a calendar. Whitaker figured out one meal at a time;

Lisa planned the following week's meals on Sunday. Whitaker didn't look at receipts; Lisa analyzed every line item.

In a way, she'd become the structure he needed. He liked being told what to do and where to go, the flighty writer towed by the put-together redhead. If someone had asked him what they were doing on a coming night, he'd just say, "Talk to Lisa. She's in charge."

But the pressure of a second book had weighed on their marriage. It was such a simple request: one hundred thousand words. The publisher had sent him an advance without even hearing what his idea was. His agent had chomped at the bit to read an excerpt or a synopsis. Whitaker had felt like he was in the World Series, and he was at bat in the bottom of the ninth. There'd been pressure. But the pitcher had already told him what pitch he was going to throw. A fastball, down and to the right. All you had to do was swing. You couldn't miss it.

All you had to do was swing.

But the typist still couldn't hit the ball.

Unsurprisingly, he'd become difficult to live with. At first, Lisa had ignored his breakdowns and doubts and become his cheerleader. "You can do it, Whit. Stop thinking so much and let your fingers move." Had she been excited about another book or the fact that they were going to start trying for a baby once he was finished?

"Es imposible, mi amor." Their conversations easily bounced back and forth between languages.

After two years, the publisher had stopped accepting excuses and demanded a draft. Anything at that point. They'd needed to see that their giant advance hadn't been a waste of time. Whitaker had felt like a bug being flushed down the toilet. Round and round, down and down, no way to escape. That fact that the giant advance had preceded him down the toilet hadn't helped things one bit. He cringed at the memory.

Whitaker had soon become an *imbécil*. Lisa's word, though he wouldn't disagree. Still, she'd persevered as his cheerleader. She'd turn the other cheek when he fell into the darkness. He'd lash out at her, and she'd take him into her arms and tell him to take deep breaths.

"I don't love you because of your book, Whit," she'd promised him. "And I wouldn't stop loving you if you changed careers. I just want you to be happy." What more could you ask of a partner?

He thought of the last time he'd seen her, a year ago. They'd met at a coffee shop, and he'd finally gotten a chance to thank her for her support and to properly apologize for being such a poor husband. He wasn't sure if their meeting had made her feel any better, but he'd been able to find the closure he needed.

Whitaker was suddenly aware of his thoughts and couldn't stand how he got stuck in the past. It wasn't that he still loved her or craved her. No, seriously. It was just that first love and the crushing power she had over you—especially when you'd been married to her. Whitaker didn't want her back. That ship had sailed. But he kind of wanted her to call him and say that she'd messed up, that she missed him. That none of her lovers since had been as good. Purely unfounded narcissistic cerebration of a man fearful that no one may ever love him again.

Letting Lisa go, Whitaker stood, barely aware that he'd left the composition books on the patio. What did it matter?

Imbécil out.

Chapter 14

WHAT GOES UP? NO, SERIOUSLY.
WHAT GOES UP?

Throughout the morning, Claire repeatedly checked to see if somehow her ringer was off. Why hadn't he called? For a moment while watching the water this morning, she'd let herself believe there was no way he would say no. Some things were indeed meant to be. At nine, she broke down and called him. He didn't pick up, and his voice mail was full. What a shocker that was.

At nine thirty, she couldn't take it anymore and drove back to the Bank of South Florida. It was clear that the Whitaker of today needed prodding. She was nearly shaking as she asked the mother of the soldier if Whitaker was in. When he didn't pick up her call, the woman said she'd walk back to his office and check.

Claire watched her until she disappeared down the hall. If he would just say yes, everything would be okay.

But . . .

If he said no again, she might have to stop. She'd have to find someone else. What a mean trick the universe would have played on her.

When the woman returned, Claire watched her footsteps, which pounded to the beat of Claire's heart. Claire almost wanted to turn and run. She wasn't ready for a final answer from Whitaker.

"He's actually sick today. Do you want his cell or email?"

Claire swallowed. "No, thank you. I have it."

She drove to Gulfport, nodding to the one-drop rhythm of a Burning Spear song. "Please let him say yes," she said, repeating herself four times.

His Land Rover was in the driveway. Maybe he was so enthralled with the story that he'd called in sick so that he could finish reading and even start writing. That would be the life break she needed.

Claire knocked on the door to no avail. She knew he was in there, though. Mrs. Claire Voyant could feel it. She knocked again and rang the doorbell. When she peered through the window, she could see a coffee cup on the table and a blanket wadded up on the sofa.

"Whitaker, I know you're in there. I went by the bank." She checked the doorknob; it was locked.

No way she was leaving without talking to him. No way could she endure another sleepless night. Besides, he honestly resembled a child to her, so she didn't mind treating him like one.

Raising her voice again, she said to the door, "I'm walking around to the back. Please, Whitaker."

Claire rounded the side of the house and looked through windows. As she reached a window in the kitchen, she caught sight of him. Feeling like she'd hooked a fish, she rapped harshly on the window.

"Please open up. I see you!" She was totally being a stalker but didn't care.

She continued around the house. His backyard was overcome with tall grass and weeds. She climbed the steps to the back door, tested the knob, and then knocked again. "Whitaker Grant!"

He finally appeared, wearing a bathrobe. His hair was all over the place. Pulling back the door, he looked at her as if she'd done something unthinkable.

"I'm sorry," she said. "I know you're sick, but I just had to hear your thoughts. Did you read it?"

"How do you know I'm sick?" He had coffee breath.

"I really don't mean to come off like a stalker, but I went by your work again." She put up a hand. "Before you say anything, please know that I need to get his book finished. It's . . ." She shook her head. "A higher purpose is pushing me. I can't sleep. I can't do anything without thinking about it."

"Claire, you can't hunt me down at work and go looking through my windows. I'm sick and tired and obviously not accepting company."

She ignored him and cast an eye toward the backyard. "Do you need a number for a landscaper?"

He let down his guard and rested an arm on the doorframe. "I'm going for a more natural habitat, a place for wild things to roam."

"You're a mess, you know that? You can't get mad at me for stalking you. *Someone* needs to be checking on you."

His voice rose an octave. "You're coming in hot today. Is this the real Claire?"

Something about this man. His whole "thing" was comical, like a cartoon character who'd come to life. She put her hands on her hips. "I'm seriously considering Baker Acting you."

"Aren't you a firecracker? I kind of like this side of you."

"I have my days." Enough small talk, she decided. She lifted her glasses and rested them on the top of her head. "Did you read the book? Start it, at least?"

Whitaker's grin vanished, and his eyes ran away as he let go of the doorframe and backed up a step. After the longest minute of her life, he ran a hand through his hair and sighed. "I did. Most of it."

By the tone in his voice, she knew a no was coming, and she waited as if his mouth were a firing squad of anxious trigger fingers. "And?" She winced, bracing for the worst.

"It's good. He's a good writer. But it's not for me."

There it was. Finality. Claire almost lost her balance, and her breath leaped from her lungs. "What? Why is it not for you?"

"I can't finish his book. I gave it a chance. It didn't speak to me, and I can't help you. This is my final answer. I'm so sorry. And I'd like to help you find someone who's much better than me."

They were facing each other as if about to duel. "There is no one else."

"Sure there is." He clasped his hands behind his back. "Why do you feel this need to get his book finished, anyway? It won't be his words."

Rather aggressively, she took a step toward him, entering his house. "You know what the saddest thing in the world is?"

Whitaker backed up.

"For someone to die without accomplishing their dream. This book meant so much to him, and I know he wanted to get it out there. It's the *only* gift I can still give him."

"It's just not for me." Whitaker's tender heart showed through his eyes. She could see that he wanted to help her, but that he didn't feel he could. That didn't cut it, though. He needed to toughen up.

Whitaker shook his head again, crossing the *t* in finality.

Claire was so sad that when he opened his arms to her, she fell into them. He pulled her in and hugged her. Did she really have to find another writer? She wrapped her arms around his waist and squeezed him. "Please, I'm begging you. Please write the book." She hated hearing herself beg but felt like she was fighting for her life.

"I'm sorry," he whispered, squeezing her tightly.

She held him for a while and didn't know why. Part of her wanted to punch him, to wake him up from this fog he was living in. They both squeezed hard and held on longer than usual, and to Claire it felt like they had both needed this hug—any good hug—for a long time. She certainly had.

Claire let go first. She descended the two steps and backed up into the tall grass, wiping her eyes.

A cricket sprang from her feet to find a better hiding place.

Whitaker whispered an apology. "Can I walk you to your car?"

Claire shook her head and started back around the house.

Whitaker called after her, but she ignored him. Enough trying to get this guy to help. He was a lost cause. Why was she wasting her time?

And why the hell did she think that all of a sudden her life was so special? Just because she'd found the courage to go dancing everything would be okay? Suddenly Whitaker would say yes and he'd finish what would be considered the finest novel of all time? They'd erect statues of David in downtown St. Pete?

Oh, how absurd.

When she twisted the key in the convertible, the reggae came blasting out. She quickly reached for the knob and turned it all the way down, until it clicked off.

Before she pulled away, Whitaker called for her from the front door. Had he changed his mind? She'd seen this pivot before at the bank. He was so indecisive. Her heart soared. Maybe the world did follow some kind of order.

Then she saw him holding up the composition books, and she dropped her head.

"You forgot these," Whitaker said, handing them to her.

Without a word, Claire set the composition books on the passenger seat and pulled away. Screw the no-smoking thing. As she left Gulfport and drove back to the beach, Claire snapped on her glove and wrapped the scarf around her hair. The smoke entering her lungs delivered a tiny sense of relief, but her mind quickly returned to Whitaker, who dampened her mood.

When she crossed onto Treasure Island—while working on her second American Spirit—blue lights flashed in her rearview.

"This can't be happening," she said, taking one last toke. She pulled into the parking lot of a Putt-Putt course and waited. A young family was giggling as they each attempted to putt their balls through a plastic pirate ship.

Claire looked at the cars passing by on Beach Boulevard. The only problem with having a convertible was everyone noticed you.

The officer stepped out of his car and marched her way. He had a very deep tan and filled out his uniform nicely. A small shaving cut marked his chin. "Ma'am, you're driving way too fast. Twenty miles above the speed limit."

Removing her glasses, Claire shook her head. "Sorry, I felt like I was creeping."

"You were eighteen over. I should write you a reckless-driving ticket." He pointed to her hand. "Why do you have a glove on your right hand?"

Claire couldn't believe she'd forgotten to take it off. "Oh, that's . . . it's so I could have a cigarette and no one at work would know."

He looked at her strangely. "I'd like you to step out of the car."

"I have this whole routine. Glove, scarf, gum, hand sanitizer."

"Are you drunk?"

Claire dropped her chin. "No."

"Step out of the car right now."

A boy yelled "Hole in one!" from somewhere behind the pirate ship.

"Are you joking?" Claire asked. "It's ten in the morning. You think I'm drunk? What am I . . . a serial killer too?"

The officer opened her car door. "Let's go."

"If you only knew what I'm dealing with right now. You and your little speeding tickets are the last of my worries."

With the subtle threat only a person with a badge can pull off, he said, "Get out of the car, ma'am."

Claire relented. Several people on the Putt-Putt course were rubbernecking. So much for discretion.

The officer ushered her into the back of his patrol car and ignored her as he climbed behind the wheel and logged on to his computer. Claire was furious, but he ignored her further pleas.

Finally, he said, "You want to take a Breathalyzer for me?"

"Fine."

The officer let her out of the back and handed her the Breathalyzer. He gave her instructions. "As hard as you can. There you go."

When the digital readout stayed at zero, she offered a smile. "Told you."

He nodded. "Seems like you're having a bad day, so I'll let you off with a warning."

Her shoulders fell in relief. "Thank you. I'm sorry for being a . . . you-know-what."

"I've dealt with worse. Hope your day turns around."

The officer wrote her a warning and patted the top of the car as she drove away. It didn't take her two minutes to put the glove back on and light another. This one was justified, and she puffed with fury as she processed the last hour of hell.

Once she neared the café, she followed her regimen to erase the evidence of her habit. Confident she'd succeeded, she pulled into her space and walked into work. Every chair was occupied. Beyoncé was coming out of the speakers.

Claire marched behind the bar and turned down the music. She looked around, waiting to find the guilty DJ. Jevaun, who was busy making a line of Bloody Marys, shook his head and said in a Jamaican rhythm, "You know it wasn't me."

Claire decided not to ask him to betray the guilty party. Instead, she eyed the line of drinks as he dropped long sticks of celery into them. She could smell the fire from his homemade Scotch bonnet hot sauce. "Will you make me one of those?"

"You got it, Claire. With a kick?"

"Yeah, with a kick."

While she waited for her drink, she watched her operation. Her eyes always went to the guests. Was there anyone unhappy? No one was waiting impatiently for a check. Most wore smiles or were stuffing their faces.

Jevaun set the drink down in front of her. Celery and a house-pickled okra poked out of the glass. "One of those days?"

"Do you ever feel like the bad won't stop?"

Always the Rasta philosopher, Jevaun waved his finger. "The bad never stop, but Jah always prevails. You gotta turn the bad to the good, girl."

She nodded and took the drink. "I'll be in my office if anyone needs me. Oh, and please change the music."

"I gotcha."

Claire sneaked the Bloody Mary past her diners, closed her office door, and sat behind her desk. What an awful day. While working through her emails, she gulped down her Bloody Mary and chomped down on the vegetables.

She couldn't wrap her head around why Whitaker would say no after reading David's incredible story. The money alone was enough. Reeling with anger, she googled his name. The first thing she saw was the cover of his book. Then his face. A charming young man with a bright future. The same man she'd met only a few feet away in the dining room so long ago.

"What a lie," she said.

Finding Whitaker's website, she angrily clicked around, as if each mouse click were a kick to his shins. The last blog entry was from six years before. She clicked on the Books section, only the one book available. She clicked onto his Facebook page. A picture of Whitaker and two of the actors from the *Napalm Trees* movie served as his profile shot. She looked at the date of his last post. It was late last night. The post read: The past is an alligator, but he's not as fast as me. She was shocked to see that hundreds of people had liked or commented on his vague post. Was he even relevant anymore?

She scanned more posts. He was tremendously active. He didn't have time to help her, but he certainly had time to write entire diatribes on Facebook.

As she polished off her Bloody Mary and her rage hit an all-time high, she decided to post on his wall. She wrote: Whitaker Grant is a selfish blowhard who pushes old ladies into the street. Claire laughed and stifled a burp as the hot sauce crept up her throat. She deleted her words and tried again.

> Whitaker Grant is a has-been and a never-was. His artistry is as fake as his humanity. I'm sorry I wasted my time reading his first book, and it's a blessing that he'll never punish us with another.

Claire posted the message and then read it again several times. She almost deleted it but decided he deserved even worse. In seconds, a notification posted. He was private messaging her.

> Really? I can't help so you decide to trash me on my Facebook page? What's that about?

Claire sat up straight and typed: You can help me. You've decided not to.

Whitaker: I can't help you because I can't write anymore.

Claire: You could at least try. Clearly, you have nothing better to do.

Whitaker: I'm deleting your post. Please don't harass me. Honestly, if you could climb into my skin for a moment, you'd understand.

Claire: I don't do pity.

Whitaker: I'm not looking for pity. I'm just looking for forgiveness. I've hurt enough people in my life and don't want you to be the next. You're actually the only person in the world that isn't driving me crazy right now.

He added a few seconds later: And that's saying a lot considering you're stalking me.

She typed: You said the book doesn't speak to you. Why?

Whitaker: I don't know. It just doesn't.

Claire: That's not a fair assessment.

Whitaker: I'm not giving you an assessment. He's a fine writer. Someone can make it a great book.

Claire: You are that someone.

Whitaker: Stop it.

Claire: Think of the press you'll get. I'll make you look like a hero. Whitaker Grant stepped in and finished my dead husband's novel.

A long pause. Was he coming around?

Whitaker: I have to go. Take care, Claire. I'd appreciate you refraining from further cyberattacks. And maybe we could hang out sometime if you ever forgive me.

Claire: Wait.

Then he was gone.

Chapter 15

IMBÉCIL

Whitaker stood from his desk and put his hands on his head. He stared at his communication with Claire displayed on the screen. "Why can't she get it?" he asked. "I would destroy that book. What's the point in reading it? And why is she so upset with me?"

The typist paced back and forth, the guilt of lying doing its best to strangle him. Sitting back down several minutes later, he typed: What?

He watched the screen, waiting for a response. Nothing. He stood again. Needing to relieve himself, he left his office. The backyard was closer than the bathroom, so he walked out into the tall grass, looked around for neighbors, and then gave back to the earth.

Returning inside, he decided it was time for lunch. He was craving a tuna melt and began to collect the ingredients. He opened the can of tuna and drained the oil. As he emptied the fish into a bowl, he couldn't stop thinking about her. Why was she so insistent? He didn't have a choice but to lie.

Trying to distract himself, he said, "Alexa, play something really sad."

The small white device on the far end of the counter lit up. In a robotic voice, Alexa responded, "Shuffling 'Feeling Down' from Spotify."

Whitaker immediately recognized the piano intro of a Coldplay song. "You think Coldplay is sad? Alexa, play something really, really, really sad."

Alexa tried again. A pop song began with an artificial beat.

"Alexa, you don't know a damn thing, do you?"

The robot replied, "Sorry, I'm not sure."

"Alexa, do you have a soul?"

"People all have their own views on religion."

"Alexa, have you ever had your heart ripped out?"

"Sorry, I'm not sure about that."

"Yeah, you'd know. You'd know all right, Alexa." He scooped some mayonnaise into the bowl. "There's nothing worse in the world. In a way, you're lucky. I could unplug you right now, and you wouldn't know the difference. Me, I'm stuck here while my ex-wife explores the dating scene in my own town. My home-fucking-town. And for no explicable reason, I've just lied to the only other woman I've been interested in since." He thought about the ring on Claire's finger. "Not that she's available. Do you know what that's like, Alexa?"

"Hmm, I'm not sure."

"You're a lucky girl. But I'll give you some advice, Alexa. Stay away from me."

Alexa missed the point. "Stay away is usually defined as stay clear of. Avoid. Did that answer your question?"

Whitaker grinned. "I guess you understand me as much as anyone. Alexa, play Roy Orbison."

Roy Orbison's "Crying" filled the kitchen, and Whitaker wept while he chopped celery. "Now that's a sad song."

Whitaker sang with the Big O as he dropped two slices of bread into melting butter in a pan. "Crying" had to be the saddest song in the world, he decided. He unwrapped two slices of cheese and placed them on the bread. "Crying" was the saddest song, and a tuna melt was the saddest dish in the world.

When his sandwich was golden brown, he set it on a plate and sat on the floor. He'd eaten hundreds of these over the years.

"Alexa," he said. "Play 'Everybody Hurts' by R.E.M."

Michael Stipe was soon singing the second saddest song in the world. Whitaker took a bite out of the sandwich and quickly pulled it away with a curse. The hot butter burned his tongue. He set down the sandwich and fell back against the cabinet, closing his eyes. His tongue was burned, and his kitchen smelled like fish. This was what it was like to be godless, mission-less, worthless. A prisoner in solitary confinement. He'd finally reached rock bottom.

Whitaker coughed into another cry and covered his face. How unmanly and feeble of him to spill tears. His father would tell him to "buck up." Jack Grant would never allow his son to cry. But dammit if Whitaker could help it. As the sandwich cooled on the floor next to him, Whitaker not only listened but felt the music as his life unraveled before him. He had failed his dreams; he'd failed his family. He'd even failed a poor widow by lying to her.

What a sad man he was.

And everybody hurts . . .

⌒

Claire was separating two tables after the lunch service when Whitaker appeared at the door. His eyes drooped like those of a short-nosed dog. Guests were still lingering, finishing the last of their meals. She had no intention of hurrying them.

He crossed the restaurant and stopped five feet from her, on the other side of the square table.

She pushed a chair back under the table harshly, the legs scraping the wooden floor. "What are you doing here?"

Clasping his hands behind his back, he said, "I need to tell you something."

Claire crossed her arms. "What?"

"I didn't read the book." He bit his lips after the confession.

Claire felt sick. "You lied to me?"

"Yes, I lied." He reached for his mustache but gave up and dropped his hands. "I read a chapter, or most of the first chapter. It's good. I just . . . I've got my own stuff going on. I figured that if I lied, I could get you off my back."

Claire scolded him with her eyes. "You're an asshole."

"That's about right. But I wanted you to know. It's not the book. His writing's great. I would love to help you. It's just my life sucks. On top of it all, I just heard about my ex-wife dating again. I don't even know why I care, but I do. It's a beautiful reminder of how worthless I am."

Claire returned to pushing the chairs back. "Doesn't make lying to me right."

Whitaker joined in the task, pushing one of the chairs back on his side of the table.

"Please don't touch my chairs. You've done enough, seriously."

Whitaker backed off and smiled cynically. "I hoped by coming here you might give me the books again. Let me give it a real read. Even if I can't pull it off, maybe I can convince someone better than me to help. Either way, I'd like to read the story. It's good so far. Way better than I had imagined."

Claire sighed. "I'm not sure you deserve to read his story now. I can't believe you lied to me. You have no idea what an awful morning I've had."

Whitaker nodded. "I can imagine."

She blew out a blast of air and looked away. What good would come of being hardheaded now? He was offering to read it. Should she let him?

Claire leaned over the table and centered the basket of hot sauces and salt and pepper. "I appreciate you coming here. And, yes, I'll let you read it. But you're still an asshole."

"No argument there. For the record, I did try to warn you."

She didn't respond.

Once she'd finished setting up the tables, Whitaker followed her out to the car. As she gave him the books this time, she felt hope again. Reticent hope, but hope nonetheless.

Whitaker held up the books chest high. "I won't lie to you again. Ever. I'm sorry."

"Just read it this time, okay?"

"Yeah, I will."

Chapter 16

THE KNIGHT IN TARNISHED ARMOR

Whitaker swung by the grocery chain Publix for a sub, and while he was in line for his bachelor staple, a younger guy with a flat-billed hat said, "You're Whitaker Grant, aren't you?"

Whitaker nodded. "Barely."

"I loved your book, man. It's incredible to run into you. I used to write a lot in school and been thinking about trying my hand at a novel. I can kind of feel the words running toward me."

"Of course you do. Like a flood in the lowlands. That's how it starts."

"I guess so. Do you have any advice for an aspiring writer?"

Whitaker turned away from watching the woman in the hairnet putting together a chicken-tender sub with extra shredded lettuce and yellow mustard for the customer in front of him. He looked at the young man who'd addressed him and saw an innocence that might not be able to handle the war of the written word.

"Writing will wrap its bony fingers around your heart and squeeze until there's nothing left. Everything you are goes onto that blank page, and the sad thing is . . . you may not like what you read. And the readers may not either. Then what are you to the world?" Whitaker raised his hand and flashed his fingers toward the sky. "Poof."

The innocent young man's mouth dropped.

Whitaker finished with, "My advice: run the other way."

"Damn, dude. Writing really beat you up, didn't it?"

"It's not for the faint of heart." Whitaker turned back toward the sandwich bar.

"I appreciate your honesty." The words drifted over the typist's shoulder.

"That's about all I have left now," he said through the side of his mouth. It was finally Whitaker's turn in line, so he stepped up and ordered a turkey and bacon sandwich with all the toppings, heavy on the vinegar. The sandwich Jedi in the hairnet put together a masterpiece of a sub that could barely be contained by wheat or wrapper.

When he got home, Whitaker settled onto the sofa and tore into his sub. Vegetables and condiments spilled out onto the coffee table.

"Integrity and a good sandwich," he said with a mouthful. "I guess some people have less than that."

He took another bite, shaking his head at the marvel the sandwich lady had put together. Once he'd plowed through the first half and washed it down with Doritos and a Coke, Whitaker picked up the first composition book, accidentally putting a fingerprint of oil on the first page next to David's note to Claire. He dried it off with a napkin and flipped to the first sentence.

"This is where it all begins, right?" Whitaker said. Addressing the author, he said, "David, why did you choose to write that first sentence? What compelled you to tackle a novel?" Another lesson Whitaker had learned in writing was that there was only one true reason that you wrote a book: because you had no other choice.

Was that true of David? Was this a story he had to tell no matter what, as if his life depended on it? And what pains had he suffered along the way?

Whitaker put his feet up on the sofa and reread the first chapter.

The protagonist, Kevin, found a young boy named Orlando breaking into his car in the driveway. He wore white sneakers. His brown hair fell over his hardened eyes. And he'd just smashed the passenger-side window with a crowbar when Kevin saw him from the den. Racing out the door, Kevin attempted to grab him, but Orlando swung the crowbar. Kevin barely dodged the attempt. With adrenaline kicking in, he slammed Orlando to the ground and pinned him down with a knee.

With his eyes now wet with fear, Orlando pleaded, "Don't call the police. They won't give me another chance."

"You should have worried about that before you broke my window, punk!" Kevin yelled, while pressing Orlando's face into the concrete.

"Please, I'm begging you." He spat pavement dust, the toughness bleeding out of him.

"You want me to let you go so you can do this to someone else? This isn't my first rodeo."

The chapter ended with Kevin indecisively staring at his phone with his pointer on the final "1" button, as if it were his finger alone that controlled the boy's future.

Surprisingly, Whitaker found himself invested in the main characters. As he moved through the pages of absolutely stunning handwriting, several realizations came to him. He paused after the first chapter to mull them over.

Whitaker knew nothing about Claire's husband. (Wait, was it husband or ex-husband? Maybe deceased husband?) He hadn't even seen a picture of David, but he knew that by reading these words and by getting to know Kevin, he was also getting to know David.

In the story, Kevin was in his midthirties and wading through a midlife crisis of sorts. Wasn't everyone in their mid to late thirties? Was David suffering from a similar fight? Was he a happy guy? Was he searching for something? How was his marriage with Claire?

The beginning pages revealed that Kevin had been dumped recently and was feeling like he might never marry. Did this predicament say anything about Claire and her marriage to David? It certainly made

Whitaker empathize with him. There was nothing worse than a woman telling you it was over.

Whitaker got the feeling that David was a solid guy, the kind of man Whitaker might have been friends with. The writing was pretty good, but more importantly, he had a lovely view of the world and a unique sense of humor. When it came to writing from the heart, David had the ability. You could teach a writer to follow the rules, but you couldn't show someone how to pour his heart onto a page.

When Kevin gave Orlando the choice of going back to juvie or working in the yard to pay off the broken car window, the reader, including Whitaker, was given a deep glimpse into Kevin's soul.

Whitaker fell back into the story as he reveled in David's novel. By the time he reached the end of the first composition book, he was absolutely immersed. Things would need to be touched up if he accepted the project, which was a possibility taking root. There were, of course, grammar issues amid David's artful calligraphy, and spots with too much telling. There were sections of dialogue that lacked description or motion and often descriptions that required finessing.

But that wasn't the point at all. It was good! The characters came alive in Whitaker's head. David had done a great job of giving Sarasota life.

Whitaker flipped back a page and reread a particular sentence that had caught him. "The beach was an overturned saltshaker pouring out into the Gulf, and above, a stratus cloud eased its way toward Mexico like a pelican fat on bait fish migrating south."

Several weeks into story time, Kevin opened up to Orlando, telling him how his fiancée had left him the day before their wedding. In return, Orlando shared the details of his broken past. A victim of her own difficult childhood, his mom had been a drug addict and often prostituted herself for her next fix. Orlando was a product of a one-night stand. She'd gotten clean long enough to get him back but then overdosed a week later. Orlando had been found sleeping next to his mother's dead body. After seven failed placements, he had given up on the chance of family and had decided to age out of the system in his group home.

The first book of the novel ended with Kevin flashing two tickets to Islands of Adventure to visit The Wizarding World of Harry Potter. Orlando was a huge fan. The words jumped off the page. "Consider this a bonus. You think you can miss a day of school?"

"You're joking, right? Are you really taking me to Orlando? Like the two of us going to Harry Potter World? I've never been to a theme park." Orlando paused.

Whitaker reached for the second book and kept going, shredding through pages. He could see Kevin as if he were sitting there next to him, a man waking from a dream, connecting with a paternal instinct long lost, realizing that by giving to this boy, he was feeding himself too. Though Whitaker was a long way from recognizing any paternal instincts, reading about Kevin was almost like looking in the mirror.

Kevin was a disaster of his own unique making, though, playing online poker at work, stealing coworkers' food from the community fridge, gulping down cable news and screaming at the talking heads. Whitaker roared with joy when Kevin hit bottom, bingeing on *Desperate Housewives* while pounding wine spritzers.

The typist paused. Should he accept the project, Whitaker knew he'd have to get to know David's life more. What were his quirks? Had he pulled these ideas out of thin air or had they morphed from his own decay? Whitaker would have to get to know Claire more as well. How had she affected his life?

David had clearly done extensive research on the foster system, and Whitaker wondered where that knowledge had come from. If he did tell Claire yes, that he'd finish the book, he'd need to dive into his own research. He was completely unfamiliar with the life of a child ping-ponging through the system, but he was more than intrigued to learn more.

Getting back to reading, Whitaker wondered if the middle of the story would fall off. Often, writing the first part was easy, but it was keeping the middle alive that made or broke a book.

Whitaker took a few bites of the second half of the sandwich and washed it down with more Coke. He kicked his feet back up and dove into the second book. After another great scene, Whitaker sat up and said, "I'm going to get paper cuts, David. I can't believe how good this is."

And then . . .

I have to write this book. There it was. The decision. *I want to help this book come to life.* Whitaker looked at his arms and chill bumps had risen. A story had literally landed on his lap, and he couldn't believe he'd almost ignored it. What if he hadn't read it? What if he'd stuck with the lie to Claire? He thought this book might have the answers he was looking for. Might he be so bold as to say Claire was right? He was meant to finish this book.

Sure, helping Claire appealed to Whitaker. Between her persistence, vulnerability, and, let's face it, beauty, she was a hard woman to say no to. Despite the complication of this book being written by her deceased husband, he couldn't deny the attraction he felt toward her.

But it wasn't just Claire that fueled his sudden desire to finish the book. Or David's story and the potential satisfaction of helping this dead man come back to life, as Claire said, giving him this final gift. Ultimately, it was because Whitaker saw himself in Kevin. Two selfish fools navigating the world with broken compasses. The only difference was that Kevin had located the Dog Star and found his way back home.

Whitaker craved a way back home, and he wanted to be a part of this journey.

If he had to name one issue with accepting the project, it was that he felt slightly scared. What if he couldn't do it justice?

Deciding that being scared was not always a bad thing, he continued reading. Wanting to know if Kevin could truly save the boy,

Whitaker threw himself right into the third and final composition book. Knowing this story would end prematurely broke Whitaker's heart. Claire was right. This story needed to go all the way to print.

Whitaker's heart hurt when Orlando and Kevin got in their first argument. Unable to forgive Kevin, Orlando disappeared, running away from the group home. Kevin spent days looking for him and feared the worst. With only a few pages left, Kevin finally found a clue, hearing that Orlando had returned to his old ways, running with young criminals bound for prison or the grave.

Whitaker had a terrible feeling that either Kevin or Orlando was going to die. And he wasn't sure he was emotionally prepared.

Then it was over. Whitaker flipped through the blank pages that filled out the rest of the composition book. "You have to be kidding me."

He dialed Claire's number, noticing the clock on the cable box read 8:18. In shock, he glanced outside. The teasing colors of dusk confirmed he'd completely lost track of reality.

When she answered, he said, "Where's the rest of it? Don't tell me it really stops here, in the middle of the third book."

"Yes, that's why I've come to you."

"Have you looked everywhere? He couldn't have left it like this."

"Yes, of course, I've looked. So you read it?"

Whitaker's heart was racing. "Yeah, I read it." He paused, collecting himself.

"And?"

"It's magnificent, Claire. It really is. I'm so sorry I put you off this long. I'm thoroughly invested."

He could hear her choking up. "Are you okay?"

"Yes," she said through the crying. "I'm just . . . just happy."

"You should be. He left you a great story. Are you sure you've looked everywhere? I mean, are there other drafts? He wouldn't have thrown away the first two." Whitaker stood. "I have so many questions.

Did you know he was writing it? Had you read any of it? Do you know the ending?"

"I don't know the ending at all. You saw his note to me. He wouldn't let me read it, and he didn't tell me anything about it. And I can't find anything else. Maybe he threw the other drafts away."

"Why would he do that? I still have all my drafts."

"I don't know. I've gone through everything. The house is empty and sold. All I have left is a few of his business files, his books, his desk and chair. There are no other drafts."

"Did he write at home or maybe he left something at his old firm? You said he was an architect, right?"

"I cleaned out his desk at work after he died."

"Can we meet? My brain is exploding right now."

"You'll finish the story?" she asked.

"Yes. But there have to be other drafts, more to it. If this is the third draft, then he had to have written the ending. We have answers to uncover first. Are you busy?" He could hear the rapidity of his voice but couldn't slow down. "Can you come over? Like now?"

"I'll be there in about thirty minutes."

When Whitaker hung up, he ran to his bedroom to get dressed. Seeing the bed that hadn't been made in weeks, he realized what he'd just done. Invited a woman into his house. He looked around and felt downright embarrassed. An impressive collection of old water and coffee cups had collected on the bedside table. A layer of dust had settled on the floor. She couldn't see this pigsty.

He grabbed his phone again and called her. She didn't pick up. He cursed and dialed again. No answer. "This can't be happening."

The disheveled typist ran to the mirror. His hair was ragged, and his mustache needed trimming. There were red vinegar stains on his shirt from the sandwich. "Shiitake on Sunday morning!" he screamed. "Fuck all and hell!" He shucked his clothes and raced into the shower.

After the fastest cleansing in human history, he toweled off and looked back at the phone.

She *still* hadn't called back.

He tried her again. No answer.

After another string of curses, he threw on some clothes, closed the door to his bedroom, and ran into the living room. He took the pile of clean laundry still waiting in a basket next to the sofa and pushed it into the closet. Then he picked up the articles of clothing draped all over the living room floor. He picked up the shrapnel of sandwich vegetables from the table and rug and put them in the sandwich wrapper. He took two more bites and then ran the leftovers to the kitchen. He looked at the clock. She would be there in less than ten minutes.

Whitaker didn't know what to do next. He unplugged the Xbox and hid it in the closet. What forty-year-old plays video games? As an added touch, he pulled two dusty Hemingway books from the shelf and displayed them on the coffee table, just in case she noticed. Much better than the copy of *Make Your Bed* by Admiral William H. McRaven, a gift from Staff Sergeant Jack Grant, which Whitaker shamefully shoved into a drawer. He straightened the pillows on the sofa and chairs and ran to the kitchen.

The accumulation of dishes was embarrassing. He looked at the daunting pile and then back at the living room and foyer. Not ready to tackle the kitchen, he raced back to the living room and ran the vacuum over the rug. He was repulsed at the crackling sound of the vacuum as it sucked up dirt and grit. With a mad dash to the bathroom, he grabbed the Poo-Pourri from the toilet. Back in the foyer and living room, he pumped out a few spritzes.

The smell overtook the room, so he turned on the fans and opened the windows. Though he was starting to think he wouldn't let her inside, he knew he needed to start on the kitchen. During the course of the cleaning, Whitaker kept telling himself that he was a disgusting man, and that this nonsense had to stop. How embarrassing for someone to see inside his world.

For God's sake, what if Lisa had somehow come to her senses and returned to him? Opening his front door, he'd say, "Oh, hi, Lisa, it's been so long!"

She'd open her arms. "Whitaker, I miss you. Please take me back. Make love to me. No, not here. Take me to the kitchen floor."

"No, Lisa. You don't want to see my kitchen. Or the living room, or the bathroom. Not even the bedroom. Can we make love in the backyard? Hold on, the tall grass and the crickets. How about the Land Rover? No. Let's do it on the front steps!"

By the time Claire knocked, he'd decided there was absolutely no way she was coming inside. He opened the door, and her beauty shot a pulse of nerves through him. He'd been so concerned about her seeing his house that he hadn't mentally prepared himself for the fact that he was about to take a woman out—not on a date, but still.

"Hey." He smiled and worked hard to appear confident. "Give me just a minute. I'll grab my computer."

"Where are we going?"

"I thought we'd sit outside somewhere." He looked past her to the sky. "It's so . . . nice out. I tried to call you, by the way."

Claire raised an empty hand. "Sorry, I was in such a rush that I left my phone."

"That explains it. Anyway, give me a moment."

"Can I use your restroom, please?"

Whitaker froze. Oh boy, there was the question he hadn't seen coming. Not much of a knight in shining armor if he couldn't lead her to the bathroom. He opened his mouth to say no, but stammered. Then he thought he'd suggest she use the backyard. *Though it's not ideal for making love, the grass is tall, so you'll have plenty of privacy.* Not the most chivalrous suggestion, he decided.

It occurred to him that he had forgotten to clean the bathroom. He felt like punching himself in the face. What an idiot! Still, he couldn't tell her no. Not unless . . .

Not unless he told her the plumbing was broken.

Hmm, then she'd ask about the second bathroom. *Oh, Matteo, what do I do now?*

With tremendous trepidation, the knight in severely tarnished armor nodded and opened the door wider. "Come on in. Please excuse the mess."

Chapter 17

Two Damaged Souls

While driving into Gulfport on the way to Whitaker's house, distracted by her thoughts, Claire had slammed on the brakes just in time to avoid a muscular man in a sleeveless shirt and flip-flops, walking a German shepherd. It was a few minutes before nine, a mild blue glow to the night sky.

Claire was desperate to hear what Whitaker had to say. He was now the only other person on earth who had read the manuscript. And he liked it! The fact that he'd read it in a day and invited her over immediately said it all. He'd been desperate to ask her about other copies and drafts. Her stalking had apparently paid off.

When she entered his house for the first time, a strong citrus scent attacked her nostrils. The walls were bare and furniture sparse, as if he'd just moved in. A surprisingly fancy houndstooth sofa stood out in the center of the living room like a giant wedding ring in a dark alley. She'd heard he had been married, so this house was obviously his post-divorce bachelor pad.

Pointing to his left, Whitaker said, "The bathroom is down the hall there. First door on the right."

Claire thanked him and followed his direction. She could see a laptop resting on a folding desk in a room at the far end. Had to be his office. No wonder he was having difficulties writing.

Finding the guest bathroom, she flipped the switch. She saw the Poo-Pourri spray and figured that was what he'd used to spray the house. How bachelor of him.

When she returned to the living room, he sprang from the sofa. "Please don't judge me too much by my mess. But I guess you now get an idea of where my head is these days. A proper midlife crisis."

"No judgment here." At least, she was *trying* not to pass judgment.

He crossed his arms. "I want to say again how sorry I am for lying. As you can see, I'm in even worse shape than Kevin is in the beginning of the story, as far as midlife crises go. But that doesn't excuse me lying to you."

Claire totally agreed but chose not to respond.

Whitaker sighed. "Frankly, I'm so embarrassed by this place I suggest we go somewhere else."

Back outside, she moved her purse from the passenger seat of the convertible, and he climbed in with a messenger bag. He gave her directions to a wine bar only a half mile away, and they shared small talk as they made the short drive south.

"I can't imagine running a restaurant," he said, glancing at her, "especially a successful one. What's your secret?"

"I grew up in my father's diner, so it's all I've ever known." She looked up for a moment, as if her father were among the stars waking in the darkening sky. Leo had been such a good father, even after her mother had left them to start her other family. Claire could still hear his roaring laugh that would pour out of the kitchen and make all the guests in the dining room smile. Who knew? If he were still alive, Claire still might have been in Chicago running the diner with him.

With her eyes back on the road, Claire imagined Leo aligning the stars in her favor, helping her preserve David's legacy. Despite Whitaker's many faults, he seemed like a genuine and kind man—very different from David, but hopefully the right choice to finish the book.

Whitaker ran a hand through his longish hair. "As many restaurants as I've seen open and close over the years, it must truly be in your blood. Seems like there are so many things you have to perfect: the menu, the staff, the setting. And only if you knock them all out of the park can you survive your first year."

Claire could have added many more to his list but got his point. "Our first year wasn't exactly easy, but let's just say I knew what to look for. My dad opened Leo's back in the seventies, and it became an institution in the Loop. I learned from a lot of his mistakes."

It was nice remembering her father, but she was eager to get into the discussion about the book as they parked along the main street in Gulfport. They sat outside under a yellow awning lit up with Christmas lights. Music akin to that of Buena Vista Social Club tickled the night air, which was just cool enough to make one consider long sleeves or pants. Alcohol-infused laughter came from the only other occupied table, where two couples were enjoying a night out on the town.

A young man with a seashell necklace burst out of the front door spitting Spanish with a Cuban tilt. Claire knew a little Spanish from school but couldn't keep up.

Whitaker stood and embraced the man, machine-gunning him back fluently.

After a minute of back and forth, their faces in close proximity, Whitaker turned and introduced his friend Miguel to Claire. "You might know Leo's South on the beach," Whitaker said. "That's her place."

"Oh, of course. My wife and I love your food. I'm so happy to have you." Miguel turned to Whitaker. "For you, my friend, I've procured a Galician godello from a very small producer that will be right up your alley."

"Ribeira Sacra?"

"Even higher. Valdeorras."

"Ah, how adventurous of you. A river wine planted by the Romans."

As Claire listened, she began to understand what a budding Renaissance man Whitaker was. He was still a cartoon character, but one of unexpected depth. And she had to admit he was a good-looking man, attractive even.

Miguel turned back to Claire. "You'll love this white. A kiss of barrel, a little age to it. Still, nice and bright but not too tart. Kind of like my friend Whitaker here."

"I'll take that as a compliment. All but the age part."

"Will this work for you?" Miguel asked her, beaming from the banter.

Claire smiled. "Who doesn't like Roman river wine?"

Miguel clapped his hands together. "Excellent. May I suggest a bowl of olives and my *tortilla Española* to start? You're hungry, aren't you?"

"Famished," Claire said.

Once Miguel had retreated back under the yellow awning, Whitaker retrieved his computer and the composition books from his bag and set them on the table. He opened up his computer, revealing a green sticker that read: CROSS ME, AND I'LL PUT YOU IN MY NEXT NOVEL.

Claire tried to be patient while she waited for him, but she wanted to say, "Okay, Whitaker, let it out!"

Once he was settled, Whitaker finally said, "I love this book. David was a wise man, wasn't he?"

Claire thought of the times when she'd come home from a long day at the restaurant and snapped at him for no particular reason. Most of the time, he would hear her out without reacting—sitting with his legs crossed, allowing her to vent. Typically, the move would completely snuff out her anger. That, to her, was wisdom—and was one of the reasons she loved David so much.

Swallowing the memory, she said, "Very much so."

"I'm a bit scared that I'm not worthy, to be honest, but I'd like to help."

His humility, as opposed to the pity seeking she'd seen before, was endearing. "You're worthy, Whitaker. I wouldn't have asked you otherwise."

"Thank you." He talked as he clicked. "How much of the story is true?"

"What do you mean?"

"Well, we writers all put ourselves into stories. Especially early on in our endeavors. How much David is in Kevin?"

Claire thought about it. "They share some similarities, I guess. Same age. The same humor, of course."

"And both going through some difficulties?"

Claire cocked her head.

"If you want me to do this, you'll have to let me pry some."

"I know," she said, pondering Whitaker's question. "I'm not bothered by the question. More, just trying to think of his difficulties. I mean, he worked too much, I guess. But he wasn't really struggling. Almost the opposite, like he'd found the secret to life." Claire remembered looking at David sometimes, wondering how he could possibly be so happy. Not that they had a reason to be sad anymore, but he was often on a totally different plane of existence, of enlightenment, even.

"Which speaks to my point about wisdom. I can sense it."

"David had his midlife quirks, too, though his seemed to lean toward healthier vices, like running and biking, and then writing, of course. Once we realized we weren't going to be parents, I opened Leo's, and he became an exercise junkie, always training for the next marathon or triathlon. Some people buy Harleys. He bought road bikes." Claire could see David's shaven muscular legs protruding from his neon-green cycling shorts. "Then he read your book and started writing. He threw himself into it just as much as he had into his training. He was that kind of guy. Why do anything less than full throttle?"

"I could have taken a few pointers on negotiating the midlife bridge. He sounds much more put together than me."

Claire tilted her head. "Um, you think?"

"Okay, let's not get carried away. You apparently enjoy picking on me, but please know that I'm a fragile being with sensitive feelings."

"And an awful mustache." Claire couldn't help but poke at him some. It was too much fun.

"Ouch." He covered his mustache as if she was about to attack it.

Claire burst into laughter. "You know I'm kidding."

"I'm glad knocking me down lifts you up." She could tell by his smile that he was having fun too. He handled being tormented well, almost welcomed it.

"I'm only teasing," she promised. "Please forgive me. But what is this mustache thing anyway? Some sort of statement piece?"

"I guess you could call it that. David bought a bike; I grew this. Same thing."

Another shared smile.

"It's not that bad, is it?" Whitaker asked.

"I can see the appeal for other men your age. If you're looking for a girlfriend, you might want to rethink it."

Whitaker smiled the smile of a man who'd spent a long time thinking about relationships and had endured the pain of lost love. "Most certainly not looking for a girlfriend. Maybe the mustache is my deterrent. Like how a single woman wears a ring."

Claire glanced at the rings and felt her shoulders slump. For an instant, she felt a defensive anger, almost rage, bubble up, but thankfully she caught it just in time and held her tongue.

Whitaker followed her eyes to her finger. "Oh gosh. I didn't mean it like that." He sighed. "I feel like a jerk. I was talking about women in general—"

Claire took in a long breath. "It's fine. I know you didn't mean anything by it."

Miguel appeared, saving the couple from any further awkwardness. He uncorked the bottle and offered Whitaker the first taste. He sniffed and nodded. "That'll do, my friend."

Once Miguel left the table, Whitaker apologized again, and then raised his glass to Claire. "To David."

She clinked his glass with hers. "To David."

They both drank to her husband and the gift he'd left.

After enjoying a sniff and sip but not making too much of a spectacle like some wine snobs, Whitaker said, "I'll try not to put my foot in my mouth again, though we may have to explore some uncomfortable spots. I don't know that I have the chops that I used to, but I'll tell you this. I will pour my heart into this project and treat it exactly like it's my own."

The reality of David's book coming to life suddenly struck her, and she felt like crying and leaping for joy at the same time. Claire took another small sip and set her wineglass down. "I know you will."

Whitaker jumped right back into the guts of Claire's life. "How was your marriage?"

Claire tensed and felt almost combative as the area between her eyebrows tightened. "What kind of question is that? This story has nothing to do with our marriage."

Whitaker put up both his hands apologetically. "You're right. I'm sorry."

Seeing the kindness and gentleness in his eyes, she knew he truly meant no harm. Claire took another long breath and shook it off. Apparently his mouth didn't come with a filter. She could either accept working with him and all his peculiarities or get up now and walk away.

No, Claire had to trust her instincts, the ones that had led her to him in the first place. And in doing so, she had to give him the benefit of the doubt. He wasn't prying; he was helping.

"No, it's fine," she finally said. "I don't mean to be defensive. Our marriage was great, like better than ever. We'd already passed our rough spots and were in a strong place. We were having a lot of fun."

Taking a welcome divergence, Whitaker asked, "Any idea where he drummed up this story? Saving a boy in a group home. Orlando. Sarasota. It's an impressive premise, the whole idea of a sad and lonely man finding purpose in helping a young man who deserves a lift up in life."

"Yeah, it's beautiful. And, yes, I do feel like he wrote the book as some sort of cathartic exercise." By now Claire knew the answer all too well, having exhausted the idea that this book was how David had experienced being a father.

"You alluded to it earlier," Whitaker said. "Please elaborate."

More laughter came from the other table, and Claire was tempted to turn around and tell them to keep it down.

Claire crossed her right leg over her left and folded her arms. "David always wanted to be a dad. It was his dream for so long, but we had trouble getting pregnant. We tried and tried. We were that couple that did way too many IVFs and IUIs, and it started to eat at our marriage. You can only deal with getting your hopes up so many times before you fall apart. It got bad once the doctor told us we had to stop. I was a wreck, especially. We toyed with adoption, but that didn't work out either." The word *adoption* squeezed her heart.

Whitaker raised an eyebrow. "How did that not work out? Aren't you guaranteed a child when you adopt?"

"Yeeaaaah, but . . . it's a long story." And she really didn't want to ever revisit it again, but she knew she needed to. "We thought we had a baby. Came home early from a trip with assurances from our lawyer. We met the mother, and she loved us." Claire looked up and added, "You have to meet the mother and get her approval before you can meet the baby. So the baby was in the nursery. We went home feeling like it was happening. But we received a call that night, as we were getting the nursery ready. A different adoption agency had come in and talked the mother into giving the baby to another couple. Apparently, they'd offered her money under the table. Our lawyer was furious; we were destroyed."

Claire took a big sip of her wine to slow her elevated heart rate. Those days had been so awful, sitting on the floor in the nursery holding the toys and touching the clothes she'd begun to collect, the ones that a baby might never touch.

Once she'd collected herself, Claire told Whitaker what she'd never told anyone. "That was it for me. I couldn't keep trying. David attempted to make me feel better, promised me we'd eventually find our true baby. I told him I was done." The confession stopped in the air in front of her, and she fought to hold back a cry. "And I said . . ."

Whitaker reached across the table. "We can do this later."

Claire shook him off and coughed up the words as if she had to get them out before they choked her. "I told him that if he loved me, he'd have to let this dream of ours go. That I couldn't bear another failed attempt. I told him we weren't meant to be parents."

Claire felt the tears collecting under her eyes. But she didn't want to cry, not anymore. "He hugged me and told me that I was all he ever needed, that we didn't need a child, that he couldn't be more content." Claire scratched the table, feeling David's breath on her neck. And she could hear the bitterness in her tone as she said, "But apparently, according to his secret book, he wasn't content at all. It reads to me as if he wrote it to experience what it was like to be a father. I guess Orlando was the child he never had." Claire touched her flat, empty belly. "What we could never have."

Whitaker put his elbows on the table. "Don't let yourself get caught up in regret. You two went through a lot. Like you said, he was happy when he died. That's what matters most."

Claire nodded. "I know." Whitaker had a good point, and it was probably the one positive that had gotten her through the first three years.

"Okay," Whitaker said. "Enough prying. And, Claire, we can always wrap up and go at it again tomorrow."

"No, let's keep going."

Whitaker wrapped his fingers around the stem of his wineglass. "Why Sarasota for the setting? Was David from there?"

Claire shook her head. "No, but he traveled there sometimes. He was doing projects all over Florida. He's actually from Tampa."

"Oh, gotcha. You're from Chicago, right? You met up there or . . . ?"

Claire loved the story of how they met, but everything was pressing down on her. One of the tears she'd attempted to suppress rolled down her cheek, and she turned so that he wouldn't see it.

But he did see it. "You know what? Let's take a break. This is all tough. We have plenty of time to talk. I think you get the picture. To do this right, I have to understand him. And I suspect to understand David, I need to understand you too."

"Yeah, I get it." Claire quickly lifted her glasses and wiped her eyes.

Leaving the topic, they made small talk for a while, getting to know each other more. Claire started to feel better and latched back on to the excitement of finishing David's book. It was a nearly epic gift that she was giving to him. And she liked that Whitaker was her choice. Her intuition had been correct. Though his prodding hurt, it showed her how serious he was going to take the project.

As they shared the bowl of olives and *tortilla Española*, Whitaker asked, "What is it you do outside of running the café, not that you have any free time? But do you have any hobbies?"

Claire popped an olive into her mouth and chased it with a sip. "I have a cat." The wine had helped calm her, and she was enjoying herself again.

"Ah, you're a cat lady. That explains a few things."

She finished chewing. "I didn't know it until I found him at the restaurant. It was love at first sight. His name's Willy. One-Eyed Willy." Claire could almost feel Willy rubbing up against her ankles.

Surprising her, Whitaker broke into an unabashed Sloth-from–*The Goonies* impersonation, saying, "Hey, you guys."

Claire burst into laughter and covered her mouth.

Whitaker stuck his fork into the *tortilla Española*. "Who doesn't know One-Eyed Willy? So outside of obsessing over eighties films and taking care of One-Eyed Willy, what makes you tick?"

With her laugh still lingering, she said, "Lately, I've been trying to reconnect with the beach. Bought a little place on Pass-a-Grille recently. I think it's fair to say I've neglected the brighter side of my world since David died. It's been a long three years."

"I know what you mean." He raised a hand. "My pain pales in comparison to yours, but I've had my troubles too. I've barely looked at the water in forever. It's such a shame. We live in one of the most beautiful places on earth, but life can get in the way, and . . . and then you forget to take the time to appreciate the things that actually matter."

How right he was. "Exactly, but I'm trying to find the magic again. And as far as hobbies, I used to be into photography. For a minute, I wanted to be the next Annie Leibovitz. But that's gone to the wayside too. This is going to be my year, though." She hammered the table, feeling a lovely sense of possibility coming over her.

Claire turned the conversation to him. "So what about you? Why the long two years? A divorce, right?"

Whitaker stretched his arms. "I guess the whole town knows."

"You kind of did that to yourself, you know. You wrote a book and went and got famous."

"That I did." He put his hands behind his head. "Anyway, yeah, a divorce. A terrible divorce. Not like we were fighting. It was actually a *gentle* divorce as far as those are concerned. I guess you could call it a

Divorce Light." Claire didn't laugh, so he tried to clarify. "You know, Bud Light. Divorce Light."

Claire offered an aware grin. "I get it."

"Anyway," he said. "Let me pop the top on my Divorce Light and share a sip." He made a whooshing sound, as if he were opening a can.

"Oh my God," she said, shaking her head in near disbelief. "So if the joke doesn't work, just keep trying?"

Whitaker lifted an imaginary can and then pretended to gulp it down. Then he crushed it and tossed it over his shoulder. "Don't worry. I'm earth friendly. That was a recycling bin behind me."

Claire found herself laughing again, and it felt wonderful. "Not bad. Your routine could use some work, but I could see you being funny."

In an instant, the curve of Whitaker's lips reversed. "There was no fighting. I was checked out. She called me on it, gave me a yellow card. I ignored it. And then she was gone. I was so wound up in trying to write again, trying to express myself. When all I really should have been doing was loving her."

Claire imagined Whitaker being a handful to live with, but a ton of fun, nonetheless. "You still love her?"

"Nah, it's not like that. I mean, I love her as a person, but we've both gone in opposite directions. In fact, she's now dating again according to the bomb of a text a friend dropped on me recently."

Claire brushed her hair behind one ear. "How did you take the news?"

"Ended up lying to a kind woman who owns a café on Pass-a-Grille. Told her I had read her husband's book, when in actuality I was suffering yet again from an old scar that doesn't want to fade away. I honestly don't know why it bothers me, but it does."

"Well, aren't we two wounded animals?" Claire said, raising her glass to him. "You actually make me feel better about myself."

Whitaker raised his own stem. "I'm glad my decline can give some- one else hope, almost like a seesaw. I go down, you go up. Maybe this whole thing I'm going through isn't for naught."

She enjoyed her wine and then, "A seesaw. I like that."

Whitaker smiled at her appreciation of his comment. "I'll try to keep my feet on the ground for you. Keep you up in the air."

It took a moment for Claire to get his meaning. "No, what goes down must go back up, right?"

Whitaker slowly lifted his hands, palms up, and said with a calm delivery, "Then our seesaw shall defy odds and rise in balance."

Claire had to give it to him. He had an interesting mind. She put a bow on the topic by asking, "All this struggling because you can't figure out anything new to write?"

"That's pretty much it."

"But now you have a story," she said.

"That's right. Now I have a story." He took a long, slow breath and pinched his mustache. "And I'm scared to death . . ."

After a pregnant pause, Whitaker said, "You should pick up your camera again. It would be good for you. Do you have any work I can see? Judging by your amazing sense of style, I bet you're more of an artist than you let on."

She couldn't help but get excited while thinking about taking pho- tos again. "I still have a couple pieces here and there. Sold most of them at the café."

Whitaker topped off both of their glasses. "I don't know if you noticed, but I have a few open spots on my walls. Will you take a pic- ture for me? I'll buy it with the money I'm getting for this book I'm writing."

She cocked an eyebrow, a smile playing on her lips. "Yeah, I'll do that."

"Can I ask one more serious question before we call it a night? And you don't have to talk about it if you don't want to."

Claire felt more ready for his questions now, like he'd earned her trust. "Shoot."

Whitaker asked his question as if he were touching a doorknob that might be hot. "How did David die?"

Claire nodded approval of the question. She'd spent enough time reliving that day that it wasn't always a torture to explore. "A drunk driver. He was coming off 375 into downtown St. Pete. About four in the afternoon. A man driving a Honda Accord with a missing back bumper changed lanes without seeing David. Ran him off the road into a telephone pole."

"Oh God, that's awful. I hope the guy's in prison."

"For about five more years. God, if you only knew how much time I've spent hating that man. It's probably a good thing he's behind bars."

Whitaker nodded understanding. "How did you find out?"

"David was supposed to bring someone by for dinner. Three years later, and I still don't know who it was. I assume he was on his way to pick up the person . . . I don't know. They never showed up. But I'd prepared all the fixings for fajitas and was waiting for them to walk in the door to fire the shrimp. They were supposed to be there at five, and I kept dialing him over and over while I waited at the dining room table."

Claire could still remember that moment so vividly, her fingers jabbing the buttons on the phone, her eyes on the empty chairs. "Something didn't feel right. I must have called him thirty times. Then there was a knock on the door. When I saw the chaplain's white collar and the police officer standing behind him, no words were needed."

Whitaker reached across the table and put his hand on hers. "I can't imagine." After a pause, he asked, "You never figured out who he was bringing to dinner?"

Claire shook her head. "No idea. I guess it doesn't really matter, but it's certainly always niggled at me."

"Yeah, it would anyone."

"And they found a Yankees hat with the tag still on it, which, if you knew David, was even weirder. He hated the Yankees—despised them. So why would he have a brand-new hat in his car? I guess it was for a client, but even so, I can't see him supporting the Yankees in any way."

Whitaker let go of her hand. "Doesn't seem fair you've had to deal with these questions for so long."

"Well, it's not like answers will bring him back. I'm just trying to get by now."

"I think you're doing better than getting by. I'd be in a lot worse shape than you. So would most of the population. I think you're a fighter and an inspiration."

Claire thanked him. "I'm nobody special, that's for sure."

"I completely disagree."

Miguel appeared, lightening the mood. Whitaker asked for the bill, and once Miguel had left, Whitaker asked, "Can we do this again tomorrow morning? I promise we will only talk about what you're comfortable with."

"It's fine, really. It's been a long time." Claire was committed to doing whatever it took to help him finish the novel.

Chapter 18

Green Light, Go

Strolling alongside Claire on the beach the next morning, Whitaker found himself in awe. It was truly sad how he'd let the Gulf of Mexico's coast disappear from his purview in the past years. No, he might as well live in some no-name town a thousand miles inland. How dare he lose sight of the tropical beauty surrounding him.

He loved the feel of the sand on his feet, the way the sharp shells lightly stabbed his pads like an aggressive pressure point treatment. He loved the salt water as it rolled over his ankles, the birds diving into the water, the herbal scent of seaweed drifting by, the light chop on a breezy day like today.

The woman beside him grew increasingly fascinating with each story and anecdote she shared, and he'd begun to understand her. Though she could be so quiet and in her head sometimes, he could feel the electricity that ran through her. The beach was indeed her domain.

"This is where I fell in love with reggae. Fourteen years old, listening to Bob Marley on the beach. When I'd leave my grandmother and return to Chicago, bracing myself for another brutal winter, it was a way to bring me back here."

"I wonder if we ever crossed paths," he said. "I was here all the time."

"Possibly." Claire pulled her eyes from the water and looked at him through her dark lenses. "So what new conclusions did you come to? You're not going to bail on me, are you?"

"No, not now. I'm committed to giving this my all."

"I couldn't sleep last night, worried you might change your mind."

He shook his head. "I didn't sleep last night either. I read the book again."

"Again?"

"Well, most of it. It's really good. Needs some work, but the bones are solid. I was wrapping my mind around some of the larger issues. And I think the biggest is getting your blessing. I know this is David's novel, and I want to respect his memory. But if I'm to take it on, I need to feel free to roam." He stopped walking, and she did the same. "I don't want to sound like a jerk, but I don't know how else to say this."

Whitaker removed his Maui Jims, wondering how to best say what he was asking. "If I'm to write it, it has to be mine. In a sense, you need to give me the story. I can't be second-guessing the muse, and I can't have you second-guessing her either. I'm not saying I want to put my name on the book. But you have to let me take creative control. I can't run every scene or change by you; I can't work that way."

Claire crossed her arms and looked back to the water, as if for approval. "I understand. The story will be yours. But I think both of your names should be on the cover."

"I'd like that." He looked at her. "I will put everything I have into it, Claire. That's about as true as I could ever be to the story and to David." Upon seeing her face light up, he said, "Here's the other thing. I don't want you telling anyone. Not yet. I don't need the pressure. If for some reason I can't pull this off, I need to be able to walk away."

"It'll be between you and me."

Whitaker began walking along the tide line again, and she followed. "I woke up and almost shaved my mustache, some sort of step toward a new me." As the words left his mouth, he heard David Crosby singing "Almost Cut My Hair."

"Oh, you did? What prevented you? It might have been a wise move."

"The fear that I might be morphing into normalcy."

"Let me assure you, Whitaker. You are anything but normal."

That made him smile, even if it wasn't a compliment.

Whitaker dodged a fiddler crab and held up a finger. "I did shower—with soap—and then stretched and did a few push-ups. If you knew me well, you'd know that is a sign of a breakthrough. Me touching my toes is like Rocky carrying logs through the snow while training to fight the Russian."

"I can definitely see the likeness."

Whitaker held up a curled arm. "You can't see them right now, but there are muscles here."

She pinched his bicep. "Yeah, I think you might have left them at home."

A little girl ran by chasing another girl with a bucket of water.

Whitaker said with a straighter face, "You've given me a gift, you know. Something big."

"Bigger than your muscles?"

Whitaker looked down to his bicep. "Believe it or not."

After a laugh, Claire turned serious again. "It's David's gift to both of us. I wish you'd gotten to meet him. I think you two would have been friends."

"It would have been an honor. To win you over, he must have been one of a kind." Whitaker didn't mean to be overly sentimental, but it was a touching moment for him. He could only be honest.

They turned back once they'd reached the Don CeSar. Umbrellas were popping up left and right, sun worshippers readying themselves for a lazy day of reading or simply watching the people and the boats pass by.

When they returned to his car, Whitaker said, "I'd better get to work."

"Yeah, me too. Will you keep me posted?"

"You know it." Whitaker considered hugging her but offered his hand instead. "I'll be in touch."

⌒

"No time like the present," Whitaker said to himself, sitting down at his desk and setting the composition books at his side. He was indeed scared. Anxious. And an emotion so distant that it seemed almost foreign was rising inside him like lava from a dormant volcano. He felt *excitement.* As he'd driven home from the beach, he could barely wait to get started. Not typing. Writing.

Opening up the first book and setting it down next to his laptop, he started a new file. As he saved it, he saw the graveyard of unfinished Microsoft Word documents buried in a file called Open Projects. Maybe he would finally close a project this time.

Whitaker formatted the document, titled it, and typed the first line. He smiled. Something told him that he was starting something big. His instincts hadn't spoken to him in such a way since *Napalm Trees.* It was a good stab at a first sentence, at least nothing to tweak quite yet. He kept going, adding a few lines here and there, ideas that seemed to come out of nowhere. Whitaker couldn't quite see Kevin's house west of the Tamiami Trail in Sarasota, so he brought out the setting more. Growing up only an hour away, Whitaker knew Sarasota well enough.

As he typed, Whitaker felt as if he were having an out-of-body experience, his fingers dancing across the keys, the fingers of a robot racing to enter lines of computer code that might save the world, the line between him and David and reality and fiction blurring.

A phone ring stole him away from his work. The ring wasn't necessarily loud, but to Whitaker it was as loud as the fire alarm he'd gone into battle against nights before. He pulled back from the computer. He noticed sweat under his arms. The screen was full of words. He looked around, and another chill ran through his body, inching up his spine. He stuck his arms out to stretch and took in a giant breath. What had just happened? Whatever it was, it felt good.

Deciding to ignore the call, he went back to work.

Finally, he looked at the clock on the wall. Three hours had passed.

Whitaker returned to the document and scrolled up. Pages and pages of words. He could feel the muscles in his forearms weary from the chase. He'd done it. He'd found her.

He'd found the muse.

"Where in the world have you been, my sweet lady?" he asked, the hairs standing up on his arms, tears rushing to his eyes. "Don't leave me again."

Sex was the only feeling he could compare this to, and it was the kind of sex you have when the whole world lights up around you, a million fireflies dancing in the dark, your partner a sorceress of delight, a long steady climax of unbridled joy. The drug he'd missed finally coming back. A fix of the finest order.

Whitaker looked down at the terrazzo tile floor. And he imagined seeing something nearly transparent—almost like a snake skin—but it wasn't serpentine. It was the skin of the typist. The writer had finally shed the unhealthy skin of the ego that had been holding him back. The typist was no more.

Chapter 19

THE DUSTY CAMERA

One afternoon a week later, after leaving Whitaker's house for another interview, Claire drove back to Pass-a-Grille and returned to her bungalow excited about finding her camera. She'd learned on a dated film camera, back in Chicago when she was working her father's diner during the day and taking college courses at night, but she'd upgraded to a digital camera with the rest of the world once she'd moved to St. Pete. What were the chances it was charged?

With Willy curiously staring at her, Claire eagerly rifled through the closet in the second bedroom until she found her camera bags. Three of them. One with the body and her favorite lens, and then two other bags full of other fun lenses like her fixed 100 mm and her wide angle. Bringing all three bags into the living room, she plugged one of the batteries into the wall and spread her camera equipment out on the dining room table, relishing in the world of photography she'd left behind.

Claire reached for her computer, deciding it would be a good time to do her scheduling for the coming week. To everyone's surprise, she'd not been working herself to the bone. Not that she was letting things slide, but she was no longer the person responding to emails three seconds after receipt. She wasn't ordering food and alcohol well before it was needed. Her life's motion was becoming a bit more "just in time," as opposed to "doesn't hurt to stay ahead of things." Apparently, Leo's South wouldn't burn down if she took a few hours off here and there.

After the battery had charged for an hour, she looked out the window, and her heart fluttered, seeing the golden hour approaching. What a perfect time to get back in. She prepped her main rig, finishing by twisting the hood onto the lens, and rushed toward the water. It was the last day of February, and the cool late afternoons had a San Diego feel about them. But spring was certainly coming. Reaching the dunes dotted with patches of sea oats, she was pleased to see a rather empty beach, at least her stretch.

An older man with a curve in his back was moving along the middle of the sand working a metal detector. She'd always wondered if people ever found anything worth the search. A couple sat in chairs facing the water with cocktails in their hands. She smiled and waved when she saw one of the mascots of Pass-a-Grille. "Hi, Kenny!" He had the deepest tan in town and strolled up and down the beach strutting his fluorescent pink or green mankinis.

"A beautiful afternoon to you, Claire!" No one on earth could pull off such a skimpy affair, but Kenny tried and did so with pride. He always hiked it up high, revealing way more of his bottom than anyone would want to see. And he didn't care one bit. He'd happily jump into a photo if you asked him.

Claire was searching for a more interesting subject for her first day back. Halfway to the water, she sat in the soft, dry sand. She wasn't one to shoot a million pictures like many in the digital age. She liked to frame and prep each shot. Only after studying the light and its effects on the subject would she adjust her lens and go in. Maybe, like David, who used handwriting in the digital age, she was an old soul still clinging to her canister of film and her old Nikon that she'd used and abused in college.

Claire put her eye to the viewfinder and moved the camera along the water, exploring the shades of blue. Other than a school of fish dancing on the surface a few yards out, the Gulf was as still as a lake. She saw a pelican flying toward her from the horizon. With very little time to react, she adjusted the aperture, cranked up the shutter speed, and backed off on the zoom. Then she lay on her back in the sand and waited for him.

With a final glance for confirmation, she verified he was still coming her way. The moment the bird came into view, she pressed the shutter button. His wings were spread wide, and he was gliding thirty feet above her. The camera clicked away with a burst of four shots, the most she ever took at one time. "Thank you, Mr. Pelican."

She sat up, removed her glasses, shook the sand from her hair, and looked at the images. The first two were blurry, but then she found the one she liked. The bird was perfect, so utterly magical as he slid across the sky, not a care in the world. "Do you know how good you have it, Mr. Bird?"

She dug her feet deeper into the sand. *It's good to be back*, she thought, looking at the photos, reminding herself how much she used to love being out here. She stood and walked down to the water, one hand holding her camera. She noticed a dolphin riding the horizon but knew it wouldn't be a good shot. Something about dolphins—it was tough to capture their grace on film, at least without the advantage of a boat's closer proximity. She strolled south, revisiting those halcyon summer days when she and David had met here and shared the clumsy and ravenous kisses of first loves. These were memories to be cherished, not to be torn apart by.

She paused to shoot a few seashells and then stopped when she saw a log in the water, pushing onto the shore. In her years on the Gulf, she'd never seen such a big log wash up. Such an occurrence might happen much more often on the East Coast because of the crashing waves and strong current, but the calm waters of the Gulf rarely brought in anything larger than small pieces of driftwood, many of which she'd collected to decorate her bungalow. Thinking there might be a good shot there, she walked up to the log and readied her camera.

Her mouth dropped. It wasn't a log.

A manatee was hovering in several feet of water, his prickly whiskers, squishy eyes, and broad nostrils poking through the surface. She gasped with joy. She'd never seen a manatee on the beach side. They typically favored the inland waterways, but the water was so calm today he must have felt like exploring. He was a giant ten-foot-long puppy dog, and perhaps the most beautiful sight she'd ever seen. He had to be close to a thousand pounds.

Claire didn't want to scare him away, so she slowed and knelt. She silently lifted her camera and adjusted the settings. "Can I take a few pictures of you, my friend?" she whispered. Knowing he might be timid, she fired off a few early shots before he sneaked away. Then she inched closer, moving quietly.

He didn't budge.

Claire couldn't believe how big and beautiful he was, the cow of the sea. So gentle and innocent. If she could have, she would have sunk fully into the water and wrapped her arms around him.

Only a few feet away, she took more shots. He had the look of a hound dog, with a giant snout, and she could see his entire body. He noticed her and backed up several inches.

She captured another shot and then quietly dropped her knees into the water, her kneecaps grinding into the sand. She didn't like the view from up high; she wanted to be lower down.

"I'm not going to hurt you. Please don't go."

As if he understood her, he paused and let her take more shots. She moved in closer, her lens hovering over the water. She could barely believe what was happening.

Moving even closer, she reached out to the big brownish-gray sea potato. "Can I touch you?"

Her arm scared him (for some reason, she was sure the manatee was male), and he moved backward.

She could tell he was leaving. Holding the camera high, she stood and watched as the manatee backed up into the small surf, took a wide turn, and disappeared.

Claire stood there watching the water, the awe of the experience filling her up. She remembered why she'd connected with the ocean in the first place. Was this vision of a manatee a sign of some sort? She remembered a time when she loved being alive. There was a time when she woke desperate to jump out of bed. She told herself to remember this feeling and know that all she had to do was be receptive.

The Gulf of Mexico would do the rest.

Chapter 20

HE'S ON FIRE

The day after she encountered the manatee, Claire enjoyed the kind of day at work that reminded her of her good fortune. It felt good to give back, to have established a place where people could start their morning with delicious food and conversation among friends and loved ones, a place where teens could congregate at the beach without getting drunk and stoned. And as she said goodbye to her employees, she could tell they felt the same way, that there was purpose to be found in working there.

After cleaning the house, she relaxed in the hammock with Willy and read a few selections from *The Essential Rumi*. She reached for a cigarette but decided against it. Feeling so carefree and peaceful, she shook her head at the wasted hours in which she'd wallowed in the madness of David's death. She so wished he could see her now, the widow finally coming alive and accepting that death was a part of life.

Between poems, Claire exchanged text messages with Whitaker. He told her he hadn't eaten all day, and that he'd called in sick—yet again—from work. Having already paid him a deposit and seeing how invested he'd become, Claire wouldn't be surprised if he quit his job soon. She told him she'd bring over a pizza, and they could visit more. She had come to look forward to their daily chats. Her whole life had been so involved around work that she'd forgotten what it was like to truly connect with someone.

There was no shortage of good Italian food in Florida, a result of the Southern European snowbirds bringing down their cuisine. Claire picked up a pie at her favorite spot, Tony & Nello's in Tierra Verde. Though not the fanciest, it was as authentic as you could find outside of Italy, and the smells of oregano, garlic, and ripe tomatoes rising from the box made her mouth water as she returned to her car.

Pulling up to Whitaker's house, she noticed the park was crowded with people walking their dogs, running, and throwing Frisbees and baseballs. They must have all just returned home from work. Pizza in hand, she approached Whitaker's front door. Before she knocked, she heard a car door open and spun around.

"You're early," Whitaker was saying, stepping out of the back seat of his Land Rover. She could tell he'd lost some weight.

"What in the *world* are you doing?"

He wiped the sweat from his forehead. "I was just cleaning my car."

"In the back seat with the door closed?"

He took the pizza from her. "You know how I mentioned that I'm having a problem with someone not picking up poop in the park?" He dropped to a whisper. "I . . . was . . . on a stakeout. I find that hiding in the wayback and watching through the tinted glass is my best vantage point."

"You may just be the most ridiculous man in America."

"You think there's someone outside of America more ridiculous? A Russian Whitaker dressed in camouflage hiding in a tree stand in Gorky Park tracking potential offenders with a sniper rifle?"

She couldn't help smiling but said sternly, "Sniper jokes are not allowed right now."

"Fair point," he conceded. "Sometimes my humor runs away from funny."

It wasn't an awkward moment at all. She'd come to enjoy their banter immensely and didn't mind when he crossed boundaries. But in a more serious tone, she felt an obligation to say, "You realize this whole dog poop thing is you distracting yourself from doing the hard work:

breaking through your writer's block. You're latching on to something you think you can control because what you *really* want to control—your writing—seems out of your reach."

"I suppose it could be interpreted that way."

Noticing his sudden discomfort, she steered away from exposing any more of his wounds. "Isn't it hot in the wayback?"

"Not bad with the windows down. And I bring a cooler with drinks." He pulled back the screen door. "Let's head inside. We don't want to give away our position."

Following him, she asked, "Did you find the perp?"

"Not even close. I'm beginning to think that whoever it is has a military background."

"They're that stealthy, are they?"

"Incredibly so."

They sat at the table in Whitaker's dining room. Knowing her way around by now, she asked if he wanted something to drink on the way to the kitchen. She did a double take when she noticed a bowl of lime and lemon wedges resting on the counter near the fridge, just like she'd told him David used to do. One wedge of each in his ice water.

When she returned to the table, she asked, "What's with the lemons and limes?"

"I figured you'd notice," he said, taking his first bite of pizza. "God, that's good." He finished chewing. "Just trying to get into his head, you know. I keep feeling like I'm missing something. The writing is going really well, but I'm only working with what he's already written. What I'm nervous about is the actual last part of the book. I want to know where he was going." He laid his slice down. "What his thought process was. I feel like he knew how it was going to end, whether he'd written it out or not. Does Kevin save Orlando from getting into deeper trouble, or is it more tragic? Does one of them die?"

Claire frowned. "No, I don't think anyone dies."

"Me, either, but it's important to stay true to the story, not necessarily to make it a happily ever after just because."

"David was a happily ever after kind of guy." *Even though his life didn't go that way,* Claire added to herself.

Whitaker picked up his slice. "That's good to know. I'll tell you, he definitely knew a lot about the foster care system. Any idea where that came from?"

Claire shook her head. "I wouldn't put it past him to have done a lot of research. Like I said, when he got into something, he fully committed himself." She reached for her first slice and fought to keep the cheese from sliding off the end.

"I've been doing some research myself. Read everything I can get my hands on. And I've connected with a few people involved with the system here, so I'm getting a better feel for what this world is like. I've also reached out to the lead agency for child welfare in Sarasota, who is contracted by the state to run the foster system down there. They manage the case managers, track the kids, all that. If they'll talk to me, it will bring a much more truthful feel to the story."

"Look at you, Sherlock. I'm actually impressed."

"Well, I was in journalism before I tried my hand at a novel."

Claire folded her slice. "I guess I knew that. It's just that sometimes I underestimate you."

With a mouthful, Whitaker said, "That's very easy to do."

"You went to Emory, right?" As he nodded, she asked, "An English major?"

Another nod, still chewing. With crumbs spilling out, he said, "A triple major in French, Spanish, and English."

"Impressive! How about grad school?" She finally dug in, noticing how perfect the sauce was, not too rich with a nice zing.

With a final swallow, he answered, "A one-way ticket to Europe was my grad school. I sold just enough of my work to newspapers and magazines to keep me afloat."

"What kind of stuff were you writing?"

"It was mostly travel pieces. I wrote for my high school and college newspapers and built my portfolio from there. Back then, it was so much easier to make money freelancing. So mostly travel, but they'd accept almost anything I proposed."

"And *Napalm Trees* was your first dive into fiction?"

"No, I wrote a collection of short stories in college."

"Why don't you publish it?"

"It was absolute trash. And long gone by now."

She wiped pizza sauce from her lip. "We really do need to talk about this dog poop thing, the investigation. It's not normal. You know that, right? You're staking out your neighbors."

"It's my civil *doody*."

Claire rolled her eyes. He didn't know how to stop with the humor. "I wonder what your alma mater would say about you now."

"Perhaps revoke my degree. But they kind of like me over there in the English department. I'm somewhat of their darling."

"If they only knew . . . So what will you do when you catch the offender? A citizen's arrest?"

He shook red pepper flakes onto his next slice. "I was thinking about that the other day. I really don't know. Maybe I can give him the evil eye, and that will be enough." He showed her his best evil eye, which was more adorable than threatening.

"Oh, that will put the fear of God in him."

"Can I just say something?" Whitaker asked. "Enough about me. *You've* really come alive in the past few days. I don't mean it to sound like I'm hitting on you, but you're so much more beautiful when you're happy. And so fun to be around."

"I feel happier," she admitted, welcoming the compliment. "Thank you. And you look pretty good yourself."

"Thanks for noticing. Turns out all I had to do was run a few miles in the mornings and stop eating like a goat. But anyway, it's nice having you around."

Claire blushed. "You too."

"Not to mention, you're the only one who thinks I'm funny these days."

"Or I'm really good at faking it."

Whitaker raised his hand. "Medic, please. Someone just stabbed me in the heart."

Claire laughed, and there was nothing fake about it.

After cleaning up, they moved their conversation to the living room. "I woke up in the middle of the night," Whitaker said, resting his feet on the coffee table, "and for a minute I thought I was him. I was in a group home, waking up in a bunk bed. It breaks my heart thinking of all the kids out there who grow up without parents." He shook his head. "To think I've spent so long in a mental gutter while children like Orlando are out there fighting real battles. I need to get over myself sometimes."

Sitting on the other side of the couch, Claire let his thoughts settle in the air. "I can't wait to read what you're writing. I can tell you're changing. For the better, I mean. Just don't do what David did and keep it all from me. You have to share some of it. At least a few teasers here and there."

"Soon enough," Whitaker said. "I'll share soon enough."

"I will sneak into your house in the middle of the night if I have to."

"Is that a threat or a promise?"

Though she couldn't deny feeling guilty, it felt nice to be hit on, to be wanted. Whitaker was attempting to hide his feelings for her less and less. "I don't know," she said. "Is that a flirt or a blunder?"

Whitaker showed all his teeth. "I'd say a blunder of a flirt."

Their eyes locked, and Claire could see that he was waiting for her to say something, to take a step forward.

Instead, she looked away.

Chapter 21

MAY THE FOURTH BE WITH YOU

After three weeks of writing David's novel, Whitaker made the final decision to quit his job. He didn't tell anyone but Claire the news. He still had royalty checks from *Napalm Trees* coming in and a few last stocks he could sell; plus Claire had given him 20 percent of her promised offer. It wasn't possible to continue trying to help people invest when all Whitaker cared about was the written word.

He looked at his decision like there was no better way to invest the rest of his money other than in his dream, a dream that he'd already proved lucrative in the past. He hadn't hinted about the project to his agent yet, because he wanted to see how the ending came out, but he knew he would be all over it. Same for the publishers.

Whitaker didn't have time for a day job anyway, even if it was less demanding than the one his father had offered. Writing this novel was taking everything he had, demanding countless hours of editing and polishing, plus tons of research. He'd built a small network of experts in the foster care world who'd welcomed his questions either by phone or over a cup of coffee, and something was happening that he hadn't anticipated. The knowledge he was gaining was sure to give *Saving Orlando* an air of authenticity, but his motivation to learn had grown beyond the project. With each heartbreaking story he heard, he felt increasingly attracted to the cause of helping these children and knew he'd be involved one way or another long after this book hit the shelves.

~

A little over two months after Whitaker's blunder of a flirt, Claire finally got a chance to hear part of what he'd been working on. It was May 4, and they were both sitting on the houndstooth sofa at his house, halfway turned toward each other. TNT was running a *Star Wars* marathon, which played on the muted television. Whitaker had made a run to his cellar downtown, and they were drinking a fifteen-year-old Barolo.

Maybe it was the wine that had given Whitaker courage. He'd printed out his selection and was reading the passage where Kevin took Orlando to Longboat Key. Orlando had never been in the water. He didn't know how to swim and was terrified of sharks and jellyfish and other potentially dangerous creatures.

Whitaker licked his finger and turned to the next page. "Standing waist-deep in the still water, I yelled back to him, 'Come on!' Rigid and afraid, Orlando looked back at me like he'd seen a fin circling. I tried again. 'You're not living if you're not totally freaked out!' Something must have rung true in those words, and the boy who'd become a son to me broke into a run, splashing into the water as if he'd done it only yesterday. A smile burst out of him as I cheered him on with everything I had. What wonder had ever dazzled me more than this moment?"

Once Whitaker had finished, he waited eagerly for her response.

"Don't get me wrong," she said, working hard to hold back a grin. "It's amazing. You're really plugged in, aren't you?"

He tossed the stack of papers onto the coffee table with frustration. "But there's a 'but' coming. I hate 'buts.'"

"It's just—"

"Be gentle," he interrupted. "I know I look like some sort of barbarian, but I'm really a softy. I'm the guy who dwells on reader reviews,

169

good or bad. Anything less than telling me I'm a writing god can send me into a tailspin."

"I was just trying to say . . . it's hard to take you seriously with that mustache. Can we shave it off already? I can't look at you without thinking you're . . . I don't know. You look like some guy I've come across while on a safari in Africa. You look like you belong in a Jeep chasing elephants. All you need is some aviators and one of those vests with a million pockets. Maybe a cigar and a camera with a telephoto lens."

"Here we go again," Whitaker said, picking up his glass of wine.

"I'm trying to help; that's all. If you're wondering why the women aren't flocking to witty Whitaker, know that it's probably that thing above your lip."

"I can't shave now or I'll risk losing the muse. It's almost a Nazaritic vow at this point. Shaving might be like Samson cutting off his hair. The muse might get upset. Besides, I don't see how a man can experience a true midlife crisis without some sort of mustache or beard expression. It's how we recognize each other when passing on the street. You know, a fraternal thing, like Deadheads and their tie-dye shirts. I feel like I'm in a brotherhood with David and Kevin all fighting to find our purpose."

Claire raised a hand. "Let's back up to the muse. For some reason, I don't think she cares about your mustache. I mean . . . if she's a she. I've never met a woman who actually likes a mustache."

"Tell that to the thousands of women who've gushed over Tom Selleck since he first blessed us with his masterpiece of facial art."

"Whitaker, I hate to tell you, but you are no Tom Selleck."

He furrowed his brow. "I'll try not to let your sharp insult damage my fragile ego. Of course, we all know Tom Selleck is in a class by himself. Just his short shorts alone set him apart." Smiling, he turned even more to her and put his arm on the back of the sofa. "As far as the muse, I've never actually visualized her. She's just kind of there. This celestial being that shoots out words."

"Like an alien?"

"Hmm, I don't know."

They were looking right at each other.

"What makes you think she's a woman?" Claire asked.

Whitaker gave a look like he'd eaten a bad oyster. "Oh God, I hope she's not a man. You may have just paralyzed my creativity permanently."

"Let's hope not."

Whitaker looked up to the ceiling, debating the possibility of a man fueling his words. "Nah, men don't have the kind of words I like. Men are big ugly humorless brutes. They're like airplane wine; they have no sense of place." He pressed his lips together and shook his head. "No, my muse is a tall brunette. She may carry a sword and shield. She rides a white horse. And when she speaks, the wind blows and the trees rustle. The birds sing back to her in collective song. The clouds spread, and the sun beams through the blue sky."

Claire rolled her eyes. "Your muse is Wonder Woman? Of course she is. You're such a guy."

Whitaker closed his eyes, clearly searching for an image. "Okay, yeah, basically Wonder Woman." He put a finger to his chin. "But I like her in glasses like yours. A sword and shield and glasses."

Claire dodged the compliment. "Now I know why you're having a hard time getting into another relationship. I thought it was just the mustache. But it appears you're perfectly satisfied hanging out with the Wonder Woman in your head. And instead of kisses, she gives you words."

"I like words but . . ."

"But what?" Claire asked.

"I do have interests outside of my muse. There is someone."

"Do tell." Claire didn't like how this admission felt.

"It's complicated. Like really complicated."

Claire scratched an itch on her arm. "Life's always complicated. So who is the lucky lady?" She tried to act excited for him.

Whitaker smiled hesitantly. "I'm the lucky one."

"Who is it?" she asked again, knowing it was jealousy she felt. She could dress it up any way she liked, but it was pure jealousy. She didn't want him to like someone. He was hers. Her writer. Her friend. They were having so much fun together. She tilted her head.

"What's holding you back?"

"Well, I'm finishing her husband's book right now."

Claire's heart stalled, a car stopped at a green light.

He waited for her to say something.

Remaining silent, she looked at him and then away.

"I think you're a very rare and special woman. Knowing I'm going to see you is what pulls me out of bed in the morning."

Claire's heart started back up.

He inched toward her. "I've wanted to kiss you for a long time, but I've been afraid. Afraid to cross the line."

Claire had wanted to kiss him too. She looked at him, looked through him. Saw the caring being radiating from his soul.

He pushed her hair away from her face and touched her cheek. When she didn't move away, he moved his face closer. Butterflies took flight in her stomach, and want took over. She became instantly aware of her lips and felt them opening, needing his kiss.

Their lips soon came together, and she felt light all over, as if she might float away. Oh, the nearness of him. To be touched again, to be desired.

Whitaker put his hand on the back of Claire's head and pulled her closer. She let go of her inhibitions, her body tingling as she fell further into his embrace. Their lips touched for the first time, a kiss that should have happened much earlier. A sense of warmth and excitement rushed over her as her lips parted, letting their tongues touch.

He slipped his hand up the nape of her neck and, tilting her head slightly, kissed just below her ear. A shiver rose up her spine. Despite his whiskers, he was a good kisser, gentle but passionate. Was this how artists kissed? She'd never dated one. His lips knew their way around a woman just as his pen knew its way around paper.

When they pulled away from each other, their eyes linked. Smiles played at their lips. She nestled into his arms, resting her head on his shoulder. He kissed the top of her head. Claire felt a tremendous sense of connection, and for the first time in forever, she didn't feel alone. Actually, feeling alone felt like a distant memory.

"I thought I'd be waiting on you forever. And I would have. You know that?" He kissed her head again. "I'd wait a lifetime for you."

She snuggled deeper into him, hearing his heartbeat. Her eyes had closed, and she was relishing his words and the feel of his arm around her. For the first time in years, she felt protected, as if she didn't have to go it alone anymore. He was the kind of guy who could lift you up even in the dreariest of days.

Claire raised her hand to his chest and opened her eyes. Before she could say what she'd intended, the sight of her diamond ring and wedding band stopped her short. Memories of David splashed over her like she was standing at the base of a waterfall. His last words. "Infinity times infinity." She became hyperaware that it wasn't David's arms around her. She felt like she'd done something wrong.

She pushed up and away—her words came out in a jumble. "I . . . I . . . We." She shook her head as she stood and backed away. "We can't do this."

Whitaker frowned and his blank eyes expressed frustration but not confusion. She knew she didn't need to explain further.

"I'm sorry," she whispered. "But I need to go."

A quick nod. "I understand."

Claire turned to look for her purse. She wanted to say something else but had no idea how to explain what she felt inside. None of this was Whitaker's fault. Her purse was hanging next to the binoculars on the coatrack in the foyer. She moved that way.

"Hey, Claire," Whitaker finally said. "It's okay."

Slinging the purse on her arm, she looked back at him. He got up from the sofa.

"I can't do that again." She touched her heart. "He's still here. I don't know how to explain it. But he's still here, and it doesn't feel right."

"I get it," Whitaker said, approaching her.

Claire inched away, reaching for the doorknob behind her, afraid to feel more of what she'd just felt.

Whitaker stopped his approach. "Go home. We can talk later."

She looked into his kind eyes and nodded. "Yeah."

With that, she turned and left his house.

As she climbed into her convertible, she heard him calling for her. He walked to the car and leaned down to her level, resting his hand on the door. "It's okay to be confused, you know. I definitely am."

Claire nodded and averted her eyes momentarily.

"Seriously," he continued. "Don't beat yourself up. It's okay to have feelings for someone else. You're too incredible of a being to live the rest of your life alone. It doesn't have to be me."

She drew in a long breath, wondering what to say. No one could ever replace David, and she'd rather be alone than spend the rest of her life pretending to love someone else as much.

Catching her off guard, Whitaker reached over and took the fingertips of her left hand. "You don't have to respond. I'm just saying . . . be easy on yourself."

Claire pressed her eyes closed. She wanted to tell Whitaker that she did have feelings for him, but she couldn't allow herself to act on them.

Finally turning to him, she said, "Thanks for understanding. I'm so sorry."

Whitaker let go of her hand. "Let's talk soon, okay?" She nodded, and he stood and began to back away. "And, hey, Claire."

"Yeah?"

He held up his hand and offered the Vulcan salute. "May the fourth be with you."

She shook her head with an ever-so-slight grin. "You're confusing your sci-fi." But she knew he knew that. A smile eventually forced its way out, but she was sad and guilty and lost inside.

He patted the door and turned away.

Chapter 22

Long-Stemmed Question Marks

The day after the kiss—the first time Whitaker and Claire hadn't seen each other since they started the project—Whitaker found himself struggling to sit down and write. Looming like the sentence awaiting a prisoner, the end of the plot was coming, and he was terrified. Tackling the blank space ahead would take everything he had. Some days he felt like he would be ready; today he did not.

After pondering for a long time what he might say, he had finally broken down and texted her. If I could, I'd send you a bouquet of long-stemmed question marks. I just want to know what you're thinking, and that you're okay.

She hadn't responded. He could only imagine what she was going through and knew it had nothing to do with him. How could he blame her for still loving her husband?

But what rode Whitaker like an Indy driver running a track on spent wheels was the idea that she might never kiss him again. He liked her. A lot. Spending this time together over the past two months had been a joy. The sad widow he'd first met had many layers worth exploring. Not to mention, she'd broken him out of his chains. He'd held off sharing his feelings for long enough, and it truly felt like he was kissing his muse.

When he finally sat down to write, he toyed with the opening paragraph for a while. It still wasn't there yet. Distracted, he looked at his phone again and wondered what was going on with Claire. Part of him feared she might burst through the door any minute and take the composition books back. What if she felt like Whitaker had disrespected her with the kiss? What if she felt like he'd taken advantage of her? A bouquet of long-stemmed question marks, indeed.

Two hours later, she finally called.

"Hey," Whitaker said. He bit his finger, wondering what she was thinking, what she might say.

"I'm sorry for running out like that."

"Don't be." He felt like she'd just stuck a needle into his balloon.

Almost like she was reading his mind, she said, "I'm just not over him, Whitaker. I still feel his warmth next to me in the bed. I still see his smile. I'm not ready to move on. I don't know that I ever will be. It's not fair that I led you on."

With a combination of heartfelt sorrow for Claire and a self-pity that could be heard in his voice, Whitaker replied, "I get it, Claire." Trying to toughen up, he stressed, "Trust me. I get it."

"Thanks for understanding."

Whitaker looked at the blank page. "Why don't we take today off, okay? I'll call you tomorrow." He looked at the words on his screen. "Let's not let this get in the way of what we're trying to do. Don't beat yourself up. We're all lost sometimes."

"You're a good man, Whitaker Grant. Don't let anyone tell you otherwise."

"Thanks, Claire."

He could have talked to her all day. But where would that have gotten him? Another round of heartache, a graveyard of roses?

~

Three days passed before she visited again. He opened the door to find her standing on the stoop with her arms crossed. She wore short, ripped denim shorts and a deep V-neck. Three necklaces of varying lengths hung down her chest. Whitaker noticed turquoise beads, a few tiny silver medallions, maybe a feather. Though he could have gotten lost in her V-neck, he kept his focus on her face.

She removed her glasses and folded them. "I'm sorry I disappeared."

"I know. You don't need to explain."

Her eyes drew him in more than the V-neck. Pupils the color of tigereye crystal, thirsty for life, unsatisfied yet undeterred.

A wave of the afternoon heat pushed past her into the foyer. He invited her in, and they faced each other awkwardly. Other than the coatrack with a set of binoculars and an umbrella, the room was empty and echoed as they talked.

Claire fiddled with her keys. "How's the writing coming?"

He shrugged. "Good. Maybe another week, and I'll be ready to tackle the ending. I'm really proud of everything else."

"The part you read me was really touching. I can't wait for more."

"There are some great nuggets in there."

"Look, Whitaker. I'm sorry, seriously. I've been beating myself up."

"Don't beat yourself up. Your husband died. I get it. You have every reason to . . . I don't know . . . to not get out of bed in the morning. I think you're awesome to even do that." He clasped his hands in front of him. "Just know that I care about you. I mean, as a friend. I'm here for you and always happy to listen. Don't run out on me, okay?"

A tear slid down her cheek and settled near her jaw. He stepped toward her, wiped it away, and pulled her into a hug. "We can't stop now. Are you with me?"

Claire sniffled into his neck, nodding.

As he held her, he realized he might have a larger role to play than simply finishing David's book. And maybe it wasn't in dating her, in losing himself in her eyes. Not everything in life can be a romance.

Maybe he was supposed to help show this wonderful woman the light again, even if that meant she found someone other than him to grow old with. We all needed that selfless person, someone willing to jump into our own darkness and drag us out of it—even when they get nothing in return.

But the truth was . . . Claire had definitely pulled Whitaker out of his own steady decline. Now, it was time to return the favor. If you cared about someone enough, their happiness trumped your own.

⁓

As the middle of May came around, Whitaker was reaching the end of David's manuscript but was stalling some. That was okay, though. His stalling had led to many more hours of polish with the rest of the manuscript, and each scene leaped off the page. But he knew that he was only hours of work away from facing the flashing cursor and the blank space. He kept telling himself to have faith. The only way he could create an ending worthy of David's story was to take himself out of it and let the great mystic take over.

He'd been writing so much lately that he was starting to feel some pain in his wrists and arms, carpal tunnel of sorts. But he knew he couldn't stop. On this Saturday morning, he'd soaked his arm in ice and popped a couple of Advil, and now he was writing standing up at his counter in the kitchen.

Whitaker pondered a question. What was it that had made David suddenly empathize with the boy in the beginning? Was it simply the realization that Orlando was eleven years old, a long way from being a man? No, it had to be deeper.

As a dramatic rendition of a Henryk Górecki symphony rose from his Amazon device, the idea came to him. An ensemble of violins and cellos sawed on their strings, and Whitaker said, "Alexa, turn it all the way up." A solo soprano sang in Polish of the Second World War, a melody that pulled at Whitaker's heart. He plugged in and let his fingers and imagination fly.

Growing up in Sarasota, Kevin was going through a rough patch when he met a teacher who taught him to sail and asked him to join his crew in a weekly amateur race. Through sailing, the world had opened up to him, and he had found the father he never had. When fate brought Orlando to Kevin's door, it was time to pay it forward.

Whitaker finished typing the flashback, amid a crescendo in the Górecki symphony—the soprano belting out several impossibly high notes—and he lifted his arms in the air. "There it is!" David's presence filled his body as tears filled his eyes. He didn't even know where some of these sentences had come from.

What a feeling it was, a story rising from the source. He'd searched for the truth about Kevin, but it turned out all Whitaker had to do was stop searching and let his muse give him the words. He smiled brightly, wiping his eyes. What a wild adventure, this writing life. Nothing could be more frustrating and discouraging, but times like these made him feel like he was on top of the world. Someone had once told him that when you experienced such moments in the creative process, you were cocreating with God. No matter what religion or what one believed, how right that was. This was where he belonged, connecting to the muse, putting her words on the page, a vessel for the story.

Only as he came down from his high did he remember about dinner tonight. He had to tell his parents he'd quit his bank job and that he was not accepting a position with Grant Construction. That would go really well. His right wrist began to throb in pain. The writer wondered how much Sadie and Jack knew already. St. Pete could be the smallest town in the world sometimes, and the matriarch and patriarch of the Grants often knew things before they happened.

Instead of dwelling too much in the thought, Whitaker left the kitchen and went to find his running shoes, the only way to exorcise these demons.

Chapter 23

THE SUPPORT GROUP

Claire was back in the circle of widows in the support group, eager to speak this time. She'd just caught them up with her progress in getting David's book finished.

"I'm . . . finally feeling hope," she said, reaching for her lemonade and taking a sip. "I've been taking life far too seriously, taking myself too seriously. And I guess what Didi has been teaching me is that it's not about me. It's about living for those who don't have the option to anymore. It's about dancing for those who don't have legs. It's our duty to whomever we call the creator and to our husbands whom we've lost." Claire shrugged. "I guess that's what I'm finally seeing. All of you have talked about it before, but it took me a little while to grasp."

Feeling much more comfortable under the microscope, Claire looked up through the ceiling to the sky. "I want David to be happy for me, and I want him to be proud. I want him to see that I can get through my struggles. If there's one thing he would have left me with, I know he would've told me to find happiness again. Whatever that looked like. I will get this book out there, and hopefully that can be a way of honoring his life. I won't stop there, though. I can't sit around wasting time anymore. I love him so much, and, dammit, I'm going to live my life to the fullest. For both of us."

Claire looked at the other widows, whose bottom lips were turned out—women who'd also had their lives flipped upside down. She smacked a determined fist against her thigh. "For all of us."

Claire swallowed a rising tide of emotions and paused to collect herself. She felt her shoulders drop and let out a sigh that could have blown up an oversize pool float in one breath.

One woman clapped, and then the rest followed. Claire met each of their eyes and saw their nodding heads and wet faces. In all the meetings she'd attended, the group had only broken into applause a few times, and their reaction meant everything to her. Claire knew that she was finally breaking out of the cocoon of grief. This was her moment. She'd done it. She'd found the other side of life after David.

Still clapping, a woman stood up and then another. Within moments, the entire circle of women were standing and clapping and cheering her on. Didi offered Claire a hand and lifted her to her feet. Her friend hugged her and then others followed, and for several minutes all of them stood in a circling embrace, the power and hope of thirteen widows—from all walks of life—overcoming the nightmares of losing their soul mates.

It was unquestionably the most touching moment in Claire's life.

Once they'd all returned to their seats, Lashonda, who was sitting across from Claire, reclaimed the floor. "Thank you for sharing." She looked at everyone. "As Claire said so eloquently, we must find a way to live a life full enough to count for the ones we've lost. We owe that to our husbands."

Claire was on a roll now and didn't want to stop until it was all out. "Do you mind if I add one thing?"

"Please," Lashonda said.

Here I go. "It's a big deal, at least to me." She put her hand to her mouth for a moment. "I kissed another man a few days ago. It was the first time I've kissed someone other than my husband since before I married him. More than a decade ago." She let the words settle. "I feel so torn up over it. Like I'm cheating, but I know I'm not."

The admission came loaded with a closet full of feelings. Sure, there was guilt, so much guilt. The rings around her finger tightened as she confessed. But at the same time, there was an unabashed freedom in saying it out loud. What she'd mulled over for several days now, ever since she had left Whitaker's house, was that she was not a cheater. She had not cheated on David, and no one would argue otherwise. As obvious as that fact was, she had to keep reminding herself.

Between bouts of guilt, she had also realized how much she'd enjoyed kissing Whitaker. She'd loved the feel of being in his arms and couldn't deny the attraction she felt toward him. And she was reminded of what it was like to share intimacy with a partner, to not be alone.

After Claire thanked everyone for listening, Lashonda said, "My first husband's been dead for nine years, and I'm still sad about it. But you know what I've realized? I believe we can have more than one soul mate." She shook her head. "We're all raised to want to find 'the one.' We're all raised to think that there's *one* man out there waiting for us, a magical person we're meant to spend our lives with. And it's only a matter of time until we find him." She raised her hands. "The love of our life. How about the *loves* of our life?"

A round of nods.

Lashonda waved her hand in the air, shaking her shoulders with it. "It's a hard concept to grapple with, but it's true. I've been blessed with two soul mates. When I met my first husband, he was it. I never needed anyone else the rest of my life. We had a great marriage." She frowned. "But then he was gone. When I fell in love for a second time, I felt guilty, but I concluded that loving another man doesn't mean that you have to stop loving the first one. I love both of my men equally. In different ways, but equally." She patted her chest. "I have room inside here for both of them."

Claire wiped her eyes along with the rest of the women in the circle.

After visiting with several of the widows after the meeting, Claire left with Whitaker on her mind. What she hadn't shared was that she was worried that she was attracted to Whitaker for the wrong reasons. Yes, she saw the charm of Whitaker Grant. He was just about the wittiest person she'd ever met, and he was brilliant and handsome. If he continued to clean himself up, he'd be one of the most sought-after bachelors in Florida. She certainly couldn't deny that she enjoyed spending time with him.

But who had she really kissed that day? Was it Whitaker? Or had she put a mask of David on his face? What a sick thought, but she had to come to grips with the possibility. It wasn't fair to lead Whitaker on if he were nothing more than the closest she'd ever get to David again, a mere replacement.

One last doubt remained . . . How could she ever truly love someone as much as she loved David?

Chapter 24

BAD NEWS BEARS

Downtown, Whitaker eased into a spot next to Straub Park under the shade of one of the many giant banyan trees, their long, straggly vines conjuring up Tarzanian memories from the playground of his youth. A light rain had fallen long enough to dampen the ground, and the acres of grass shined green in thanks. Across the street, diners broke bread under the umbrellaed tables that stretched for blocks along Beach Drive.

Whitaker strolled past the Museum of Fine Arts, remembering the day he'd given a writing lecture from between walls that hosted some of the finest art in Florida. It had been a long time since he'd strolled through a museum, since before Lisa had left. God, when was the last time he'd attended any of his city's offerings? Had he lost touch with the city he'd professed his love to?

Established more than a century earlier, the Baywater Yacht Club stood between the lines of restaurants along Beach Drive and the legions of boats bobbing in the marina. Whitaker circled to the front of the building and passed under the flagpole that had been designed to look like a ship's mast. Though he always felt like a fish out of water, Whitaker had been visiting this club since he was a child, and familiar faces welcomed him as he worked his way to the dining room. Lines of the black-tied commodores who'd run the club looked back at him from their black-and-white photographs on the walls.

Whitaker hated dressing up and felt awkward in his khaki pants and pink polo shirt, but he'd tucked in his shirt to avoid his father's scrutiny, which could sometimes draw blood. The floors of the grill were covered in a carpet the colors of autumn, and Whitaker thought the pattern might have served well as window curtains for his deceased grandmother's house . . . back in the 1970s.

Upon seeing their son, Staff Sergeant Jack Grant and his wife, Doña Quixote, stood from their table, which was draped in blue. Sadie came around the table, hugged Whitaker, and kissed him on the cheek. He complimented her blouse and then turned to his father, taking his hand. Having left his veteran's hat at home, his bald spot was shiny on the top of his head. He wore pressed khaki shorts and a Tommy Bahama shirt. No one offered a stronger grip than Jack Grant. He made sure of that. Whitaker had often wondered if Jack sat in his office tugging on a cigar and squeezing a stress ball, working his hand muscles, making sure he was always the dominant one. Jack could turn a chunk of coal into a diamond in one squeeze.

"Son, it's good to see you. You're looking fit."

"Thanks." Whitaker squeezed hard, determined to crush his father's grip. But there wasn't a chance in hell.

As the three of them sat, Whitaker looked around the room. Half the tables were occupied, many by the remaining snowbirds spending their last few weeks before sailing north for the summer. Looking toward the small bar with two wine fridges behind it, Whitaker nodded at one of the managers he'd known for a long time. Returning his eyes to the table, Whitaker marveled at the sixty-four forks aligned perfectly on the left side of the stack of twenty-seven china pieces decorated with ocean scenes. He looked at the twenty-five knives, wondering which one he should use first. And then the six water glasses lined up next to the four different wineglasses. Sometimes he had a hard time deciphering reality from his exaggerations. The club wasn't *that* fancy. Nevertheless, all he needed was one lowball glass filled to the rim.

As the three of them tested the waters of conversation, Whitaker noticed Jack was particularly silent, which was scary. This evening was obviously a dinner invitation that came with an agenda. For some reason, Whitaker had hoped that maybe, just maybe, Jack and Sadie had wanted to spend some time with their oldest son. Truth be told, Whitaker was very excited—slightly hesitant but eager, as well—to share his new project with them. He hoped they'd notice the fire in his eyes. The Whitaker sitting there before them was a new man, one who worked out and cared about what he put into his body.

Abandoning his grunts and nods, Jack finally cut through the niceties. "We heard you left your job."

Whitaker thought it was absolutely amazing how Jack's minimalist delivery could rumble an entire block like thunder. It took Whitaker paragraphs to say something as powerful as Jack could in one short, terse sentence. He could be a character in a Hemingway novel.

After recovering from his father's thunderous assertion, which felt oddly like an accusation, Whitaker fingered the napkin on his lap. "Nothing gets by you in this town."

"The Grants have been here a long time, Whitaker. I know everybody. I probably built that bank and don't even remember it."

"You probably did, Dad." Whitaker shifted in his seat and decided to give his parents the answers they were looking for. "I quit, but it's different this time. I'm actually writing again, like really writing. With purpose. I've started a new project that's incredible." Whitaker turned up the corner of his mouth in excitement. "I can't talk about it yet—I don't want to jinx it—but, trust me. This is a big deal. I can't wait to share more with you."

Whitaker looked at his mom, who was smiling and nodding eagerly, as if she'd jumped back into her college cheerleading outfit just for the occasion. He looked at his dad, who still hadn't broken his stare.

Whitaker grinned at the absurdity of his father. What could you do but just smile at the man? He was *the* Jack Grant, the builder of St. Pete, the somewhat great father who truly wanted the best for his children. But he was also Jack Grant, the overly confident man who not only wanted the best for his children but was damned sure he knew better than his children what *was* best for them.

Placing his arms on the rests, Whitaker broke into an audible chuckle.

"What?" Jack said, refusing to let his lids slide into a blink. The father-son staredown.

"Nothing, Pop. You're one of a kind. And I can feel myself wanting to please you. Seriously, you're going to be proud of me and this project, and I'm already nearing the end. It's maybe the best thing I've ever worked on. Not just in writing, but maybe the best accomplishment of my life. And the thing is . . . it's not only about me. I'm helping someone else out." He couldn't keep the news from them another moment.

Bouncing his eyes back and forth between his parents, he said, "A woman—a young woman—came to me with a novel that her late husband had been working on. She asked me to finish it for him. To my great surprise, I was absolutely floored by it."

"That's wonderful," Sadie said.

"Yeah, I'm really lucky to have been included." He wondered if he should share any names. Of course they knew of Leo's South on Pass-a-Grille. He decided he'd best leave the details for later.

The server appeared, setting a basket of breads and butter on the table. After listening to her recite the specials, Sadie ordered a glass of chardonnay, and the men ordered cocktails. Whitaker was tempted to find something on their impressive wine list, but fermented grape juice wasn't going to cut it tonight.

Jack placed a hand on the table. "Hold on. So you're ghostwriting?"

Whitaker breathed through the defensive feeling wedging its way in the door. "I guess you could call it that . . . but in the most significant sense of the word."

Jack nodded and his wheels turned.

Sadie reached for one of the dark pieces of bread. "I can't get over how great you look. You've trimmed up."

Whitaker tried to ignore the venom in his father's comment and appreciate his mother's compliment. "I have indeed. I'm telling you, this book is bringing me back to life. Everything's finally making sense again, and this woman is paying me a lot of money. I think this project will put my career back on track."

He looked at his father. "Dad, I know you want me to come work for you, and I really did think about it, but I need to see where this goes. You're the one who tells me I'm always so stuck on myself. It's different now. I'm helping this widow get over her husband, and she's a really nice girl, and we've become friends. You'd love her."

"Who is she?" Sadie asked. "Do we know her? You're talking about her like you're interested in her. She your age?"

"She's a long way from entertaining another relationship, so I'm trying not to even go there in my head. She still wears her wedding rings. I'm not trying to get in the way of that."

"Be careful, honey," Sadie warned. "I see the same look in your eye that I did when you met Lisa."

Whitaker figured Jack was about to chime in with his own warnings about Claire, but Jack surprised the writer with a curveball. "What's the story about?"

Whitaker was absolutely dumbfounded by his father's query. Not because of the specific question, but because his father was showing interest. His mother had always asked about his novels, but to hear his father show curiosity was such a soothing feeling. Even if Jack was forcing it, who cared? His question was one of those instances over the course of Whitaker's life where Jack had shown how great a father he could be.

Whitaker looked at his dad. "It's about a guy my age going through the typical impediments we midlifers go through. All the stuff that drives you crazy. But this guy looks outside of himself and helps a young boy who needs a lift up in the world. He's an orphan living in a group home. No father to speak of. His mom pushed him out of a moving car when he was three. It's not a sob story, very uplifting. So far, at least. But I've been doing a ton of research, trying to understand the foster care system. It's heartbreaking to learn how many kids come from broken homes. We're all just skating by ignoring them, thinking we have enough to deal with."

Whitaker pushed himself up straighter with the armrests. "Did you know more than a *hundred* kids a month are taken from their parents in Pasco and Pinellas Counties? Some months more. We don't have the support system to give them homes. Parents are afraid to adopt or even foster. Children are living in *hospitals* right now, because it's the only place with empty beds." Whitaker took a breath. "I think this novel will help bring awareness and maybe help a few kids. If I could even help convince one family to take in a child in need, then I'd be happy." Whitaker shook his head and repeated a notion he'd read online. "Who are we as a community if we can't take care of our children?"

Jack crossed his arms high on his chest and breathed in deeply. His belly visibly expanded against his button-down shirt and then contracted again.

Whitaker braced himself as a sharp pain ran through his forearm to his wrist. "What is it?"

"That's all fine, son. Sounds like a fun little project. Or hobby, or whatever it is you call it now. And it's nothing you couldn't do while working for me. Something to do on Saturday mornings. Like fishing is for me."

The pain reached Whitaker's fingers, and he stretched his hand. Did Jack really want to go to war right now? Could Whitaker bite his tongue? "Look, Pop. I am so appreciative of the job offer. Seriously, I am honored that you'd go out of your way for me. And I know it's a great job, and a million men would be lucky as hell to be offered such a position. But I'm not them, and I'm not you. I look at you, Dad. The things you've accomplished as a soldier, an entrepreneur, a father, a husband, a community leader. It's all so commendable, and I'm inspired." Holding eye contact, Whitaker gently set his throbbing fist down on the table. "But I'm not you. I have to give back my own way."

Whitaker pointed at himself. "I'm an entertainer. I change people's lives with words. Or at the very least, show them a different perspective, or, hell, put a brief smile on their face. Writing is the thing I can give most to the world, and that's why I have to do it. Doing anything other than writing is just pretending, or faking it. I don't want to die a pretender."

The two men continued staring at each other, and Whitaker had no idea what his father was thinking. But Whitaker knew he was doing what was right, and even if he couldn't get through to his father, he had to stand his ground.

"How is the story going to end?" Sadie asked, attempting to deflate the tension.

Whitaker smiled at Jack and finally broke eye contact. He turned to Sadie. "That's the tough part. What this guy has written is so good, but he left it hanging right before the climax. The kid I told you about is in trouble."

The server set the drinks on the table, and they tossed them back while talking more about the story. Jack forced his way back to at least faking interest. The conversation moved into lighter conversation as they ate. Whitaker had always enjoyed the fried shrimp plate, but he opted for a kale Caesar topped with a piece of tilefish instead.

Once the topics of conversation were as empty as the twenty-seven plates, Whitaker sensed Jack and Sadie had more on their agenda than asking him why he'd left his job.

When he caught them looking at each other as if urging one another on, Whitaker decided he'd go ahead and rip the Band-Aid off. "So what is it? You're not telling me something."

Sadie looked at Jack and then patted her mouth with her napkin. They both looked at Whitaker but didn't speak.

"Might as well get it all out," Whitaker said, moving his hand in a circular motion.

Jack looked at his wife. "Let me tell him."

Whitaker could feel the acid from his salad dressing creeping up his esophagus. Anchovies and bad news. Was their surprising interest in his story an attempt to butter him up for what was to come? For the life of him, though, he couldn't imagine what it was. Had someone died? Did one of them have cancer? There was no cancer ever diagnosed that could kill Jack Grant.

After a sip of bourbon, Jack dropped the hammer. "We ran into Lisa's parents yesterday."

Hearing Lisa's name rise from his father's mouth was not a good feeling.

"They told us Lisa is engaged."

There it was again. A few words and Jack Grant had brought down Thor's hammer.

Whitaker stared into his father's eyes and then lost himself in his own head. Lisa was engaged. Lisa was getting remarried. Lisa was in love with another man.

He felt a hand on his arm. It was his mother's. He looked at her and then looked back down at the remainders of kale and corn bread croutons and dressing on his plate.

Sadie squeezed him. "You knew it had to happen."

Whitaker patted his mom's hand and then pulled away from her.

Jack cleared his throat. "From what they told us, it happened very quickly. A few dates and then he proposed to her. They're marrying in Martha's Vineyard on May of next year. He's a surgeon."

Whitaker processed the information his father had shared. He felt his rib cage imploding. Why, dammit? Why did Lisa still have so much control over him? After all this time, she still owned him. Whitaker felt like lifting the table and pushing it over, letting the fleet of china and glass smash onto the floor.

Another man—a better man—was taking his ex-wife. She was in love with him.

"What should we do for dessert?" Sadie asked in a jolly, high-spirited tone. Were those pom-poms in her hand?

Whitaker stood from the table and tossed his napkin onto the chair. "I'll pass on dessert. Thank you very much for dinner."

"Whitaker," Sadie said. "Don't do that. Don't let her break your heart again."

"She's not breaking my heart. It's just not something I need to hear right now. Mom, Dad, thanks for dinner."

Racing out the back door before he encountered any more familiar faces, he grappled with this awful news. Everything that he had built these last two months—all the happiness he'd found—rushed out of him. Why? He didn't miss Lisa like Claire missed David. He didn't see her shadow crossing the hall. He didn't still feel her warmth next to him on the bed. It was the loneliness, that fucking abyss of not being wanted by anyone. Whitaker replaced by a goddamn surgeon, Lisa never looking back. And then Claire, still hung up on a man she would never see again. Even the dead were more lovable than Whitaker.

Using Staff Sergeant Jack Grant's analogy, Whitaker felt like he'd spent all this time building a giant mansion, only to find out the foundation was made of cards.

And Lisa, the Queen of Hearts, had knocked it down.

Chapter 25

The National Treasure

Whitaker collapsed onto the houndstooth sofa face-first. How was it that he had fought so hard recently to overcome the struggles of a decade of washed-up-writer syndrome, only to be toppled with a crappy reminder of how bad of a husband he'd been? How bad of a person, really. Claire had probably saved herself a lot of heartache by stopping his advances. Who was to say he was any more put together now?

With his eyes fixed on a spot on the wall, his mind danced clumsily through the years of marriage. He flashed back through all the smiles they'd shared, and each memory stabbed him like the barb of a stingray, each stab leaving venom to poison the bloodstream. He'd been nothing short of an asshole.

He recalled the day she'd sat him down and given him the first of several gentle warnings—warnings he didn't take seriously. "This is your wake-up call, Whit."

He saw himself on that day, shaking his head, assuring her that he was focused on coming back, that he was inching back, grasping with everything he had. "I swear to you, Lisa, give me a little bit more time. I can see the end of this nightmare. Let me get this next story out, and I'll be back. It will be about us. I just can't let this career I built slide."

"What you don't see, Whitaker," she'd said, "is that you're trying too hard, and you're thinking too much. Let's focus on us and having fun. I have a feeling you'll get your stories back."

She was right, but he wasn't listening.

The worst of life strikes you when you're at the top, Whitaker decided. Because at the top, everyone and everything was out to get you.

He found himself imagining the surgeon, who must have family up on Martha's Vineyard. As much as Whitaker wanted to put a hit out on him, he hoped the man would treat her with the love and respect she deserved, doing what Whitaker had failed to do.

It wasn't heartache, was it? Had he a choice of Claire or Lisa, he'd choose Claire. No doubt. So why was this news so difficult to process? Because of the failure and the rejection, the lonely bed he'd made for himself. Whitaker Grant might be a great writer, but he was a terrible lover. And what mattered more than love?

If for nothing more than to have some company, he flipped on a cable news channel. Then he opened his Facebook on his phone. He typed Lisa's name in the search bar and found her. He clicked on her profile page and realized that she had unfriended him. This unfriend- ing was something new, because he had recently stalked her. And it felt like she'd cut the head off their relationship. Like all the years they had shared together didn't matter anymore. The total elimination of every- thing they had ever had.

Crossing into new territory, Whitaker went to several of her friends' pages and poked around. He scrutinized a few shots of Lisa, but he saw no indications of a new man in her life. Thankfully, he didn't see a surgeon from Martha's Vineyard running across the beach in slow motion in his scrubs, his stethoscope poised in his right hand, ready to test the beat of Lisa's happy heart. Whitaker stopped to look at his lost redheaded lover with friends at the Grand Prix in downtown St. Pete in March.

For a flash of a moment, he recalled the day he and Lisa had attended the Grand Prix together. The morning before the first race, Lisa had found a review online calling him a "national treasure." Though Lisa had spent the day laughing at the comment, he'd ridden his high horse for weeks. Today, he would have been happy with anything close to such a lovely designation. He would even have found delight in something more mediocre. He'd even take "neighborhood treasure" at this point. Whitaker Grant, the "crown jewel of Gulfport."

The next morning, Whitaker finished brushing his teeth and looked at himself in the mirror. In his father's voice, he spat, "Private Grant, are you a typist or a writer? Get. Your. Ass. In. That. Chair. Now." He saluted himself and then followed his own orders.

Returning the laptop to the desk, Whitaker sat down and worked his way to the document. He had to get something out, even if only a few words. He looked at the picture of David and tried to tap into Claire's dead husband. "Please share your story with me," Whitaker said. "I'm here, ready to type, but I don't know where I'm going."

Whitaker lifted his fingers above the keys. "Let's go, David. Give me something to work with."

No words came. Not even letters.

His fingers waited above the keys like a dog ready to chase after a ball the owner had no intention of throwing.

Something was missing.

Whitaker tried desperately to remind himself that every single writer on earth faced these demons. Even Hemingway hated himself sometimes and hated writing and doubted every single word in every sentence.

The best writers, though, *they* trudged through it. Whitaker sat up again, trying to muster the energy and faith needed. With his fingers at the ready, he tried to make a choice. That was all writing was in the end. Choices.

He couldn't type one word. He couldn't make one choice. He couldn't hit the ball.

Claire walked barefoot in the wet sand, searching the heavier patches of shells for sharks' teeth. Her camera hung from her neck, the memory card nearly full with the shots of her rediscovered passion. This was her special place, to be on the beach, walking in the rays of the rising sun, an abundance of life dancing all around her.

With her eyes closed, she could hear a seagull calling its mate, the wind blowing against her ears, the waves crashing onto the sand, the shuffling of the shells. The bliss of her youth on this beach had returned.

She looked up to see a black skimmer flying across the water, its beak skimming the surface, searching for food. Her grandmother Betty had first introduced her to this bird. With oversize orange-and-black beaks, they looked almost top-heavy, and, to Claire, resembled a toucan. During one of their many beach walks, Betty had told her that they had vertical pupils that helped cut the sun's glare.

It had been a few days since she'd seen Whitaker, and she missed him. Even when she did her best to think of something else, distracting herself, his name would flash before her one letter at a time. W.H.I.T.A.K.E.R.

When she returned to her bungalow, Claire checked in with him. Only a few seconds into their call, she detected that something was bothering him. "What's going on with you?"

After a long beat of silence, he said, "I don't want to rain on your parade, Claire. It thrills me to hear you so happy and bubbly. But I'm having a tough time today. I . . ."

Claire sat down on the rocking chair on the porch, knowing bad news was coming.

"I can't put my finger on the ending. I don't know where David was going. I feel like I'm lost."

Claire swallowed her disappointment and said encouragingly, "Maybe you need to walk away for a few days. You've been staring at the story nonstop for months. Seriously, have you even taken a day off?"

"No, but it's not that. The muse doesn't reward you for taking vacation."

"Enough about the muse." Claire stopped before saying more. *Be gentle, Claire.* "What can I do to help?"

"That's just it," Whitaker said. "I don't know if there is anything anyone can do to help. I've stared at David's last line for days. This is exactly why I didn't want you to tell anyone."

Knowing she needed to give him encouragement, she made a firm decision on an idea she'd been pondering. "I've been thinking. I want to give you something."

"What's that?"

"It's a surprise. Why don't you take the day off from writing and relax. Put your feet up and stop thinking about it. I'll be over this afternoon after I close the restaurant. Okay?"

"All right."

Claire took a quick shower and rode down the beach to the café. After an hour of computer work, she helped the chef with inventory. Just before closing, she asked Jevaun if she could borrow his truck. He followed her back to her bungalow and helped her lift David's desk and chair into the truck bed. After watching him drive away in her convertible, his dreads blowing in the wind, she stepped up into his Chevy. The woven steering wheel cover was the colors of the Rastafari: red, yellow, and green. Don Carlos was singing through the speakers. She turned it up and drove across town, moving her head to the Jamaican grooves.

When she pulled up, she found Whitaker slumped in a chair in the front yard under the kapok tree, which had shed its white fibers all over the yard, spreading its seeds. He was shirtless in surf trunks, and she couldn't help but notice how much leaner he'd become.

He pulled on his shirt and greeted her when she climbed out. "New truck?"

"I borrowed it so I could deliver your gift."

Whitaker looked into the back. "A desk?"

"They're David's. A Victorian pedestal desk. And the chair is Herman Miller. I figured it would be an upgrade."

"From my card table? I'd say. But you don't have to do this."

Claire walked to the back and dropped the tailgate. "I thought they might help you tap in. Really, I don't see how you get anything done in that awful office of yours. I can't think of a less creative space in the world."

Whitaker pointed to his forehead. "This is where the creative space is supposed to be. But I'll take any help I can get."

"I think we ought to clean up your office and make it more writer friendly. I'm sensing some blocked chi in there—whatever the opposite of feng shui is."

"I don't disagree, but I'm dealing with it. Just hit a slump; that's all."

Claire saw the pain in his eyes. "What you need is a hug." She stood onto her toes, opened her arms, and pulled him in, wrapping her hands around his neck. "You're such an awesome man, Whitaker. And an amazing writer. Don't get discouraged."

He whispered a thanks, giving her a light squeeze.

Claire kissed his cheek, surprising even herself. Whitaker lost his breath. She felt his heart kick. Not wanting to push away, she ran a hand through the hair on the back of his head and pulled him tighter. "I believe in you," she whispered into his ear.

When she finally took a step back, with a flutter in her stomach, she looked at his face. He was as surprised by the kiss as she was.

She quickly spun toward the truck. "Now help me get this out. I'm not leaving until your office is worthy of your words."

As they struggled to ascend the steps with one of the desk's pedestals, Claire was thinking about two things simultaneously: how nice it felt to be in his arms and that they should have taken the drawers out to make this easier. She almost said as much when a pair of lovebugs landed on her arm.

"They're out in full force today, aren't they?" Claire said, blowing them off her arm.

"Like locusts."

"Oh, c'mon, they're adorable."

Claire spent the next thirty minutes helping Whitaker clean up his office, getting rid of trash and vacuuming and pulling distractions off the wall. He didn't need that damned movie poster looking down on him. Or the picture of him and his ex-wife walking into the movie premiere. As she pulled the photo down, he told her about his ex-wife remarrying, and everything began to make sense.

"Now you're telling me." Claire set the photo down in a cardboard box, trying to pretend that the news didn't bother her. "No wonder you're hurting. I bet nothing brings on writer's block like heartache."

"It's really not heartache," Whitaker said. "I'm just reminded how awful of a husband I was. Makes me feel bad that I wasted so much of her life."

Claire wasn't sure whether she believed him about the heartache, but his statement made sense. "Don't be silly. I'm sure she doesn't feel like you wasted her life. You might be a handful, but you're still amazing half the time. I bet she misses you. You think that surgeon can make her laugh like you used to? I doubt it."

"I appreciate that."

Claire hoped he wasn't giving up. She hoped the despair in his eyes wasn't the white flag of surrender.

Chapter 26

A KNOCKOUT

As the next morning's sun cut through the window and sprayed his face, Whitaker woke with mild (or perhaps tepid) determination. Wiping the sleep from his eyes, he marched into the kitchen in his boxers, brewed his coffee, and worked himself into the right mind-set.

Walking into his office, he took in the new digs. David's desk and chair. The sparkling window looking out to the backyard. The stacks of books organized on the shelves. He looked down at the floor and was pleased to see the shine of the terrazzo tile.

He sat in the chair, which pushed into his mid back and forced him to sit up straight, reminding him of the old days. The writer always sat up with perfect posture. The typist wrote in a slouched position that would have made a chiropractor weep with hopelessness. Whitaker glanced at the picture of David, hoping the man would give him inspiration. But Whitaker felt only guilt. Guilt for not having the stamina and faith to finish his story and equal amounts of guilt for having feelings for his wife, even kissing her. Whitaker turned over the picture on the desk.

"That's enough, Whitaker." It was go time. He stabbed out words that felt cheap and elementary, but he pushed his way through, writing the scene where Kevin finally found Orlando.

After reading back over twenty minutes' worth of work, Whitaker cursed himself. "No, no, no!" He felt so angry inside. All of it was shit. Where was David going with this story? More than anything, Whitaker felt just like Kevin, like he'd lost his connection with Orlando. Where was the boy and why was he so angry? Had David intended for him to die?

While pouring another cup of coffee, Whitaker realized he'd left his phone in the Land Rover. He threw on a bathrobe and left the house. Snatching it from the cup holder, he checked his messages while standing in the yard.

Reading a short text from his brother, a pair of lovebugs landed on his phone. Blinded by his frustrated writing session, he smacked the screen, knocking the bugs to the ground. He looked down to the sidewalk and saw that he'd killed one, and the other, still attached, was flapping its wings, certainly sensing the death of its mate. Whitaker couldn't bear the thought of one having to live the rest of his or her life alone, so he did the only thing he knew to do. Shoving the phone in his pocket, he stomped down on both bugs with his bare foot, extinguishing their pain forever.

He glanced at the smashed bugs and hated himself for what he'd done. He raised both hands in the air and brought down two fists. It couldn't get any worse.

Casting an eye toward the park, wondering if anyone was watching his absurd meltdown, he noticed a German shepherd taking a squat. The man on the other end of the leash, wearing a muscle shirt and a hat turned backward, was patting his pockets. When the dog finished his business, the owner twisted around, surveying the land. He didn't notice Whitaker, who'd crept into the shadow behind the Land Rover.

With apparently no shame or care for his neighborhood, the man continued along the grass, his dog walking dutifully by his side.

"Hey, man!" Whitaker yelled, running shoeless across the street to the park. "You didn't pick up your dog's poop."

The man turned around, and Whitaker eyed his build. He was a good three inches taller than Whitaker and shaped like a boxer, top-heavy with traps that looked like they needed their own zip code. Steroids much? A skateboarder could do rail slides on them. Of course Whitaker's archnemesis had to be a bodybuilder. That was the way the typist's life worked.

The Incredible Hulk said in a deep voice, "Yeah, I left the bags at the house. I'll get them on the next turn."

Whitaker was not going to be deterred and stood his ground. "I've heard that before." He pointed back toward the poop. "You can use your hands or a leaf."

The bodybuilder laughed at first, but then his face straightened. "Get lost." He tugged at his dog, and they moved on.

With determined steps, Whitaker followed them.

The man turned and waved one of his big arms in the air. "You might want to mind your own business if you know what's good for you."

Clenching his fists, Whitaker weighed his options. Considering the man's size and the fact that Whitaker had not fought anyone since high school, the typist didn't think he had a chance. But an idea came to him instead. This dude might have muscles, but Whitaker knew he could defeat him in a more passive game of wits. If he could snap a picture of him, then Whitaker would plaster the guy's face on signs and put them all over the neighborhood, with a nice tagline like *This man does not pick up after his dog.*

Whitaker smiled at the potential. He fished the phone out of his pocket and quickly snapped a shot.

"What the hell are you doing?"

Whitaker raised two fingers to his own eyes and then pointed to the perpetrator. "I'll be watching you." For a moment, Whitaker felt victorious, like a gangster establishing his domination over the neighborhood.

The bodybuilder didn't move like a bodybuilder; he moved like a butterfly, like Muhammad Ali.

Whitaker saw the bull logo of the University of South Florida engraved on the man's class ring a millisecond before Whitaker's head snapped back and . . .

With no grasp of time, Whitaker came to and realized he was lying in the grass. Lovebugs were dancing all around him. He reached for the pain raging around his jaw. He turned his head and saw the cracked screen on his phone.

The man and his German shepherd were a hundred yards down, walking away from him.

Chapter 27

THE "DELETE" BUTTON

Whitaker sat down in David's chair and looked at his cracked phone. He clicked on the folder that held all his new projects, including *Saving Orlando*, and highlighted it. He rolled his mouse cursor over "Delete."

This was all he had to do. Delete. Let things go.

He couldn't take much more of this fucking roller coaster he was riding on through this wrecked world. Why the hell had he committed to this project?

Removing his hand, he slumped into his chair and frowned. Of course he couldn't delete *Saving Orlando*. He couldn't do it to Claire or to the children like Orlando who needed a voice. He might not be able to finish the project, but someone else could take what he'd done and continue.

The doorbell rang, and Whitaker sat up and wiped his eyes. He felt Claire's presence. In the spirit of finally deleting the writer and saying goodbye to these youthful dreams, he grabbed the three composition books and the picture of David from his desk and carried them to the front door.

"What the . . . ?" She pulled back the screen door and reached for his face. "You've got blood everywhere."

He wiped his chin. "I finally found the culprit in the park. And he was bigger than me. A *lot* bigger than me." Whitaker told her what had happened.

"Honestly, Whitaker, you deserved it. I'm having a hard time pitying you."

"Perhaps."

"What do you mean, perhaps? You know I'm right."

Whitaker did, in fact, know she was right. But he didn't want to talk about it. Instead, he said, "I need to talk to you about something else. Can we sit?"

She sat in the chair next to the sofa. He sat on the end of the sofa closest to her, the pain of letting her down already gnawing at him.

He collected his thoughts and then looked her in the eyes. "I can't do this. I can't finish David's book. I have no idea where it's supposed to go."

"What? You're getting there, Whitaker. You can't give up now."

"I'm finally realizing that it's the writing that's been holding me back. For some reason, I've been chasing the next story and the next word as if it's finally going to give my life meaning. As if it might make me happy. But what I realized today, finally, after all these years, is that writing is the enemy. It's not my calling. Yes, I'm good at it. That doesn't mean I need to be doing it all the time. It is ripping me apart. All along I've been chasing the exact thing that is eating away at me." Whitaker made a crushing sound with his fist. "Crushing me."

"You can't quit now," she said. "You're there. At the end. We are there."

"Yes, we are there at the ending. And I've explored several possibilities—five or six, at least, and they don't feel right. It's like a higher force is preventing me from concluding his story."

She moved onto the sofa next to him and put her hand on his. "Please don't stop now." A tear sneaked out of her eye.

"Claire, I can't tell you how I feel inside, and I can't tell you what it's like, but I can tell you that if I don't stop, like right now, it's going to kill me." He added, "You can have everything I've done. For free. And I'll pay back what you've given me so far. Let's find someone else to finish it. Together. I believe in the project. I want to see this through. I just don't want to be the one writing the end. Simple as that."

The headshake of disappointment. "You're letting fear win. You have some serious inner-critic issues that beat you sometimes. Stop all this feeling sorry for yourself. I'm so tired of hearing it. Seriously."

"Me too! I don't want to talk about it anymore. I want to throw my laptop in the trash and get on with life. If I keep trying to write, I will die unhappy and alone."

"You're not alone." She took his hand and repeated, "You're not alone."

Whitaker wasn't sure about that. They might have built a nice friendship, but in the end she was sitting there for her husband. He took the stack of composition books and the picture and handed them to her with yet another apology. He hated to hear himself apologizing, whining. She was right. Enough already!

She accepted them with her head down.

"I need you to take these and go. Believe me, we will find someone way better than me to take *Saving Orlando* home."

"I'm not taking these back." She set them on the coffee table. "What are you going to do, Whitaker? Go find another job you don't love? You can't stop writing."

"I most certainly can stop writing. I'll go to work for my father. Even saying it out loud makes me feel lighter, like there's less on the line."

Claire shook her head. "I'm so sick and tired of feeling like I'm begging you, but this isn't about me or David's story. This is about you pulling your head out of your you-know-what. Stop with all this whining and woe-is-me. It's not who you are. You know what? Don't finish the damn book if you don't want to, but to say you're hanging up your pen is nothing short of cowardice. Quit acting like the world owes you something and grow up. They are just words, lined up one after another. Stop taking yourself so seriously."

As if she could ever understand. Whitaker stood and took the books and picture back off the table. He held them out. "Take them. Please. They're not safe in my hands." He said that last bit as a way to force her to take the books. He wanted them out of there. He wanted this responsibility off his back.

Claire took the books and went toward the front door. Watching her walk away might have been the saddest thing he'd ever seen. Cue the Roy Orbison and a tuna melt.

"I'll email you what I have so far. And I'm sorry, Claire."

Once she was gone, Whitaker returned to David's chair and clicked his way back to his OPEN PROJECTS folder. He could finally let go of his ego, and he could finally settle into being a normal human. He dragged *Saving Orlando* to an email and typed Claire's address into the form.

Whitaker moved his mouse to the "Send" button but hesitated. This was it, his goodbye to writing. Yes, a retreat and surrender. Perhaps a cowardly one. But also the start of a new life.

Whitaker pressed his finger down but pulled back at the last moment. He lifted up the mouse and slammed it as hard as he could onto the desk. It shattered, plastic shrapnel shooting out across the desk.

It wasn't enough to satisfy his rage. So many people had commented over the years that they could never imagine Whitaker losing his temper. How wrong they were. Swiping his right hand along the desk, he knocked everything off: the laptop, the writing books, the broken mouse, the cup of cold coffee, the lamp. The bulb of the lamp sparked in a final blue flame as the cold coffee spread like a pool of blood.

Just in time, he saved his laptop from the coffee and set it back on the desk. Pulling the computer open, he prayed that it was still operational, that he hadn't lost the latest iteration of *Saving Orlando*. As the display lit up, he reached for the mouse by rote until he remembered that he'd smashed it. A longtime hater of the trackpad, he fortunately had a spare in the desk.

Whitaker put his hand on one of the iron pulls of the drawer and tugged. It slid a couple of inches into an abrupt stop, like it was caught on something. With his anger still lingering, he jerked on the drawer until it broke free and came flying off the casters. As it crashed onto the floor with a boom, something white slid out, a piece of paper, maybe.

A photograph?

It must have gotten stuck behind the drawer. Out of breath from his tirade, he reached down. It was an image of two people standing in front of a baseball stadium. Whitaker recognized the man in the picture instantly. It was David.

A young boy stood smiling next to Claire's deceased husband.

"What is this?" Whitaker asked. Chill bumps fired on his arms, and he had a sudden sense of lightness, like he was flying. He stared hard into the boy's eyes.

"Who are you?"

Chapter 28

Pop Culture

With David's unfinished story in her hands, Claire traipsed down the steps of Whitaker's house and went to her convertible. Though a very small part of her hoped that Whitaker might change his mind, she could see the defeat in his eyes—his white flag waving shamefully. And she didn't know if she was strong enough to help him dig out of it.

This felt like the end.

Setting the composition books on the seat, she took a moment to look at David's picture. "I'm so sorry, David. I'm trying my best." It was as if he'd come back from the grave to ask her to write this story, and she was not fulfilling her part of the bargain.

Then the sound of a door opening and closing. Turning, she saw Whitaker leaping down the steps, waving something like a piece of paper up in the air, yelling for her to wait.

"What in the world, Whitaker? What are you doing?"

He wasn't the man she'd left moments before. He was glowing as he handed her a photograph.

"What is this?" She took the picture from his hands and looked. Her body went rigid.

Whitaker asked, "Who is he?"

Claire was staring at the photograph in shock. David and a boy were standing in front of a baseball stadium. The sign above their heads read: HOME OF THE BALTIMORE ORIOLES. David was wearing a green polo shirt and seersucker shorts. And he was holding his arm around a boy she'd never seen before—a white kid with a broad nose and straight brown hair partially covering one eye.

Whitaker was asking again, "Who is he?"

Claire shook her head and looked again. "I don't know."

But she did. She did know.

"I think that's—" Whitaker paused.

Claire and Whitaker said at the same time, "Orlando."

Claire looked up at Whitaker, who was now leaning with both hands on her car door. She looked back down at the photo. "What are they doing in Baltimore?"

Whitaker pointed to the stadium in the background. "No, that's Ed Smith Stadium in Sarasota. It's where the Orioles have their spring training."

Claire nodded. "I've never seen him before. I don't understand what's going on." She could barely wrap her head around what this picture had to say, all the possibilities.

Whitaker circled to the other side of her convertible, picked up the books, and climbed into the passenger-side seat. "We need to find Orlando."

She was still staring at the picture. "Where did you find this?"

"Behind the drawers."

"How did we not see it before?"

"I don't know. Must have been stuck between the runners." Moving along with his thoughts, Whitaker said, "Something crazy is going on right now, Claire. I feel like you were meant to give me that desk, and I was supposed to find this picture. And now we're supposed to find the boy."

Claire turned to him. "Five minutes ago, you were telling me you were done."

"I know! But that was before the story fell into my lap. This is it. This is the lead I was waiting for . . . and thought would never come." He lifted up the three composition books. "I can't stop now. What if Orlando is truly in trouble? I mean, in real life."

He was right. Claire's mind was racing so quickly, she couldn't process the next steps. "Where would we even start?"

The man beside her had suddenly come alive and was apparently thinking more clearly than he had in a decade. He said enthusiastically, "Probably by getting me out of this robe and into something more presentable."

She looked him up and down. "I agree."

Whitaker looked to the sky and back. "I don't know about you, but I'm going to Sarasota. Orlando would be fourteen or so now. I'm going to find him. I'm not coming back until I know he's okay. And I have the ending." Whitaker turned fully toward her with bright eyes. "Are you with me?"

Claire felt blindsided by the idea but couldn't imagine not going. She wanted answers as badly as he did. Was Orlando okay? How much of the story was actually true? And what was this secret life David had been living? "Yes, I'm with you." She wanted this book finished more than he did!

"Come here," Whitaker said, opening up his arms.

Their hug was awkward as they fumbled over the center console, but once their arms wrapped around each other, he pulled her in. "What a ride, Claire."

And she found herself not wanting to let go of him. How much longer could she keep her feelings for him a secret?

They discussed the logistics as they returned to his house. Claire offered to drive to Sarasota. While she waited in Whitaker's driveway for him to pack a bag, she asked a coworker to take care of Willy. Then Claire took a picture of David's photo with her phone and sent it to his close friends and family members, asking if they knew anything about the boy. She was in touch with them enough that reaching out wasn't a complete surprise.

The news settled in her mind, and she wondered how David could have had a relationship with a boy without her even *knowing* it. What else had he been doing of which she was unaware?

Tapping her fingers, she reminded herself that she had always trusted David implicitly. Why was she jumping to conclusions? It's not like he had a wife and family down in Sarasota. This wasn't a picture of his son. Right? David could have gone down one time to a game and met this kid, something as simple as that. To that end, she texted the picture to a couple of David's old friends too.

As Claire pulled away with Whitaker riding shotgun, she drove with great anticipation. They were closing in on answers. Though she was terrified of learning the whole truth, she knew that they were onto something amazing. She had a feeling that Whitaker was right. The end of the story was waiting with Orlando, and those two cutting across town in her convertible right this moment was meant to be.

"How in the world are we going to find him? A picture and a first name. That's all we have. Assuming Orlando is his real name. I don't know what's truth or fiction anymore."

"Why don't you reach out to the people you've been interviewing? I'm sure someone can lead you."

"That's actually a great idea." He took out his phone and worked away for a while.

Driving over the bridge from Deadman Key to St. Pete Beach, Claire asked, "Are we getting ahead of ourselves? Assuming the boy in the picture is Orlando is a pretty large leap. It could be anybody." The possibility felt too much like a fairy tale.

Whitaker was infectious with his recovered excitement. "If that is not Orlando, I will go to work for my father, and I'll never write another word. The rest of my life. And I will never complain about it again." He leaned in toward her. "I know with everything that I am that that boy is Orlando."

Claire weaved past a slow Jeep. She had to agree with Whitaker and continued his argument. "Why else would he have the photo in his desk? The desk where he was writing the story."

"Exactly."

Whitaker followed her inside her bungalow. "This place is so you."

"What does that mean?"

"I love it, quirky and artsy. Feels nice in here. And look who we have here." Whitaker reached for Willy, who was rubbing his back on Whitaker's leg. "You must be the infamous One-Eyed Willy." He held him up and looked at his face. "Yep."

Whitaker hung out with Willy on the couch while she packed. When she returned to the living room, he was dangling his fingers above, and Willy was trying to paw him. "He's a good one, an old soul."

"He's my little buddy. Pretty much saved my life."

"I believe it." He changed the subject. "You know, I've driven by this house so many times. It's funny how two people are meant to cross paths, and it's inevitable, but they might only be feet away from each other for years before the uniting. How crazy is it that I used to write in your café and now we are here together solving what could turn out to be a real mystery?"

Claire looked around to make sure she hadn't forgotten anything. "It was your book that brought us together."

Whitaker nodded. "And then David not wanting to read it."

Claire smiled at the memory. "David was never someone to like pop culture."

"Pop culture?" Whitaker said dramatically, standing from the chair. "*Napalm Trees* is a literary behemoth. There was nothing pop about it."

"Pop means popular. Your book and your movie were popular."

"Taylor Swift is popular. John Grisham is popular. What I wrote is a Tom Waits album of literature. And believe me, not everyone loved it. I've read every review ever written, and some people don't agree on its merits."

"I stand corrected, Mr. Waits. What I was trying to say was that David didn't like to be a follower. To read your book was to follow everyone else."

"Anyway . . . before I cower into the fetal position at the thought of writing pop, are you ready? It looks like you packed for several months. Are we going on a cruise around the world?"

Claire looked down at her bag. "I wanted to be prepared."

~

While driving toward the bottom of the peninsula, Claire called one of her managers, making sure things would run well at the café in her absence. The more she and Whitaker talked, the more she believed in their mission. She needed to know who this boy was, how he and David knew each other, and how much of the story was true. Had the man she'd married and grown to trust actually been living a second life? Once again, she found herself angry at him, but this time she had just cause. And what else was there? What else had David been hiding?

Claire turned up the reggae as they left St. Pete and crossed the vast stretch of Tampa Bay on I-275, which separated St. Pete and Bradenton. The wind picked up immediately, but it was too beautiful a day to put the top up. Slivers of thick jungle dotted with oak trees and several varieties of palms bordered the highway, and, beyond that, the sparkling blue of Tampa Bay on both sides.

Rising high over the water on the new cable-stayed bridge, Claire looked at the gangly mangroves of the Terra Ceia Aquatic Preserve and then the northern finger of Anna Maria poking out into the blue. How many times had David crossed this bridge?

After their descent, she looked over and noticed Whitaker reddening from the sun. "Do I need to put the top up? You're looking like a steamed crab."

Whitaker smiled. "I've been hiding in my dungeon for months."

"I can see that!"

"So before you called my book *pop culture*, we were discussing how often our paths have crossed. Think about every step that has led us to this drive. At some point, you decided to open up a café on Pass-a-Grille."

Claire turned down a Raging Fyah tune. "That was about ten years ago."

"Ten years ago," he emphasized. "Think about that. You opened the café about the same time I published my book."

"That's right," Claire agreed. "Books were my escape from all the stress of starting a new business." As the words left her mouth, she realized how much of her life had been a giant escape. Opening Leo's South had been an escape from the sad reality of living a childless life. David had been making plenty of money, but what the heck else was she going to do with her time? How else accept the death of her potential motherhood?

"I remember you coming up to me that day at the café. I thought you were just another girl hitting on me."

"You're such a dirtbag." She hit him on the leg. "I most certainly wasn't hitting on you. I was happily married."

"I got that. It didn't take you long to bring up David and flash your ring in my face. It's just funny to think about. How lives intertwine." He added, "I wish I'd been more open to your request to finish his book from the beginning. I can't believe I lied to you and kept trying to back out. I'm so sorry."

She was touched by his sincerity. "Well, now that you're out of your cave, think about this. Everything you and I have both been through was meant to be. I might never have found that picture if I hadn't given you the desk."

"And if I hadn't stormed into my office, almost deleted everything I'd written, and—"

"Almost deleted the files?"

"I didn't do it." He wagged his finger. "Thought about it for a second but didn't do it."

Claire's eyes widened. "Why in the world would you consider deleting months of work? You're such a drama queen, a bona fide kook."

Whitaker smiled and stuck out his fist for a fist bump. "Here's to two kooks looking for answers in a world full of question marks."

"The long-stemmed variety of question marks, no doubt."

"Bouquets of them." Claire gave him a bump and then took his hand. "Thanks for doing this with me. Thanks for caring."

Whitaker blushed. "Thanks for resuscitating me." With that he unbuckled his seat belt and nearly stood as he raised his head above the windshield. With his curly hair blowing in the wind, he yelled a call of freedom and happiness.

When he looked back to her, Claire was smiling so hard she could have kissed him again. She looked back to the steering wheel and to her rings. She'd promised herself she wouldn't kiss him again until she'd taken the rings off for good.

The time had come.

Out of nowhere, several pink flamingos crossed over the highway. "Look!"

Whitaker turned toward the sky. "If that's not a sign we're onto something, I don't know what is." He plopped back down and buckled his seat belt. "In terms of symbolism, an encounter with pink flamingos is a sign of good fortune, especially on a journey."

"Really?" Claire lit up.

"No," Whitaker admitted. "But it sounds possible."

Claire shook her head. "You're ridiculous."

"Do you know what a flock of flamingos is called, though? It's not a flock."

She took her eyes off the road for a second and glanced at him. "What is it?"

"A flamboyance of flamingos."

"Oh, c'mon."

"And a group of manatees is actually an aggregation of manatees."

"Really?" Claire studied his poker face. "No, I'm not falling for your distorted lies."

Whitaker's voice raised an octave. "Distorted lies? I am bathing you in the glory of the English language. Oh, and by the way, I wonder if they have a Clarion Inn in Sarasota. Only seems right for Claire to stay at the Clarion."

Smirking, Claire shook her head. "Does your mind ever stop?"

"All I know is that if we stay at the Clarion, they better serve éclairs. Because you know what I want? To eat éclairs with Claire at the Clarion."

Claire couldn't suppress a laugh for a moment longer, and though she didn't tell him (and maybe should have), she marveled at how much richer her life was with this man in it—absurdity and all.

Chapter 29

SAVING SARASOTA

Whitaker and Claire stopped for grouper bites and peel-and-eat shrimp at Woody's River Roo in Ellenton before continuing down to Sarasota. A guitarist worked his way through a set list of acoustic classics as they discussed possibilities and strategy. Still coming to grips with the discovery of the photo, their conversation ping-ponged without focus like they were two severe sufferers of ADD. "I can't believe this is happening."

"Me either. I wonder what . . ."

"But how could he have . . . ?"

Shrugging shoulders. "What are the chances he's still . . . ?"

Whitaker was having a ball, chasing down a lead that could be life changing. It was almost impossible to believe that Orlando was a living and breathing boy, but at the same time he was willing to bet his entire writing career that it was true.

Back on the highway, he looked at Claire in her gold-rimmed prescription sunglasses, driving her convertible with the top down, singing with the reggae that seemed to ooze from deep within her, and he wondered where he'd be without her. Probably halfway through a miserable first draft of *I Hear Thunder*, figuring out how the character was faring in his attempt to break free from the Mafia. *I'm serious, Matteo. I'm done.*

Every time Claire's phone dinged, Whitaker would check to see if she'd gotten lucky fishing around the photo to friends and family. And one by one, they responded that they had never seen the boy in their lives.

The burning question that kept returning to their conversations was, How do you find a boy in foster care with a first name and a picture? They'd jumped the gun by hopping in the car to drive down to Sarasota, but what else were they going to do? Whitaker certainly wasn't going to sit around his house and wait for answers.

He had reached out via text to a couple of his contacts, including a case manager in St. Pete and a woman named Carissa at the local child-placing agency, but he hadn't heard back yet. He and Claire had agreed to drive straight to the placing agency's office.

Inside a one-story office building close to downtown, the young man—possibly an intern—at the front desk wasn't nearly as impressed with Whitaker's local celebrity as much as he was with Claire's brief story. He did warm up once Whitaker mentioned Carissa, though. "She's out of the office today, but let me ask Sophie if she has a minute to help you." A few minutes later, Sophie came around the corner wearing a pink suit jacket. After introductions, she led them to an empty meeting room with a large chalkboard covering most of one wall. The words THINK WITH YOUR HEART, NOT WITH YOUR HEAD were written in large block letters in the center.

Once they were situated in the chairs around the long conference table, the woman in pink looked at Claire incredulously. "So you're trying to find a young man who may have known your deceased husband?"

"Yes, exactly." Claire handed her the photograph. "We think my husband, David, was possibly helping him, perhaps acting as a mentor. Honestly, I'm not sure. I just know that this boy has some answers I've been looking for."

"And you've heard, I'm assuming, how much effort the state puts into attempting to protect the children. I'm not saying you two have any ill intentions, but there are many parents we'd like to prevent from discovering their child's location."

"Yes, I totally get that."

Sophie looked at the picture. "What's his name?"

"Orlando."

"You don't know his last name?"

Claire shook her head. "All we have is the picture and his first name—or what we think is his first name."

Sophie blew out a slow breath and shook her head as if they'd just asked her to find a sunken ship in the Gulf.

"And his age," Whitaker chimed in. "We think he's about fourteen."

"If my husband was mentoring him, you know, spending time with him, wouldn't he have had to register in some way? Wouldn't there be paperwork?"

Sophie nodded. "He would have had to do a background check, get fingerprinted."

"Which would be in the boy's file?"

"Yes, but not something you could access."

Claire was scrambling. "Is there a way to reach out to every case manager in the area via email with the photo?"

The woman stifled a grin. "Not that I'm aware of."

Claire sighed. "What do we do then?"

"There are a few websites where children that are up for adoption are listed . . . with pictures. I'd start there." She named four sites as Claire typed them into her phone. "These are only children up for adoption, not everyone in the system. And they're not exhaustive lists by any means, but at least it's worth looking through." She tapped her pen in thought. "DCF won't help you without a court order."

"DCF?" Claire asked.

Whitaker knew the answer. "Florida Department of Children and Families."

Claire removed her glasses. "What else do we do? What would you do?"

Sophie pondered the question. "It's a tough one. You could perhaps convince someone to share the list of licensing agents, the ones who license all the homes. They know their kids. But I don't know that they'd help you. We're all working to protect the children."

"Could you help us get the list?" Claire asked.

"I don't have it." She looked at Whitaker. "Maybe Carissa can help you. I'd try Google. I'm really sorry, but they take this seriously. Honestly, you're going to run into a lot of brick walls. Please don't tell anyone I told you this, but I'd say the best thing you can do is try to get lucky on social media. You can find a lot of Facebook groups with foster parents in the area. Maybe they can help you."

Whitaker had joined a few local groups involved with the foster care system as part of his research, but he'd never posted before. It wasn't a bad idea. He'd do anything to find Orlando, even if that meant using his celebrity and getting the media involved.

Back in the convertible, Claire drove them into town. Sarasota came off cleaner and wealthier than St. Pete—perhaps more populated by semiretired snowbirds with disposable income. Whitaker had always loved the vibrancy of Sarasota and appreciated the juxtaposition between it and St. Pete. If they were colors, St. Pete would be orange and purple. Sarasota was bleached white and light blue.

They checked into their rooms at the Sarasota Modern, which they'd booked online on the way down. Hearing the Latin electronic beats easing through the lobby and seeing the pool with its fancy cabanas, tall palm trees, and slick outside bar, Whitaker felt like he was in Miami for a moment. Claire said she'd go through the list of websites, looking at pictures in her room, while Whitaker worked Facebook from his. They asked the concierge for restaurant recommendations and agreed to meet back in the lobby in an hour.

After a quick shower, Whitaker perched up on the balcony overlooking downtown and logged into Facebook. Finding a few of the groups he'd been stalking, he announced himself and mentioned that he was helping someone locate a boy, but all he had was a picture and a first name. Hopefully, he could appeal to someone who could help.

~

Claire propped three down pillows behind her on the bed in her room. A group of children were playing Marco Polo in the pool below, and Claire loved the sound of their voices sneaking through the cracked balcony door. With the picture of David and Orlando in her hand, she pulled up the first website the woman at the placing agency had shared and navigated to the available children.

Her heart sank as she put her eyes on the first page. The children were of all ages and colors. Some of the pictures showed two or three siblings. Big, bright smiles, all of them staring at the camera, as if they were all asking for help. Or, at least, for a family. Though Claire was still furious at David for lying, she found herself looking through his eyes, seeing the importance of supporting these beautiful beings that had been dealt a difficult hand.

Claire rolled her cursor over a teenager holding a basketball. She was laughing in the picture—a gorgeous smile—and her image had been captured at the perfect moment. Clicking on the photograph, Claire discovered several more shots. One depicted the girl spinning the basketball on the tip of her finger.

Claire stared at her pictures a long time before wiping her eyes and clicking away. This would take longer than she thought. And it would take more out of her than she could have ever imagined.

It didn't feel right to rush through the pages. She clicked on each child and took a moment to attempt to understand them, to imagine the strength these young boys and girls had tapped into in order to survive and thrive. It broke her heart to think about how many more were out there, not just in Florida but all over the world. Every one of them belonged down in the pool playing Marco Polo.

Clicking on a boy about Orlando's age, she broke into a full-on cry when she read the words at the top of his profile. *Status: On Hold.*

Her mouth went dry. *How could we live in a world where a human is on hold?* Was he being tested out by a family? Like one might test-drive a car? Claire put her hand to her chest and looked into the boy's eyes. She wanted to reach through the screen and pull him out, to save him from the hard times he was enduring. She wanted to protect him so that he could grow up gradually, not all at once like she imagined most of these kids had been forced to do.

Claire lost hope in finding Orlando as she reached the end of the last website. Lying there on the bed, she set the computer down and breathed through what she'd just experienced. No wonder David had taken to Orlando. What could possibly be more important in life than helping a child thrive?

But why? Why the hell had he not brought her in earlier? Why hadn't he included her? Staring at the blank screen of the television in front of her, she tried to imagine how she might have handled it if he'd told her about Orlando. She liked to think she would have welcomed Orlando with open arms.

Claire texted Whitaker, updating him and telling him she would need a little extra time to get ready. She sat up, putting her feet on the carpet. Somehow, despite the thousands of children who needed help, and despite David and his lies, she had to keep on living her life.

And that was it, Claire thought. Your heart was ripped to shreds and then you had to turn right around and keep living. But she had a feeling that these children, this thing David had been doing, wasn't going to leave her. The compulsion to do her part had wedged itself into her heart. For now, though, she stood and went to the shower.

With the long healing cleanse, sadness began to leave her. She committed to figuring out a way to carry on what David had been doing, not for him, but because she'd stumbled upon the call herself. There was no way she could be shown this world and not commit a part of her life to doing something about it.

Knowing Whitaker had reached this conclusion as well, her thoughts went to him. And she felt a sudden urge to be near him, to hear his voice, to share her emotions with him.

With a towel wrapped around her chest, she dried her hair and then walked to the closet to debate wearing the baby-blue dress she'd brought. Not risqué but certainly a little much for two friends getting a bite to eat. She had wanted to wear it tonight, to imply her feelings for him, but something else needed to be done first.

Returning to the bed and taking a seat, she held her hand out and looked at the wedding band and diamond David had given her.

A flash of good and bad memories hit her, and she nearly saw his face as she spoke to him. "I hate my anger toward you. It seems so unfair to make all these assumptions about you lying to me without you being here to defend yourself. I want to believe this was the only lie you've ever told me. That you truly just wanted to protect me and were terrified of how I might react. To that end, I'm going to try to forgive you, but . . ." She clenched her fist. "You're making it hard."

Claire paused and focused on what she really wanted to say. Looking at the rings again, she said, "I think I'm doing what you'd want me to do. I like him, David. What a weird thing to say, something I never could have imagined. But I know you'd understand. He makes me laugh, and I feel so good around him, like the way I used to be with you. It's different but also kind of wonderful. Don't think for a moment that taking off these rings means I'm forgetting you, and it has nothing to do with me being mad at you. It's just time I accept that you're gone."

She worked both rings off and clasped them in her hand. David wasn't speaking to her, but she thought that if he was, he'd say something like, "What took you so long? Go for it!" And, hopefully, he'd say, "I'm so damn sorry for keeping Orlando from you."

Claire was standing in an all-too-tempting, short light-blue dress, looking at her phone. He couldn't help but peek at her long legs, which eventually led down to rose gold thong sandals. Before he was caught, he forced himself to divert his eyes. He needed to tread carefully. When she turned, he noticed how low her dress was cut, and he thought to himself, *Not fair at all.*

Before he was busted exploring dangerous territory, Whitaker turned to the door and said expeditiously, "You look great. I think our Uber is here." In hindsight, he'd never spoken two sentences so quickly in his life. Didn't she realize what she was doing to him?

She'd suggested they leave her car with the valet so they could enjoy a bottle of wine. Once he'd located their ride, he opened the back door for her and noticed she'd removed her rings. Was that recently? He couldn't recall the last time he'd seen them. More importantly, *why* had she removed the rings? Was this her way of saying she was finally ready to take the next step? Knowing him, he might read into this bit of good news and get his hopes up, only to find out she'd left them with a jeweler for polishing.

Either way, it wasn't a question he would run by her, which forced a rather quiet ride through town. The ball was in her court, period. He'd already made his move, and she surely understood his fear of rejection. Removing the rings wasn't going to cut it as a green light. If she wanted to take their relationship into romantic territory, she needed to fly a banner behind a plane.

Why was Whitaker being awkward? Had he noticed her naked finger?

Claire thanked him for opening the door for her and stepped into the quaint Italian restaurant the concierge had suggested. It was six o'clock and already packed. Being a restaurateur herself, she couldn't help shaking down the restaurant's first impression.

The first thing she noticed was the opera music, and it fit well—authentic, not hokey. Just the right volume. The lights were dimmed down nicely. A man was shaping dough in front of a real brick oven. Golden candelabras with years of dripped wax stood on a center table along with several large bottles of wine. The hostess welcomed them with a smile and led them to their seats by the window, where a small candle burned atop a white tablecloth. It was feeling more and more like a date, but she was the only one who knew it. Or was she?

As they both perused menus, Whitaker said, "I could eat Italian every day of the week."

"I know this about you," she said. "That's why they all know you at Pia's in Gulfport."

Their server approached the table and, in a heavy Italian accent, said, "Excuse me. Happy to have you here. What to drink?"

Whitaker tapped the table. *"Lista dei vini, signore."*

The server lit up. *"Sei Italiano?"*

"No, no, amo il cibo Italiano." From there, Whitaker fell into a lengthy exchange with the man.

To stoke his pride some and to keep his confident smile going, she said, "Even after three months of knowing you, I'm still trying to process the fact that you're fluent in four languages."

"Thank you. It's just about the only thing I do well."

She wasn't sure that was true and had a feeling there were many more layers to be pulled back. "What did you two talk about?"

"I told him my roots are far from Italian, but that I loved Italian food so much that I had to learn the language. And then I told him I considered it a travesty that they grow cabernet sauvignon and merlot in Tuscany and asked if he had a nice Sangiovese. He's bringing it now."

"What's wrong with cabernet and merlot?"

"Absolutely nothing, but sadly, many Italian farmers pulled out their ancient indigenous varieties to plant grapes more familiar to the Americans, who happen to be the largest consumer of Italian wines in the world. Though there are many Tuscans who would disagree, I think they are putting their business before their art—something I'm not a fan of."

"What are you supposed to do if you don't recognize the wines on a list, then?" She squinted momentarily. "I'm asking for a friend."

Whitaker took a sip of water. "Good question. Take a chance or ask the server or somm. That's what they're there for."

"You're just full of surprises, aren't you? I've always hated that I can't speak another language." It was true, a deficiency that had always bothered her.

"Oh, c'mon. You didn't learn Spanish growing up?"

"A few words, but I'm a long way from fluency."

"Hang around long enough and maybe I can help."

Claire *was* actually thinking about hanging around him for a while. Did he know that?

"Repeat after me," he said. *"Prometo aprender otro idioma antes de cumplir los treinta."*

Claire said, "Whoa, whoa. That's a lot to say."

"A couple words at a time." He walked her through it.

"What did I just say?" Claire asked, going along with this little game of his.

Whitaker leaned in toward her. "I promise to learn another language before I'm thirty."

Claire chortled with delight. "Thirty! I wish."

"Did I get your age wrong?"

Was he joking? "You really think I'm under thirty?"

"We've never talked about it. It's not polite to ask a lady her age."

"For your information, I'm well over thirty, and we'll stop there." She blushed. "Thank you for the compliment." Claire adjusted in her seat. She liked seeing Whitaker open up and continued to play her part in being a good conversationalist. "So how do you say, *My name is Whitaker, and I'm an intriguing, sensitive, and complicated man?*"

Whitaker flashed a smile. *"Mi chiamo Whitaker e sono un uomo intrigante, sensibile e complicato."*

Claire loved to hear him speak. He helped her repeat it. "How about in Spanish?"

Sounding like a completely different person, Whitaker spat out his translation. *"Me llamo Whitaker y soy un hombre intrigante, sensible y complicado."*

"And French?"

In more of a high-pitched song with guttural edges, Whitaker said, *"Je m'appelle Whitaker et je suis un homme intriguant, sensible et compliqué."*

"Compliqué," Claire repeated. "What a lovely language."

"It really is, both beautiful and angry at the same time."

"Okay, mister. How about Japanese?"

Without hesitation, Whitaker broke into Japanese.

Her mouth dropped. "I don't believe it. What did you really say?"

"Your fish is old." He shrugged. "It's the only thing I know how to say."

Claire inclined her head and said quietly, "Let's hope my fish isn't old."

They shared a plate of *spaghetti alle vongole* and discussed the next day. They had not expected to hit so many roadblocks in the search, but it made sense that everyone was bound by law to protect the children. Using Google, Whitaker had found a short list of licensing agencies. They would start there and visit each one. And they'd both attempt to spread the word via social media.

After polishing off the bottle of wine, they finished the meal with two glasses of limoncello. Claire was feeling both light-headed and distracted. She was sure by now that she wanted to kiss him tonight but didn't know how to initiate it. Was he waiting on her to make the first move? Didn't he know she was completely out of practice?

Back at the hotel, she stood facing him in the lobby, wondering if he might ask her to the bar for a nightcap. "That was a good meal," she said flatly, anxiously.

"A beautiful meal. A great recommendation. Want to meet for breakfast early? I'm diving into a little more research now."

She couldn't bring herself to suggest a nightcap, not that she needed one. Agreeing to meet at seven, they both entered the elevator and rode up in silence. Why couldn't she just plant one on him? He was obviously still interested in her. The looks he gave her, the way he listened. He'd already tried once. What was she afraid of?

When the door slid open on her floor, she stepped out of the elevator and offered a quick smile. "Thanks for dinner."

A handsome smile back. "My pleasure."

And then the door closed, and she stood there cross armed for a while, wishing she could try again.

Chapter 30

WHAT'S BETTER THAN CEREAL FOR BREAKFAST?

Upstairs in his room, Whitaker sat on the couch again, flipped on cable news, and opened up his laptop. Apparently, his name was still recognizable, as he'd drummed up quite a few comments in the Facebook groups. As part of his post, he'd asked if he could post Orlando's picture. Several people, one even in all caps, had typed: DO NOT POST HIS PICTURE. Others suggested that surely someone at the placement agency could help. Another said he should talk to the *Sarasota Herald-Tribune*. One woman told him to PM her, which he did. He almost posted that Orlando could be in trouble and that the search was time sensitive, but that didn't feel entirely true. Three years had gone by.

After checking, Whitaker brushed his teeth and climbed into the comfy bed with David's composition books. Now that they were onto the truth, maybe he could learn more. He began reading, taking in the story with an entirely different view. No wonder David had struck a chord; he'd based the story off his own life.

Whitaker yawned as he moved to the second composition book, but something was telling him to keep going. What if a clue lay within these sentences?

Three hours later, Whitaker was flying through the third book, utterly lost in the story. He felt like he'd drunk a cup of coffee. Amid

David's skilled handwriting, Whitaker ran across a scratched-out word that brought him back to reality. There were plenty of mistakes that David had corrected with his pen, but this one in particular stopped Whitaker in his tracks. David had originally written that Kevin was driving south on MLK Jr. Street toward Orlando's group home. He'd scratched out "south" and written "west." Not that big of a deal.

Unless you know that MLK in Sarasota doesn't run south.

But that it does in St. Pete.

Whitaker sat up straighter and pondered the mistake. He tried to put himself in David's shoes. How do you accidentally mess up directions? If David was writing a scene in Sarasota, he'd be picturing the scene as it was taking place. He'd be driving west in his head on MLK in Sarasota. To accidentally write the word "south" meant that David was picturing the scene in St. Pete.

The boy was real.

What else in the story was real?

And had they known each other for days, weeks, or months? Whitaker had a feeling it was more like months. Whatever the answer, it seemed more plausible that they'd met and bonded in St. Pete.

Ah, but what about the picture at the Orioles game in Sarasota? If David were taking Orlando to a game, why not go to a game in St. Pete? Why would they drive all the way to Sarasota?

But why would David have moved the story to Sarasota in the first place? Well, David had obviously fictionalized the majority of the story. David was Kevin. Sarasota was possibly St. Pete. Then Orlando was almost surely a fictional name. Perhaps David had moved the story to Sarasota to further separate truth from reality and to protect Orlando. To that end, he would never use Orlando's real name.

Whitaker looked at the time. It was four in the morning. He could barely wait to break all this to Claire.

Claire woke with Whitaker on her mind. He deserved to know that she'd turned a corner in her overcoming the loss of David. And that she couldn't stop thinking about Whitaker. She imagined his breath on her neck, his arms wrapped around her, protecting her from this sometimes harsh world. Removing the rings was definitely not enough of a message. Why couldn't she just kiss him already?

When she sat down at the breakfast table downstairs, Whitaker sprayed her with a line of words that moved too quickly for her morning brain to comprehend. She put up a hand. "Hold on, slow down. It's early." *And I was thinking about us.*

Whitaker paused. "Are you sure you never met Orlando?"

"Good morning to you too." The salty smell of bacon wafted over from a table nearby.

"Sorry. Good morning." He couldn't stop himself. "I came across something that suggests this story really took place in St. Pete. We're in the wrong city."

The nugget of information woke her up. "Why do you say that?"

He told her about his discovery.

"Wait. You read his entire book again?" She couldn't believe it.

"Just about. I didn't sleep last night."

Claire's eyes widened, thinking that he looked just fine. "You are one determined man. I think you're reaching. Just because Kevin was going south instead of west on MLK?"

"It's more than that. It's not the first time he's slipped into a St. Pete setting instead of Sarasota. I can't recall the other example and couldn't find it, but I remember thinking it was weird. I'm telling you. We're in the wrong city. Think back. Don't think about the name Orlando. I'm not even convinced the boy's name is Orlando. He made up the name Kevin. Why not make up all the characters? Anyway, think back to your time together. Did David ever have anyone help him with chores? Did he ever talk about a kid he'd met? Were there any other parallels to your life?"

"Don't you think I've already gone there?"

"I'm telling you, Claire. Orlando—or whatever his name is—is in St. Pete. Or, at least, he was. It's not just the subtle mistakes with the setting. It's that David wrote this book based on a real-life experience. I think he spent a lot of time with Orlando, like more than we are considering. And if so, that wasn't happening in Sarasota." Whitaker wiped coffee from his mustache. "To that end, I refuse to believe that no one in David's life knew of Orlando. I understand that David was hiding him from you. But he had to have told someone."

Claire stared out the window, watching cars pass by. She didn't like being reminded that David had been hiding things from her. "I sent the picture to his two best friends, all his brothers and sisters, and both his parents. They'd never seen Orlando before."

"How about his work? Did you send it to them?"

Claire shook her head. "No. I haven't really talked to any of them since the funeral."

Whitaker dipped his chin. "I think we should drive back and visit his office. You said it was on Fourth in St. Pete?"

Claire nodded, trying to process Whitaker's change of position. "I'm still not convinced enough to think we need to leave Sarasota right now. I think we should stop back by the agency. Did you hear from your contact there, Carissa?"

"Yeah, she texted me last night. Said we can chat today. But she can't help us if it's in Sarasota. Remember, we'd be dealing with the placing agency in St. Pete." Whitaker shook his head. "All I can say is I've spent three months reading and tweaking your husband's story. I've gotten to know him. When you're writing, you see this scene in your head, and you're putting it down on paper. If he'd made up the scene, he wouldn't have screwed up the direction. It's way too much of a coincidence. I think Orlando was in a group home in St. Pete. I think David met him somehow, probably a story similar to what we've read."

Claire dropped her head, feeling the painful impact of a potentially even bigger lie living between David and her. As difficult as such a grand deceit was to accept, it was equally hard to argue with the man in front of her. He was on a mission, and he was showing the genius that he'd been hiding for so long.

One more thought came to her. "What about the picture? David and Orlando were obviously here at some point."

Whitaker nodded confidently, as if he'd already thought about it. "David brought him down here to a game. Maybe it was a team Orlando liked."

Claire was beginning to process all the possibilities, if in fact her husband had been keeping this secret from her. "Or maybe he didn't want to run into anyone he knew. Someone that might tell me they saw David and a boy at a game."

"Yeah," Whitaker agreed. "I thought of that too."

They both ate homemade granola with fresh berries and raw wild-flower honey, and they talked about their next moves. After paying the bill, Whitaker asked, "Why don't you send the photo to the guys at his firm?"

Claire set down her spoon. "No. I'd rather go by in person."

"Fair enough," Whitaker agreed, taking a last bite. After chasing it with a sip of coffee, he said, "I need to run and grab my things. Meet back down in twenty?"

Claire nodded, and they both stood, walking in tandem toward the elevator. Claire's heart rate quickened. She'd decided it was now or never.

Whitaker pressed the button, and they waited.

Claire felt like she was going to faint.

Once they'd entered and the door closed, Whitaker made a comment about the weather.

Claire took a deep breath and looked at him. It was in his warm eyes that she found her composure. She stepped toward him and put a hand on his chest.

Confusion painted his face.

"Do you ever plan on trying to kiss me again?"

He swallowed. "I . . . I've wanted to."

She moved closer, her face inches from his. "Don't give up on me, okay? I like you. A lot."

"I like you too," Whitaker whispered, touching her waist.

Letting herself go, Claire kissed Whitaker, and her heart soared.

When they reached her floor, the bell dinged, and the door opened. Whitaker took her hand. "Don't go."

"We can't stay in here forever."

Whitaker stole another kiss as she slipped out of the elevator. "I'll meet you in a few."

The door closed.

Her desire for him was undeniable. She felt it all over.

Back in her room, she retrieved the wedding band and diamond ring from the soap dish in the bathroom. Holding them tight in her hand, she said, "I'll always love you, David. Infinity times infinity." As she placed the rings inside a compartment in her Coach makeup bag, she wrestled with the guilt of moving on. David would have really liked Whitaker and would be so happy for her. Even as mad as she was at David, she still cared what he might think.

Waiting for Whitaker, Claire sat cross-legged on the white leather sofa in the lobby. Electronic chill played on the speakers, but she wasn't paying attention. She was thinking about their kiss.

Whitaker came around the corner with his bag on his shoulder.

Claire gasped. He'd shaved his mustache. "Aren't you handsome?" she said, standing. "What got into you?"

He ran a finger above his upper lip. "It was time; that's all."

"Then you deserve a reward." She approached and planted several kisses on his lips. By the time she let go of him, he certainly knew how much she liked him.

Chapter 31

An Oliver Twist

Back in St. Pete, as the orange ball in the sky signified noon, Claire and Whitaker pulled into the parking lot of David's old architecture firm, Wyatt and Jones, on Fourth Street. Focusing on steel, brick, and sharp angles, the result was one of the most stylish in St. Pete, and David had been instrumental in the design.

As Claire turned off the car, Whitaker asked, "Do you want me to wait here?"

Claire thought about his question for a moment. There was nothing to be ashamed of in bringing another man inside. And she could use the support. "No, please come in. You should see the inside. It's really a sight to see."

They walked around to the front. The bamboo entry doors were flanked by vertical gardens called green walls. The succulents and moss glistened from a previous watering. Pulling back one of the doors, they entered the high-ceilinged space, and Claire felt a ripple of nervous anticipation. She hadn't been here since she'd come in to pick up David's belongings only days after his death. It had been a day of hugs and tears shared by Claire and all his coworkers, who'd told her how much he meant to the firm. Someone had even called David the mascot.

Light poured in from the large windows, making the giant potted plants very happy. Other than a few patches of exposed brick, the walls and floors were shades of white. Twenty men and women were either sitting or standing at their electric desks. The noise of phone calls, printers, and brainstorming filled the room.

Stopping halfway through the lobby, Claire pointed to her right, seeing David's old workstation. "That's where he used to sit. When he started, there were only eight of them in the firm. It looks like they're growing."

"I wonder if my dad's been in here. It's quite the building."

"Yeah, they used to be crammed into a corner suite in the office park across the street from the Publix. They built this maybe six years ago."

"I can't believe I've never noticed it before."

"It's funny how you might be right next to something, but you don't notice it until you're meant to." Claire turned to Whitaker to make sure he caught her meaning.

He certainly did. "Isn't life something?"

Claire scanned the room, noticing several familiar faces. A man named Zeke in chinos and a plaid shirt spotted her and nearly jumped out of his chair, coming their way.

"Claire," he said, flashing his teeth, opening his arms.

"Hi, Zeke. It's so good to see you."

Zeke gave her a tight squeeze. "You look great," he whispered.

Claire thanked him and looked back to the center of the room. She hadn't seen most of these people since the funeral. "Lots of new faces around here."

"I know! We're growing like crazy."

"So is St. Pete."

"That's exactly right. It's a good time to be an architect."

Claire gestured toward Whitaker and introduced him as her friend.

Zeke looked at Whitaker for the first time. "I know you."

"Oh yeah?" Whitaker said, his ego grinning.

"Yeah, you're the barista from down the street, right? Made my iced cappuccino this morning?"

Claire froze, unsure of how to react. She kind of wanted to laugh.

Whitaker's face went white. "Uh, no, actually, I'm not a baristo." Slicing a hand through the air, he added, "Wrong guy." A nervous chuckle followed.

Zeke grinned. "I'm kidding. I loved your book."

A handsome smile rose on Whitaker's face, accepting defeat in this quick game of wit. He reached for Zeke's hand. "Well played, sir. Well played."

The three shared a laugh, and several other of David's former coworkers herded around them. After more hugs and introductions, Zeke asked, "What are you doing here, by the way? You should stop in more often. We miss you."

Claire took the floor, feeling David's old life circling around her, watching her. She wanted them to see she was doing better. "We're trying to get to the bottom of something and need your help." She cast her eyes toward the others. "It's a long story, but I'm trying to find a boy David apparently knew." Claire dug into her purse. "We found this picture in his desk yesterday."

Claire handed the photograph to Zeke, and the other coworkers squeezed in around him to take a peek.

"That's Oliver," Zeke said.

Claire's heart buckled.

Whitaker stepped toward her and put a kind hand on her lower back.

"Yeah," a woman named Eliza agreed, looking at Claire. Eliza had joined the firm the same year as David and was a similar age to Claire, so they'd gravitated toward each other at work events and found they shared similar political views. "David caught him breaking into a man's car."

"That's weird. He didn't tell me. When was this?" Claire asked.

"Gosh," Eliza said, her freshly applied lip gloss glistening. "Maybe a year before . . . you know." Eliza shook her head. "David made Oliver track down the owner and pay him back for the broken window."

"Yeah," Zeke said, "David actually gave him a few small jobs around here to make the money."

"What kind of jobs?" Claire asked.

"A little bit of everything. Cleaning windows. Picking up trash. Washing our cars. Oliver was only eleven or twelve or something. So he wasn't a huge help, but he was a good kid, under the circumstances. From what David told me, Oliver had been dealt a pretty bad hand."

Whitaker stepped in. "How long was Oliver hanging around here?"

Eliza lifted a shoulder. "Not long. A few weeks. I'm surprised David never mentioned him to you."

Claire's voice cracked. "I am too."

Everyone was silent. Treading so closely to the topic of David's death was dangerous business.

Claire once again found herself at the center of a pity party and didn't like the feeling. Before it got weird, she offered the best explanation. "Probably just another day in the life at the office." Sometimes, when she'd asked about David's day at work, he had said something to the effect of, "Just another day in the life. I'd rather leave it at the office and focus on us."

Zeke returned the photograph. "I didn't know about him taking Oliver to a baseball game. Actually, I didn't know he'd hung out with him outside of the few times here."

Everyone shook their heads, assuring her they didn't know either.

"That's the Orioles stadium down in Sarasota, right?" Zeke asked.

Claire nodded.

"What a cool thing to do for him," Zeke said. "Taking him to a baseball game."

She smiled, trying to ignore the thoughts of betrayal. Of course, David had had a life at this office that she hadn't always been caught up with. That was the way office life was. But still. Helping a young boy was the kind of thing he would have mentioned over dinner. Unless he was hiding it to protect her. Her stomach churned.

Claire wasn't thinking clearly. She looked at Whitaker, encouraging him to take over.

Whitaker read her look and asked Zeke and the others, "Where is Oliver? Or where was he? Any idea how we can find him?"

"Yeah," Eliza said, apparently eager to get a word in. "I don't know if he's still there, but David said he was living in a group home down the street, that big gray house with the white columns. Actually, I saw it for the first time shortly after David died. For a second, I thought I should go tell Oliver the news of David's passing, but I didn't know they were still in touch." At Whitaker's urging, Eliza shared specific directions.

"What's this all about?" Zeke asked. "Trying to learn more about David?"

Claire suppressed a rising sadness and looked at everyone. She didn't want them to see her fragility. Sticking the photograph back into her purse, Claire said, "David was writing a book when he died. About a man helping save a child from a group home. Now we know his novel was inspired by Oliver."

Zeke looked at Claire and then Whitaker. "So now we know why you're standing here."

"Yeah, Whitaker is helping me research the story."

"And to write it," Whitaker added. "I'm finishing the story for her. I don't know if any of you knew, but David was a heck of a writer."

Claire choked up. It was the first time Whitaker had gone public with the news that he'd taken on the project.

"Oh yeah," Zeke said. "He loved to talk about writing. He mentioned he was working on something. I'm glad you're going to finish it for him." Zeke looked back at Claire. "Please let us know what we can do to help. Of course I want to read it the moment it's ready. I'm sure we all do." He looked back at Whitaker. "Make sure you do David justice. He was one of the finest men I've ever known."

Whitaker offered a nod, and Claire smiled. "Thanks, Zeke." Though inside, she wasn't smiling. She was questioning Zeke's kind words. Apparently, no one knew who David truly was. She felt a tectonic shift of anger deep inside.

When they returned to the car, Whitaker dropped into the passenger seat. "They're a nice group."

"Yeah, David loved working there." Claire slid into her side and returned to the more important topic. "Did we really just find him? I guess Orlando is Oliver."

Whitaker closed his door. "I think we're hot on his trail."

What Claire failed to mention was that she was scared to death.

⌇

Showing he was there for her, Whitaker reached past the empty Gatorade bottle in the cup holder and took Claire's hand. "Hey."

Claire let out a sigh and turned to him. She had yet to turn on the ignition. The parking lot was empty of pedestrians.

"This is really deep stuff, Whitaker. And it's become completely evident that David was protecting me. I mean, his coworkers knew more than me!" Claire drifted off for a moment. "David didn't want me to know that he'd become a father to this boy. Doesn't it feel that way to you?"

It definitely felt that way, but Whitaker wanted to be gentle. "Kind of, but I think he was acting more like a big brother—to the boy, not to you. We'll know much more when we find Oliver. But, yes, I think he didn't want to bring you down as he worked through his own pain of not being a father." Whitaker felt an urge to point out the lighter side of their discovery. "But, hey, Claire. I have a feeling Oliver was helping him in a big way. And I'm sure he planned on telling you eventually.

It's not like he was keeping some big secret. He met a kid at work and tried to help him out."

Claire squeezed his hand. "I know. There's no use jumping to conclusions. I feel like such a bitch. I can't help thinking back to that day when I told him to stop pestering me about a baby." She clenched her fists together. "I was so stupid! He wanted to be a father, and I was so selfish that I couldn't see through my own mess. If we would have kept with our adoption plan, we could have had a child that year." She touched her belly and sighed. "I was so hardheaded. I think I wanted a baby just as much as him, but I somehow suppressed it, like an extended form of shock when you're numb to the pain."

Whitaker turned more toward her and brushed her hair away from her face. "You can't go tearing up the past like this, Claire. I get where you're coming from, and I know it hurts, but don't go beating yourself up. We're all trying to survive. And we all make mistakes."

"What an epic mistake I made."

Whitaker did not find it easy to see her beating herself up. She'd been through enough. "As you and I both know, everything happens for a reason. Even mistakes. We wouldn't have this gift of a novel to remember David by if everything up to this moment in your life hadn't happened. I think David wrote it to tell you exactly how he felt. What better way to share with your partner?"

"He could have tried sitting me down and telling me the truth." Claire dropped her head in exhaustion. "Thank you for going on this journey with me. I'm so glad you're here."

"Me too."

Though Whitaker was afraid of crossing boundaries, he moved closer and kissed her. To his surprise, she put her hand on his face and kissed him again and again.

"David would have liked you," Claire said. "You two could have been great friends."

"I don't doubt it." For a moment, Whitaker found it odd to kiss her and hear David's name in the same breath. But then again, David would always be a part of her. That was the way it needed to be if he wanted to grow a relationship with her.

Letting go, he sat back and put his arm on the door. "Now, let's go find this kid."

~

The gray house with the white columns was tucked into a corner lot a few blocks away from the architecture firm. Two cardinals resting on the stoop flew away when Claire closed her car door.

Whitaker and Claire ascended the steps, and she wondered how many times David had done the same. Her pulse pounded relentlessly as she looked up to the windows of the second floor. Would it be this easy? A boy she'd read and dreamed about for months waiting behind this door, ready to share David's secrets?

Whitaker led the way and reached for the doorknob. It was locked, so he rang the bell.

"No turning back now," Claire said, knowing the answers waiting on the other side of the door could destroy her.

"We could turn and run if you want to. I am really nervous right now."

"I don't care what's on the other side of this door. I'm not moving until someone answers."

They didn't have to wait long. A rather large man in an oversize T-shirt with his hair greased back opened up the door halfway. "What can I do for you?"

Claire put her hand on Whitaker's arm, letting him know that she wanted to take charge. "We're looking for a boy who lives here. Or used to about three years ago. This is a group home, right?"

The man had a slight lisp. "Yes, it is, but I'm sorry. I can't help you."

Another brick wall.

Claire put up a hand. "No, wait. I understand that you're not able to share information, and I get it. But this is a special case." Claire searched for the strength to be convincing. "My husband died three years ago, and he used to work at the architecture firm just north of here on Fourth. I've found a picture recently of my husband and this boy, and it seems my husband was helping him out of some trouble, doing some mentoring. I just want to talk to him a little bit. His name is Oliver."

The man shook his head and started to close the door. "Even if someone named Oliver did live here, I wouldn't tell you. I'd lose my job."

"What can we do then?" Whitaker asked.

"You'll need to go through the placement agency. They're the only ones who might be able to help you. But, honestly, I'm not sure they will."

"Wait, please," Claire said. "Would you just take a look at this picture?" Claire didn't wait for a response. She held out the photo and watched the man's eyes, hoping to see the twinkle of recognition.

He glanced at it briefly. "Again, I'm sorry. You need to go about this legally."

Whitaker backed up. "He's right."

As much as she wanted answers, Claire knew the man was indeed right. But they were so close. Turning away, she broke into a cry and started down the steps, following Whitaker.

She heard the man sigh behind her. "Look."

Claire glanced back optimistically.

"He's not here, okay? He wouldn't have been here that long anyway. He'd either be reunited with his birth parents, placed with a foster family, or, hopefully, adopted. I hope that helps. It's all I can do for you."

Claire pretended to wipe tears from her eyes. "What's the name of this place? Just so we can tell the placement agency."

"The Oakwood House."

Claire and Whitaker thanked him and returned to the convertible.

Buttoning his seat belt, Whitaker asked, "Did you just fake a cry?"

Claire turned to him with a smile playing at the corner of her lips. The things she was capable of to get at the truth.

"You manipulating scoundrel. How dare you."

She put the car in "Drive" and pulled away. "How did you know?"

"I've heard you cry enough over the past few months. It's the first time you crying didn't break my heart. That's how I knew."

Claire hung a left. "I'll do whatever it takes to find Oliver."

"Yeah, me too."

~

They stopped for tacos on Central and sat outside overlooking a stunning graffiti portrait of a woman trapped and floating in a fishbowl, which covered the entire side of an old brick building.

"I know exactly how she feels," Claire said before biting into a chip. She was sitting opposite Whitaker.

He drank a sip of water from the red plastic cup in front of him. "I think we all do."

Whitaker's phone lit up, and he read a Facebook message to himself. "Well, look at that. The placement agency wrote me back. Sent me a contact. A woman named Laura. Let me try her." He left a message on her voice mail and followed up with a text message.

After downing a salty chip with the particularly smoky and delicious salsa, Whitaker looked at Claire, who was still lost in the graffiti. "You still with me?"

She looked at him. "Yeah, sorry. What an emotionally draining day."

"I can only imagine. But you know what? We're getting somewhere. What a meaningful journey we're on. And we will find Oliver. I know it."

Claire dipped a chip into the smoky salsa.

Before she could retract her hand, Whitaker grabbed a chip from the basket and playfully stabbed hers, knocking off the salsa.

Claire gasped as she looked at Whitaker's guilty, smiling face. Whitaker watched the tension relax in her body. "You can always make me smile. Thanks for that."

They met eyes and shared a lovely moment.

"I like making you smile," Whitaker whispered. After they ate their chips, he put his hand on the soft skin of her wrist. "I know this isn't the right time to ask, but I'm doing it anyway." He ignored the fear of rejection creeping up his throat. She'd kissed him this morning. What did he have to worry about? "Would you allow me to take you out tonight?"

She removed her glasses and wiped her eyes. "Look at me. Do you really feel like taking me out?"

"Ten thousand million percent yes. I've wanted nothing more for months. I like you. You like me. Let's do this."

She set her glasses down on the table. "Is this how the intriguing, sensitive, and complicated Whitaker Grant asks women on dates?"

He could look into her eyes forever. "I'm just cutting to the chase. Enough of this already."

Whitaker's phone rang, and he looked at the screen. It was Laura from the agency returning his call. "That was quick," he said to Claire.

Leaving the table, he answered. "Hey, Laura, thanks for getting back to me. Now, may I ask what you do, exactly?"

"I do a little bit of everything these days. Been at this more than thirty years. Was a case manager for fifteen years. Fostered kids for much longer than that. Now I'm a director here at the agency."

Her confidence excited him. "Then I've found the right person."

"We'll see. So you need to find a boy with only a picture and a first name?"

"I know it's not a lot to go on. We do know the group home where he was three years ago."

He glanced over at Claire, who was watching him pace back and forth along the sidewalk.

"And if it made it into the file, my friend's husband was acting as a mentor and had surely gone through the background check process."

"That helps. But three years is a long time, Whitaker. I hope the boy's not even in the system anymore. We try to place them as quickly as possible. Either way, on any given day, we're dealing with over three thousand children. Removals and placements are happening all the time."

"Understood. Pardon the cliché, but I know it's a needle-in-a-haystack thing. Nevertheless, I think Oliver would want us to find him."

"I'll tell you what. Text me his picture and the other info and let me think on it. I'm not promising anything, but if you'll be patient, I can turn over a few stones. How about that for a cliché?"

"Not bad, Laura. I like you already." Whitaker eyed the fish tacos being delivered to the table. "I'll send the picture right over. And thanks. Thanks so much for everything you do."

"Once you get to know some of the children, it's easy to do."

"I can only imagine." Whitaker thought about Orlando and Oliver. "Okay, my friend is about to eat my tacos. I look forward to hearing from you."

Once he'd ended the call, Whitaker texted Laura the photo and other info and then sat back down. "I am carelessly optimistic. It's a matter of time now."

"She thinks she can help?" Claire asked.

"She knows she can help. It's just a matter of her being careful about it. She wants to do whatever's best for Oliver. Now about that date . . . Is tonight too soon?"

Chapter 32

I'm Getting There

Whitaker had not taken a woman out on a proper date in a long time. Several hours after she'd dropped him off, as he rode along the beach toward her house in his especially clean Land Rover (he'd also fixed the broken belt), he found himself terribly nervous, his mind scrambling, his body jittery. He kept telling himself to relax, that he'd been spending almost every day with this woman for half of a year. Ah, but things were most certainly different now.

It was seven and still bright outside, and the warm breeze was blowing hard against the palm trees along Pass-a-Grille Way. Whitaker eased to a stop in front of her house and tried to compose himself. This was his chance. He'd craved her for so long.

Whitaker wanted a partner to share the fun times with. He wanted someone to remind him of what the fun times were. Claire could be that partner. She was the one who'd lifted him out of the abyss, and she was everything that Whitaker ever wanted, and he was getting his chance. What a lucky guy.

"You'd better not screw it up," Whitaker told himself, stepping down from the Rover. He straightened his white linen shirt and ran his hands along his hair, hoping he still had some game left in him. He walked into the porch, noticing a copy of *The Good Earth* by Pearl S. Buck on the hammock. He knocked.

Claire opened the door, and the light bent as Whitaker searched for the right words.

She was wearing a one-piece jumper, and it pushed and pulled in all the right places. Her long hair shone as it fell past her shoulders. She looked at him through her glasses. "Hi."

Whitaker smiled and reached for her hand. He pulled her in and kissed her. "You look amazing."

"You look more handsome than I've ever seen you." She touched his naked upper lip. "And I so love your face without a mustache." Another kiss.

Whitaker felt his impulses trying to breach the castle walls, but he reminded himself that he needed to treat her with a tremendous amount of care tonight.

"Come in for a second." She took his hand and pulled. "I have something for you."

"Oh yeah?" Whitaker asked, letting her drag him inside.

Whitaker waited with Willy while she scurried into the kitchen and returned with a beautifully wrapped present, clearly a piece of framed art, a couple of feet tall. As she handed it to him, she said, "You're the one who encouraged me to pick up my camera again, so I thought it only fitting."

Whitaker carefully untied the elaborate gold bow and pulled back the emerald paper. Holding up the reclaimed wood frame, he looked at the photograph. It was a picture of a manatee in the surf.

"You took this?" he asked, looking at her, blown away by her skill.

"Yeah. Like a month ago."

"What the . . . ? Where in the world did you find a manatee in the surf?"

"Right out here." Claire pointed toward the Gulf. "I don't know if he lost his way, but as you can see, the water was pure glass, so I guess he was exploring."

Whitaker returned his wide eyes to the photograph. To get a better view, he leaned it on the sofa and stood back. The manatee was looking right at him, his puffy eyes lingering above the water. Whitaker pinched his chin and bathed in her art, noticing the way she'd framed the shot: low and tight.

He turned and took her hand. "It's the greatest present anyone has ever given me. Really. I'm so touched." He pulled her in, and they embraced. "And I thought I was the artist. You have such a talent."

Claire thanked him modestly. "Now take me to dinner. I'm starving."

Whitaker didn't eat out like he used to, but there was a time when he'd gallivanted all over town chasing the newest restaurant, the latest exciting bottles of wine. At the height of his foodie obsession, before the grand collapse, Brick & Mortar on Central Avenue had been one of his absolute favorites. It turned out Claire and David had dined there several times as well.

The outside tables were occupied, the diners enjoying a breeze from the fans above. Passing by a wine barrel featuring the evening's menu, Claire and Whitaker walked into the boisterous and crowded space. A woman with hair the color of obsidian and a welcoming smile led them to their table. A hanging steer skull looked down on the patrons sitting on stools along the bar.

Whitaker helped Claire into her seat and sat opposite her. The foursome next to them was working on a bottle of Château Blaignan, and their laughter was loud. But *not* annoying. Who could get mad at people for being too happy? The old Whitaker could, but hopefully the typist was six feet under for eternity.

The writer reached for the wine list straightaway and recognized a few names he'd been reading about lately. The owners had always procured a fine list of producers that leaned toward conscious farming and minimalist intervention. By the time their server arrived, he was ready. He pointed to the chosen one. "I think we'll do this Morgon. And if you don't mind dropping it in ice, that would be lovely."

With that out of the way, he turned his attention to his date. Claire was working her way down the food menu. Her light-brown eyes and those glasses made him smile. That they'd gone so long just as friends amazed him. To think there was so much more between them to explore.

She looked up. "What?"

"You make me happy; that's all."

"Right back at you."

Once they'd both scanned the menu, Claire asked, "Have you given any more thought to the ending of *Saving Orlando*? Have these new developments with Oliver registered?"

Through the window, Whitaker watched a heavily tattooed man toss his little girl into the air. They were both giggling. "I'm trying not to go there yet. I want to meet him, Claire. I want to shake his hand. I want to see that he's a real boy."

"Yeah, me too."

Chills fired on his arms as he thought about it. "What will you say to him? What's your first question?"

"Oh gosh." She looked off toward the noisy bar. "I have so many. Ultimately, though, I want to know why David hid him from me. And if there was anything else he was hiding. How about you?"

Whitaker blew out a long breath. "I guess I want to know how much of the book is true."

They paused when the server appeared with the wine. Whitaker gave the cru Beaujolais a good sniff and sip and relished in the vibrancy, the way the red fruit danced on his tongue. He signified his approval with a thumbs-up, and then they fell back into conversation.

Though she'd told him a lot about her life growing up in Chicago, he pushed further, learning more about her with each anecdote. The moment he told her he wanted to meet her mother, he realized he'd opened up a door he might regret. No, nothing to do with meeting her family. He would love that.

But after she admitted it might be a while before her mother visited St. Pete, she said, "The bigger question is: When am I going to meet Jack and Sadie Grant?"

Whitaker dabbed his mouth with the napkin. "Oh, you don't want to do that."

"Of course I do."

And of course he wanted to introduce her. A few months ago, he might have dodged the question. Or lied and said he would set something up, only to put it off as long as possible. Though he felt a prick of anxiety, he liked the idea of sharing her with them.

Whitaker spread the napkin back over his lap. "I'll set something up. Jack and Sadie would love to meet you."

They stayed at the restaurant for three hours, talking nonstop and enjoying superbly plated, creative, and colorful dishes that paired brilliantly with their gamay. They shared a shrimp-and-white-bean appetizer, and then she opted for the bouillabaisse. Whitaker abandoned all discipline and chose the homemade noodles with slow-braised short ribs. They didn't stop there. The bread pudding, smothered in fresh whipped cream, was the best they'd ever had, and they fought over it with their forks.

Along with their food high, Whitaker was high on Claire, and he thought it wild how far off in the distance Lisa felt. He hoped Claire felt the same about David.

It was as if Whitaker and Claire hadn't even known each other until then. They'd been so focused on the project that they hadn't let themselves explore the lighter topics, the ones so enjoyable to new lovers. No, their love wasn't love at first sight. It was more of a slow burn that had started little fires everywhere in his heart.

As they stood to leave and she put her hand on his arm, he could feel the fires uniting now, one collective wildfire burning in his soul. He didn't know much for sure in this world. He didn't even know how he would pull off the ending of David's book. But he knew that he loved Claire.

When they returned to her bungalow, Whitaker escorted her to the porch door. He found himself nervous again, two opposing voices playing tug-of-war in his head.

Amid a symphony of night sounds, Whitaker pulled her toward him. "I'll keep trying the social media angle, but I have much more faith in Laura. Let's give her a chance before we do anything else too drastic. I'm not against making our search more public, but I'm not sure we need to."

Claire drew a line with her finger from his chest to his navel and whispered, "Fingers crossed."

They kissed, and as they pulled away, she said, "I'm getting there, Whitaker. Trust me."

"I know you are." He put his cheek to hers. "I'm not going anywhere."

As he returned to the Rover, a smile rushed over him. He couldn't put a finger on it, but tons of good was coming. Out of this whole mess he'd made, something wonderful was well on its way.

⌇

With a cup of coffee and two fried eggs in front of him, Whitaker pondered Claire's request from the night before. She wanted to meet his parents. What a loaded idea. But he wasn't as opposed to the notion as he'd thought he might be. The typist might have pushed a meeting off for days, weeks, or even months. But that skin had been shed.

In its place, the writer felt nearly eager to share his current life with his parents. The last time he'd seen them, he'd scurried out of the yacht club with the sad news of Lisa's engagement. And he'd certainly felt their eyes on him during his absurd and most certainly childish retreat.

"What did we do wrong in raising him?" Jack had probably asked Sadie once Whitaker had left, begging the server for another drink.

"Oh, Jack, he's still growing up; that's all."

"He has gray hairs. I was fighting for my country at half his age." His grip would have tightened around his empty glass. "I swear to God, kids these days."

Whitaker had spent too long wondering how that conversation had gone. But now he just wanted them to be involved. To meet Claire, to hear the story of Whitaker and Claire's journey. And to share their incredible discovery that Oliver was alive.

For a second, as he cut into a deliciously runny yolk, Whitaker wondered why he wasn't more hesitant. Sure, there was a possibility that Jack could say the wrong thing. He most certainly would embarrass Whitaker to no end. But it didn't really matter.

Whitaker liked Claire, and he wanted to share her with the ones he loved. And he did love his parents. So damn much. Perhaps all the grief he had with his giant family had been of his own making. Perhaps he was the problem. Either way, that was all in the past. With this new lens on life, Whitaker reached for his phone.

"Mom, good morning."

"Hey, sugar. Aren't you up nice and early."

Whitaker found himself surprised that he didn't feel suddenly defensive. The typist might have said, "I get up early every morning to write." But, no, the writer said, "I know. Actually, I woke up feeling so alive today. I don't know what's gotten into me."

His ex-wife might have told him she was his biggest fan, but in truth that role had always been filled by his mother. With her pom-poms shaking, Sadie cheered, "I love to hear that! I know you've been going through some stuff. And I've tried to call."

"I know you have. Thank you for worrying about me. I had a little setback but feeling much more together now. Actually, I wanted to see if you and Dad wanted to come over this weekend for dinner. I'd like you to meet Claire."

A pause, the lull between waves. Whitaker imagined Sadie raising her hands as if he'd made a touchdown. Then setting her pom-poms down and doing a toe touch. "Let's go, Whitaker. Let's go!"

Unable to contain herself, Sadie jumped down from her cheerleading stunt and said, "We'd love to meet Claire. And Saturday night is great for us. Your dad is fishing earlier, but he'll be back shortly after lunch."

"Excellent." And Whitaker found himself scratching his head, wondering where his sarcasm had gone. He was actually excited.

When he hung up, he cut into his egg again. "Walter, what's gotten into me?"

In his stately tone, Walter replied, "We're all glad to have you back, young Whitaker."

Once the caffeine had fully kicked in, Whitaker realized what he'd just committed to. Sure, he'd been keeping a neater house as of late. But not neat enough for the rendezvous spot for Staff Sergeant Jack Grant and Sadie to meet Claire. He had four days and knew he'd better make the best of them. The writing could take a back seat for a while.

First and foremost, the outside needed some serious attention. Had there been an HOA in his neighborhood, they would have thrown him out years ago. Pulling on some cutoff shorts and beat-up tennis shoes, Whitaker left the house and walked shirtless to the shed. Lizards dashed away as he pulled open the plastic door. The smell of mildew hit him hard. Though he hadn't planned on it, he decided that cleaning out the shed needed to be his first order of business. He removed everything.

Once he'd filled his trash can with useless dried-up cans of paint, old plastic pots, and unknown chemicals due to their labels fading or having peeled off, he filled his push mower with gas and got started.

A John Deere might have been a better choice, as the little mower had to work extra hard to cut down the jungle he'd let go wild. But she eventually got the job done. He moved on to the Weed eater and trimmer, working all the way around the house, bringing his humble abode back to life.

Proud of how things were turning out, he made two trips to Home Depot to pick up outdoor furniture, mulch, a few plants and flowers, and even some touch-up paint for the columns on the front porch. By the time the sun was setting, Whitaker collapsed into his bed with a sense of pride tucking him in.

The following day, a pot of coffee led him into his second project. The inside. Yes, he'd gotten rid of the filth that the typist had been dwelling in, but it was still nowhere near where it needed to be. He carried out several awful pieces of furniture that belonged in a frat house. He moved the other furniture and rolled-up rugs to vacuum and polish the floors. He cleaned out the refrigerator and scrubbed down the kitchen and bathroom. It was another all-day affair, but he felt invigorated doing it, like this was the last missing piece in rediscovering his true self. Instead of finding himself repulsed at what he'd been, he held on to the excitement of where he was going.

On Friday, he ran all over town, shopping for new furniture, bedsheets, new dishes, and silverware. It was time to start living up to the man he wanted to be. After a string of more errands after lunch, he stopped by two local art galleries and fell in love with three pieces he ended up taking home. As the sun came down Friday night, he toured his house with a great smile on his face. In three days, he'd turned what had been a post-divorce prison into a house he was happy to live in and to welcome people into.

On Saturday morning, he went for a long run and then rode over to the farmers market, which had just moved from the waterfront location over to Williams Park for the summer. He picked up what he needed for the night's meal and also some more flowers for inside. Ending his exhausting four-day makeover, he swung by his wine cellar on the way home.

By the time Claire knocked on the door a few minutes before five Saturday night, the house was in the best shape it had ever been, and Whitaker was in the kitchen in his apron stirring the beurre manié into his favorite preparation of coq au vin, a dish he'd obsessed over while living in Paris in his twenties.

He walked casually to the front door, pulled it open, and breathed her in. Claire wore an off-shoulder knee-length white dress, and her hair was pulled back into a ponytail. It took a moment for him to grasp that they were now a thing.

"You look lovely." Whitaker took her hand and kissed her and smelled the jasmine of her perfume.

Claire walked inside. "Oh my gosh, is this why you've been hiding all week? Your place looks . . . like not your place." She stopped in the living room and turned back to him. "Bravo, Whitaker."

"I'm glad you like it." He pointed to the wall on his left, by the entrance to the hall. "What do you think?"

She followed his finger to the photograph of the manatee she'd given him framed in reclaimed wood. "Oh, it looks great."

"Now I can pass by it every time I go into my office to write. A reminder of my muse."

Claire smiled and spun around. "And new furniture? I actually like your house now. It's adorable. And you have great taste. Have you been watching too much HGTV?"

"I've seen a few episodes lately. Wait until you see the backyard."

The doorbell rang, and they both turned. Whitaker took a long, slow breath. "Here we go."

He pulled back the door. "Hi, guys. Welcome."

"You shaved!" Sadie exclaimed.

They shuffled through the door in their country club attire, and Whitaker introduced them to Claire. In what Whitaker considered a bold move, Claire hugged Sadie and then Jack. "It's a pleasure, Mr. and Mrs. Grant."

Jack's sunburned and stern face melted into a smile as he briefly removed his veteran's hat. "It's so nice to meet you, Claire. Please call me Jack."

"Yes, sir. And thank you for your service."

Claire might as well have picked him up and placed him in the palm of her hand, a tiny replica of the army man, a G.I. Joe. "You're welcome," he said, with the pride he duly deserved.

"I don't want to embarrass Whitaker," Sadie told Claire, "but you must be the one he's cleaned his act up for." She made a show of looking around the living room as they moved farther inside the house. "I am just so impressed."

"I am too," Claire confessed. "He's really turned it around."

Sadie shook her head. "The last time I was here—"

Whitaker stepped forward, smoothing his hands together. "All right, everyone. Let's not make this entire evening about picking on Whitaker. We haven't even had a sip of wine yet, and I'm already blushing."

In the kitchen, Whitaker uncorked a rather blousy Meursault that he knew his mother would enjoy. They gathered around the island as he poured the glasses.

"I'm so happy to see you wearing an apron again," Sadie said. "What's on the menu tonight?"

Whitaker pulled the top off the dutch oven, and a blast of steam and savory aromas rose into the air. "I thought we'd go French tonight. Coq au vin. Then cheese and a salad to finish off."

Sadie spun her glass. "I'm surprised you still knew how to turn on the stove."

"Well," Whitaker said, "I did learn cooking is *not* like riding a bike. It took me a little while to get back into the swing of things. Nearly cut my finger off earlier." He showed them a Band-Aid wrapped around his index finger.

"Well, I'd say you're off to a good start," Jack said, glancing at the cheese and charcuterie board Whitaker had prepared.

"Thanks. So before we eat, I thought we could sit out back and chat for a while. Claire and I have so much we can't wait to share."

Leading them outside, Whitaker looked past the small patio with his new furniture to the short green grass and then the fresh mulch running up against the fence. Feeling a nice breeze, he eyed the clouds rolling in from the east. A perfect night to sit outside, as long as those clouds didn't bring rain.

Descending the back steps, Claire asked, "Where are all the wild things? Did a landscaper come over?"

"It was all me, believe it or not."

"But where will the grasshoppers go?"

"They're welcome to stay if they'd like."

The breeze picked up.

"I'm really impressed," Claire admitted. "Actually, I'm surprised you even know *how* to start a lawn mower." Whitaker could tell she was putting on a show, trying to light Jack up.

It worked. If Jack hadn't been convinced by her yet, she'd surely won him over now. He grunted with joy. "Believe it or not, Claire, this young man used to help me keep the finest yard in the neighborhood. We were like a platoon of the army's finest out there every weekend."

Whitaker shook his head as they sat around the table and umbrella. Why resist? "I don't know what happened to me. Books pulled me away from small engines and landscaping. But fear not. I have returned and am quite eager to spend my Saturdays like most humans in America. My forties will be the decade I fell in love with yard work."

Ready to move on, Whitaker turned to his left. "You might know Claire's restaurant, Leo's South, at the beach?"

"Oh, sure," Jack said. "Now I like you even more. I've eaten there a few times over the years."

After a few minutes of restaurant talk, Claire said, "And Jack, I hear you're a fisherman."

"Yep, as a matter of fact, I took some clients out today."

"How'd you do?"

"We slayed 'em. A big grouper and five red snappers. The season just started, thank goodness. It would have hurt to throw them back."

"You should have brought some over, Dad."

Jack turned to Whitaker. "Last time I brought you fish, you let them rot in your fridge."

Whitaker raised his hands up in peace. "Fair point."

Jack turned back to Claire. "If you eat fish, I'd love to share some with you. Red snapper is about my favorite."

As Claire assured him she would love some, Whitaker looked at his mother and grinned. What else could you do when you were dealing with Jack Grant?

They focused on Claire for a while and eventually reached the topic of the book. Whitaker grabbed another bottle of chardonnay and they told the entire story, starting from Claire's knock on his door.

What struck Whitaker most about that night was the question Jack asked once the story had been told. Each word did what many of Jack's did, Thor's hammer dropping down. But this time they were words of encouragement.

As Jack and Sadie were still trying to wrap their heads around the story and the fact that Oliver was a real boy, Jack leaned in, bouncing his eyes back and forth between Whitaker and Claire. "What can we do to help you find him?"

Whitaker had never loved his father more.

Chapter 33

The Skyline of Havana

Claire had been sure that she was the worst to dance salsa in the history of the Gulfport Casino, but as she watched Whitaker attempt to follow the instructor, she knew otherwise. Whitaker had no rhythm and so little control of his feet, she wondered how he even managed to walk.

But you know what? It didn't matter. She'd never laughed so much in her life, and she liked that he could handle the ridicule. Even Didi was having a hard time concentrating and had one eye on Whitaker's penguin feet fumbling about.

Now into the second week of June, it had been two weeks since Claire and Whitaker's first date, and they'd spent nearly every day together. Claire couldn't believe it, but she was falling in love. Not falling . . . she was right into the depths of it, at the bottom of the canyon of love after a long descent, as Whitaker might say. He was an explosion of color that she welcomed and couldn't do without. As she watched him dance like a fool and laugh like a child, she knew that he had come into her life for a much bigger reason than finishing David's novel. And she'd learned that behind all his fun and games stood a man of substance. Whitaker would never replace David, but Claire was intent on loving Whitaker in a new and different way.

Three days before, per Laura's suggestion, they had agreed to fingerprinting and background checks. Considering they'd had no luck working the social media angle, the woman's request felt like a great break in the search. When Whitaker had asked Laura if she was making progress, she said, "I can't make any promises right now."

After the instructor moved to the next couple, Claire asked, "How can someone who speaks fluent Spanish, among several other languages, possess no dancing skills whatsoever?"

Whitaker took no offense and said with a smile, "That's like saying just because you can speak Russian you can dance *The Nutcracker*."

"I would pay a lot of money to see you dance *The Nutcracker*. Even more money to see you in a leotard." The image drew a smile.

"Baby steps, Claire. Baby steps."

As the next track came on and the Latin beat set the pace, she asked, "Well, shall we make an attempt?"

Whitaker moved into ready position, his hands in the air, waiting for her. "Let's do this."

After attending for several months now, she was starting to get the hang of the dance. She counted for him, encouraging him along. "Forward, two, three. Back, two, three. There you go, not as bad as I thought."

"Oh, c'mon. Cubans everywhere are cringing."

"That's not true," Claire assured him. "I can almost see the skyline of Havana in your eyes."

He smiled and kissed her. "Look who should be the writer."

After the class, Claire, Whitaker, and Didi rode together to one of Claire's favorite restaurants, Chief's Creole Café, in an area known as the "Deuces" on Twenty-Second Street. During segregation, this part of town was the bustling Main Street for the black community, and just up the road the Manhattan Casino had hosted some of the most important names in show business, including Duke Ellington, Louis Armstrong, Nat King Cole, and James Brown. Now this neighborhood was making a comeback.

They walked past the giant mural of Louis and his trumpet on the side of the restaurant and walked through the open gates. Mr. B, one of the owners, chatted them up for a while and then sat them outside under the pergola. A bottle of Crystal Hot Sauce graced every table.

Sipping on sweet tea, they snacked on the complimentary fried okra, chatted casually, and perused the menu of New Orleans fare. They ordered the jambalaya, the crawfish étouffée, a shrimp po'boy, and beignets to share.

Claire popped an okra into her mouth. "So what's new with you, Didi? I'm sorry I've been distant." Claire hadn't called her friend in more than a week.

"Oh, I get it. You two have been busy. And clearly developing a little thing."

Blushing, Claire took Whitaker's hand, and they met eyes. The guilt she'd felt when they'd first kissed had all but gone away, and in its stead she found such wonderful comfort in knowing they had each other. "This man has certainly gotten my attention."

Whitaker leaned over to kiss her. "And you mine."

Didi clapped her hands together. "Oh, how happy this makes me."

Claire broke away from their kiss and turned to Didi. "So where's your Spanish lover?"

"Long gone. There's just too many men in the world. I can't seem to stop."

"You broke his heart?"

"I'm sorry to say that I ripped his heart out and crumbled it in my hands, if I'm being honest." She dropped her head. "He's *still* calling me."

Claire couldn't imagine living Didi's roller-coaster life, especially when it came to dating and men. She turned to the only man she needed. "Imagine a younger, better-looking Antonio Banderas. That's whose heart she broke."

Whitaker inclined his head. "I'm not sure anyone is better looking than Antonio Banderas."

Didi threw her hands up in the air. "Oh, he was great, but there are plenty more. Who wants Spanish food every night? I love jamón as much as the next girl, but sometimes I'm craving doner kebab . . . or wiener schnitzel, sometimes beef bourguignon."

Whitaker and Claire died laughing. More power to Didi if that was her thing.

Mr. B sat another party nearby as Didi added with lower volume, "And sometimes, a good-old-fashioned hamburger."

"That's a lot of protein," Claire said, wiping her eyes.

Didi touched her chest and batted her eyelashes.

Whitaker measured an inch with his thumb and forefinger. "And sometimes you crave crawfish and shrimp."

Didi shook her head amid the laughter. "You're the one that ordered the shrimp. I'm a lobster girl." She held her two hands out, well past shoulder's distance.

Claire and Whitaker laughed to tears as Didi regaled them with stories of chasing men around the globe. In the middle of Didi's story about a date with a Hollywood celebrity, Claire noticed Whitaker's muted phone light up on the table. She knew exactly who it was and nearly lost her breath.

When Whitaker saw that it was Laura from the local child-placement agency calling, he quickly excused himself and took the call as he walked farther up the sidewalk. A white egret with its long neck and legs was poking its way up the sidewalk ahead of him.

"Sorry it's so late, but I have really good news," Laura said. "I've located Oliver and spoken with him. He agreed to meet with you."

Whitaker's eyes watered, as if the entire world suddenly made sense. "What?"

"I found him a few days ago but had to get his permission before we moved forward. Can you and Claire meet him tomorrow?"

Whitaker turned and started back toward the table. "Yes, definitely. Where? What time?"

"Bay Vista Park at the end of Fourth Street South. Nine o'clock in the morning. He'll be with his case manager. I'll text you her number once we get off the phone."

"Thank you so much, Laura. This means everything to us."

"Just take care of Oliver. That's all that matters to me. I don't know what you're expecting, but he's been through a lot. Just know that. Okay?"

"Absolutely."

Her tone turned more somber. "I've told him about David's passing. He needed to be prepared."

"How'd he take it?"

"He's a tough kid, as many are in the system. But it certainly tore him up. He's looking forward to meeting Claire. I think he has a lot of questions."

I think everyone does, Whitaker thought. "Where has he been?"

"He's been living with a great foster family near the park. Been with them for two years now, and he seems happy and stabilized. That's why you need to proceed carefully."

"We will. I promise." Whitaker realized how little he understood about the life of a foster child. No amount of research could paint a true picture. He thanked Laura, said goodbye, and returned to the table.

The women were staring at him.

Whitaker couldn't help but smile at their victory. "She found Oliver. And we're meeting him at Bay Vista Park down south at nine tomorrow morning." He put his hands on Claire's shoulders while she was still seated. "We did it, Claire." He could feel the tension running through her.

~

"You haven't spent the night with him yet?" Didi asked, driving Claire back to Pass-a-Grille.

"Not yet, no."

"What are you waiting for? If you don't want him, I'll take him." Didi pressed the pedal hard as the light turned green.

"I want him," Claire said. "We're just taking it slow."

"Nothing wrong with that. I think you two make an adorable couple." Didi put up her hand at the person driving in front of her. "Get in the right lane, slowpoke!"

"Trust me. I like him a lot. Just working through the last of my stuff. He knows how I feel about him."

Didi glanced at Claire. "Are you terrified about tomorrow?"

Claire breathed in the heavy question. "Even Whitaker couldn't put into words the trepidation I feel."

"It's going to be all right."

"I know . . ." Claire hoped so desperately that Oliver was David's only secret. It was the only one she could possibly bear. "There's still this nagging feeling eating at me. What if I find something out that destroys my love for him?"

"You may." Didi switched lanes again. "But something tells me you will love him twice as much after tomorrow."

Claire smiled and lost herself in the stars. That was a nice thought. Either way, she wouldn't miss this meeting for the world.

Chapter 34

THE SILVER LINING

In a weak attempt to distract Claire from her morning thoughts, Whitaker pointed out a Tampa Bay Rays player's waterfront home on the way to Bay Vista Park. It didn't work. She had a one-track mind and couldn't believe this was actually happening. Reaching the southeastern tip of St. Pete, they pulled into the parking lot of the park, which was on Tampa Bay.

A gazebo stood at the end of a long pier that faced the Sunshine Skyway Bridge, which had taken them to Sarasota almost three weeks before. People were making good use of the park today. A line of trucks with boat trailers waited to ease their boat down the landing. The playground was full of kids swinging on the swings, climbing the towers, and sliding down poles.

As she reached for the car door handle, a tsunami of anxiety hit her. To think it all came down to this.

"I don't see him," Claire said, scanning the park through the windshield as her skin tingled.

"They'll be here." He put his hand on her arm. "Remember, as nervous as we are, he is too. He's been through a lot."

Snapping the car doors shut, they crossed into the lush grass. Claire scrutinized the people around the playground. No kids old enough to be him. Then she saw him near the seawall.

Finding it suddenly hard to breathe, she pointed and muttered, "I think that's him." Actually, she knew it was him.

Whitaker followed her gaze toward the sheltered picnic tables on the southern end of the park.

A woman and a boy were standing up from one of the picnic tables. Claire knew the woman was Kari, Oliver's case manager. She was dressed like a teacher in blue pants and a blue-and-white striped shirt. Oliver wore a baseball shirt, mesh shorts, and bright running shoes.

Claire's throat closed for a second, and her heart scraped at her rib cage. Amid the nervous jitters pecking at every part of her, the fear of potentially learning things she'd rather not know, she also felt a good deal of excitement, like this adventure she'd been on since finding the composition books had led her to this exact moment.

They walked in silence toward Oliver and his case manager. Though the boy in the photograph was eleven, the young man standing before them was one and the same. He was taller than in the photo, maybe three inches shorter than Whitaker. He had brilliantly blue eyes that looked both curious and skeptical. His hair was the same as it was in the photo, straight and long, long enough to cover his eyes if he didn't push it to the right. He was a good-looking boy, still so young. Too cute to be called a man, still a few months from sprouting. Awkward he was, but only because everyone was awkward at fourteen.

Claire said the first words. "You must be Oliver." She reached for his hand, and he shook weakly, averting his eyes. She instantly thought of the pictures she'd scanned through back at the hotel in Sarasota. Why wasn't he among them? Did he not want to be adopted?

After introductions, Kari gestured toward the picnic table. "Why don't we sit down?"

"That's a great idea," Claire said, trying to sound upbeat and positive.

Claire and Whitaker sat opposite Oliver and his case manager. Two men were playing a game of chess at one of the tables under a gazebo.

"They told you about David?" Whitaker asked.

A nod, Oliver's sadness coming through.

Claire and Whitaker had already put together that no one had told Oliver about David, and they could only assume he had been left wondering for three long years.

"I'm so sorry you had to find out this way," Claire said, a foreign feeling rising up inside of her, something so distant she couldn't place it at first, but it was powerful and thrilling.

"That's okay."

Whitaker took over. "We're still trying to put the pieces together, but you knew him for a while, it sounds like."

"A year or so."

These short answers were breaking her heart. Claire had forgotten what it was like to be fourteen, but hearing the boy's high-pitched yet changing voice reminded her. Fourteen was when you were finally finding yourself, growing into your body, discovering your identity.

"Did you have any idea what happened to him?" Claire asked, already knowing the sad answer.

Oliver shrugged. "I don't know." He looked to the parking lot and back again. "I thought he was mad at me."

"Didn't you have a way to get in touch with him?"

"Yeah, my case manager—the one back then—had his number. But I didn't want to call him and bother him."

"He didn't run off on you," Claire assured him. "Is that what you thought?"

Oliver nodded, and the foreign feeling, still unidentifiable, rose up her spine.

Everyone took a long breath, barely hearing the noises from the playground.

"Let's back up," Whitaker said. "Do you know who we are?"

"Kari told me. You're a writer." Oliver glanced at Claire, his eyes still darting and insecure. "You're Claire. I recognize you from the photos on David's desk."

Her heart suddenly burned, the other feeling going away. "I don't know where to start, Oliver. He never told me about you."

"I know."

"What do you mean, you know?"

Oliver looked at the table. "He wanted to tell you for a long time. Couldn't figure out how."

"What was the big deal?" Claire heard anger in her voice and reminded herself to calm down.

He shook his head, eyes still down. "He just said you were sad about never being a mom."

Claire tightened her face, controlling the rush of emotions.

"But David was going to tell you," Oliver assured her, like he was standing up for him. "We were supposed to go to your house for dinner one night. He wanted me to meet you."

"What happened?"

"He never came to get me. I didn't see him again."

Claire's voice cracked as she asked, "Was that in February? Three years ago."

Oliver thought for a moment. "I think so."

The entire weight of the world came dropping down on top of her. "That's the day he died, Oliver. I'm sure of it. He told me he was bringing someone over." She set her hands on the table. "Of course it was you. He was hit by a drunk driver around four o'clock. On February 18."

Oliver crossed his arms and squinted, looking past Claire's shoulder to nowhere. Claire could tell he was counting back. Oliver choked up, and his eyes grew wet. He was pressing his mouth together, fighting off a cry. He turned right, looking at the gravel bed below.

Everyone let him process the news.

For more than three years, she'd wondered who was supposed to have dinner with them. And Oliver was the answer. David *was* going to tell her about him.

"I thought he just—" Oliver stopped and shook his head, biting down hard on his emotions. Kari put a comforting hand on his back.

"I thought he was mad at me and decided he didn't want me to meet you."

"No, honey," Claire said. "He never would have done that. From what I can tell, he cared about you so much." That foreign feeling came rushing back, but more familiar now. It was love but different somehow.

Oliver was floored by the news, his whole body folding in.

"After the accident," Claire said, "the police found a Yankees hat wrapped up as a gift in his car. Was that for you? Are you a Yankees fan?"

A tear nearly shot out of his eye. "Yeah." His lip trembled.

Claire's heart ached, feeling the boy's pain from across the table, a lifetime of fighting to survive, fighting to find a place in the world. Bad news, death, abandonment. It was all he knew. She was witnessing a boy discover that he hadn't been abandoned after all, that the world maybe wasn't as bad as it seemed. Or was it? David was still dead.

In the silence that followed, she heard an engine starting up on one of the boats near the landing.

Oliver rubbed his eyes, still climbing back from the news. "I thought he was just like all the others."

Tears flowed like waterfalls from the adults. Claire swallowed, now knowing exactly what the foreign feeling was. It was the inner mother inside of her trying to escape, the instincts she had suppressed so deeply that she'd forgotten about them. Until now. Looking back at Oliver, she saw him as his mother might, and her heart ached for him.

"Who could blame you?" Whitaker asked, wiping his eyes. "No one knew to tell you. Claire didn't know anything about you until recently."

As Claire processed her years of running from the mother within her, Whitaker told Oliver briefly about the book, then added, "Apparently, you meant everything to David. He was writing a book about you. Not exactly about you, but based on your relationship with David. We think you really changed his life."

"Yeah, I knew about the book," Oliver said. "He talked about it sometimes."

"What did he say?" Claire asked, caught off guard once again at how well Oliver possibly knew David.

"Just that he was writing a story with me in it. Like, you know, a kid based off me."

Whitaker took over. "He didn't finish it, but the kid is in trouble in the book. Were you in some kind of trouble?"

Oliver looked at Kari and back to Whitaker. "No, I wasn't in any kind of trouble."

"But you said you and David had gotten in an argument."

Oliver nodded. "I had skipped a baseball game, and he started lecturing me. I didn't like it. So we got in a fight. It was the day before I was supposed to meet Claire. That was the last time I saw him. He dropped me off at the group home and told me he'd be back the next day to take me to meet Claire. I was kind of a jerk but told him I'd still go."

Claire squeezed Whitaker's hand and asked Oliver, "I don't understand why he didn't give me a heads-up that you were coming, at least. Why the surprise?"

Oliver shrugged. "I don't know . . ."

She could tell he was holding something back. "What is it?"

With his eyes back on the table, Oliver muttered, "I really don't know . . ."

Claire's heart stopped. Had David wanted to adopt this young man? Was that the unspoken truth? Of course it was. She could have been this boy's mother! No wonder these feelings were coming at her so hard.

Attempting to collect herself, she said in a shaky voice, "He should have told me about you from the beginning." And Claire had to ask.

"Was there anything else he was keeping from me? I guess you wouldn't know."

Oliver glanced at her and shook his head.

This young boy might have been her son. It was all too much, the revelations, the deception.

Thankfully, Whitaker stepped in. "He took you to a baseball game down in Sarasota? What was that all about?"

"The Yankees, Orioles, yeah. How'd you know?"

Coming back to reality, Claire dug into her purse. "The only reason we're here is because we found this picture in his desk." She slid it across the table.

Oliver stared at it for a long time. "I can't believe he's dead. And I've spent all these years hating him." He kept staring at the photo until a smile came.

"Was it a good day?" Whitaker asked.

Oliver looked at him, much brighter this time. "The best. Are you kidding me? Starlin Castro hit one out of the park at the bottom of the eighth, bases loaded. I jumped up and spilled my hot dog all over David, ketchup and relish and everything."

He handed the picture back to Claire.

She shook her head. "No, it's yours. You keep it, please."

Oliver pulled it back with a thanks.

Needing a break from the intensity, Claire asked, "Where do you live? What's your life like now? We tried to find you at the Oakwood House." She couldn't believe she was talking to a boy who might have become her son if David had not been killed. How would she have reacted when they'd come in the door? She wasn't sure.

"Oh, yeah," Oliver said. "That was a long time ago. I'm with a family now."

"You're adopted?" Claire asked with a shaky voice.

"No, I'm living with a foster family. Very different than a group home. There's five of us in there right now."

In a soft, exhausted voice, Claire asked, "Can I ask where your parents are?" Maybe the answer could help Claire understand him.

Oliver looked at Kari, who was dabbing her forehead with a handkerchief, then back at Claire. "Whoever my father is, he doesn't know I exist. My mom's somewhere up in Georgia, in and out of jail. She's an addict."

Claire's bottom lip jutted out. "When's the last time you saw her?"

"Two years ago. She tried to get me back, but then went bad again. Her rights were terminated when I was twelve."

Claire found herself nodding at the strength of this young man. "That's gotta be tough."

"It happens."

So many questions, but they couldn't drill him forever. They talked for twenty more minutes, much lighter conversation exploring his world. Oliver told them that he loved sports, but baseball was his favorite. He also loved food and cooking. And he had really good grades. Claire wanted to clap for him as he talked about the good in his life.

Then Kari said they had to leave.

Whitaker looked across the table. "Do you think we could meet again, Oliver? Claire has asked me to finish David's book, so we can get it out there. A testament to David, a way to remember him. I have a feeling you could help." Whitaker looked at Claire. "And I know Claire would like to visit with you more."

Claire nodded. "Absolutely."

"Can we take you out for a bite to eat sometime?" Whitaker asked. "The boy in the book loves hamburgers. Do you?"

"Yeah, for sure."

"Then I've got the spot. But first I'd love to—" He corrected himself. "*We'd* love to meet your foster parents and see your place. See what your life is like. Would that be okay?"

"Yeah, I think so."

"How about this? I'll reach out to Kari later today and go from there."

Oliver agreed, and Claire wasn't sure whether she'd ever see him again.

It wasn't until they were back in the Rover and pulling back onto Fourth that Claire snapped, completely breaking down. With her elbows pressing down on her thighs, she cried into her hands. So many lies. For months. Had she been connected at all to David in their marriage? And to think she might have been a mother. To think that boy could have been her son. If he'd just told her from the beginning, everything might have been different.

Chapter 35

SALT WATER IN THE WOUND

Claire was supposed to go straight to the restaurant after their meeting with Oliver. That didn't happen. Barely able to make it inside her front door, she dropped her glasses on the coffee table and trudged through the living room and into the bedroom. Her whole world throbbed, the pain of David's secret life drowning her, drowning her sudden rediscovery of motherhood. Maybe this was the only lie he'd ever told her, but it was an epic deception, something she certainly couldn't forgive easily.

What made him think he should keep Oliver a secret for a year and then suddenly spring him on her as a surprise guest? Had he thought she wouldn't understand unless she actually met the boy? *Give me a little credit, David!*

She didn't know what was worse. His decision to lie about Oliver—essentially treating her like an immature child—or her part in his death. Fury and guilt wrestled for her attention. If she hadn't been so caught up in her own self-pity, he wouldn't have felt a need to keep Oliver's existence a secret, and he wouldn't have been in his car at that exact moment on his way to pick up Oliver. Her selfishness had murdered him!

Dropping onto the bed, she hammered a pillow with her fists until she had nothing left. Then, exhausted, she curled into the fetal position and wept. Willy jumped up, and she pulled him in close. She cried about her own selfishness at first. How could she have been so self-involved, closed off, and unreceptive that she'd taken away David's dream? What kind of partner was she?

The first lesson you learned in marriage was that you couldn't put yourself first. You were supposed to both give equally and put aside yourself for the collective. She hadn't done that. She'd been in so much pain over David's infertility that she'd been unable to see past it, unable to breathe through it, like the serpent of infertility strangling her. Her selfishness had strangled the mother she could have been. Claire was right back to where she'd been when they had first learned of his weak sperm and low count, back when she was holding her own head under-water, drowning herself.

The first few months of "trying" were not exactly tough, but bear-able. "Be patient," David had said, after their first negative pregnancy test, the one after she was sure she was experiencing morning sickness and had begun daydreaming of cute baby outfits. They tried again and again, one negative test after another. They were timing their sex as per-fectly as possible, and after any rather forced session, she would spend thirty minutes with her legs high up in the air.

Then the doctors' visits and the tests, the mother inside of her los-ing faith.

Claire remembered stumbling out of their fertility doctor's office in silence. Unless she left David, which wasn't an option, she was not going to be a mom. What a bitter pill to swallow.

Only when David had broken down in the car, telling her between bouts of crying that he was sorry he couldn't give her the life she'd always dreamed of, did she feel his pain. She was able to pull her head out of her own sadness for long enough to understand. He'd felt like a failure. She'd been able to see it in the way his shoulders had shaken while he'd cried into his hands. She'd been able to see his manliness crumbling.

She'd pulled him in and hugged him and told him it was okay, that she wasn't angry; maybe it was meant to be. She'd meant it. She couldn't stand seeing David in so much pain, and he didn't deserve it, and she was determined not to let herself blame him.

She'd whispered into his wet neck and shaking shoulders that they would work with the doctors and do whatever it took. Turned out, doing whatever it took didn't guarantee a baby.

Claire cried harder, feeling that emptiness, that missing part of her.

Perhaps subconsciously, she had blamed him. But she'd never told him anything other than "It will be okay. What's meant to be will happen." Even as she had said the words, though, she had wondered if they were true.

As those lonely months had passed by, as their desperate attempts failed, one after another, Claire remembered losing touch with who she was. That sadness had turned to anger and defeat. When they'd signed the first papers moving forward with adoption, she hadn't been excited like many potential parents might be. She'd already pushed herself back under the water for the last time, sealing her fate.

Claire had missed the most important part. He'd had dreams too. Of being a father. Of raising a child. Of being a young one's hero. Of giving a little one the tools with which to take on the world. Little did she know she'd been holding him under the water too.

After they'd hit the first snag with their adoption process, she'd told him to let it go. She couldn't keep trying. Another fail would have ended her.

Ended them.

She'd barely considered what he'd been going through. How could she hate him for keeping Oliver from her when it was her own selfishness that had led them to a childless life? They could have adopted! As she now understood, there were so many children who needed them.

Curled up on the bed with Willy in her bungalow on the beach, Claire cried and cried, and could feel her lungs filling with water, almost as if her body were gasping for its last breaths.

And only after her body and soul were dried up did she fall into a sad sleep. She woke hours later to a thunderstorm, fed Willy dinner, drank a glass of water, and returned to bed. While she settled back into her brokenhearted coma, her phone rang in her purse in the living room. She didn't bother. The phone kept ringing and dinging with calls and texts as lightning flashed through the windows.

At daybreak, Claire felt the sun splash through the window onto her bare back. The sun had no right to shine today. She closed the blinds, shutting out the world, and crawled back into the bed, wallowing in despair.

Then a knock on the door. And several more. She heard Whitaker calling her name.

All cried out by now, she stared at the white of the ceiling and waited for him to stop knocking. To leave her alone. To let her find her own way back.

Sometime later, she climbed out of bed and went toward the porch. She needed to see the sun, to breathe the salt breeze.

Whitaker was sitting in a rocking chair reading *The Good Earth*. The ground was wet and lush from the rain the night before.

"What are you doing here?" she asked, pressing open the screen door to the porch, wiping her eyes, wishing away the darkness covering her face.

One-Eyed Willy slipped past her and jumped onto Whitaker's lap.

Whitaker put down the book and gave the cat some attention. "Checking on you."

"How long have you been here?"

"All morning. Didn't you hear me knocking?"

Whitaker set Willy and the book on the table and stood and hugged her. "I know this is tough, but please don't shut me out," he whispered.

Silence. He had no idea how tough this was.

"What can I do for you?" He took her hand and met her eyes.

Claire turned her head toward the street. An old VW van with a paddleboard on top crept by. "There's nothing you can do."

"I tried to call you last night. I talked to Oliver's foster mom. She said he was free this afternoon at three. I texted you the address."

Claire nodded, biting down on a bitter rising cry. "I can't. Not right now."

"What do you mean you can't? Claire, we found him. Don't you want to talk to him?"

"Yes, of course. But not today." She started inside, holding the door for him, indicating for him to follow.

"I'm not going to see him without you."

Claire pivoted and faced him in the center of the living room. Whitaker was being gentle, but she felt a red rage on the verge of eruption, the kind of anger that didn't care where it was pointed. She crossed her arms. "Why do you need to go see him? So you can finish the book? So you can go and get famous again—off David's story this time?"

He side-eyed her. "How could you say that? Forget the damn story. I'm invested in Oliver. And apparently I'm the only one."

"How dare you!" she snapped. How dare he assume anything about her. He had no idea what it was like to experience your partner die. To open the door to a policeman with red eyes and the saddest news in the world. The only struggle he'd ever known was his privileged little fight to be a writer, to chase his calling.

Whitaker moved to her and opened his arms. "I'm sorry. I didn't mean that."

Well aware of her irrationality, she turned away. When he tried to touch her, she shook him off. "You will never understand. Honestly, you need to leave. It will only get worse from here."

"What the hell does that mean?"

"Just go, Whitaker."

"Claire," he said, stepping away from her, "it's not about you." He talked to her back. "I'm sorry to be a jerk, but it's not. Not anymore. I am so sorry you lost your husband. I can't imagine. But don't you see there's something larger at play here than your loss? David was doing something special. He gave hope to a boy that didn't have any. He showed him what it was like to be loved. I can say this to you because I'm just as guilty most of the time: stop thinking about yourself and think about Oliver. Think about all the good your husband did for this boy. Stop thinking about how your husband lied to you. He was trying to find his own happiness while protecting you at the same time. He was trying to do good. He didn't tell you because you might not have been able to handle it. He didn't tell you because he loved you."

Claire didn't like being spoken to this way. Her dried-up tear ducts ground like an engine without oil. Anger, fear, sadness, regret. Guilt.

She finally spun toward him. "Don't you think I know all that? And don't talk to me like you knew David. Just because you read his book doesn't give you the right."

"I've done more than read his book." Venom filled his eyes. "And I think I've been closer to him than you have the past six months."

How dare he.

"Get out!" she screamed.

Whitaker raised his hands, repeatedly pressing his palms down. "Calm down, Claire. I'm sorry. I know you need some time."

She pointed to the door and, through clenched teeth, demanded, "I want you out of my house."

Whitaker lowered his hands slowly, his eyes on her the entire time. He nodded three times and turned. He stopped with his hand on the knob.

"If you only knew how much I cared about you. And I've tried to show you—even while you've done your best to push me away. I am all about you and me. There's nothing I want more. Not even another book deal, if that's what you're thinking. Now, I'm not saying I'm perfect. So far from it. But if you want us to happen, I need you to put in some effort." His voice dropped off. "The person I know you really are."

Then he left through the porch, the door once again snapping shut after him. Claire dropped to the rug in tears as she heard him telling Willy goodbye.

Chapter 36

The Parents with Wings

There was no way she could let him visit Oliver without her. Dodging geysers of guilt and sadness springing up all around her, she walked to the beach, hoping to find a calm patch in the madness. She sat cross-legged at the tide line and let the water wash around her, a search for healing in the waters that had once given her hope.

Though there were no miraculous miracles, Claire was reminded of that foreign feeling once again, the mother that she could have been, the mother she wished her own mother had been, a fearless woman who always pushed aside her own problems for the benefit of her son, be it Oliver or a child she carried in her own womb.

Tapping into this strength, Claire returned home with love swelling in her heart. She made it to Leo's South in time for the breakfast rush and dug in deep all the way through lunch.

Jevaun had even noticed her change. As he ran a knife through a grapefruit, he said, "You doin' all right today, yeah?"

Claire gave him a smile rich with confidence, and he nodded back—as if he knew exactly what she'd been through and where she was now.

Using the address Whitaker had texted her, Claire pulled into the drive-way behind his Land Rover. The large Italian-style house was in an afflu-ent neighborhood in the Southside called the Pink Streets, so named for the streets colored with pink dye—a way to distinguish the area, first done back in the twenties. The house had a fancy red-tile roof and was surrounded by a line of manicured hedges. An ADT Security sign poked out of the fresh mulch near the front steps.

Whitaker stood on the steps, watching her in surprise. She hadn't given him a heads-up, perhaps the last of her hardheadedness asserting itself.

Claire opened up and stepped out, and he met her halfway.

"I'm really sorry," she confessed.

He bit his lip.

"No, really. I had no right. And I didn't mean any of it. I'm just a basket case right now. We're about to walk in and see where he lives. I feel like I'm just stepping deeper and deeper into David's secret life, and I'm just terrified. That's all. It has nothing to do with you."

He pulled her into a hug. "I forgive you. And I understand. It's heavy stuff."

She squeezed and whispered another sorry.

Letting go, Whitaker said, "I'm glad you came."

"I guess I have no right to be mad at you for going without me."

He touched her chin. "I think I've been beat up enough for the day."

After knocking on the door, Claire heard some commotion before a brunette in a USF Mom apron revealed herself. Probably in her early fifties. She greeted them with a smile that could melt ice. *So this was what a woman with a true heart of gold looked like,* Claire thought.

"Jacky?"

"That's me." She had a soothing voice and a calming demeanor that illustrated a certain poise under pressure.

They followed her inside and heard boys laughing somewhere deep within. "You must forgive me," she said to Whitaker. "I have had my hands full, so I haven't had the time to read your book. But I did see the movie. It was a gorgeous story."

"Thank you very much. Even from the little bit I've heard, what you do sounds so much more amazing."

Claire looked at the shiny floor's hardwoods, the neat row of children's shoes lined against the wall. "How long have you been doing this?"

"Gosh, most of my life. Almost thirty years. We just passed the two hundred mark."

"Two hundred kids?"

"Yep, two hundred boys have been through here."

Claire smiled in awe. She couldn't even imagine.

Jacky turned to lead them through the house. Lots of cheery decor: paintings of flowers, bright-colored rugs. "We all have our calling. I grew up in the system, and there were a few adults along the way who saved my life. How could I do anything else? But thank you for saying so." She turned left down a hall packed with photographs—presumably from the boys who'd lived here. "Oliver's in the shower. He'll be down in a minute. Oh, and Kari's in the kitchen."

"How many kids are living here?" Claire asked, taking her time to look at the photographs, her heart heavy and hopeful at the same time.

"We have five at the moment. One boy was just adopted, so we have an empty bed waiting for someone."

Claire turned away from a photo. "How long will that take to fill?"

"We're putting our feelers out. Not long."

Whitaker shook his head. "How do you do it? I can barely take care of myself."

"Never a dull moment," she drew out.

They entered an enormous kitchen with three circular dining room tables, two built-in large refrigerators, and a giant island. They'd clearly remodeled to cater to these boys, their loves.

Kari, Oliver's case manager, was sitting in a chair in the corner by the window. She looked up from her computer. "Hi, guys."

Claire and Whitaker said their hellos.

"I'll be here if you need me. Just hammering out some emails."

Jacky took a plate of cookies off the granite island and held it toward them. "We bake a lot around here."

Claire and Whitaker each reached for one.

"How could I resist?" Claire took a bite of the chocolate chip cookie, which was still warm and gooey in the middle.

Whitaker moaned with delight.

"I've had three already," Kari admitted from her chair. "It's dangerous coming over here."

Jacky set the plate back on the counter and looked at Claire. "They're made with coconut sugar. And they're vegan. I'm trying to teach them about eating healthier without cramming it down their throats. These boys have eaten a lot of fast food in their lives."

"How can you possibly cook for so many?" Claire followed her question with another bite, tasting the coconut this time.

"You're running a restaurant," Whitaker added, catching a crumb falling from his mouth.

"Oh, they help," Jacky assured them. "A couple of them have a real talent in the kitchen. Oliver's one of them."

An idea came to Claire. She brought up Leo's South, and though Jacky had never eaten there, she'd heard of it. "Well, I'd love to host all of you for breakfast or lunch sometime. On me, of course. And I could give them a tour of the kitchen, introduce them to my chefs."

"Oh, they'd love that! Would you like to meet everyone?"

Claire and Whitaker nodded eagerly.

Walking into the living room, they found four happy young boys of various skin colors sitting on beanbags playing UNO. Her nerves toyed with her as she took in the scene. Two guitars rested on stands next to an amplifier. There was a keyboard near the window, which looked out back toward the pool. Board games filled the built-in bookshelves. And she noticed an Xbox set up under the television.

"Everyone," Jacky said, "meet Claire and Whitaker."

A collective chorus of "Hi" greeted them.

Claire waved and met eyes with each of them. "Nice to meet you." She couldn't have imagined navigating the world without stable biological parents at such a young age. And yet here they were, more than dealing with it.

"Who wants to tell Claire and Whitaker what we did today?"

They all seemed eager to speak, but one young man beat the others to the punch. He had big blue eyes and flashy silver braces. "We went to a nursing home."

"Yeah, and what did you do?" Jacky asked.

The other boys were giving her their full attention.

"We helped them out with their phones and tablets."

"That's incredible," Claire said, looking at the boy with braces and then the others.

"You wouldn't believe how helpful they were."

"Oh, I can believe it." Whitaker turned to the boys. "My mom has no idea what she's doing with technology. Just entering the right password is an accomplishment. And she's only just learned how to use emojis. Let me tell you something, gentlemen. Baby boomers should not be allowed to use emojis."

"Jacky never knows her password," one boy said.

Everyone smiled.

"It's true," Jacky admitted. "I don't."

Jacky poked each of them about their favorite subjects in school and then said to Claire and Whitaker, "They all have As and Bs. Not one C in the bunch right now."

As Claire and Whitaker made a show of being impressed, Jacky looked back at her children. "But I want to see even more As. Because you know why?"

The boys looked at her, waiting for an answer.

"Because I know you have it in you."

Once the children had returned to their activities, Jacky gave them a tour. Though she shouldn't have been surprised after seeing what Jacky was capable of, Claire was still taken aback when she saw how clean the boys' rooms were. The beds with Tampa Bay Lightning comforters were made with military precision. The carpet stood tall from a recent vacuum.

"My father would salute these boys," Whitaker said. "I can't even make a bed so well."

"It's the first thing we do when we wake up," Jacky said.

Back in the kitchen, Jacky offered them a glass of ice water, which they happily accepted. Kari was still working away. Jacky invited them to the large backyard, which was lined by a tall white vinyl fence. They sat by the well-maintained pool under the shade of an umbrella. A basket overflowed with footballs, Frisbees, soccer balls, and other activities. Beyond the pool, a tall oak tree with a long branch running along the ground stood alone in the Bermuda grass.

They discussed the wild string of events that had led Claire and Whitaker to this moment. "I know we dropped some heavy news on him yesterday," Whitaker said as he wrapped up his story. "How's he handling it?"

"Oliver's a tough kid. Sometimes I can make the mistake of thinking he can handle anything. He's very good at hiding it sometimes. He had such an awful childhood, so he's learned to dig in and deal. But I know he's not immune—just tougher than you and me."

"I don't doubt it."

"It's easy to think of Oliver as a young adult," Jacky said, "but he's only fourteen. I don't know about you, but fourteen was difficult for me."

Whitaker itched his arm. "I have a feeling my definition of *difficult* is much different than yours and Oliver's."

Jacky smiled and nodded. "His therapist has come by three times since Oliver found out about David, including yesterday after your meeting at the park. To an extent, Oliver feels like it's his fault. That if he hadn't broken into that car, David would still be alive."

Claire's stomach tightened. "That breaks my heart. And it couldn't be farther from the truth."

They spoke about the stages of grief and what Whitaker and Claire could do to help Oliver work through his emotions. Jacky was seasoned in helping children work through trauma, and Whitaker listened intently as she expounded on what it was like to be fourteen and in Oliver's shoes.

"Can I ask a strange question?" Claire asked, taking a detour in the conversation. "I don't mean anything by it, just trying to learn." He looked at her. "Why haven't you adopted him? I mean, it seems so hard to be a foster parent. You're always saying goodbye."

Jacky nodded. "I've raised my kids, and they're all grown up. Fostering is something I do because it fills me up inside. Some of these kids don't want to be adopted, which is fine by me. And the ones that do, I want to help them find their forever homes."

Something about that idea of a forever home struck Claire hard. Not like a punch in the face, but like a rumbling earthquake below her feet. Was that what Oliver wanted? A forever home?

"How does that work?" Whitaker asked. "I mean, the adoptive process."

"I'll get a call from their case managers about a prospective parent, and we'll set up a matching meeting. If it goes well, we have a few more meetings. If it's meant to be, then these parents start the adoption process."

Claire could see the face of the mom she'd met so many years before, the one who'd ended up giving her baby to someone else. She shook the memory and asked, "What does Oliver want?" And she thought she knew the answer.

"Oliver is a little jaded after having such a tough go with his mom. I think he might be happy aging out of the system."

Claire's heart kicked at her chest. A reel of another life Oliver might have lived spun by in her mind. She could see David and him fishing from the end of the dock at their old house in Coquina Key, Claire joining them with a picnic lunch.

"Is that why I didn't see his picture on the websites?" Claire asked. "The Heart Gallery and the others?"

"Yeah, he doesn't like being on there. It's tough for some kids, especially teenagers, to be on display on the internet. Other kids might pick on them."

Claire totally understood. "And he could stay here until he's eighteen?"

"Absolutely. I don't play favorites, but Oliver is truly one of a kind. Such a sweetheart. If I was ever to consider adoption again, he's the first that comes to mind. You should see the way he cares for the other boys. He's the leader, always showing the new ones the ropes."

They turned to the sound of an opening door. "Well, there he is."

Oliver walked outside onto the patio, dressed in jeans and a green polo. He attempted eye contact but dropped his head again nervously.

Claire and Whitaker stood and shook his hand.

"How's it going, buddy?" Whitaker asked.

Oliver shook his hair off his eyes. "Good."

Claire couldn't tell if Oliver was being sincere.

After they shook, Whitaker said, "If you ever meet my dad, be careful shaking his hand. The man will crush your bones."

Oliver pretended to laugh.

As the others sat, Jacky stood and excused herself. "I'll help with dinner. I'm sure y'all have a lot to talk about."

After she'd left, Claire asked, "Is Jacky married?"

"Yeah, Jerry. He's at work."

"What's he do?"

"He's a software developer. Works for a start-up downtown."

"Cool guy?"

"Yeah, super cool. They're both great."

It made Claire happy to know he'd found a good home. Even if it was temporary.

Whitaker sat back and crossed his legs. "Not that you're asking, but I tell you, Oliver, I spent most of my twenties and thirties thinking about myself. Then I meet someone like Jacky and realize what a selfish shit I've been."

Claire eyed him.

Whitaker covered his mouth. "Sorry for the curse."

Oliver smiled, and Claire realized it was the first time since they'd met. "You two are such boys."

Claire watched Oliver and Whitaker share a knowing smile. Then Oliver flipped his hair off his eyes again and said, "Yeah, I'm really lucky."

"I'm thinking about taking that bed that's available," Whitaker said. "I'd sit by this pool all day every day. Do you think you'll be here until college? If you're going to college, that is."

Oliver nodded. "I want to go to Duke."

"Duke? Wow."

"All depends on how I do next year."

"Do you have the grades Duke requires?"

Oliver was perking up, speaking with more assurance. "I didn't in ninth grade, but this past year I was kicking ass." He stopped himself. "Oops, sorry."

Claire shook her head at them as Oliver and Whitaker smiled again.

"How about baseball?" Claire asked, moving on. "Could you play for them?"

"No, I'm not that good. I'll keep playing in high school, but I doubt a college will want me. At least, not a big college."

The thump from a car's bass shook the ground as it drew near. Once it quieted, Claire asked, "What position do you play?" She knew very little about baseball but was suddenly much more interested.

Oliver punched his palm. "Pitcher."

"Pitcher?" Whitaker said. "How fast is your fastball?"

Oliver raised an inquisitive eyebrow. "Why does everyone ask that?"

"I don't know. I guess for those of us who don't know a lot about baseball, it's the logical question."

"I'm high seventies at best. There's a kid on our team throwing in the nineties sometimes. And he throws a mean slider, just buckles right-handers."

Whitaker offered an encouraging smile. "I'd love to come see you pitch next year."

"Cool," Oliver said casually, as if he didn't take Whitaker's promise seriously. Perhaps wanting to steer away from talking about himself, he asked, "So what do you need to know for this book?"

Whitaker sat up straighter. "That is exactly the question I've been wondering to myself for months now. I truly don't know. It's weird talking to you, actually, like you just walked off the page."

"Yeah, I guess so."

Claire jumped in. "Oliver, if it makes you feel uncomfortable, we don't need to talk about the book or David. The last thing we want to do is upset you."

"I don't mind," Oliver said. "Is the book any good?"

"More than good." Whitaker looked at Claire for a second and then returned his eyes to Oliver. "Would you like to read it? You kind of have to, actually. Assuming you're interested."

"Yeah, sure." Oliver finished his water.

"Awesome. We, of course, want your permission to publish it. You might get kind of famous. David made you out to be a pretty cool cat."

Oliver smiled at the idea.

"Claire and I are desperately curious to know what's true and what he made up. Maybe you and I can come up with the ending together. It's difficult taking another man's idea and adding to it. But now that you and I know each other, I have a feeling you could help me finish. If you're up for it."

Oliver took his time thinking about it.

Claire thought he couldn't have been more adorable, and she wanted to see him smile again.

He finally said, "Yeah, I'm up for it."

"The story ended abruptly, like I told you. Orlando is in trouble. I think David used his creative license to drum up some drama. Doesn't seem like you were in too much trouble back then." Whitaker was fishing some.

Oliver looked back to the house for a moment. "I was when he caught me, but he kind of helped me out of it. I stopped hanging around the wrong kids and started playing baseball. He's the one who talked me into trying out."

Claire smiled, wishing she could have been there. A flash of anger returned, thinking all David had to do was tell her from the beginning.

"That's awesome you're still playing," Whitaker said. "If I was in your shoes and thought he'd run off on me, I might have slipped back to my old ways. Know what I'm saying?"

A shoulder shrug. "I guess I have a good coach. He looks out for me. Comes by here sometimes. And I have a therapist who's helped some."

"Dude, you got it going on. Seriously. You could probably teach me a thing or two."

"Isn't that the truth," Claire agreed.

Oliver offered a closed-lip smile, and Claire could see they were getting through to him. And it wasn't about getting answers out of him. It was about seeing how she and Whitaker might get involved with his life, help him continue on this positive trajectory.

Claire decided to dig deeper. "So what does your therapist say about all this . . . how to handle it? I could use a few pointers."

"He says that every time I feel guilty, I should think about something else. Like a good thought."

She clasped her hands together under the table. "That's pretty good advice. I guess if you accept that your guilt is unwarranted, which it is, then thinking about something happier is probably a good practice."

Oliver was suddenly staring at the table, biting his lip.

Claire set her right hand on the table, palm down. "I didn't mean to pry, Oliver. I'm so sorry. Let's not go there, okay?"

"I don't care what anyone says," Oliver admitted, squinting. "If he hadn't been trying to help me, he wouldn't have gotten in the accident." He sniffled and wiped a tear before it rolled down his cheek.

Claire felt a sudden hollowness behind her rib cage and glanced at Whitaker. They were both stumped. She didn't know Oliver well enough to get up and hug him. It wasn't appropriate. Instead, she leaned in. "If he had never met you, he might have died with something missing. But instead he died with a full heart, happy that you were in his life. Trust me. I didn't know about you, but I knew something was going on. He'd never been so happy in his life. I thought he was just in a good place, but it was because of you." Claire choked up. "Trust me, it was you. I'm so grateful that he met you."

Oliver covered his face with his hands and cried into them.

Claire looked at Whitaker again and then stood and knelt next to Oliver, putting a hand on the boy's shoulder. "Don't blame yourself at all, please. I know all about feeling guilty, and it's a waste of time." She felt sick inside and could barely handle seeing him so sad.

Oliver cried harder, his adult shell cracking, revealing his inner child.

Choosing to respect the boundaries, Claire resisted the urge to wrap her arms around him.

When Jacky came out later and invited them to stay for lasagna, they happily accepted. And it was the most filling—and fulfilling—dinner of her life.

Chapter 37

The Hat

Three days later, Claire was sifting through boxes in her guest bedroom while Willy watched her from the bed. She'd planned dinner with Whitaker and Oliver later and wanted desperately to give Oliver the Yankees hat but wasn't exactly sure where she'd hidden it.

After David's accident, a policeman had given her everything that had been inside David's totaled car. Something had told her to keep the hat, and it wasn't just the mystery of it. Though she had wondered why it had been in the car, she'd chalked it up to being a gift for a client, a gesture he was no stranger to. Still, she'd elected to hold on to it, tossing it into a box with a few other items of David's that she hadn't been able to part with: his letter jacket from high school, his suit from the day they married in Chicago.

Taking the pinstripe hat out of the box, she sat with it in her hands, her back up against the wall. Willy jumped down to join her, and she welcomed his company.

Claire was finally feeling better. She'd spent three days thinking about David, wondering how he might have reacted had the tables been turned, wondering if she was getting this all wrong—if she had any right at all to be mad at him. No matter where the blame lay, it was time to move on, time to forgive him.

How could she condemn him for fighting through his own struggles without drowning her in them too?

Running a hand through Willy's fur, she said, "Enough wasting life, Willy. I don't know how you've lived with me so long."

~

Along with much of St. Pete and even Whitaker's new novel, the story of the Chattaway began in the 1920s. Painted hot pink and parakeet green, the cash-only restaurant was quintessential Florida, a dive joint with mostly outdoor seating that always promised live music and a good time. Whitaker remembered feeding the koi here when he was a boy. And though he had not yet taken the plunge, the owners had been hosting a proper afternoon tea with their vast collection of china for longer than he'd been alive.

It was a mostly clear night, warm, and humid. Several green parrots were perched on a telephone wire looking down at the commotion. A man with a guitar sang Jimmy Buffett songs on the stage. Claire and Oliver were sitting across from Whitaker at the picnic table. They each held menus.

"All right, then, Oliver," Whitaker said, "who would win in a cage match? Batman or Spider-Man?"

"No, no, no. You can't compare Batman and Spider-Man. They're totally different. If someone is going to fight Batman, it would have to be Iron Man. That's a fairer fight. Think about it. Batman and Iron Man are both rich. They both have all this technology—"

"Yeah," Whitaker interrupted, "but it depends on what they have with them in the cage. Spider-Man still has his webs and ability even when he's Peter Parker, right? How about Batman? He needs all his gadgets. Same with Iron Man. Actually, I might argue that Peter Parker could take both. He'd wrap a web around them, then spin a hammock in the corner and watch them starve to death. Batman's got nothing."

Oliver held up a finger. "Well, for one thing, Batman is much smarter. Same with Iron Man. Like, two of the most brilliant guys on the planet. Neither one of them would get stuck in a cage without their gadgets. And even if they were forced to, they're both in incredible shape. Batman is a martial arts master. He wouldn't let Spider-Man get a web around him."

"My God, you're good," Whitaker said, looking at Oliver and then Claire, who was smiling as she perused the menu. "He should be a lawyer."

Whitaker had hit oil when he'd brought up comic books, a passion they clearly shared. It was through comic books that Whitaker had fallen in love with reading as a child and what had led to his love of gaming as an adult.

After ordering, Whitaker and Claire homed in more on Oliver's interests, and Whitaker watched sadly as Oliver began to pull back. The boy who was so giddy over Batman and Iron Man earlier was starting to quiet down, his long diatribes returning to the one- and two-word answers he'd been giving at the park and at Jacky's house.

Claire must have noticed, too, as she started pushing the conversation toward Whitaker's writing. Whitaker sensed it was time to embrace his role as the court jester. He briefly told them the idea behind *I Hear Thunder*.

"Imagine this. My character—very handsome and dapper—comes in to sip on a bottle of rum with another bootlegger. He's wearing a three-piece suit with a Smith & Wesson hidden somewhere inside."

Claire looked at Oliver, smiling. "Sounds like a bestseller to me."

Oliver turned up a corner of his mouth.

"And a blockbuster movie. I'm confident Brad will do my character justice. Don't even worry about it."

Oliver was toying with a saltshaker, still checking out from the conversation.

Whitaker looked at Claire, and they shared a moment of understanding. How could they reel him back in?

Claire tapped Oliver's arm. "Have you even seen *Napalm Trees*?"

"No," Oliver admitted. "I mean I've heard of it, but I haven't seen it."

"What!" Whitaker said, struck by the sadness of a life without movies. "Don't tell me you never get to see movies."

"No, we do. I just don't watch old movies."

"Old movies!" Whitaker exclaimed to Claire and Oliver's delight, the court jester coming alive. "Oh my God, I'm getting old. Just a minute ago, I was still feeling like I was part of the young guard of St. Pete. One of the young artists pushing the boundaries." He shook his head. "Not anymore. Now my movie is lost to the young generations, another *Ben-Hur* or *The Sound of Music*."

Oliver shook his head. "Never heard of them either."

Whitaker dramatically dropped his forehead to the table. When he came back up, he said, "Thank you for putting me in my place, dear Oliver."

"You're welcome," Oliver said, his smile coming back.

"You'll have to forgive Whitaker," Claire said to Oliver. "All he wants is to be relevant."

"And yet I'm so far from it."

"Oh, I think you're digging your way back," Claire said.

"With a very tiny trowel. What I'd give for a backhoe."

What an odd threesome they were, Whitaker thought, looking around at the other tables. But here they were having fun, and Whitaker had the feeling that Claire was as happy to be there as he was. And hopefully Oliver too. What Whitaker wanted to say, but didn't know how, was that Oliver was not the only one looking for a tribe.

As they shared an order of hush puppies, Oliver opened up again, telling them both funny and heartbreaking stories from his past. Working his way backward through the years, he finally came to the last time he'd seen his mother. "I first entered the system when I was ten. Then my mom got sober, and I went back to live with her. I remember being so happy. She's messed up, but she's still my mom, you know? Even when she'd hit me, I'd still hug her back. We did okay for a while, but then she started getting high again. A neighbor saw her hurting me and called the cops. They dropped me back into the system. I kept hoping we could try again, that she'd get sober, but it never happened."

Whitaker heard a young man speaking but sensed the remnants of the little boy inside Oliver's fourteen-year-old shell: the kind heart, the hidden innocence, the fragility of a child still trying to make sense of it all. He remembered what he was like when he was fourteen. Cocky and all knowing, happy to tell you what you should believe or how you were wrong. Those attributes had served him well as a writer but had certainly dredged up trouble along the way.

Oliver was completely different. Certainly not as confident as Whitaker had been. Definitely hesitant to trust anyone. But Whitaker also detected a note of wisdom, like Oliver had seen it all before. There were times when Whitaker would be talking to him and suddenly feel like he himself was the younger of the two.

Another notion became obvious. Oliver was not the kind of boy you could lie to. He'd been the victim of lies all his life, and he'd been hardened by them. He'd come to believe people were guilty until proven innocent. It reminded Whitaker of an idea he'd heard during his research for *Saving Orlando*.

You couldn't tell kids who've been hurt you love them; you had to show them.

Then the food came . . .

⇛

Claire watched Oliver eating his hamburger with only ketchup and mayonnaise and fries. Fourteen years old was such a difficult age, even if you were raised in a normal environment. It wasn't fair that Oliver had to deal with so much more than traversing the typical rites of passage.

His mom had abandoned him and apparently abused him physically. He had no father to speak of. Somehow, he'd turned out okay. A bit rough around the edges. She could tell he had his issues, as anyone in his case would. But he was a fighter, a kid trying to do his best.

Okay, he'd broken into a car, perhaps even run with a rough crowd—if David's comparisons between Orlando and Oliver were accurate—but he could have gone down a much worse path. He could have been much angrier at the world. Instead, he seemed to be trying. And trying his best was all you could ask of a boy—no matter his circumstances.

Though they'd hit a few stumbling blocks in their conversation earlier, Claire felt like Oliver had opened up with them enough to dive deeper. "What were you doing breaking into a car?"

Oliver didn't seem to mind the question at all. "Hanging around the wrong kids in school. Trying to impress them."

"You don't hang out with them anymore?"

"Nah, that was my old school. And a long time ago. Now I just hang out with the other baseball players mostly. Our coach doesn't put up with that kind of thing. Our first baseman was caught toe tagging toward the end of the season. Coach kicked him right off the team, didn't even let him explain himself."

"I've read about this toe tagging thing," Claire said, "where the kids all meet up at night in a parking lot and start racing around town."

"Yeah, exactly. Driving like boneheads."

Oliver let her steal one of his fries. Then she said to him, "I have to give it to you. Someone who's been through what you've dealt with. You have every reason to still be running with that rough crowd, breaking into cars, toe tagging, God knows what else. But here you are, playing baseball and getting good grades, wanting to go to Duke. I just think you're an awesome human and an inspiration, and I hope you know that."

Oliver blushed and looked down at his burger. "I have David to thank for a lot of it. If he hadn't convinced me to try out for the team, I might still be in a pretty bad place. Baseball is just about all I think about now."

Claire wiped her eyes and patted his back. "Did he come see you play?"

"Yeah, quite a bit. That's why we got in the fight, because he came to a game, and I didn't show. He knew I wasn't sick."

Claire imagined David sitting in the bleachers watching Oliver play. Was this when he was supposed to be going on a long bike ride after work? "So what's this Yankees obsession?"

Oliver finished a french fry. "It's the one thing I know about my dad. Sounds stupid, but my mom told me he loved the Yankees. I think that's about the one thing she knew. As much as I want to hate him, I try to picture him as a nice guy. David took me to my first game. I mean, a preseason game, but still, it was amazing."

Claire smiled, knowing she wasn't the only one still missing David. "He hated the Yankees. I'm sure you know that."

Oliver smiled back, nodding. "Yes, he did."

"He must have really liked you then."

Oliver nodded, taking a bite of his hamburger. Once he was done chewing, Whitaker watched him start to wipe his mouth with his sleeve, but at the last moment Oliver reached for his napkin.

The singer onstage started another Buffett song, "Tin Cup Chalice." Claire reached into her purse and extracted the Yankees hat. It still had a tag on it. "He never gave up on you, Oliver. I hope you know that."

"I know that now."

Claire offered Oliver the hat. "Now I know why I've been holding on to this for so long."

"That's the hat that was in his car?"

Claire nodded, holding back her emotions.

"You're giving it to me?" Surprise shot out of his eyes.

"Of course."

"Thank you so much," Oliver said, looking at the hat for a moment before placing it on his head. "It fits!" He adjusted it and then looked at her. "This is pretty awesome." He opened his arms to her, and she hugged him with everything she had.

So this is what it's like to have a child in your life, Claire thought. She had never quite been able to let go of the anger she'd harbored toward her mother for leaving them, so she'd never gotten to know her younger half siblings. A few trips to Chicago here and there, but for the most part Claire had avoided her mother's new family. Of course, Claire had employed some younger adults at Leo's, but they were closer to eighteen.

Oliver was still so young and innocent and impressionable, and though she'd only known him for a little while, she felt a vested interest in his life—the man he would become.

Looking past him, Claire saw a patch of dark clouds moving in and heard a faint groan of thunder. The wind pushed through, whipping the palm fronds above.

Oliver caught a napkin setting before it sailed into the air.

"I hear thunder," Claire announced, winking at Oliver.

Whitaker made a big show with his hand. "Okay, that's enough picking on me for the day."

"No, listen."

Another rumble, this time with more fury.

"Oh, you were serious," Whitaker said.

More thunder, and then a lightning bolt with several terrifying tentacles shot from the sky, striking the ground close by.

Claire clapped her hands together. "I think it's time to go."

Whitaker raised his hand. "Check, please!"

And the raindrops began to fall.

Chapter 38

CAN YOU SWIM?

It had been a long time since Claire enjoyed a meal in the main dining room of her restaurant. Today was a special occasion, though. She and Oliver were spending the morning together.

Whitaker had made the excuse that he was writing, encouraging them to go on without him. Claire wasn't sure if he was truly working, but she was quite sure the real reason he'd asked for a rain check was that he wanted her to enjoy some time alone with Oliver. He knew she still had so many questions, even though they'd seen him twice more since the dinner a week ago.

It wasn't even nine yet, but it was bright, warm, and humid outside. Almost every table was taken. Claire and Oliver occupied a two-top out back near the herb garden.

Claire watched him tear apart his blueberry buttermilk waffles like a shark on flesh. "I'd ask if Jacky was feeding you, but I know she is. She's a great cook." Claire and Whitaker had eaten with the family two nights before, enjoying a delicious tuna casserole.

"I'm a growing boy," Oliver said between bouts of shoveling. He wore his Yankees hat, and Claire wondered if he'd even been sleeping in it.

"Yes you are." She sipped her green smoothie, tasting the wheatgrass she'd asked them to add.

"Best breakfast ever." He licked his lips and chased his bite down with a big gulp of fresh-squeezed orange juice.

His happiness made her smile. "After breakfast, I'll introduce you to Chef. He's who holds this place together. It's fun to see the kitchen at work."

"Hold on, the guy who cooks? His name's *Chef*?"

"No, his name's Jackson, but in restaurants you call the chef *Chef*. Just like you'd call the captain of a ship *Captain*."

"Weird." Back to his waffles.

Claire watched him go, still trying to understand him. Would he have been the same boy if she and David had adopted him? Would he still play baseball? Would he be happier? Would he have more opportunities? Not that he'd been deprived where he was now. Perhaps he'd have different opportunities.

After another sip of her smoothie, she set down her glass. "Have you ever been to summer camp?"

He set down his fork. "Yeah, to Boyd Hill. But last year was my last year. I'm too old now."

"I didn't know they did a summer camp. Tell me about it." Boyd Hill Nature Preserve backed up to Lake Maggiore in the Southside of St. Pete and was home to an abundance of wildlife—and supposedly even the most experienced birder's dream.

"It's really cool, actually. Last year we learned about survival."

"What do you mean?"

Oliver picked a blueberry skin from his teeth. "You know, like which plants you can eat . . . or use for medicine. How to build shelters. First aid."

"How cool. I never learned that stuff. Have you seen any alligators out there?"

"Tons. Huge ones. And we get to hold owls and snakes—"

Claire dropped back in her chair. "Oh, count me out."

As he told her more about his summers, she realized Jacky and the other adults involved with his life worked hard to give him the same experience any child should be entitled to, and that made Claire happy. They talked about his favorite subjects in school and his closest friends. She could tell he was learning to trust her and discovered he only held back or returned to his shorter answers when they spoke of the past.

She stirred her smoothie and tried to put herself in his skin. When she'd been his age, she was chasing boys. "Can I ask you something kind of personal?" After a nod of approval, she asked, "Do you have a girlfriend?"

Oliver shook his head. "Nah, not right now. One dumped me a few weeks ago."

"Oh, Oliver. I'm so sorry."

Oliver pumped his shoulders. "Yeah."

"Well, I'm always here if you want to talk about it."

He thanked her and looked down at his empty plate.

Had she crossed a line? Or was he just sad about the breakup? "I have a feeling you're one of the cool kids. Girls always like baseball players. I sure did when I was fourteen."

Oliver looked back up. "I wouldn't say that I'm one of the cool kids."

"No?"

He shook his head. "No, definitely not."

"There will be other girls. Better girls." Claire noticed a table with empty water glasses but didn't want to disrupt her conversation with Oliver, so she tried to ignore it. "Growing up is so tough. I wish I could say being an adult is easier, but I haven't found it to be that way."

Oliver set his hands on his lap. "Is Whitaker your boyfriend?"

Claire's face tightened for a moment, and she looked around the crowded restaurant, almost as if other diners were listening in. No one was paying attention to them.

"Yes, he is." Claire felt lighter to have admitted it. "Does that make you angry with me? Because of David, I mean."

Oliver quickly shook his head. "No way. That was a long time ago."

Claire nodded, looking at the water glasses again. Where was their server? "Yeah, I know. Believe me, it wasn't easy. I've wrestled with the idea of dating again ever since I met Whitaker. But in the end I know David would want me to move on. And I think he would have liked Whitaker."

"Yeah, Whitaker's awesome."

Realizing she could concentrate better outside of her restaurant, Claire started to stand. "Well, why don't we go meet the chef and then take a walk along the beach? When's the last time you did that?"

"I guess last summer. Jacky took all of us."

"Have you ever found any sharks' teeth?"

He shook his head.

"Let's go see what we can find."

After enlisting a server to fill the water glasses and introducing Oliver to everyone in the kitchen, Claire led Oliver along the sidewalk and over the dunes. They left their shoes by a bench and strolled along the water. Patches of buttery cumulus clouds thickened up the sky. A long way out over the Gulf, a series of darker nimbus clouds promised a coming rain shower. The rainy season was officially underway. Their conversation came easily, and she was grateful to Whitaker for giving them this time together.

Claire taught him how to look for sharks' teeth, and they combed the sand for shiny black triangles. But after twenty minutes, Claire could tell he was losing faith. "Don't be discouraged. It took me years to find my first one."

He tossed the black shell he'd thought might be a tooth into the water. "This is not easy."

They were working their way north along the tide line toward the Don CeSar. It was sea turtle–nesting season, and volunteers from the

Sea Turtle Trackers had come out early one recent morning to mark the nests with wooden stakes and orange tape. Claire explained the struggles of a baby sea turtle trying to get back to the sea after it hatched.

Returning their focus to the hunt for sharks' teeth, Claire said, "It's a game of patience and determination. My grandmother taught me, and I'd be happy to pass along my secrets."

"Is she why you moved to Florida from Illinois?"

"Yeah," Claire said, picturing her grandmother's face. "She gave me my love of the Gulf. We would walk up and down this beach every morning, and she'd find at least five teeth every time her feet hit the sand."

Several more minutes into their search, they came across the famous Kenny in his green mankini, strutting past them. He wore gold aviators, which reflected the rising sun. Claire and Kenny exchanged a hello as they passed.

Once Kenny was a safe distance away, she turned to Oliver.

"Oh my God," he said, "you know that guy?"

"Everybody knows Kenny."

Oliver burst into a laugh, and Claire couldn't help but laugh too. But she didn't want Kenny to hear, so she caught Oliver, wrapping her arms around him. "Shhh."

Oliver laughed even harder, pulling her hand away from his mouth.

Claire turned, and if Kenny had heard them, he wasn't worried about it. He was happily moving down the beach, his mankini pulled up in the back as high as ever.

As they both collected themselves, Claire said, "Whatever floats your boat, right?"

Oliver was still shaking his head. "That should be illegal."

As they renewed their Don CeSar route, Oliver asked something completely out of the blue. "Hey, Claire, can I tell you something?"

"What's that?" she asked, hearing by his tone it was of great importance to him.

"I'm sorry that I broke into that car and messed up things with you and David."

Her throat closed momentarily. "What are you talking about?"

"If I hadn't been such a punk, none of this would have happened." With all the defeat in the world, he said, "He'd still be alive."

Claire grabbed his arm and stopped him from walking. A fire burned in her heart. "Never once have I thought that way. You had nothing to do with him dying."

Oliver looked toward the sand.

She lifted his head up by his chin and looked him in the eyes. "I am so extremely thankful that you came into our lives. And I'm so happy that David was able to feel what it was like to be a father before he died. I don't ever want you to think you had something to do with his death. You didn't. You hear me?"

He offered an unsure nod.

She let go of him. "I've felt the same way, like it's my fault. Like he'd still be here if I hadn't been so vehemently opposed to adoption." She shook her head. "We can't think like that."

Oliver nodded again, and she pulled him into a hug. He squeezed hard, and she knew he'd needed to get that off his chest.

They kept walking and talking, and the gloom of David's death left their conversation. Soon they were laughing again.

When she finally spotted a tooth, Claire yelled, "Ah, gotcha!" She reached down and retrieved the black tooth, which was about a half inch tall. She handed it to Oliver.

"No way," he said, lifting his palm closer to his eye, examining her find.

"Hold on. You've never seen one?"

"I've seen them at Boyd Hill, just didn't think we'd find one." He looked left to the water and then held up the tooth. "I don't understand how anyone goes swimming in there."

"Sharks want nothing to do with people. Besides, that tooth is probably ten thousand years old."

"Well, I'm sure he had kids and then his kids had kids."

Claire smiled. "Baby sharks are called pups."

A wave ran up around their legs. "Did you ever learn to swim?" Claire asked, recalling the scene in David's book. "No big deal if you haven't, just wondering."

"Yeah, I can swim. But I like swimming in pools better. Where you can see what's in there with you."

Though the storm crept closer, the sun was breaking through the cumulus clouds, and the temperature rose several degrees instantly. Oliver removed his shirt, revealing his super-white stomach and chest. She noticed a pink scar, about four inches long, running from his clavicle to his shoulder. Though she had no idea where it came from, she could only imagine. And instead of letting the scar sadden her, it only served to make her feel even more compassion for him.

After walking a little farther, they sat in the sand. A couple was setting up a University of Florida Gators tent behind them.

Claire tapped his arm with the back of her hand. "Hey, I had an idea the other day. I want to start a foundation in David's name to support foster children in the area."

"That's pretty cool." He was digging a hole with his heels.

"I thought you might be interested in being the spokesperson."

Oliver tossed a shell toward the water. "What do you mean?"

"I'd need someone who can speak from experience, tell people what it's like for you. You could be that young man. You can help me raise money and bring awareness to all the children in need. I think you'd be great at it. And it would be awesome for your résumé—especially a Duke application. What do you think?"

He picked up another shell. "Would I have to talk to, like, a lot of people? Like public speaking?"

"If you wanted to. Public speaking is something you get used to. Might as well get it over with before college."

He dug the shell into the sand. "I hate getting in front of people."

Claire turned to him. "What? You're a pitcher, standing all by yourself on the mound."

"Yeah, but that's different. I'm just throwing a ball."

"Public speaking is basically throwing fastballs with your mouth."

Oliver rolled his eyes.

"Seriously." Claire wiped a bead of sweat off her forehead. "I know you'd be good at it."

"Can I think about it?"

"Of course you can. There's no pressure. It was just something I thought you might enjoy."

He stopped moving his feet. "I guess you're right. I do need to get over the public speaking thing at some point."

"We can take baby steps," Claire said. "You don't have to go address Congress. I was thinking we could visit some of the other foster homes to start out. I bet some of the kids newer to the system would love to hear how you've figured out your way. It could make a big difference. They'd look up to you."

A thread of excitement ran through his words as he said, "Yeah, I could do that."

Claire pushed up from the sand and offered him a hand. "Let's get dried off and go do something fun."

As she pulled him up, he asked, "Like what?"

"We could go annoy Whitaker while he's trying to write."

Oliver snorted. "That sounds kind of fun."

Chapter 39

LET'S GO, YANKEES

Two months later and the Florida sun had officially baptized August with its first one-hundred-degree day. The humidity hung thick in the air, slowing everything and everyone down.

Whitaker and Claire had been spending a lot of quality time with Oliver, visiting his foster family's house, taking him on adventures, even slowly introducing him to the Grant family, starting with Jack and Sadie—who'd welcomed him with open arms (or, as Whitaker had halfway joked, welcomed him with the Grant family's vampiric bite). Oliver was not nearly as reserved as he had been when they'd first met him at the park. There were still hints of skepticism in his eyes and body language, but he'd come a long, long way.

Whitaker had secretly been writing, but he wasn't worried about word count or delivering the perfect ending. He was having fun, writing from the heart. He wrote when the moment moved him, and he went where the story pulled him. But the pressure wasn't there. He didn't wake feeling the need to impress anyone. He didn't wake feeling constrained by his ego.

He woke excited about telling the story that was coming alive before his very eyes, the breakthroughs of an egocentric man and the waking of a boy who has every reason in the world to keep on sleeping.

It wasn't hard to put that on paper.

When Claire asked how things were going, he'd say with a grin, "I'm getting there."

When she'd asked him this morning, he didn't admit that he was only paragraphs away from typing "The End." What only he and other writers could know was that typing those two words was the same as a mountaineer stabbing his flag into the peak of the mountain he'd just traversed, and he felt it coming.

Regarding that brunette librarian with a sword and shield that he called the muse, he'd been reminded of the most important lesson in writing. She certainly rewarded those writers who found the discipline to sit in the chair every single day, but she most rewarded those who remembered that there was life outside of a story, that a true writer must find his awakening in the real world.

Namely, Whitaker was in love, having found his real-life muse. Never had he cared for a woman as much as he did for Claire. He often caught himself watching her sleep or doing a task as mundane as putting away the dishes, losing himself in her movements and her facial expressions. She was a wonder that never ceased to tingle his senses. He still craved to hear her speak, especially as her voice rang with more cheeriness and positivity with each passing day.

And Oliver. One thing Whitaker knew for sure. David hadn't done the boy justice in *Saving Orlando*. And absolutely no words could. Not even if Whitaker knew every language in the world could he describe the beauty and resilience of Oliver. He was one of a kind.

That was why when Jack Grant had surprised them all a week ago, telling them he'd bought additional tickets to go with his two season tickets for the series opener of the Yankees–Rays game, Whitaker's heart had nearly burst out of his chest. Not only had his father bought the tickets as a way to officially accept Claire and Oliver into their lives, which was enough of a powerful message in and of itself. But Jack was continuing to contribute to the loving cocoon wrapping around Oliver, and that was what the boy needed: people in his corner, caring for him.

Claire was perhaps even more active than Whitaker in building this circle of love. Whitaker had seen the mother in her come alive, and she was there for him all the time, working closely with Jacky and Oliver's case manager, making sure he had everything he needed, thinking of the things that only a woman with motherly instincts was able.

~

Due to the migration of the snowbirds and the century-long history St. Pete and Tampa Bay had with the New York Yankees, Tropicana Field in downtown St. Pete came alive when the Yankees came to town. Though the covered, air-conditioned stadium was home to the Tampa Bay Rays, Yankees fans often outnumbered the frustrated Rays fans, who wanted new management and a new stadium. It didn't help that many in the Rays administration had been doing everything they could to move the stadium out of St. Pete.

It was a damn fine day to go to a baseball game. And an even finer day to take Oliver to the *first* regular-season game of his life. Whitaker, Claire, and Oliver climbed out of their Uber at the front door and quickly found some shade under an oak tree to wait on Whitaker's parents. When the Yankees came to town, it was always a packed house. Decked-out Rays and Yankees fans moved in hordes toward the stadium, an occasional chant rising up from the excitement.

Oliver was wearing a white Yankees jersey with black stripes and the hat Claire had given him, and he looked to be bursting at the seams, ready to get inside and take his seat. Claire and Oliver were joking with each other as Whitaker scanned the crowd for his parents.

There they were.

Staff Sergeant Jack Grant was limping across the street in his veteran's hat. Sadie was next to him, overdressed for a game, waving excitedly all the way until she reached them. Though Oliver had only known the Grants for a little over a month, no one had spoiled Oliver more than Sadie. She treated him no differently than her other grandchildren.

"Hey, Dad," Whitaker said.

Jack stuck out his hand, but Whitaker opened his arms and wrapped them around his father's shoulders. Holding back a cry, Whitaker said, "You're one hell of a guy. You've made his whole world."

Jack patted Whitaker's back before letting him go. "He's a great kid. I wish I could give him the world."

"This is a good start."

"Well, I'm more excited than he is. And I hope he doesn't mind, but I want to see my Rays tear the Yanks apart. We're only two games back." Jack smacked Whitaker on the shoulder and moved on to Oliver and Claire.

Whitaker hugged and kissed his mother. "Where are your Rays colors?"

"They've never been my colors, darling. Besides," she said, peering over at Oliver, "I think I'll pull for the Yankees today." Then she winked.

Whitaker turned in time to see Jack pecking Claire on the cheek and then shaking Oliver's hand. Oliver looked up into Jack's eyes.

"Now, that's a handshake, son!" Jack exclaimed.

Oliver busted out a grin that nearly brought Whitaker to his knees. Every time his father had pushed him to the edge, Jack would break from his hardened veteran shell and stun the world with the love that was so evidently still alive in his heart.

It's funny to think how we process experiences differently, Claire pondered, watching Oliver's reaction when he saw the seats, which were six rows behind the plate.

"Are you kidding me!" he yelled, spinning his head around, taking in the bright lights and loud music, then putting his eyes on the field.

When he sat down between Claire and Jack, he said, "This is the greatest day of my life. Thank you, Jack. Thank you, thank you, thank you."

"You're very welcome. As long as your Yankees lose, I'll bring you back." Jack hit him on the leg.

Oliver smiled and returned his eyes to the action.

When the Yankees took the field, Oliver stood, put his pointer finger and thumb against his mouth, and blew out a loud whistle. Bursting with energy, he pointed at each player, calling them out by name, throwing out stats too. Claire, Whitaker, and Oliver had watched at least five games together on TV recently, and Claire had learned more about baseball in the last month than she'd known in her entire life of being a fair-weather Cubs and Rays fan.

They ate popcorn and peanuts, watched the players warm up, and listened with joy as Oliver continued to spit out numbers like a statistician, teaching them all a thing or two. A cameraman working his way down the steps stopped to take a picture of the five of them. Jack paid forty bucks for a package of various-size copies.

Once batting practice was finished, as Oliver was chomping at the bit for the game to begin, Jack tapped him on the shoulder. "Hey, Oli, come with me. I want to show you something. We'll be right back."

Oliver looked at him in surprise, and Claire thought he might turn him down. The game was about to start! But no one turned Jack Grant down. Especially when he'd bought the tickets.

Oliver and Jack ascended the steps and disappeared.

"What's that all about?" Claire asked Sadie.

"I have no idea. You know Jack. Probably wants to show him the water tank with the stingrays."

Sadie looked back and forth between Claire and Whitaker. "I like you two together."

Claire wrapped an arm around Whitaker's neck. "Me too."

"I think I'm bringing up the rear," Whitaker said, cracking a peanut shell. "But I guess someone has to. It's a shame I inherited my father's looks and not yours, Mom."

A vendor in the aisle yelled, "Ice-cold beer!"

"I think you and your father are the most handsome men in this stadium."

"I agree," Claire said, smiling with Sadie.

A few minutes later, while Sadie poked around on her phone, Claire said to Whitaker, "What a great day, huh? I'm not sure anything makes me happier than seeing him smile."

Whitaker leaned over and kissed her with peanut breath. "I'm right there with you."

The three of them stood to let a couple in blue wigs and Rays uniforms pass by with nachos and sodas. The smell of the pickled jalapeños rose up into the air, and Claire was tempted to snag a chip. When was the last time she'd had ballpark nachos? Maybe years. The two die-hard fans squeezed in next to Whitaker, and he made small talk with them.

Just as Claire opened her mouth to ask where Jack and Oliver were, she saw them on the field near the dugout. She hit Whitaker on the leg and pointed. "What are they doing down there?"

Whitaker was shaking his head in wide-eyed surprise.

The vendor was coming back up the steps yelling, "Ice-cold beer!"

Claire looked closer and saw a glove on Oliver's hand.

The announcer cut through the noise of the crowd, saying, "Welcome to Tropicana Field!" His voice echoed throughout the stadium. "We'd like to start off today's game with the ceremonial first pitch!" More echoes.

Putting it all together, Claire looked at Sadie. "Did you know about this?"

Sadie shook her head.

Claire grabbed Whitaker's shorts.

The announcer continued, "Today's ceremonial first pitch will be thrown by a young man representing the David Kite Foundation, a nonprofit working to change the lives of foster children in Pinellas and Pasco Counties."

Claire couldn't believe her ears.

"Please welcome Oliver Hastings to the mound."

Claire stood so quickly she knocked the popcorn out of Whitaker's hands, and it spilled all over their feet. Whitaker and Sadie stood, too, and they cheered like this was the last game on earth.

As Oliver walked toward the mound, Claire took a peek at Jack, standing on the sidelines with crossed arms. He wore the kind of proud grin you might see on a grandfather.

Claire turned her eyes back to Oliver. His smile stretched to his ears as the catcher handed him a ball and gave him a pep talk. Then Oliver strutted up to the mound as if he'd made that walk a million times.

Before winding up, Oliver looked up and right, searching for where they were sitting. Claire, Whitaker, and Sadie screamed his name until Oliver found them. With the ball tightly clutched in his right hand, he pumped his fist.

Claire melted, and so did everyone around her.

As Oliver wound up, she so hoped he wouldn't embarrass himself. He didn't need the shame of a bad throw holding him back. In fact, for a second, she felt angry at Jack for putting such a huge responsibility on him.

Please make it to the catcher, she prayed.

Her fears were unwarranted.

Oliver's windup was gorgeous, and he slung the ball with grace. It hit the leather of the catcher's glove with a smack that could be heard all the way up in the seats. Claire cheered even louder, only to be outdone by Whitaker, who was screaming shamelessly.

Claire turned to Sadie and hugged her. "What an amazing idea."

Sadie nodded in agreement, wiping tears from her eyes. "Jack knows a lot of people in this town, doesn't he?"

That was the day that Claire fell in love with baseball. And the first day she truly understood what it might mean to be a Grant.

Chapter 40

I Don't Hear Thunder

I have a story. Wrapping up the ending now. I'll have something
for you in a few hours. And by the way, you will love it.

This was the message Whitaker texted his agent early in the morning
after the game. He'd been sitting at David's desk since 3:00 a.m. writing
with grand inspiration. One-Eyed Willy had sneaked into his office at
about five and was perched on the bookshelf watching Whitaker type.

His agent had finally responded back at six. Give me more.

Whitaker pulled himself away from the ending to respond: Not yet.

I Hear Thunder?

No, Matt, not I Hear Thunder. I am the fucking thunder. Brace
yourself. Story imminent. Over and out.

Whitaker closed his messaging app, turned off his Wi-Fi, and went
back to work. His fingers danced like they never had before. The end
of the story came as if it had been there all along. Of course it had!
Whitaker had been so caught up in his own ego that he'd feared his
sentences might not be as crafty as they'd been in *Napalm Trees*, his
wordplay not as lofty, his descriptions not as sexy. What he should have

focused on was the story! You can string together the most beautiful sentences in the world, but without a story you have nothing.

He'd figured out the missing piece, the glue that bound Kevin and Orlando. He'd originally considered the possibility of Kevin or Orlando dying. That might have been a tearjerker.

But it wouldn't have been true. It wouldn't have been true to what David wanted and where David was headed.

And the lesson Whitaker had learned over the past six months was that David was headed toward a love story. One big beautiful love story.

The writer's fingers continued to fly, and tears rolled down his cheeks as the story nearly told itself. A new character had entered Kevin's life, turning his world upside down. Turning Orlando's world upside down.

The power Whitaker felt in his fingers was indescribable as he wrote the last words. It was as if each stab of the key came from not only his finger muscles and forearms but even his shoulders. Not only was his whole body involved, but his soul as well. And it was his soul doing the heavy lifting.

The writer finished the last line, knowing it was right in every way.

He pressed the return key and typed triumphantly: "The End."

Whitaker sat back in David's chair, basking in victory like a warrior after battle. He looked at the gash in the wall, which he still hadn't repaired. He enjoyed the reminder that came with it. What a journey this had been. To think this was a writer's life. Each book a dive down into the abyss, the best stories coming from the deepest of depths, wringing every emotion out of you, leaving you deathly tired but utterly alive. And once you'd finished and felt like you'd given all you had, you had to wake up and do it all over again.

In his Walter Cronkite voice—deep and exact—Whitaker asked himself, "Who in their right mind would put themselves through this every day, Whitaker? Why not take the road more traveled?"

"Because, Walter. This is what I was born to do." Whitaker caught himself from slamming his fist down on the desk. He didn't want to wake Claire.

He still had work to do. Turning toward Willy, he said, "I'm gonna make your mama proud, little guy."

Whitaker scrolled back to the beginning of his writing session and spent another two hours editing and polishing what he felt was a very fine ending. Once he'd read the last lines again out loud, he decided it was time for her to read it.

As the printer dealt out page after page of *Saving Orlando*, Whitaker sat back with his arms crossed, pondering the night before, how very perfect it was. He felt her presence behind him and rotated in the chair.

Claire was standing at the door, wearing her glasses and a Chicago T-shirt—the band, not the city. "What are you doing out of bed so early?"

Whitaker made a dramatic effort to look her up and down. "I'm wondering the same thing myself."

Claire turned her head to the printer. "What's that?"

Whitaker didn't have to say it out loud. A smile rushed over him.

"You finished, didn't you?" She stepped farther into the room.

"Every last word." He rose to standing and leaned in for a kiss.

"How does it feel?" she asked.

"Like the battle has been won."

She drew a shape, a heart maybe, with her finger on his chest. "I want to read it."

"Soon enough."

"No," she said, pushing him away. "I'm reading it today."

"That's why I'm printing it out. But we have a little time until it finishes. You can't walk in here like this and not let me hold you for a little while."

"Is that all you're looking for?" Claire asked, looking at him like he'd stolen a cookie out of the cookie jar. "A little snuggle?"

"For starters." Whitaker pulled her close and spoke into her ear. "No more words this morning. I've said all I can say." He kissed her cheek.

"You have until the printer has printed the last page."

"That doesn't give me much time. I should have written a second epilogue. Maybe an afterword too."

"Unless you've been holding back, I think you'll be fine."

"How dare you."

~

With a cup of Earl Grey tea steaming beside her and Willy nestled up to her leg, Claire was sitting on one end of the houndstooth sofa holding the stack of white paper making up the last section of *Saving Orlando*. Whitaker was pretending to read *A Gentleman in Moscow* in the chair next to the sofa.

"I can't read it with you watching me," Claire said, flipping to the next page.

"I'm not watching you. I'm reading."

"I suppose a man of many languages such as yourself can read upside down if it suits him?"

He turned the book around to see the cover. "Oh, how about that?"

Claire rolled her eyes. "I know you were waiting on me to notice."

A sly grin. "Nothing gets by you, does it?" He added, "Seriously, I can't *not* watch you."

"It's good," she said. "Trust me. It's the best book I've ever read. Stop worrying."

Whitaker turned the right side of his mouth up into a smile. "Easy for you to say."

The story moved so quickly and beautifully that she was swept away again and didn't think at all about the authors. What Whitaker had done for the story was bring Kevin to life. He'd given Kevin the tools he needed to break free, the arc he needed.

Of course, Whitaker had brought a woman into the story, and Claire didn't have to make too many assumptions to read between the lines.

In his writing, David had never mentioned a woman in Kevin's life. Only that he was lonely. Making a large creative decision, Whitaker had introduced Orlando's new case manager, Amy. His last one had left her position, leaving Orlando alone again. Amy quickly stepped in with a full heart, ready to support his growth.

Only as Claire reached the last few paragraphs did she pause to take in the significance of the work David and Whitaker had written—a story of survival, second chances, redemption, and love. A tale with such power that she knew it would be enjoyed long after they were gone.

Claire read out loud the final page of the epilogue of *Saving Orlando*, savoring each thought and image.

"I spent my thirties wondering if I was worth loving. Until Amy came into my life. She lifted me up and resuscitated my senses, reminding me of what matters—the cosmic sense of what matters. It's love, of course, and after knowing her only a few minutes, I loved her. She was the one with the courage to walk blindly into the darkness to find Orlando and, like she'd done for me, she brought him back. She was our lighthouse casting hope out into the dreary fog of our lives.

"I suppose I have Orlando to thank for all of it. Only in attempting to save him did I find love, and I will be forever grateful. Before I fell in love with Amy, I fell in love with him. A different kind of love, but just as powerful.

"It was, by the way, never me who was saving Orlando. You probably knew that. How I'd ever been so confused is still a mystery to me. No, I was never saving Orlando. But to name the book *Saving Kevin* would have given away the ending.

"If you drive south on MLK and work your way toward the Gulf, you'll find the tiny chapel where I married Amy three months later. Though she could have done much better, something drew her to me. In appreciation to a world that would allow a wreck like me to marry such a fine woman, I will spend the rest of my life trying to be a better man and husband and . . . father.

"A week after marrying Amy, we took Orlando to New York to see a game at Yankee Stadium. During the seventh-inning stretch, we asked Orlando to be our son."

Claire sniffled and removed her glasses. She read the final two words. "The end."

She set the last page down on the coffee table and turned to Whitaker, wiping her eyes. "Wait a minute. You can't go south on MLK in Sarasota. Haven't we already been through this?"

Whitaker threw up his hands. "Oops. I'll have to fix that."

She side-eyed him. "If I didn't know any better, I'd think you're trying to tell me something."

"Isn't it crystal Claire?"

Claire shook her head at the man who'd finished her late husband's novel. She thought about her journey and the pain of losing a love and how empty she'd once felt inside. And then she saw her possible future, one rich with Oliver and Whitaker, and she knew that no matter how broken the road, there was joy waiting for her at the end.

Epilogue

THE BIG APPLE

Sixteen months later

"Why do they call it the Big Apple, anyway?" Oliver asked, strolling up Fifth Avenue in Manhattan, the hat Claire had given him slightly tilted on his head, his eyes and ears tuned to the sights and sounds erupting around him.

A chilly fall wind funneled between the tall buildings, and Claire zipped up her down jacket. "That's a good question. I have no idea."

"Oh, I do," Whitaker exclaimed, circling around a man slinging bottled waters. Once he'd caught up with them, he said, "Back in the thirties, this little boy in Queens was bobbing for apples. You know, you have all these apples floating in a giant bucket of water, and somebody has to go in with their teeth and try to grab one."

"I know what bobbing for apples is," Oliver said.

A taxi driver slammed his horn.

"Just making sure. You kids and your Fortnite and hovercrafts and virtual reality. Back when I was a . . ."

"Oh God, please don't go there," Claire said, walking between them.

They stopped at the end of the block, waiting for the red hand to turn green. "So anyway, the kid from Queens lifts his head from the bucket, water dripping down his face and this huge red apple in his mouth, and his friend yells, 'Holy smokes, that thing's the size of Manhattan!'"

Oliver laughed. "You're so full of it! I know you're making that up."

"Hold on," Claire said. "You made that up?"

A smile rose on Whitaker's face.

Claire punched him on the arm. "I can't believe you."

"It was pretty good, though, right? A kid in Queens."

"I don't believe anything you say anymore," Oliver admitted, putting one foot into the street.

Claire noticed and pulled him back to the sidewalk without a word. He got her message. She put her hands on Oliver's shoulders. "From now on, Oliver and I will assume everything you say is fiction."

Whitaker looked back and forth between them. "That takes all the fun out of it!"

"That's what you get when you cry wolf." And then, as if testing the waters—almost as if it were a question—he added, "Dad."

It was the first time Oliver had called Whitaker "Dad."

Claire wanted to say, "Yes, you can call him 'Dad'!" But she bit her tongue, not wanting to coddle her son. He'd called her "Mom" a few times, so this was the next step. A very exciting one.

Whitaker obviously heard the tone, too, and jumped in to squash it. Acting like hearing "Dad" was no big deal, he put his arm around Oliver. "Are you really preaching to me about crying wolf, Aesop?"

Claire breathed easier as Oliver smiled at him. There was a time when she could never have imagined marrying again, never imagined being a mother. All that had changed, and seeing her two men love on each other filled her with gratitude.

The hand turned green, and they crossed the street and moved up the sidewalk. They stopped and stared when they came upon the Barnes & Noble on their right. Posters with the cover of *Saving Orlando* flanked the entrance. Though she'd seen the cover a million times, it never got old. It depicted a man holding a boy in a headlock in the grass, both of them beaming with joy. *Saving Orlando* typed in a noble font. Two names below, separated by an ampersand. David Kite first, in a large black font. Whitaker Grant, much smaller, as he'd insisted.

Claire looked back at David's name. She so wished he could be here to see this, but it felt wonderful to know she had been able to give him this last gift, this last goodbye.

Below one of the posters, a sign read: BOOK SIGNING WITH WHITAKER GRANT, COAUTHOR OF THE NEW YORK TIMES BESTSELLER SAVING ORLANDO. TODAY! 3 P.M. Through the window, Claire saw the giant display of hardbacks waiting for Whitaker's signature. He'd talked a lot about wanting to do a second signing here (the first was almost ten years before), and she didn't need to look at his face to know how he felt right now.

Without looking down, she touched the rings Whitaker had given her, a platinum band and a vintage emerald-cut diamond. She smiled, remembering his proposal last winter, when he had secretly gathered everyone special to them at Leo's South and taken a knee in the sand in the middle of the main dining room. He'd even flown Claire's mother down for the surprise. Oh, how Whitaker it was and how quickly Claire had said yes. And then the roar of their friends and family and the other guests.

How could Claire do anything but keep on swinging, as her former neighbor Hal had taught her?

Claire reached for her two men and pulled them close, wrapping her arms around their waists. She turned her head to each of them, smiling. Other pedestrians wove by, racing in and out of the madness, juggling their phones and cups of coffee. A car horn blared, starting a cascade of horns that worked their way up Fifth like falling dominoes. A bus slid up to the curb behind them with a screech, and people of every kind piled out.

So many people, so many broken roads. But it was here Claire's broken road ended.

Acknowledgments

A huge thanks to my rock star agent, Andrea Hurst, who helped tremendously in taking this novel to the next level and pushing me to my best. It's been one lovely honeymoon of aligning stars since the first day we spoke. Thank you to Chris Werner, Krista Stroever, and Danielle Marshall of Lake Union for giving me a chance. It's a dream come true to be working with you.

Thanks to my incredible alpha and beta readers, who trudged through the story long before it was ready. You poked holes in all the right places, and I think we got 'em all! Your selflessness is inspiring.

I had a feeling exploring foster care in Florida would touch my soul, but I had no idea the extent. What a vast collection of golden hearts. You make me want to be a better human. Specifically, I'd like to thank Laurallyn Segur, Jacky and Jerry Logemann, Crystal Sterker, Amy Lawrence, and Kelly Zarle, who brought me into their world and showed me what it's like to love with everything you have. This book is for the children you continue to help every day.

Through this journey, I'm reminded of the importance of family, and to that end I owe everything to Mikella and Riggs. You are my tribe, and your love, support, and belief in my art fill me to the brim. Thank you.

Thanks to all of you who've read my books and supported me over the years. I'm one lucky guy.

About the Author

Photo © 2018 Brandi Morris

Boo Walker is the author of the Red Mountain Chronicles series. He initially tapped his creative muse as a songwriter and banjoist in Nashville before working his way west to Washington State, where he bought a gentleman's farm on the Yakima River. It was there among the grapevines that he fell in love with telling stories. A wanderer at heart, Boo currently lives in St. Petersburg, Florida, with his wife and son. For more information, visit www.boowalker.com.